# MIDNIGHT
## ON THE
# MISSISSIPPI

# BOOKS BY MARY ELLIS

**SECRETS OF THE SOUTH MYSTERIES**
*Midnight on the Mississippi*

**CIVIL WAR HEROINES**
*The Quaker and the Rebel*
*The Lady and the Officer*

**THE NEW BEGINNINGS SERIES**
*Living in Harmony*
*Love Comes to Paradise*
*A Little Bit of Charm*

**THE WAYNE COUNTY SERIES**
*Abigail's New Hope*
*A Marriage for Meghan*

**THE MILLER FAMILY SERIES**
*A Widow's Hope*
*Never Far from Home*
*The Way to a Man's Heart*

**STANDALONES**
*Sarah's Christmas Miracle*
*An Amish Family Reunion*
*A Plain Man*
*The Last Heiress*

# MIDNIGHT
## ON THE
# MISSISSIPPI

## MARY ELLIS

HARVEST HOUSE PUBLISHERS
EUGENE, OREGON

*Cover by Lucas Art and Design, Jenison, Michigan*

*Cover photos © Larry Mulvehill, 13/Gary Faber / Ocean / Corbis*

This is a work of fiction. Names, characters, places, and incidents are products of the author's imagination or are used fictitiously. Any resemblance to actual persons, living or dead, is entirely coincidental.

**MIDNIGHT ON THE MISSISSIPPI**

Copyright © 2015 by Mary Ellis
Published by Harvest House Publishers
Eugene, Oregon 97402
www.harvesthousepublishers.com

Library of Congress Cataloging-in-Publication Data
  Ellis, Mary,
  Midnight on the Mississippi / Mary Ellis.
  pages ; cm. – – (Secrets of the South mysteries ; book 1)
  ISBN 978-0-7369-6169-1 (pbk.)
  ISBN 978-0-7369-6170-7 (eBook)
  1. Women private investigators—Louisiana—New Orleans—Fiction. 2. Murder—Investigation—Fiction. I. Title.
  PS3626.E36M53 2015
  813'.6—dc23
                                                    2015000616

**Printed in the United States of America**

15  16  17  18  19  20  21  22  23  / LB-JH /  10  9  8  7  6  5  4  3  2  1

*This book is dedicated to my parents,*
*Elizabeth and Steve.*

*Where would I be if you hadn't picked me out*
*from the other squalling infants?*

# ACKNOWLEDGMENTS

Thanks to my darling husband, Ken, who helped me prowl the streets and alleys of the French Quarter and travel the back roads of Cajun Country and upstate Louisiana. A better research assistant has never lived or breathed. Without you I would have driven straight into a bayou and drowned long ago.

Thanks to James at the Stonewall Range for answering my questions about firearms, and special thanks to Deputy Janise of the St. Landry's Parish Sheriff's Department for your procedural help.

Thanks to Joe Stopak, retired fire chief and arson investigator for Richfield Village, Ohio. Your patience with answering my questions was only exceeded by your expertise.

Thanks to Peggy Svoboda, who took the time to proofread a printed copy of this manuscript with her eagle eye.

Thanks to my lovely agent, Mary Sue Seymour; my fabulous editor, Kim Moore; and the wonderful staff at Harvest House Publishers. Where would I be without your hard work?

# ONE

*Yacht* Queen Antoinette
*Somewhere on Lake Pontchartrain*

*What?* I still can't hear you, James!" Hunter Galen shouted into the mouthpiece. "Call me back in a few minutes. I'm going on deck. Maybe the signal will be stronger." Ending the call, he headed for the doorway of the grand dining salon. Around him, the birthday party was in full swing. He glanced across a room filled with smiling faces, assured that the party had been a great idea. His mother, still stunning at sixty years old, was dancing with the senior partner of the law firm that had represented Galen business interests for years. Was something going on between them—more than just a slow waltz between old friends? Maybe, but he wouldn't worry about it tonight. His mother and everyone else were enjoying themselves. In addition to delicious catering and plentiful libations, two bands—zydeco and swing—provided entertainment, with even a DJ between sets to keep the younger generation happy.

From the corner of his eye, Hunter spotted his girlfriend, soon-to-be fiancée, clinking champagne glasses with his sister, Chloe, and his sister-in-law, Cora. Together the three looked like a blonde, brunette, and redhead hair color advertisement. While he watched, Ashley Menard glanced his way, her face lighting up with a Miss Louisiana smile. That's what she once had been—or, at least, first runner-up. Tall and reed slim, Ashley's cool composure stemmed from the belief that everything she touched would turn to gold. And it usually did. She lifted two fingers in a wave before refocusing on her future sisters-in-law.

*"Don't even think of getting down on one knee until you ask Daddy,"* Ashley had warned him. Daddy. Twenty-six years old and owner of a chain of hair salons, yet she still referred to her father with a juvenile moniker. Well, this still was the old South, after all.

When the vibration of his phone jarred his attention from the party, he saw on the screen that it was James again. Sighing, he headed up the stairs for better reception. On the promenade deck above, Hunter sucked in a lungful of humid air and leaned over the polished teak railing. "Hello, James," he spoke into the mouthpiece.

"Hunter, we have to talk. This is important. I know you're tied up right now, but I had drinks tonight with old man Morrison at the bank. He wants to talk to us about the credit advance I requested. He refuses to extend the corporate credit line until we *both* come to his office. That tight-fisted—"

His colorful description of their banker became garbled as James's voice rose with agitation.

Shaking his head, Hunter gazed out at the dark water of Lake Pontchartrain. A nearly full moon reflected off of the glassy surface. Although the breeze on his skin felt cool, his anxiety level kicked up a notch. "Don't blame Mr. Morrison, James. Having us both present was my idea. You're getting us in pretty deep. Let's sit down tomorrow and crunch the numbers, but I think—"

Apparently James Nowak wasn't interested in either crunching numbers or the financial solvency of the firm. Hunter could hear him shouting but fortunately couldn't discern much of what he said.

"James! You keep breaking up. Let's talk tomorrow. You know I'm on a boat in the middle of Lake Pontchartrain at my mother's birthday party—"

The line went dead. Hunter probably would have tossed the phone into the waves if his older brother hadn't crept up behind him.

"Something wrong, little brother?" Ethan Galen spoke with his smooth-as-cream accent. Funny how three siblings could be raised together, yet only one, Ethan, could speak fluent French that even a Parisian wouldn't find fault with. Hunter and Chloe must have spent too much time in front of the TV instead of talking to *Grandpère*.

"No," said Hunter. "Just business as usual in Galen-Nowak Investments. If James keeps this up, we'll have to sail the *Queen Antoinette* to Costa Rica to hide from our creditors." He laughed with little humor.

Ethan offered a halfhearted grin. "If there's any way I can help, call my office in the morning. Right now Mother is about to address her adoring fans. I didn't think you'd want to miss that." He opened the vapor lock door leading back to the party.

While Hunter had been arguing with his partner for the one-millionth time, his family and friends—everyone in the world he cared about—were waiting for him. "Go on down. I'll be right behind you."

"Right. I'll keep the party moving along." Ethan studied his brother for a moment and then ducked his head under the bulwark.

Staring at the fishing boats bobbing on the surface, Hunter took stock of what a fortunate man he was. For the moment, all family members were speaking to one another, he had a gorgeous girlfriend, and he worked in a profession that thrilled and challenged him every day. He was no ordinary stockbroker. On behalf of his clients, he wheeled and dealed in initial public offerings, emerging markets, real estate investment trusts, aggressive sector funds, and volatile stocks that would cause the average investor to faint dead away. Fortunes were made and lost similar to a Vegas game of Texas hold 'em. His clients weren't senior citizens who lived off income generated by their portfolios. Volatility, even wild gyrations, came as no surprise to those who trusted him and invested with his firm. Hunter loved the game and always would. The buying and selling of securities made his heart pound and his blood race through his veins.

With little alternative, he shook off his argument with James and hurried back downstairs. There wasn't a business in the world that didn't run into snags every now and then. The two of them would hammer this out in the morning. Didn't they always?

In the main salon, Ethan had just finished his speech and was introducing the birthday girl. Accepting the microphone from him, Clotilde Galen looked beautiful in a peach-colored suit and high heels. She would still be a dynamo at one hundred, let alone a mere sixty. Hunter slipped into a seat at Chloe and Aaron's table.

His sister passed him a bottle of champagne and an empty glass. "You missed the toast. Try to catch up." She barely glanced in his direction, her attention directed to the center stage.

Hunter filled his flute but left it alone. The heavy fragrance of magnolia from the table arrangements was making it hard to breathe.

"I can't tell you what a lovely surprise this party is tonight." His mother's lilting voice drifted over the guests like a sentimental refrain. She spoke more musically than he could sing. "Having my friends here, along with my beloved family, my mother…" Clotilde's voice cracked as everyone's attention shifted to *Grandmère*.

Surrounded by Ethan, Cora, their young son, and her best friend, Jeanette Peteriere, the grand dame of the family smiled, the creases deepening on her gentle face. When *Grandmère's* trembling fingers lifted her champagne glass in salute, the crowd erupted with hoots and uproarious applause.

After a brief interval, Clotilde tapped the microphone with one long fingernail. "I know not everyone could see from where they sat, so I wanted to mention the thoughtful, age-appropriate gifts I received from my darling children." More hoots, more applause. "From my little girl, Chloe, who recently received her bachelor of arts degree at Tulane..." Clotilde paused, knowing her audience wouldn't pass up an opportunity to make noise. She wasn't disappointed.

Chloe stood, nodding and waving at her well-wishers while her FBI agent fiancé, Aaron, grinned with pride.

Clotilde waited before continuing. "Chloe has given me a year's worth of classes entitled 'Yoga for Senior Citizens' at the community center downtown." She waved the embossed certificate in the air. "A full year."

The crowd offered thunderous applause.

"And my son Ethan and his lovely Cora paid for my lifetime membership in *AARP*." She held aloft a second embossed document. "My entire lifetime—can you imagine?"

Apparently, the guests could imagine because many began pounding on the tabletops.

Suave and diplomatic, Ethan half stood and waved like a visiting royal monarch, while his wife beamed with pleasure. The corners of Clotilde's lips turned up into a smile as she waited for everyone to settle down again. "As much as I love my gifts, the best of all is having my children here tonight. Thank you, Ethan, Hunter, and Chloe, for inviting everyone to this lovely boat for my celebration. This was the best birthday surprise I ever received."

Clotilde's voice cracked slightly on the last word, even as her luminous green eyes filled with tears.

Kenneth Douglas, the family's attorney and friend, offered her a steadying arm as she stepped from the podium.

"Wait, Mom. Stay up there," called Hunter. He scrambled to his feet. "I haven't given you my gift yet."

Clotilde looked eager for the spotlight to shine elsewhere, but she nevertheless moved back to the dais.

"Happy birthday." He held out a brightly wrapped box.

Accepting the gift from her son, she quickly stripped off the paper. "Fixodent adhesive," she murmured. "Looks like the large, family-sized box. Thank you, dear." Clotilde lifted it high so all could see. "I'll keep this in a safe place until it's necessary. Fortunately, my teeth are all still mine." Again she tried to leave, but her younger son wouldn't allow it.

"Look inside the box, Mama," he said, relishing the moment.

Clotilde hated the endearment "Mama" and flashed him the look that said, *You're in big trouble, young man.* But like a good sport she ripped open the box. The crowd leaned forward in their chairs, with several in the last row standing so they could see.

Instead of the plastic tube everyone expected, Clotilde extracted a sheet of thick vellum festooned with fancy calligraphy, stamps, seals, and assorted vestiges of officialdom. She unrolled and scanned the document, reading aloud a word here and there.

The party guests waited. Her family waited. Even Mr. Douglas peered curiously over her shoulder.

Then her face blanched as her hand fluttered to her throat. Finally, she stopped reading and stared at her son. "What is this, Hunter? What is this paper talking about?" As the fingers holding the document started to shake, the audience grew silent.

"The yacht *Queen Antoinette*, what you referred to as a 'boat' a few moments ago, is *your* new sailing ship. Don't call her a boat anymore or you'll make her mad." Hunter waved a hand around the elegantly appointed main cabin, where forty guests had just finished dining. "She's yours, Mama. Happy birthday. The captain and crew will be a phone call away whenever you wish to sail. They can charter her out to help defray operating expenses while you're abroad." Hunter glanced at his siblings and grinned. "Oh, by the way, Ethan and Chloe went in with me on the gift. And the missing tube of Fixodent is in my jacket pocket for whenever you need it."

The crowd erupted into bedlam and rushed toward the podium, surrounding Clotilde with noisy congratulations and best wishes. Hunter overheard several aunts already asking to use the vessel for upcoming showers and parties. Despite her heels, his mother was soon lost in a sea of people. Hunter exchanged glances with Ethan, who lifted a snifter of bourbon in salute. Cora was trying to fight her way up toward the birthday girl. Snuggled against Aaron's shoulder, Chloe grinned as the two of them whispered secrets the way engaged couples often did.

Hunter scanned the guests for Ashley but couldn't find her. Usually her height in heels made it impossible for her to hide, but she definitely was not in the room. He was about to search for her in the galley when his cell phone vibrated. In exasperation, he sprinted up the stairs to the upper deck for better reception.

Once he had answered, his business partner again pleaded, cajoled, shouted, and cursed in a staccato of fractured phrases. But no matter where Hunter went on the ship, the signal was too weak to decipher anything coherent. "Wait until tomorrow, buddy. We'll sort this out," shouted Hunter into the phone. "Take it easy. Nothing can't wait until morning."

"Hunter, this is no time for you—Get back here now and— You've no idea who just walked in—"

Then he heard only the irritating sound of static. But one thing came through loud and clear, unlike their earlier attempt at conversation. James was begging. If not begging, then desperate—for what, Hunter had no clue. He stomped toward the ship's stern, where a row of fiberglass tenders waited to ferry late arrivals or early departures. Fortunately, a few crewmembers lounged nearby.

"Take me back to the marina as fast as you can." He stepped down into the nearest boat and handed the crewman a hundred-dollar bill. With a roar of a powerful outboard motor, they took off without another word.

# TWO

$\mathcal{B}$ecause a lightweight speedboat spent more time above the waves than touching water, Hunter was on dry land and headed toward the city within twenty minutes.

James had better be having a heart attack or being robbed at gunpoint to take Hunter away from a party he'd been planning for months. He clenched down on his molars as he wove his way down Pontchartrain Boulevard far above the speed limit. He tried calling James's Metairie townhouse to no avail. With few other ideas, he drove to their downtown office. Nobody in their right mind would still be working after midnight on a Saturday night, but his partner often fit that description.

They had been best friends since pledging the same fraternity at Auburn College. Something about suffering hazing rituals had forged a bond during their freshman year. Later, when they shared a passion for stocks and high-flying investments, they talked about forming a partnership after graduation. James had interned and then been hired by a conservative investment house to gain experience. He had described it as Blue-Haired Boredom, Incorporated. Rebalancing portfolios twice a year to maximize returns and generate additional income didn't float his boat. As soon as his contract expired and James felt comfortable venturing out on his own, he approached his college friend.

Hunter had gained his sea legs at big brother Ethan's insurance firm. The work was even less exciting than James's experience because Galen customers preferred conservative annuities for their financial nest eggs. In addition to that, Ethan, as CEO, oversaw every transaction Hunter made, tempering his younger brother's enthusiasm for adventurous investing. Hunter found himself playing solitaire on his computer during client phone calls to keep from falling asleep. Face-to-face meetings to discuss financial goals and risk assessment were similar to Chinese water torture. When he advised one particularly indecisive customer to "simply stash your money under the mattress where it will be safe," he knew he'd reached the end of his tenure with Galen Insurance. It was time to strike out on his own, to take a chance.

James Nowak shared the same desire to broker aggressive stocks and investments for risk-taking clients. No one liked to lose money when a market tanked or a particularly hot tip cooled off like January rain on a parade, but Galen-Nowak customers understood the risk-reward concept. No risk, no chance of high returns on your savings. Their company wasn't for the faint of heart or those who depended on interest income to supplement their Social Security checks. But just as a person shouldn't take his mortgage money to Las Vegas, Hunter tutored his clients to maintain diversified portfolios and not gamble more than they could afford to lose.

It was of no consequence that the brokerage start-up capital came from a trust fund Hunter inherited from his grandfather. James didn't have one red cent left after paying for his rehabbed condo, a new Corvette, and his steady stream of new-and-improved girlfriends. The trust fund would be paid back gradually as the business amassed clients and profits. Hunter wasn't worried about his initial investment. It was those that followed he started to question.

The parameters of their business partnership had been carefully spelled out in a contract, with everything above board. It didn't matter that James wouldn't see profits beyond his monthly paycheck for at least ten years. His salary was substantial.

Hunter forced himself to relax as he pulled into the parking lot. James's dark-green sports car gleamed even in dim light. For the second time that night, Hunter counted his blessings and tamped down an uneasy feeling in his gut. Foghorns on the river and faint sounds from the cruise ship terminal carried on the night air as he unlocked the door at the employee entrance. After a short elevator ride to the top floor, he stepped into their ultramodern office. Windows overlooked his beloved city, struggling to redefine itself after the cruel blow nature delivered the summer of 2005.

Hunter threaded his way between the secretarial desks and broker cubicles. Trash cans overflowed with almost as much debris next to them as within, while computer printouts and stacks of analyst reports cluttered every desktop. Brokerage houses looked as if they had been in a tornado's path by the end of the day. The cleaning crew apparently had not reached their office yet in their evening rotation.

Hunter felt an ominous twinge of dread as he approached the pair of executive suites spanning the back of the building. James's light was on. Equal in proportion and ambience, the two offices shared an adjoining bathroom complete with shower and double closets so that neither partner received more than the other. Hunter had even leased his own Corvette, not to be outdone in flashy horsepower. He laughed at himself, thinking how competitive young men could be.

"Hey, buddy," he called. Hunter pushed open the carved oak door. "Here I am. What is so urgent that it couldn't wait?"

His question hung unanswered in midair. Client files, usually stacked on the left, had been scattered across the floor. Coffee cups, newspapers, mail, and desktop detritus had been swept from the surface. On the computer monitor, photos of Mardi Gras floats rotated on the screensaver. Then Hunter's blood turned cold. A body was sprawled on the floor next to the desk in an odd, frozen pose. One knee was bent to the side as though he'd tried to rise but changed his mind mid-attempt. Men didn't pass out in such poses. On the carpet a dark stain fanned from the head.

Hunter's dinner of crab ragout and lobster thermidore churned in his gut like acid. Lurching forward, he uttered a strangled, "James! What have you done?"

Watching a lifetime of horror movies and cop shows hadn't prepared him to find his best friend lying in a pool of blood. Bile rose in Hunter's throat as he stumbled back. Fighting his gag reflex, he steadied himself with the desk and blinked several times to be sure his mind hadn't concocted the terrible scene.

Nowak's brown eyes stared vacantly at the ceiling. Near his right hand, on the imported Aubusson carpet their decorator had insisted upon, rested a handgun. Hunter had never seen the gun before. Several absurd notions ran through his brain. *James doesn't own a gun. He hates hunting. He would rather get his exercise hitting golf balls into a water trap or bending his nine-iron around a tree trunk.*

Hunter reached out and grasped the cold steel of the gun. He hefted its weight and balance, the smooth finish. The anxiety that had begun in the back of his mind surged into a roar of frustration. "James, what did you do? What could have been so bad we couldn't work it out?" He dropped the gun, grabbed both lapels of James's jacket, and pulled him up. It was the same Armani suit he'd bought the day they signed their partnership papers.

James's head lolled back as Hunter half shook the dead man. Fighting down a wave of nausea and revulsion, he lowered the body back to the floor. The coppery stench of blood filled the shadowy office. Hunter didn't hear the approaching sirens or shouts of identification as men entered the office. He heard nothing until someone spoke next to his ear along with the distinctive click of a round being chambered into place.

"Hold it right there, buddy. NOPD." Someone spoke with the slow drawl of upstate Alabama. "Show me your hands and get up real slow. Don't do anything quick-like. What's going on here? We got a call 'bout a robbery in progress, and look what we got instead."

Hunter stared up into the face of a New Orleans patrol officer, who was aiming his gun on the center of Hunter's chest. Another cop in a blue uniform entered the office from the right with a second piece of firepower.

The first officer kicked away the weapon and yanked Hunter to his feet by his jacket. After moving to the outer office, Hunter explained who he was and why he was there, but even after producing identification, one of the officers kept his eye on him.

EMTs, someone from the coroner's office, and crime scene techs flowed into the executive offices in a steady stream. Although a gurney went in, James never came out of his home-away-from-home. When Hunter failed to supply sought-after answers, he was handcuffed and taken to precinct headquarters. He was told he would be held overnight for questioning. Considering the family lawyer was dancing with his mother at her party, he refused the offer to have counsel present during his interrogation. He preferred to take his chances in county lockup rather than ruin Clotilde's birthday.

In the end, he spent the remainder of the evening in a holding cell surrounded by drunks and disorderlies. With such an assortment of companions, despite the luxurious accommodations, somehow Hunter knew he wouldn't sleep a wink that night.

# THREE

*Three days later*
*Office of Nathan Price Investigations*

*M*r. Price? Someone is here to see you. The woman says she's your cousin." The assistant's tone of voice indicated she didn't believe that to be the case.

Nate pressed the intercom button. "She got a name, Maxine? Or is she just a generic cousin?" He stuffed police reports and preliminary evidence findings into his battered leather briefcase. He needed to talk to the so-called witnesses who reportedly overheard Hunter and James arguing recently. And he especially needed to talk again to Hunter. He'd been evasive about the matter, as though fighting with a partner was just business as usual. Nowak's death was being handled as a potential homicide, even though evidence that ruled out self-inflicted death wasn't in the files Nate had received.

"She says her name is Nicolette Price." Again Maxine's voice betrayed her skepticism.

Nate's mind conjured up an image of a skinny, all-elbows-and-knees tomboy who had followed him around like a spaniel at family reunions, graduations, and wedding receptions. Her pale blond hair usually needed washing and hung in a tangle around her shoulders. He and his male cousins would invent elaborate schemes to rid themselves of the pest, including locking her up in the boat shed for hours at a time. He was assessing the windows for possible escape routes when the unstoppable Nicolette pushed open his door and marched in.

Well, she didn't exactly march. It was more along the lines of a totter on ridiculously high heels. Her jungle mane of frizzy hair at least had been tamed into normal curls, and the young woman no longer dressed in camouflage fatigues. However, her huge brown eyes contained the same persistent determination as before.

"Hello, cousin. Do you remember me? It's Nicki." She held out her hand, no longer adorned with huge rings and nail art.

Nate stared, a bit slack-jawed. Her conservative navy blue suit and starched white blouse were straight from a *Murder She Wrote* episode.

"Nicki Price," she said, her hand still hovering in the air. "Your Aunt Rose's daughter. I'm down from Natchez, Mississippi. What's the matter with you, Nate? I haven't changed that much." Her slow Delta drawl morphed into a tone of clipped impatience.

Okay, this was the cousin he remembered. He shook her hand to keep it from falling off her arm. "Hey, Nicki. How ya doin'? You here to do some sightseeing in the big city? I'm a little tied up today, but maybe I can point you in the right direction—"

"I didn't come to be a tourist. I'm here to help. And from what I read in the paper, you can use me." Without being asked, she sat down into the chair in front of his desk and adjusted her skirt hem carefully.

He tried not to sound as impatient as he felt. "What exactly do I need help with? I buy all my catfish at the grocery store these days, and I haven't bashed in anybody's mailbox in years."

A stony glare rewarded his attempt at humor. "That was a joke," he said, folding his hands on his desk.

"I'm here to help with the Nowak investigation. Based on what they reported in the *Times*, I believe Hunter Galen will be charged with murder. If you plan to keep him out of jail, I suggest we find the real killer or your best friend's brother is on his way to Angola."

"Nicki, how could you possibly help me?"

"I finished my courses in investigation and have taken two years of classes at Alcorn State. I'm fully trained and qualified to assist you in solving this case."

He scratched the stubble on his jaw. "I remember my mom telling me you were at Alcorn, but that seems like a *long* time ago." He put special emphasis on the word "long" just to needle her.

"I had to *work* to put myself through school." She selected her own word to emphasize, sounding peevish. "It took me longer than you because I didn't get a full ride to LSU on a football scholarship."

"Easy, cousin. It's not my fault women's sports don't command the respect or financial support they deserve."

"Sorry." She exhaled a sigh. "It's been a long time since I defended volleyball as a serious team sport."

As Nate laughed the tension in the room seemed to disappear. "Are you licensed in the state of Louisiana?"

"I read the Louisiana training manual, took their classes, and I now have my license. I applied for a concealed carry permit, but the state must finish their background check on me." She straightened her spine against the chair.

"Will you have it soon?"

The slight flare of her nostrils betrayed he already knew the answer to that one. "After I log in a few more hours at the firing range, but I'm working on it. You know I'm a crack shot, Nate."

"We don't line up soda cans on the fence rail in New Orleans and shoot 'em off with a squirrel rifle, Nicki. We have really bad guys down here. Some of *them* are a crack shot too." He spoke slowly, his words holding a note of pity, as though consoling a not very bright child. "I don't want to explain to Aunt Rose how her only child ended up in the hospital...or worse." He shook his head as he rose to his feet. "Why don't we get caught up with family gossip over supper some time?"

"I can help with your investigation, Nate, even before my permit to carry comes through. You need me, considering the way this case is going so far." Scrambling to her feet, Nicki tugged her skirt down.

"Why exactly do I need you? I have an assistant. Maxine is all the support staff I can afford at the moment. Look around, kid. The population is nowhere near what it used to be. That means fewer missing children, fewer wayward spouses, and not as many employers spying on their employees. Business is off. I can't afford to put you on the payroll just because you're my favorite cousin." He reached out to cuff her chin playfully the way he used to do.

She swatted his hand away. "I'm not asking for charity. I'm asking for a chance to prove myself. This is a high-profile case. Every little dribble of information lands on the front page or the six o'clock news. You're just one man. And apparently you're not great with media damage control. Just think how many clients may find a way to your door if you help this Galen guy beat the rap."

Nate's good humor vanished. "Hunter Galen didn't kill his partner, Nicki. I'm not trying to help him get away with murder."

"Whatever. I've gone through the training and I *can* be an asset. I'm just asking for a break. You owe me after tormenting me for years."

Nate felt a twinge tighten his gut. "Did you really think I was that rotten?" he asked, trying to sound astonished. "I thought we got along pretty good."

She shook her head, her hair floating around her shoulders

like a mane. "More like a cat playing with a mouse—real nice at first, but then the cat chomps off the little mouse's head once it gets bored."

"I never once chomped off your head." He scrubbed his face with his hands. "Look, even if I were willing to give you your first big break, where would you live? Cheap places to stay are nonexistent. And I'm not good with roommates. My advice is to go home. Get some experience in Mississippi. Cut your teeth in a small town before you come down to the big leagues."

"How many paying customers do you think I can find in Natchez? Oh, except for our next-door neighbor, who hired me to find her missing cat. She insisted I take a ten-spot, which I donated to the animal shelter. I've already given up the lease on my apartment, and I have a place to stay. I didn't plan to mooch off you."

He lifted an eyebrow. "Where, Nicolette? Where are you staying?"

She hesitated as though reluctant to divulge too many details. "In a trailer park in Chalmette with an old friend of mine. It's a short commute down St. Claude and I have a car."

"In an old FEMA trailer?" His brow furrowed with concern. "That's no place to live. Those little communities are dangerous, *ma petite*. You tell your friend to get out of there too. It's not safe for single women." He glanced at his watch. "I gotta go, but give me your number. I'll call you and we can talk more later. I'm supposed to meet the dangerous *murderer* in ten minutes."

# FOUR

*T*he moment Nicki handed Nate her number, the tormentor of her youth—the boy who once drilled holes in her pirogue and laughed while she swam to shore in green water—bolted toward the door. She stared at the back of his expensive, well-tailored suit, the kind her kin back home couldn't hope to be buried in, until he disappeared. Only one option came to mind as she glanced around the cluttered but tastefully decorated office. She did what she had been trained for. She followed him like the professional private investigator she was.

While Nicki tracked her cousin through the city streets, she arrived at three distinct conclusions. First, men in general treated traffic like some kind of adversary to be defeated. Second, Nate loved to speed to the next traffic light and then slam on the brakes. Why couldn't men just adjust their speeds accordingly? And third, tailing someone on television looked much easier than it really was. Nicki thought she had lost him for sure until she spotted his sleek black Volvo squeezing into a tiny parking space. She wouldn't have attempted to park there on a bet. Hanging back to not give herself away, she waited for another spot to open up.

After five minutes and two trips around the block, Nicki pulled her compact into the driveway of an abandoned building.

Though a hand-painted sign proclaimed the entire area a loading zone, the building looked abandoned. She'd read that police
cruisers on patrol in New Orleans were still few and far between
since Katrina. Fewer parish residents meant less tax dollars for city
services, stretching every municipal department's budget. Nicki
decided to take her chances. Parking next to the deserted building,
she walked toward the only eating establishment on the block.

A small brass sign on the windowless facade revealed nothing
about what waited inside. The Blue Lotus looked like the kind of
place she imagined a date would take her if the man truly cared.
That is, if she had time to date. Then again, nothing like this elegant restaurant would have stayed in business long back home.
Cool, tropical-style ceiling fans circulated the air-conditioning
above eight or nine bistro tables. Fortunately, her quarry wasn't
seated at any of these or her clandestine surveillance would have
been finished before she'd even had a chance to start. A horseshoe-
shaped bar dominated the room with tall rattan stools. Beneath
her feet were highly glazed ceramic tiles, while the lighting was
muted and the patrons' voices subdued. No jukebox blasted
zydeco, no rail above the bar showcased fifty varieties of beer, and
no waitresses wore cropped T-shirts and shorts. No waitresses at
all. She saw only one waiter—and he was wearing a tuxedo, no less.

*Probably no prices on the menu. Maybe no menu. Maybe you just
tell the Creole chef what you want and...and voilà!*

She walked through the bar toward the French doors and
peeked around a large plant. The outdoor patio was a lovely
surprise—five times the size of the interior portion with stone
walkways connecting intimate terraces for ambiance and seclusion. Artfully placed potted palms and hibiscus provided additional privacy between tables. Strings of tiny white lights woven
through the Spanish moss would transform the restaurant into
an enchanted fairyland come nightfall.

In the courtyard her cousin sat under a live oak talking with another man. Although his back was to her, his shoulders were broad, his hair thick and tousled, and his sport coat loose and casual. Galen—trying hard not to look rich and infamous. Nate must have said something amusing because the accused threw his head back with laughter.

"May I help you, ma'am?" A voice over Nicki's right shoulder nearly startled her out of her toe-pinching shoes.

"One for lunch," she squeaked. She felt her cheeks redden under the maître-d's perusal. "May I have that table, please?"

His gaze followed to where Nicki's finger pointed—a table hidden by a huge blooming bush, one terrace higher than Nate's. "Ah, a good table for people-watching, yes?" Grinning, he held open the door for her.

"True, but if you don't mind, I'd like to seat myself." Before the man could argue, she pulled a menu from his fingers and scurried across the flagstones. Behind her he clucked his tongue but didn't follow.

Nicki slipped into a seat, propped her menu in front of her face, and moved the vase of flowers to a better position. From her vantage point, she could watch her cousin and Hunter Galen. Investigator and client were huddled deep in conversation, their menus ignored on the edge of the table. If only she could get a clear view of their faces, she might be able to tell what was being discussed. But neither one of them would sit still long enough.

Nicki only knew what she'd read about him, which wasn't much. Newspapers in Natchez said little about rich powerbrokers in New Orleans. However, news concerning the suicide or potential murder of his friend and partner had reached even the front pages in the Delta. He was better looking than the photo run in the *Times*, yet the thing Galen really had going for him was his hair—thick, wavy, dark blond, short on the sides, longish in the back. The kind of cut worn by arrogant men who thought they ruled the world.

Finally, Nate stopped bobbing and weaving and sat still long enough for Nicki to read his lips. *We'll see that no charges will be brought against you. I promise you'll never spend another night in jail.* The hair on Nicki's neck stood on end. If this pretty boy was guilty, if he had blasted his business partner into kingdom come, she wasn't going to enjoy getting him off. But if she could prove herself to Nate—and that led to his hiring her on a permanent basis—she would be happy to hand Jack the Ripper a get-out-of-jail-free card.

# FIVE

*T*he piranhas are getting more creative these days," Hunter said, stretching out his long legs under the table. "She must be from a tabloid. My sister-in-law told me the *Times* reporters never hang out here. Not enough red meat on the menu to satisfy their appetite for blood." He shook his head with disgust.

"What are you talking about?" Nate asked, taking a sip of his iced tea.

"A woman is taking pictures of me with her cell phone while trying to hide behind her menu. Not very subtle but don't turn around. I'm curious what other tricks she has up her sleeve."

Nate frowned and scratched his chin. "What exactly does she look like? So skinny that if she stood sideways she would appear to be a boy? Is her hair the color of sawdust?"

Laughing, Hunter stole another glance at the woman peeking around the side of her tall menu. "She's fairly thin, but I wouldn't mistake her for anything but female. And I would describe her hair color as sand on the beach."

Nate snorted. "Mirror sunglasses, like from an old rerun of *Miami Vice*?"

"Do you know this reporter? Is she a friend of yours? I hope you haven't gone over to the enemy's camp." Hunter refilled his glass of ice water from the pitcher.

Another snort—this one loaded with contempt. "Pretend you're talking on your cell phone. Act like something exciting is about to happen. Keep Miss Busybody's attention on you."

"What's going on, Price? You said you had important evidence to discuss in James's murder—if that's what they're calling it now. I don't have time for games."

"Humor me just for a minute, Hunter. I think I hear your phone ringing."

Before Hunter could argue, the investigator caught the arm of a roving waiter and whispered something into his ear. Then he stood and took off in the direction of the men's room.

Nate Price was Ethan Galen's best friend—Ethan's only close friend as far as Hunter could tell. He'd had little choice but to hire him when the police suspected him in James's death. But the guy always seemed like a banana peel left on the back stairs. Exhaling a sigh, Hunter pulled out his cell and pretended to be having a fascinating conversation. After a short interval of talking to nobody, he felt silly and pocketed his phone.

Suddenly, a burley waiter picked up the potted shrub in front of the woman's table. With her cell phone in her left hand, while her right scribbled in a small, green, spiral notebook, the reporter's mouth dropped open. A doe caught in the crosshairs on the first day of hunting season wouldn't look more surprised.

With few other choices, Hunter offered her his most ingratiating smile.

In an instant, Nate materialized behind the woman's table, grabbed her by the jacket, and yanked her to her feet. Like a lioness disciplining her young, the cub was dragged down the terrace steps, hissing and sputtering.

"Hunter, I'd like you to meet my cousin Nicolette Price. Nicki, this is my client and old friend Hunter Galen, although you may find the concept of friend alien, considering the way you're creeping around and spying on us."

The conspiratorial waiter appeared with a third chair. "Sit," Nate ordered. "Tell Mr. Galen you're sorry and that you'll never pester him again. Then I want you to go home. And I mean to Natchez, not Chalmette." Nate slouched into his chair and finished his tea in two long swallows.

Hunter looked from one angry red face to the other. They eyeballed each other like dogs fighting over a bone.

"I'm not going to apologize for doing my job, and I'm not going back to Mississippi. You can disabuse yourself of that notion right now." She hissed the words from the side of her mouth while her lips barely moved as she sat down.

"What exactly is your job, Miss Price? Are you a reporter?" Hunter felt like a reluctant witness to a family squabble. "I have already issued a statement to the press. I've nothing more to say until all the evidence has been processed." He studied the young woman's flushed face. She wore a prim but wrinkled suit with a white blouse buttoned up to her throat, a thin string of pearls, and high-heeled pumps. Her matching skirt and jacket made her look like an escapee from a convent school in the Swiss Alps, but her skin was the color of heavy cream and her lips were full and lush.

"No, Mr. Galen, I'm a private investigator just like Nate. How do you do, sir?" She stretched out her hand.

Hunter ignored Nate's exasperated sigh. "I'm very well, thank you." He caught the sweet scent of peaches from her skin.

"You see? He's just fine, Nicki. But with that long drive ahead of you, you'd better be on your way." Nate took hold of her sleeve and tried to hoist her to her feet. "Thanks for dropping by."

Cousin or not, Hunter didn't like Nate manhandling a woman. "Lay off her, Price. Show your cousin a little family love.

Why don't we have lunch since Miss Price drove all the way here?" He picked up one of the menus that had been ignored thus far.

Nicki shrugged from Nate's grasp and picked up the other menu. "Thank you, Mr. Galen. That boy has the manners of a muskrat. Wait until I tell Aunt Charlotte how he's been treatin' me since I arrived." This time she used an exaggerated Mississippi delta drawl. "I would love some lunch. I already decided what I wanted before I saw y'all sittin' here." Then with a shake of her head, the drawl vanished. "I mean, when I noticed you dining with my cousin and decided to make your acquaintance. I forget myself sometimes. I'm living in the Big Easy now, not out in the sticks. I should talk accordingly because I'm a long way from Jefferson County."

"Not quite far enough," Nate murmured.

"Nicolette is right. You do have the manners of a muskrat, Price." Hunter waved over the waiter. To Nicki he said, "I'm pleased you decided to join us."

"For crying out loud, Nicki, I'm not hiring you. You can bat your pretty, long lashes all day long, but it won't change a thing."

The waiter stood by Hunter's chair, glancing with amusement from one to the other.

"Do I have pretty, long lashes, Mr. Galen?" Nicki asked innocently. "No one's ever told me that before." Her smile stretched from ear to ear.

"You do, indeed."

"That's very interesting, but I didn't come to town to bat my eyelashes, or flirt, or even sample the cuisine of this restaurant." She pivoted toward the waiter. "But since I am here, I will have a bowl of turtle soup, the shrimp jambalaya, and *Niçoise* salad."

Despite the fact her pronunciation of the French dish of cold tuna rhymed with "my cozy," the waiter didn't blink. "Very good, madam. And you, sir?"

"I'll have the same." Hunter suppressed a laugh. He'd never heard a woman order so much food. Ashley usually ordered a house salad without dressing and then picked things off of his plate when no one was watching.

Nate looked from one to the other. "Are we *never* planning to eat again? Just bring me a burger," he said to the waiter. "And I would like a beer. In fact let's all have a beer, unless my cousin prefers a bottle of Dom Pérignon or perhaps a 1959 vintage Rothschild?"

Nicki's cheeks darkened with embarrassment. "If you recall, I don't imbibe. Never have and never will, but don't let me stop you. I'll have raspberry tea." She turned in her chair to face Hunter. "To finish what I was saying, I'm here to try to keep you out of the slammer. I have completed training in criminal investigation and have offered my services to Nathan in return for a modest starting salary. Plus any expenses incurred on the job, of course."

"Of course." Hunter noticed a single dimple in her right cheek. The left contained no matching indentation, creating an appealing lopsidedness.

"Of course, nothing," Nate said irritably. "Nicki will only muddy the water. She'll make a big fuss and turn everything into a sideshow. I've never needed help before and I don't now."

He then launched into a pointless summary of Nicki's unsuccessful attempts to mediate family squabbles.

Price was really getting on Hunter's nerves. Even if he hated this out-of-state cousin who dressed like Miss Marple, he shouldn't treat her so rudely. "Stop!" Hunter held up a hand. "I'm paying the bills, so I would love to hear why Nicolette believes I'm heading to jail."

A blush rose up her neck, connecting her freckles into rosy splotches. "You may call me Nicki. It's the evidence, of course. Your fingerprints were all over the gun. There was gunshot residue on your hand—not a lot, but hey, what possessed you to pick up the gun if you didn't shoot the guy? Don't you ever watch *CSI*?"

Leaning back in his chair, Hunter paused to reflect. "Yes, I watch *CSI*. But when I found my best friend with the bottom half of his face gone and a quart of blood down his shirt after just talking to him on the phone less than an hour earlier, my thinking went a little off track." He gritted out the words, trying to control his temper. After all, this was Nate's cousin from upstate Mississippi. "And I didn't shoot the guy. I hope you never find one of your friends in a similar situation."

The waiter discreetly set their luncheon plates on the table and disappeared.

"No problem there, boss. She doesn't have any." Nate took a huge bite of his burger. "And don't say I didn't warn you."

Hunter and Nicki ignored him, preferring instead to stare each other down.

Nicki was the first to speak. "All right. That was a bit tactless. My apologies, Mr. Galen. But there are witnesses who heard you arguing with the deceased while out on your yacht. In addition, coworkers have made statements to the police that you two often fought about money." She picked up her spoon and began her meal with her soup.

"Please call me Hunter if you're going to work for Nate and therefore me. And it's not my yacht. It's my mother's."

"Ohhh, noooo." Nate dragged out both words. "Hunter, tell me you're not serious." And to Nicki he said, "I don't know when you had access, but you had no business snooping in my files."

His client turned on Nate. "When did you plan on telling me about these witness statements? And who on earth went on record at my mother's birthday party that James and I argued?" His second question was more musing aloud than for anyone in particular.

"I was about to discuss the police report today at lunch before we were so rudely interrupted." Nate leveled a glare at Nicki.

Smiling sweetly, she finished her soup and then attacked her cold salad with fork and knife.

Hunter slicked a hand through his hair. "Great. I stumble blindly onto a crime scene, and because somebody heard us arguing, the cops don't plan to look any further? They're going to present this case to the grand jury, aren't they?"

"That would be my guess." Nicki popped a grape into her mouth and chewed.

"No, and even if they do, the DA doesn't have enough evidence to formally charge you." Nate insisted. "The GSR wasn't consistent with your firing the gun. A thirty-eight throws a lot of powder. It was rub-off, and the lab report will confirm it. Besides, arguing with a business partner is business as usual, I would say."

Hunter tried some of the soup, but he had lost his appetite. His mother and grandmother should have been able to live out their days without one of their offspring being suspected of murder. If he was arrested, the ladies would never show their faces in public again. He pushed away his bowl of soup.

"Is something wrong, Mr. Galen? Can I bring you something different?" The waiter stopped next to his chair while en route to another table.

"No, everything is fine. Perhaps I'll take this with me for later." He smiled at Nicki, not wishing to hurt her feelings about the menu selections. Then turning back to Nate, he said, "I can't be arrested for this. Do you understand me, Price? I can't go to jail."

"No problem. That's why you pay me the big bucks. There is no way the DA will trump up charges based on the weak evidence they have. You had no motive to kill Nowak."

Nicki set down her fork, her jambalaya only partially consumed. "I wouldn't be so sure about that. A forensic accountant will comb through your books looking for anything shaky. You're a stockbroker, aren't you? If they find even one dubious entry, you'll be suspect *numero uno*. *Comprendes español, señor?*"

"No, a little French, but I take your meaning nevertheless." Hunter didn't like her low opinion of his chosen profession, but at this point she seemed to understand the situation better than the seasoned veteran who sat glaring at her. He tossed his napkin on the table. "I want you to hire Miss Price to work with you, Nate. Not because I doubt your competence or your dedication, but because this case could get complicated. You can utilize her recent training or expertise and bill me for her salary and expenses. You're right, Miss Price. The police need to be pointed in the right direction or all they're going to see is me."

Nate lifted his hands in surrender. "Fine. I concede defeat, but how is your mom, Nicki? Doesn't Aunt Rose need your help up in Natchez? It can't be easy for her to work and take care of herself too with her rheumatoid arthritis. If you're on the case, you can't be running back and forth."

Nicki squirmed in the chair. "Yeah, that's what she has, and it's gotten worse actually. She had to quit her job because she can barely bend her fingers. It's started to affect her kidneys and lungs too. She has applied for Social Security disability, but until she's approved there's no money coming in." Nicki glared defiantly at Nate as though daring him to say the wrong thing. "That's why I need to work a *real* job in my profession instead of toting out the early bird specials to senior citizens."

Nate whistled through his teeth. "Man, I am sorry to hear about your mom."

Hunter's gaze rotated between the two Prices. "So is it settled? You two will work together on my case?" He picked up his lunch, efficiently boxed by the waiter, and signed the check that materialized before him.

"Yes," Nate replied through gritted teeth.

"Good. Then I suggest you not idle away the rest of the afternoon while my best friend's killer remains at large. After all, I am suspect *numero uno*. Nate, look into these alleged witnesses who heard me arguing with James. Let's see if any had an ax to grind with Galen-Nowak Investments. Then give me a call tonight."

"Will do, boss. I'm on it." Nate jumped to his feet and left by the main entrance.

"Nice meeting you, Nicki." Nodding his head, Hunter headed straight for the gate that led from the courtyard to the alley next to the building.

Unfortunately, he heard the clatter of her high heels on the flagstones behind him. "Wait! What do you want me to do?"

Taking pity on her, he stopped and turned around. "Why don't you call my lawyer, Kenneth Douglas? See if any of the forensic evidence reports are back yet. He can secure copies for you and Nate. Here is my address, cell, and home phone. I'll write Douglas's number on the back." Taking out a business card and pen, he jotted down the number and handed the card to her.

"Ah, Mr. Galen? I was wondering..."

"The police techs tested my hands at the scene. There's no way the GSR will come back consistent with firing a weapon. Find out—"

"Mr. Galen?" she interrupted again.

"I insist you call me Hunter."

"Hunter, could you give me a lift to the impound lot?" She looked anxiously over his shoulder. "Who would have thought this really was a loading zone?"

"I don't understand." He opted for patience after her ordeal with Nate.

"Somebody towed away my car. I didn't want Nate to give me the slip before...I mean, there weren't any other parking spots, so

I had little choice. I parked there and now it's gone." Nicki crossed her arms over her chest in a defensive posture.

Hunter pulled out his cell phone. "Let me call you a cab, Miss Price. I need to get down to—"

"See, that's just the thing." She interrupted him again. Apparently no one ever explained to her the wisdom of allowing someone to finish a sentence. "Even if you're kind enough to spring for the cab, there's the matter of the towing fees and whatever the impound lot charges."

"Sounds like you've danced this number before."

Her face blushed to deep scarlet. "A time or two, yes. But you could make it an advance against my salary. I don't mean as a gift or anything."

Hunter glanced around for Nate, but the man was gone. With few other options, he unlocked the passenger door to his car and courteously held it open for her. "Of course, Miss Price. But you'd better pay attention to the signs here in New Orleans. As you said at lunch, you're not in sweet Mississippi countryside anymore."

"I'll do that, I promise." She ducked her head into his sports car.

After she was settled, Hunter closed her door and headed around to his side. As he got in and started the powerful engine, he couldn't decide whether having her on the case might have advantages or if he'd just stepped on a hornets' nest.

# SIX

After examining Nicki's proof of ID and taking the two-hundred-dollar advance she had received from Hunter, the impound lot released her Escort. How could they charge storage fees when no one asked them to store anything?

"Hey, cousin, you busy?" Nicki asked as she stepped into Nate's office. She'd decided to come clean about her first misstep. "I saw your light still on."

Nate listened patiently and then asked only one question. "Did you think 'No Parking—Loading Zone' was merely a suggestion?"

Nicki let his well-entitled sarcasm slide. "What are you working on?"

"Just cleaning up paperwork that should have been done days ago. Then I gotta call my mom, something I should have done weeks ago." Nate grimaced. "As sons go, I'm not the best."

"How is Aunt Charlotte?" Nicki slouched into a chair, happy that the topic of family had been broached.

"Fine, as far as I know. She's miffed about Sean moving in with his girlfriend before walking down the aisle."

"Can't blame her there. You two were raised better than that." Nicki winked at him to soften her words.

"Why did your mom move to Natchez?"

"That's where her doctor is, although those new biologics he put her on are causing unpleasant side effects. All she does is complain when I call."

"Living with chronic pain can't be easy. That would make anybody crabby." Shutting his laptop, Nate leaned back in his chair.

"It's not that. She's unhappy with life in general, as though she's mad at my dad for getting killed and leaving her to fend for herself." Nicki met his eyes and then glanced away. "Considering both our mothers are widows, they sure adjusted to the situation differently."

"My dad left behind his pension and a decent portfolio of investments. Uncle Kermit..." Nate selected his words carefully. "He didn't plan as well for the future."

Nicki laughed wryly. "Well said, Mr. Diplomat. According to Mom, my dad never lasted longer than six months on any job. And when he did get paid, he drank his money at some bar on the way home."

Nate was quiet for a few moments. "Is that all you remember? I remember Uncle Kermit smiling and cracking jokes and always catching more fish than everybody else put together."

"We did eat a whole lot of fish for supper." Nicki smiled at the memory of Friday nights. "I remember him being really sweet to me. He loved to pick me up and swing me around. Plus he brought me Chick-O-Sticks and taught me to swim. Yeah, my parents argued a lot, but to hear Mom talk now, he was an abusive tyrant. Dad never laid a hand on me, not even when I deserved a smack on the behind."

"Which was probably six days out of seven." Nate wiggled his eyebrows. "I don't think Aunt Rose is making up stories. How old were you when he died—seven or eight? Kids don't have an accurate picture of life at that age."

Nicki picked up her water bottle and pressed it to her forehead, the condensation feeling cool against her skin. "You're right. He was probably Sir Galahad to people with no expectations, those who didn't hold him accountable like my mother. Paying bills was always the impossible dream in our house." Nicki's tone turned bitter. "He acted surprised every time Mom needed money for the rent, as though the first of the month didn't come around twelve times a year. If we went six months without the utilities getting disconnected, it was a miracle. After he died and we moved in with Mamaw and Papaw, I couldn't believe how they never argued about money. I don't remember them disagreeing about anything."

"That's not true, Nicki. Papaw loved LSU and rooted for the Tigers, but Mamaw rooted for Ole Miss. She even has a Rebels' ball cap."

"How'd that happen? Our grandparents didn't even have a TV for a long time. And neither finished high school, let alone went to college." Suddenly antsy in the small office, Nicki stood and began to pace. "What do you remember about the night my father died?"

"Nothing. I wasn't there." Nate looked at his watch.

"I know, but what were you told you about it?" She paused behind his chair and gave it a shake.

"What's the point? That was what...seventeen years ago?"

"Humor me, please. I was only eight, but you were thirteen."

Frowning, Nate scratched the back of his head. "My dad and yours, along with the rest of their brothers-in-law, took off to the swamps for the weekend. They went two or three times a year to hunt or fish or just get away from their wives. No big deal."

"My dad never came home. I call that a big deal."

"Sorry. I only meant the trip wasn't unusual." Nate sounded duly chastised. "The way I heard it was your dad got into a fight during a card game and then took off in the pirogue to cool off.

That made no sense because they usually played for nickels and dimes, nothing that would cause a fistfight or hard feelings."

"And the men were drinking and got drunk," she interjected, growing impatient.

"No, *your* dad got drunk. The others probably nursed one beer all night. Your dad was the one with a drinking problem."

"That's what your mom said? That sounds pretty judgmental."

"Don't get sore, Nicki. You asked me to tell what I remembered."

"Just because my dad was an alcoholic doesn't mean he deserved to die." Without warning, tears flooded her eyes despite the passage of so many years.

"Of course not. Nobody's saying that now and nobody said it back then. We don't know how Uncle Kermit died. He left the camp around midnight and when he hadn't come back by noon the next day, the men called the sheriff. They spent Saturday and Sunday looking for him, but the swamp is a big place. When he still hadn't turned up by Sunday night, everyone went home. They had to work the next day." Nate lowered his voice. "Why are you bringing this up after all this time? It's not even Father's Day." He tried to coax a smile out of her.

"Because I plan to find out how he died now that I'm a full-fledged investigator."

You could have heard a pin drop in the office.

"Don't be ridiculous. It's been seventeen years. If the sheriff found almost no evidence back then, you don't have a hope in heaven of finding any now."

"I deserve to know more than I do, Nate. Whenever I ask my mother about what happened, she always changes the subject."

"Maybe it hurts to talk about it or she still misses him."

Nicki snorted. "Still misses a man who only gave her twenty bucks for groceries for a week but always had money at the bar? The same man who ripped up her dress—her first new one in years—because she bought it without asking him first? It doesn't seem like she's wallowing in grief to me."

"Maybe not, but you asked me for a job. If you're on the Galen case, you don't have time for a cold-case investigation, even if that's what your dad's death was."

"You have my word I'll be here for you, but nobody works twenty-four hours a day, seven days a week. My free time, however small, is my own."

"Why did I think I could talk sense to a mule?" He stood and started for the door.

"I have no idea." Nicki followed him out of the office and down the steps.

"Where are you going now?"

"To pick up a pizza and head to Christine's, boss."

Nate waited until he was halfway to his car before delivering his final shot. "Fine, but don't say you weren't warned. If you start turning over rocks, something nasty is bound to crawl out." His tone contained uncharacteristic vehemence.

For once, Nicki didn't have a smart reply for him as he climbed in and slammed the door. She just stood there and watched him drive away.

# SEVEN

$\mathcal{S}$taring down into the courtyard below, Hunter listened to annoying music while on hold with his bank. Huge puddles formed on the flagstones, giving his backyard a subterranean feel. Water cascaded over the sides of the fountain, its overflow drain apparently blocked again by algae. His mood perfectly matched the weather—one no more black or depressing than the other. Finally, his banker picked up the other end.

"Hunter? How are you, son?" asked Morrison. Despite the fact Hunter was nearly thirty, he would always be "son" no matter his age. The banker was an old friend of his father's. Five minutes of small talk ensued, wherein Morrison asked about the health of every Galen family member and expressed his sympathy over James's death.

With the niceties aside, Hunter asked about the current financial standing of Galen-Nowak Investments. The situation was worse than he thought—a lot worse. "How on earth could we have a half million in unsecured debt with your bank? Our line of credit was only supposed to be two hundred fifty thousand."

"True, true, but your partner—excuse me, your late partner— kept asking me for additional sums. He said it was strictly a short-term cash flow problem. I saw no reason not to grant his request, never having any repayment problems with your company in the past." Morrison forced an unnatural laugh. "Is there a problem, son?"

There was a large problem as Hunter saw it. To loan out half a million dollars without requiring both partners' signatures on the application sounded to him like an unsound business practice. James never should have been given so much rope to proverbially hang himself with. "No problem at all," he said to the banker. "But I need to have my accountant go over the books before I arrange a repayment schedule."

"Of course, of course." Morrison clucked his approval. "Give my best to your mother."

As Hunter hung up the phone, his mood couldn't have gotten fouler if the courtyard flooded to the level of his apartment. Walking back inside from the gallery, Hunter padded across the cool dining room tiles and sank into his favorite chair. He loved living here and never regretted moving into the six-room suite over an antiques shop on Rue Royale. Shortly after Ethan and Cora's wedding, the newlyweds left the French Quarter and moved into *Grandmère's* mansion, initially to housesit while she toured Europe. But after the arrival of their first child, they thought the Garden District provided a more family-friendly neighborhood and decided to remain permanently. The situation worked out for all concerned. Their eighty-five-year-old grandmother and her seventy-five-year-old housekeeper, more a companion than anything else, loved having people in the huge house again.

The Rue Royale apartment was elegantly decorated with exquisite fabrics, rare antiques, and priceless *objets d'art*. Hunter didn't give a fig about any of that. Instead, he loved the proximity to great restaurants, good blues clubs, and several entertainment hot spots. Provided one avoided Bourbon Street, the French Quarter was an exciting place to entertain clients from outlying parishes and a super place to meet women, who came to the Quarter for shopping and sightseeing, from college age to grandmothers looking for antiques and artwork. His charm and manners, and his penchant for making people happy, had served him well in a friendly town.

But his social days were behind him.

Ashley Menard was the loveliest creature to ever focus her light blue eyes in his direction. As gracious as she was attractive, she was a throwback to the soft-spoken, demure woman of the South's bygone era. William Faulkner had written about the type many times. Ashley had many friends and plenty of admirers. Although she hailed from old family money, she'd worked hard to build her hair salon and day spa into a fast-growing chain. Hunter was certain Ashley would make a wonderful wife and mother. After all, as his mother loved to point out, he wasn't getting any younger.

Hunter heard the click of a key in the lock and the stomp of wet shoes on the mat. Within a few moments, the subject of his woolgathering swept into the room, her cloud of perfume competing with the scent of magnolia wafting through the open French doors.

"Hunter. There you are, my darling. What are you doing home in the middle of the afternoon? Shouldn't you be at the office selling lots of stocks and bonds to amass big piles of money so you can support me in the style to which I wish to grow even more accustomed?" To emphasize her point, she dumped an armload of shopping bags onto his coffee table. Several boxes of shoes fell to the floor, spilling their contents. Hunter reached down to pick up one high heel by its narrow strap. As he placed it back in the box, he spotted the three-hundred-twenty-dollar price tag. Three-twenty on sale, no less.

"More shoes, Ash?" he teased. "You know what happened to

Imelda, don't you? You would have to start changing shoes three times a day just to wear them all."

"Who's she? And I already do, baby." She bent down to brush a kiss close to his mouth. "You know I simply had to have this heel height in navy."

"Absolutely. Anyway, I'm home because I need to go over my financial statements. Those shoes will be perfect when you visit me in the Ursulines poor house. Considering the lines of credit James took out, that'll be my next address. Oh, wait. They closed that place a hundred years ago. Now where will I go?"

"You are going to Tuscany with me on our honeymoon." She continued to rummage through the bags. "You worry too much, darling. Didn't you and James take out life insurance policies on each other? You know, just in case."

Her question took him by surprise. He and his partner had discussed it, but he didn't recall ever mentioning it over the dinner table. "No. That would have been smart, but we never got around to it."

"What a shame. Oh, Hunter, you're rich. For a second there, I thought you were really worried about money." She laughed as though waking from a dream to discover she was Cinderella after all. The glass slipper was a perfect fit.

Hunter knew this was not the time for a serious financial discussion. Ashley earned her own money, giving her every right to buy however many pairs of shoes she wanted. But he often got the idea she was in training—preparing to graduate to some higher lifestyle. Not that he could imagine what that would entail.

"Whew, shopping is hard work." Sinking onto the sofa, Ashley fanned herself with a box lid. "I'm glad I stopped over instead of taking this stuff home. Sometimes I wonder why I don't just move in."

"Because your father would come after me with a shotgun. And I've seen what he can do to a clay pigeon."

"Only if you don't ask me to marry you." Abandoning the sofa, she plopped herself down on his lap in the overstuffed chair. "Do you have to head back to the office right away?" she asked, nibbling lightly on his neck.

The sensation spiked his heart rate. "What office?" he asked, shifting her to a more comfortable position.

Ashley sighed and pressed her mouth to his. Her kiss tasted warm and pepperminty.

"'Scuse me, folks. I knocked, but y'all must not have heard me—you being busy and all. So I just came on in."

Ashley startled so hard she would've landed on the floor in a heap if not for Hunter's quick reaction. He tightened his arms around her as he said angrily, "Who in blazes are you?"

"Detective Russell Saville," the intruder said in a slow drawl, pulling a badge from his trouser pocket. "New Orleans Homicide. Are you Hunter Galen?" He asked the question with his focus never leaving Ashley.

Saville was tall and wiry, with thick, oily hair, a flat nose, and olive-toned skin. His suit stretched across his wide shoulders and muscular chest. A weapon bulged beneath the fabric of his jacket, and the man looked rough even wearing a suit and tie.

Ashley rose gracefully to her feet and smoothed down her skirt. "Are you done staring, Detective?"

"Yes, ma'am. Begging your pardon." He bowed his head slightly.

Hunter stepped in front of Ashley to break off the little tête-à-tête. She possessed the uncanny ability to make every situation revolve around her within moments. "Do you usually just walk into people's homes, Detective? What's this about?"

"Like I said, the front door stood open so I didn't wait to be invited. I did announce myself, but you must not have heard."

Hunter suddenly had enough of the man's insinuations. "Ashley, please close the front door and then give us some privacy." She did have a penchant for leaving doors, cupboards, drawers, and even car doors open behind her as though she expected a personal maid to trail behind her and tidy up.

"Yes, of course, darling." She brushed a kiss across his cheek before walking out of the room.

"Do you have a warrant, Detective? I'm pretty busy here." Hunter flexed his fingers unwittingly.

Saville's eyes had followed Ashley. "Fine-looking woman, Mr. Galen. You two engaged or anything like that?"

Hunter stared at him speechlessly. Was he serious? "Could I see your badge again, Saville? Because I don't know who you are or what you want. And I'm sure not seeing a warrant."

The cop drew out his ID again. "I don't need a warrant to ask an upstanding citizen like you a few questions. I would think you'd want to help us find your partner's killer." Saville walked to the bank of windows overlooking the garden. "Man, we're going to need an ark if this rain don't stop."

When he turned around, Hunter saw his moustache twitch. If the guy weren't wearing a gun under his sport coat, Hunter would have loved taking a swing at him. "If you're here about James, was it a suicide or not?" He exhaled his pent-up irritation.

"Oh, we're pretty sure it was no suicide. You see, Mr. Galen, when somebody offs themselves, we usually find the gun still clutched in their dead hand. All the muscles in the hand and arm tighten up. But Nowak's fingers weren't locked around any gun."

"Is that right?" Hunter knew the guy was purposely trying to bait him with his callous referrals to James's death.

"Somebody wanted this to look like a suicide, and that somebody doesn't know squat about guns—probably the intellectual bookworm type. Most likely, he or she didn't go there to kill

Nowak or they would have had a better plan in mind. Nah, they went to talk to the guy, chew the fat, and then they shot him when Nowak didn't see things their way. They hoped it would look like a suicide, but shooting him was definitely an afterthought. No robbery. No mutilation. Somebody just decided the world would be a better place if James-the-Stockbroker was dead."

"Apparently you think that somebody is me," Hunter murmured in a low voice, digging his fingernails into his palms.

"You ready to confess yet? Then I can tidy up my paperwork and move on to the next mess. I hate having open cases." Saville slouched against the windowsill, a strand of gelled hair falling into his eyes.

"If that's what you came for, get out of my house." Hunter was losing the battle to control his temper.

"Easy now, Mr. Galen. There is one more little thing. We just arrested Nathan Price. I think you know the guy. He's on his way down to central booking as we speak." A glint sparkled in the detective's dark eyes.

"What for?" Hunter closed the distance between himself and the detective.

"Why, obstruction of justice, of course. He crossed into a secured crime scene. He claims the uniformed officer on duty watching the perimeter gave him permission to take files and your computer. But, funny thing, the cop on duty doesn't remember saying anything like that." Saville's thin lips stretched into a sneer. "At the very least, we got him on impeding an investigation. With him arrested for breaking and entering a couple years ago in Metairie, we have enough to yank his PI license for a while. At least until a judicial review board takes a good long look at the guy." The sneer turned into a downright grin. "Man, you hang around with some pretty shady characters, Galen. And here I thought you college-boy types just flocked together at the espresso shop or out at the country club."

"And here I thought Katrina washed all the corruption out of the police force."

"Ouch, that hurts." Saville pushed away from the windowsill and moved within inches of Hunter's face. "I think you're just mad 'cause I figured out your little plot."

Hunter straightened his spine. "What plot would that be?"

"Maybe you blew your partner away in some heat-of-the-moment tiff and then sent over the family handyman, Price, to tidy up your mess. Yeah, I know Price has been cleaning up after Galens for years. And I'll bet you left something behind besides your fingerprints all over the weapon. You're not all that smart are you, college boy?"

Hunter's fingers balled into fists as he shifted his weight into an aggressive stance.

"Hunter!" Ashley strode into the room. "Don't let that detective goad you into doing something foolish. Nothing would please him more." She wedged herself between the two men. Apparently she had been eavesdropping and felt the need to intervene.

Hunter could feel his entire body break out into a cold sweat.

"You're a fortunate man, Galen," Saville said. "Having a woman—a beautiful woman—to fight your battles for you. Whoo-wee, I wish I was born lucky like you."

"Ashley, go back into the kitchen, please. Everything is fine here."

"And have you punch out this officer and end up in jail?" She turned toward Saville. "We're about to announce our engagement and don't need this trouble." Her lower lip protruded in a pout.

"I see your point, sugar. You surely can't be betrothed to someone in the slammer. How will that look to your mama's friends?" Saville rocked back on his heels with amusement.

Hunter relaxed his fists one finger at a time. "You're spinning your wheels, Detective. The only reason Nate was there was to find out who killed James. That's what you're supposed to be doing instead of wasting time harassing me. I had no motive to kill my business partner. Even if you slept through most of your academy classes, motive must factor in here somewhere."

Saville's grin waned and then disappeared altogether. "Motive still looms large, Galen. That's why I requested a search warrant for every financial record in your office, including your computer's hard drive. My fellow *slackers* are executing it right now. Forensic accountants will rack up plenty of overtime picking apart your books. I'm betting we find all the motivation we're looking for." Saville stepped past Galen, purposely bumping shoulders on his way to the foyer. In the doorway, he paused and launched one last salvo. "It's too bad the Galen family's other trained seal retired last summer—Lieutenant Charlie Rhodes. Man, didn't he come to the rescue more than once? But all that's over with. No more tipped scales of justice—one for the rich and one for the rest of us." The venom he aimed at Hunter had nothing to do with the Nowak murder case.

"What's the matter, Saville? Were you expecting to make chief of detectives but were passed over for someone with a brain?" Hunter knew this adolescent sparring was a mistake, but the detective had crawled under his skin. Too little sleep, too much caffeine, and too many things going wrong had conspired to make him a crabby man.

"Don't you worry. I'm smart enough to bring you down. This town's been reborn. Your kind ain't in charge anymore."

"Maybe the fact I didn't do it *might* get in the way of your personal agenda," shouted Hunter, but Detective Saville had already left the apartment, slamming the door behind him.

Hunter went to the sideboard to pour himself a drink but reconsidered. He needed a clear head. And he needed Ashley to leave. He was in no mood for her opinions on Saville's manners or anything else at the moment. "Ashley, why don't you take your purchases home and I'll call you later." He tried to keep his voice as level as possible.

After a few minutes of halfhearted resisting she left, promising to call when she returned from a work seminar in a few days. Hunter breathed a sigh of relief when her cloud of perfume followed her out the door. He had plenty of work to do. Fortunately, his assistant fretted about computer viruses or corporate espionage and had hard copies of the firm's financial records for the last five years. She kept them in a closet in his apartment, dutifully bringing over a new file every month. Pulling out the boxes of files, he had a long night ahead of him.

Detective Russell Saville wouldn't be looking for James's killer now that he'd tweaked the guy's nose. And he probably wouldn't have anyway. The guy was lazy, evident in the way he walked, and even the way he chewed gum like a cow's cud. But Saville wasn't Hunter's most pressing problem at the moment. Forensic accountants would be going over his company books as though combing hair for lice. They would soon know more about the Galen-Nowak financials than he did. And that was his fault. For too long he had let James manage the office, including the corporate money flow, so that he could devote himself to the portfolios of their large corporate clients.

That had been a mistake. He feared James's personal appetite for risky, high-flying investments may have gotten out of hand. He'd suspected James had been up to something fiscally unsound, yet he hadn't confronted him. Why? Because James was his best friend and he didn't want to jeopardize that friendship.

Hunter had never liked confrontation. In fact, he usually did everything he could to avoid it. A shrink would probably conclude the tendency stemmed from the middle sibling's role of arbitrator, which in truth would be correct. But as he carried box after box of financial reports to the dining room table, one idea niggled in the back of his mind. If he had confronted James, if he'd asked the right questions, would his partner still be alive today?

# EIGHT

*N*icki stared out the pizza shop window as the dismal rain finally dwindled to a drizzle. But even sunshine couldn't improve her overall bad day. Words from her conversation with Hunter as they went to pick up her car stuck in her craw. *"You need to work on your surveillance techniques, Miss Price. Lurking behind a menu may work occasionally, but taking pictures with your cell phone needs to be rethought. You should get one of the cool mini cameras James Bond used."* James Bond, indeed. She would have told Mr. Smarty Pants off if she hadn't needed this job. Besides, she worked for Nate, not for Hunter. She didn't care who paid her expenses.

Finally, her number was called. Nicki set a six-pack of Coke next to the pizza at the register and pulled out her wallet. She had no intention of showing up in Chalmette empty handed. Not that she was hungry after the quantity of food she'd consumed at lunch. Why had she eaten like a farmworker after her mom packed two perfectly fine tuna sandwiches for the drive to New Orleans? Maybe because the food in that hoity-toity restaurant had tasted so good. The turtle soup reminded her of Mamaw's, and the jambalaya had been loaded with shrimp instead of being merely a bowl of pink rice with bits of what could have been seafood at some point. Food like that shouldn't go to waste, and she didn't care what Hunter thought of her anyway.

She knew one thing for certain. Despite the newspaper's insinuations, he didn't kill his business partner. Men like him would never pull a trigger. They would pay someone to do it. And a professional would have staged a far more convincing suicide than that. Why would he want to kill his partner anyway? If he did have some hidden reason, Nicki planned to ferret it out. Not just to clear his name, but to show her cousin what she was capable of. She wasn't Nicki-from-the-Mississippi-backwoods anymore.

The memory of Nate's introduction still stung after all these years. He may have only been fifteen at the time—and all boys that age were obnoxious—but for some inexplicable reason his opinion meant a lot to her. She would gain his respect or die trying. The jangle of her cell phone jarred her back to the moment. *This had better be important—daytime minutes,* she thought. She had to be the last person in America without an unlimited calling plan.

"Hi, Nate," she said, seeing his name on her screen.

"Where are you?"

"I'm on my way to Chalmette. This is Christine's only night off at the coffee plant."

"Good. Stay there tonight. Be sure to lock the doors if that tin can even has locks. I sure wish you had your gun permit. Everybody else living there will be packing heat."

"Don't worry so much. I'll be fine."

"I didn't call to rag on you, Nicolette. Tomorrow morning I want you to head home to Natchez. Tell Aunt Rose I'm real sorry this didn't work out."

"Nate, no! I thought you'd agreed—"

"I did, but I'm changing my mind." His voice turned tender. "Nicki, I've been arrested for crossing the crime scene at

Galen-Nowak Investments. I'm waiting for my lawyer to post bail, but apparently the DA can't decide whether to charge me with obstruction, which is a felony, or interfering with a criminal investigation, which is just a misdemeanor."

"Oh, dear," she breathed into the phone. Her cousin wasn't fond of small places. He certainly wouldn't fare well in jail. "Did you do it? I mean, how did this happen?"

"I asked the officer on duty if I could take a few files and Hunter's computer. I showed him my ID. He nodded his head—at least, that's what it looked like to me. Then on my way to my car, cops surrounded me, slapped on cuffs, and read me my rights." Nate whistled through his teeth. "This is serious. I could lose my PI license. I had a little trouble a couple of years ago. Now I've been suspended pending a full hearing by the review board. That could take months, Nic. I've been ordered off the case. So, little cousin, there is nobody here to assist."

She tried to get in a word, but the phone line crackled as the signal faltered.

"I gotta go. They already took away my phone. Civil liberties are few and far between in the clink. I'm sorry I couldn't give you your big break." He hung up.

But he was wrong. Nate was handing her a big break on a platter. She would find out who shot James Nowak and get Mr. Charm-and-Personality off the hook. Nate would be so impressed he'd make her a full partner. Then she would be able to afford her own apartment, maybe in the French Quarter or a loft in the Warehouse District. Someplace chic in the city. No more rural free delivery for her. No more junk cars up on cinder blocks. No more mud washes doubling as driveways, and no more bashed in mailboxes courtesy of teenagers with nothing to do. Nicki would live in the Big Easy even though it wasn't all that big anymore. And for many people, it had never been easy. But she liked it.

And this case was her ticket to the big leagues.

Unfortunately, the road to her dreams contained a stopover in one of Chalmette's three trailer parks. The former FEMA village was worse than she had imagined. Cars were parked haphazardly. Doghouses, storage bins, motorcycles, bicycles—even kids' toys were chained to whatever couldn't be carted away. The tightly packed units offered no privacy whatsoever. When the neighbors argued, everyone heard them air their dirty laundry.

*This is only temporary*, she reminded herself.

After parking legally this time, Nicki knocked on Christine's door. The two friends had gone to high school together but hadn't seen each other in four years. Christine and her husband had moved from Red Haw to find employment. Both had found jobs at the coffee processing plant in New Orleans. They bought a shotgun house in Chalmette and produced two adorable children, at least according to photos in Christmas cards.

Then Katrina took the house away. A prettier girl on the production line took the husband away. And Children's Services took custody of the kids after an impromptu inspection. When the social worker found only a day or two's worth of food in the house, the children were placed with her ex-husband—correction: more often her ex's mother—an unpleasant woman who had always disliked Christine. Now plenty of paperwork and several inspections had to occur before the children would be returned.

Her old friend answered the door wearing shorts, a T-shirt, and orange flip-flops. Her left hand held the TV remote, her right a can of diet soda. "Hey, girl, you come bearing pizza? In that case, come on in."

Nicki stepped into the tightest packed, closest quarters she'd ever seen. Stuff—boxes, toys, stacks of magazines, mismatched furniture—filled every inch of space.

"Hi, Christine. Good to see you. Thanks again for letting me stay a while."

"What are friends for?" Christine said cheerily as she took the pizza box and plastic ring of Cokes.

While Nicki moved a stack of newspapers from a chair, a very large man entered from what must be the bathroom. He seemed to take up all the room's available space. Tattoos decorated his arms, shoulders, neck—everywhere not covered by his jeans or T-shirt. Even his jawline sported art in the design of a colorful goatee.

"Hi. I'm Nicki," she managed to squeak as she held out her hand.

"How ya doin'?" He glanced at her hand but made no effort to shake. "I'm outta here. Don't need to listen to chicks jabbering all evening." With a bang of the screen door, the goliath exited the trailer, allowing more space for oxygen.

Christine handed her a paper plate piled with pizza. "Don't mind him. Travis is cuddly as a teddy bear once you get to know him." The sound of a motorcycle engine roaring to life nearly drowned out her words.

Nicki silently vowed to not stay long enough to find out. She also vowed to help this woman stop making bad choices any way she possibly could.

"Before you make yourself comfy in here, I'll show you your room." Beaming with pride, Christine led the way down the minuscule hall and swung open the door to a bedroom.

At least she had run the sweeper on the small patch of exposed carpeting. Boxes of toys were stacked to the ceiling, blocking the room's only natural illumination. A stuffed rabbit's ragged ear hung from a box. Bunk beds flanked one wall, and on the opposite wall were two small bureaus. With the only source of ventilation obstructed, the smell of dirty socks assailed Nicki's senses. "This will be fine," she lied.

"When I get my kids back, you'll have to make other arrangements. But that probably won't be for a while."

Nicki saw both grief and guilt filling her friend's face. "How is your case going? Any update?"

"Nah. The lawyer says I'll be lucky to get a hearing scheduled before January. Lots of cases on the docket ahead of mine."

*The attorney probably isn't losing sleep over it either, considering how many domestic cases a legal aid lawyer handles*, Nicki thought. Christine's kids were her life. One slipup had taken away the only good thing she had.

The kitchen phone rang, breaking the painful moment and giving Nicki time to assess her new quarters. The last thing she wanted was to fall into a routine of daytime TV while recounting the ways life knocked you down. She had too much experience with that back in Natchez. It was one of the reasons she'd left. Many of her girlfriends preferred to spend their time complaining about their lives instead of doing something to change their sorry existence. Nicki didn't need to look beyond her own house to witness a hard-luck story better than any on *The Jerry Springer Show*. Rose Price's debilitating illness was a culmination of a lifetime of sorrow and disappointment.

Nicki shook away thoughts of her mother. *I've only been gone twenty-four hours.* Inhaling a breath of stale air, she walked outside to get her rolling duffel, tote bag, and makeup case. Her small amount of luggage seemed more than the room could absorb. If Christine was working the second shift, she would be gone when Nicki returned from a hard day of sleuthing. They would probably seldom cross paths, especially if Christine had visitation with her kids on Sundays.

"I can't believe how much we have to catch up on, Nic. For

starters, did they ever find out who killed your dad?" Christine's question cut through Nicki's fog as she crammed her few garments into the tiny closet.

"No, and I don't really want to talk about it. Why don't you tell me about your kids instead? Do you have any recent pictures? I haven't seen them since they were in diapers."

Christine's eyes lit with joy as she hurried for the photo album. Nicki exchanged her suit and heels for a long-sleeved polo shirt, jeans and sneakers, and the rest of the evening passed pleasantly as they ate pizza, reminisced about high school, and swapped girl talk. Christine didn't ask many questions about Nicki's college years or why she'd come to New Orleans when so many residents had found new places to live after Katrina. She seemed far more interested in gossip about their former Forrest High School classmates. Eventually, though, Christine fell dead asleep on the couch, but Nicki was so wired she couldn't sleep if her life depended on it. The neighbors' TV blared through the aluminum walls, and soon her new roommate's snores added to the cacophony. Nicki slipped from the trailer, locking the door behind her with her brand-new key. She could sleep tomorrow while Christine worked at the plant. Right now she had someplace to go.

# NINE

*N*icki headed to the address on her client's business card, 786 Rue Royale in the French Quarter. *My, oh, my. Can't they just call it Royal Street like everywhere else in America?* A quick Google search had told her all she needed to know about Hunter's background—he had old family money, high society connections, and a beautiful girlfriend whose face would not have been out of place on the cover of *Vogue*.

It was after eleven when she parked and stared at the bank of windows above a pricey-looking shop. Every light glowed brightly in Galen's apartment. Apparently, the electric bill wasn't a problem. Maybe a guilty conscience wouldn't let the guy sleep.

Her compact car, although fuel efficient and practical for getting into tight parking spots, didn't provide lounging comfort. After fifteen minutes of shifting around and jamming her elbows, Nicki got out of her car, walked across the street, and pressed the button next to Galen's wrought iron gate. When the intercom crackled to life, she identified herself and then listened to utter silence. No *who?* No *get lost?* Maybe the man couldn't remember her name after their auspicious introduction earlier that afternoon. Finally a buzzer released the latch, and Nicki pushed open the gate. Beneath a shady canopy, a brick pathway led to the steps to Galen's rarefied world. Although the passageway between buildings was narrow, clay pots of blooming shrubs and flickering gaslights softened the appearance of an average alley. She climbed the steps slowly, questioning the wisdom of her decision to contact him at his home.

"Come in, Miss Price. I wasn't expecting you." The great man himself opened the fancy carved door, looking haggard and in need of a shave.

"No butler, Mr. Galen?" Nicki asked with a smile as she stepped across the threshold.

"It's his night off. Coffee?"

"Sure. Cream and three sugars. And please call me Nicki. Since I'm beholden to you for two hundred bucks, we should be less formal."

"Cream and three sugars it is, Nicki." He moved past her through the high-ceilinged foyer without a backward glance.

Without invitation, she followed him into his kitchen—a large, airy room with an expanse of windows overlooking the garden. Everything in the room was white—tile, countertops, appliances, and the art glass chandelier. Clean, simple lines with no clutter. There wasn't even a ubiquitous toaster ready for morning. Nicki watched him fill a mug, drop three cubes from a sugar bowl in the drawer, and splash milk into the cup. He handed it to her and then walked from the room.

Nicki followed, feeling a little foolish. In the living room she took a nervous sip of her coffee. While he perched on the end of the sofa, she stood like a tourist in a museum. The room took her breath away—dark, moody, and filled with antiques. Persian area rugs covered polished hardwood floors with heavy, overstuffed furniture—the room was the antithesis of the stark white kitchen. "Nice room," she murmured. "Can I have the name of your decorator? The place where I'm staying could use a makeover."

Hunter peered around as though seeing his home for the first time. "Thanks, but I can't take credit for the decor. My brother owns the apartment. The whole building, actually. He has way more taste than I do. Perhaps he can recommend someone for you."

"Are these antiques real?" She ran a finger along the intricate scrolling of a beautiful mahogany armoire.

"I suppose so. I never asked. After he married and moved to a house, I moved in here." He stifled a yawn behind his own coffee cup.

She examined the piece a bit more. "It's real, all right. My Papaw...um, grandfather...was an auctioneer. He taught me how to tell fish from fowl, as he would say. Lots of good reproductions are being passed off in the antique world these days."

From the arm of the sofa, Hunter studied her curiously, like a scientist peering at something unknown through his microscope. "Must be an interesting line of work for your grandfather. Hunting for the next buried treasure in someone's attic."

Nicki shrugged. "No money in it anymore for legitimate dealers. Everybody wants to get rich buying and reselling stuff on eBay."

Small talk about her grandfather's vocation was apparently growing tiresome to the important man because Hunter cleared his throat and asked, "Have you heard about Nate? I sent my attorney to the courthouse to bail him out. It's a bogus setup if ever I heard one. But the licensing review board will take a serious look into the charges."

"That's why I'm here, besides the fact I couldn't sleep. I'm taking over your case."

His expression looked even less pleased than finding her at his door late at night. "No offense, Nicki, but I need a real investigator. Not some kid with an ax to grind or something to prove to her family back home."

She'd been enjoying how he said her name—soft, not harsh, and clipped like how most people pronounced it. Her appreciation of his accent ended abruptly. "I'm no kid. I'm twenty-five."

"I need a professional. They're looking at me for murder, and someone set Nate up on an obstruction charge. Are you even licensed?"

"Yes. And I'm just waiting for the background check for my carrying permit, which will be finished any day now." Her voice rose with irritation. She was being dismissed like a second grader.

Hunter ran a hand through his hair in one fluid motion. "I'm sorry, but I'm thinking about calling another PI agency—a firm recommended by your cousin."

"That lowdown, underhanded snake from a tick-infested swamp!" Nicki set down her coffee cup with a clatter.

Hunter blinked in confusion and rose to his feet. "Who?"

"Nate. He stabbed me in the back." She closed the gap and stood face-to-face with the man the cops thought shot his partner in the head. Even at this hour, his aftershave smelled hypnotic. "He had no business calling somebody else after hiring me."

"I'm sure stabbing you in the back wasn't his intention. He doesn't want you getting in over your head. This isn't finding lost cats, Nicki. My partner is dead and I didn't kill him. That means some bad guy did."

His condescension stiffened her spine. "Are you going back on your word, Mr. Galen? You talked Nate into hiring me. My involvement wasn't contingent on him staying on the case. This afternoon at lunch you saw potential in me you liked. Tell me what's changed since then."

Hunter crossed his arms over his chest. "What if I need protection from whoever killed James? Where's your gun, little missy?" He mimicked John Wayne in a C-grade Saturday afternoon movie.

He was mocking her! "Buy yourself a vicious German shepherd to stand guard. In the meantime I'll hold up the brainy end of the investigation. I know plenty about forensic accounting. I can follow a paper trail like a bird dog after a mallard."

"I didn't know that. You didn't mention anything during the initial interview about spaniels or ducks." While she held her breath, Hunter stared at her for a long moment. Then he sauntered back to the kitchen to refill his mug and top off hers with her at his heels. "I already have a team of accountants on my payroll, all supposedly experts at money trails."

"And one of them could be your partner's killer."

He released a weary sigh as he led the way to the dining room. Stacks of reports, ledgers, and files covered the entire surface. "All right, let's get started. I've been going over our company's financial records. These are the same records that NOPD has a copy of, thanks to their search warrant." Noticing her confusion, he paused. "Well, Miss Price?"

"Well, what?"

"Where's your little spiral notebook? The green one you were filling with notes in the Blue Lotus?"

"It's in my purse." She ran her tongue over dry lips.

"Get it out in case you'd like to note something."

"You mean I'm still on the case?" Nicki couldn't seem to stop floundering.

"Isn't that what you just campaigned for? Didn't you plan to get your way?"

"I sure hadn't expected it."

Hunter laughed, the rich sound resonating off the high ceiling. "Do you always say exactly what's on your mind?"

She inhaled deeply as she pulled her pen and notebook from her purse. "I do, but that doesn't always turn out well for me."

"You are a rare individual." He pulled out a chair at the table and sat down across from her. "Most of the women I know say what they think I want to hear."

"I'm not most women. I need to hit your bathroom first and stop drinking coffee. When I get back, show me last month's financial statements and we'll work backward from there." She hurried in the direction he pointed, more nervous than at any previous point in her life. Hunter Galen unsettled her. For one thing, she was attracted to him. His perfect tan reached into the hair at his temples, while the tiny lines around his eyes made him look distinguished. Even without sleep and everything that happened, he was a handsome man. But more appealing than his appearance was the fact that he believed in her, and he believed she would do what she said. She wasn't even that sure of herself. All her life, people—especially males—had doubted her, as if she were a pathological liar who had to prove herself over and over. Hunter seemed ready to trust her until proven wrong.

After she returned to the dining room and settled comfortably on a chair, Nicki stole a glance at him. She liked being believed in. She was determined to solve this case and send him back to his fancy girlfriend. Then the two of them could live happily ever after.

# TEN

*L*ight flooded the room through clerestory windows near the ceiling, bringing Nicki fully awake. Despite multiple cups of coffee last night, she had dozed off with her head on the dining room table, while her left hand still clutched her pocket calculator. A crocheted afghan was wrapped around her shoulders.

Hunter lay sprawled on the floor beside the table, flat on his back and surrounded by boxes of tax records and financial reports for the past several years. Worry lines and fatigue had vanished from his features. His chest rose and fell with each breath as he snored softly. For several minutes she watched him sleep. He looked more muscular and athletic than one would expect in a stockbroker. His pectorals flexed against his shirt with each intake of air, while his biceps stretched the material of his sleeves. *No doubt he has a personal trainer on the payroll.* She nudged his hip with one bare toe, not remembering what happened to her sneaker.

"What? What's wrong?" He bolted upright and glanced around.

"Nothing's wrong. It's morning. We both fell asleep. I hadn't planned to stay over. I have a place in Chalmette, you know."

"Yes, I remember. A FEMA trailer. But instead you got to sleep face down on hard mahogany. Sorry, Nicki. I should have offered you the guest room. I hope you'll find me a better employer than host." He slowly rose to his feet and stretched.

"For the record, it's not a FEMA trailer. That was hauled away long ago. Hey, do you still have the food you brought home from the Blue Lotus? I'm starving."

He smiled. "I've got something better in mind than leftovers after our successful night. Let's go out to breakfast. You can wash up in the bath off of my bedroom." Hunter pointed toward a hallway before disappearing onto the balcony with his cell phone.

*Even first thing in the morning, before a shower or teeth brushing, the guy looks great.* But it had been a good night. They had uncovered several reasons why someone would kill Hunter's business partner. Nowak had overextended Galen-Nowak Investments big-time. Hunter would have to come up with a healthy infusion of capital just to keep the lights on and pay broker commissions on trades already processed. None of the figures supplied by Nowak matched the books. He had some bizarre accounting practices he hadn't learned at Carnegie Business School. And he'd been churning client portfolios to generate fat commissions for himself. Not many of Galen-Nowak clients benefited from his management during the past couple of years. They would have been better stashing their money under the mattress.

Nicki spotted a brand-new toothbrush lying on Hunter's bathroom counter along with a comb. *Thoughtful guy.* She debated her options and then turned on the shower taps. The hot water coursing down her back and shoulders felt like heaven, even if she had to put on her clothes from yesterday. She lathered her hair with his shampoo, scrubbed with an incongruous soap-on-a-rope, and rinsed off. Hunter's towels were the thickest, softest cotton she'd ever touched. It felt strange using his bathroom. The man was her new client—a man suspected of killing his partner. And James

Nowak had certainly provided plenty of incentive, considering how he'd drained the company coffers, but proximity to a potential murderer wasn't making her nervous. Nicki wished Hunter was old, fat, and toothless. Then her stomach wouldn't be bobbing like a tugboat in a storm. Physical looks shouldn't affect professional relationships, but, unfortunately, they usually did.

She had a sudden urge to open every drawer and closet to see what brands he preferred. Colgate or Crest? Charmin or White Cloud? What a goose she was turning into. If she wasn't careful she'd make a big fool out of herself. The man had a girlfriend. He wasn't her type. And she certainly wasn't his. Enough said.

Nicki peeked out the door to check his bedroom before stepping out in only a towel. Empty, quiet, and eminently masculine. Wood blinds shut out early sunlight, while polished tile floors felt cool under her bare feet. One wall held an expanse of bookcases. A cluttered desk with computer monitor sat between two French doors leading to another balcony. His bed was massive and dark wood, with four posts thick enough to support the roof of a building. A tapestry quilt had been pulled up to the navy silk pillowcases. *Tasteful. It must be nice to be rich.*

But the best surprise was a pair of cut-offs and a T-shirt stacked on his blanket chest. She felt certain they hadn't been there when she went into the shower. She quickly dressed in the borrowed clothes and went looking for her benefactor.

Hunter was barefoot and whistling out of tune as he filled two mugs in the kitchen. Comb tracks were still visible in his freshly washed hair. In his chino shorts and a polo shirt he looked as though he planned to play a few rounds of golf later. "I sure hope one of those is for me," Nicki said as she settled into a chair.

He met her gaze as he handed her a mug. "I'm afraid breakfast will have to be takeout. I just got a call from the captain of the *Queen Antoinette* and he needs to see me. Some kind of small problem that needs to be settled with the dockmaster. He called my mother, but she was flummoxed by the whole matter. She's still new at this."

Nicki sipped the strong brew. "What exactly is the *Queen Antoinette*?"

"A sailboat. Well, a yacht actually. It was a birthday gift from my brother and sister and me." When he finally noticed her outfit, a grin filled his entire face. "Hey, those duds never looked so good."

"The shirt is too big and the cutoffs are a little tight through the hips, but clean clothes sure feel better than day-old ones."

"There you go again—saying exactly what's on your mind."

"You don't pay me to be subtle. We don't have to worry about breakfast. I can hit a drive-through on my way home." Nicki finished her coffee and then set her mug in the sink. Turning around, she said with a smile, "You and your sibs give great birthday presents. I've never been on a sailboat before."

"You've never been on a boat?" His shock sounded genuine.

"I was in a pirogue a few times in the swamp and a rowboat on the lake by my grandma's."

"It's hard to believe that's the extent of your seafaring. Didn't you grow up a few miles from the Mississippi and within a couple hours of the Gulf of Mexico?"

"Wait. I went on a flume ride once at Six Flags. Does that count?"

"It does not." He shook his head. "How about a cruise ship to Cancun or a gambling riverboat?"

She shook her head.

"No powerboats for water-skiing? A ferry boat across the river?" He scratched his stubbly chin.

"What part of 'I've never been on a boat' don't you understand, Galen? Lots of people in this country could say that."

"Sure, if they live in the middle of Iowa or Nebraska. Natchez is on the largest river in the United States."

"I've looked down at the Mississippi from a bridge."

"In that case, we could take care of this today. How would you like brunch on Lake Pontchartrain? I can call the captain back and tell him to alert the crew. The *Queen Antoinette* can be ready for a morning sail by the time we drive to the marina."

Nicki stared at him without blinking. *Going out on a yacht in his clothes? What if I get seasick?* "I don't know anything about sailing."

"You don't have to. That's what the crew is for."

"Look, I work you, Galen. I don't think this is a good—"

"We both need to eat and compare notes as to what we discovered last night before falling asleep. One quick spin around the lake and that's it."

He construed her silence as acquiescence. "Prepare yourself for a new experience, Miss Price. One you will tell your grandchildren about." Hunter rummaged around in a drawer, the matter apparently settled.

"What if I throw up?" Nicki winced at her choice of words. "I mean...get sick?"

Having found whatever he sought, he lowered his head to meet her eye. "That's why I'm giving you this." He handed her a tube of Dramamine. "Take two with water and eat some crackers. Never go on water with an empty stomach unless you're certain you don't get seasick. Swallow those down and let's go. I'll call the captain right now." He pulled a box of saltines from the cupboard and gave them to her as he punched a number into his phone.

There was no point arguing. Hunter Galen was obviously used to getting his own way, even if she wasn't. Nicki munched crackers all the way to the marina, already queasy from his fast and furious driving. He wove in and out of traffic as if he were in a virtual reality game.

"Relax. You'll be fine." He gave her bare knee a shake. "It's Lake Pontchartrain on a lovely day, not the Bermuda Triangle during the perfect storm."

His fingers lingered a moment too long. The physical sensation running up her spine and pooling in her stomach did nothing to set her at ease.

*Do you understand me, Price? I can't go to jail.*

Remembering the arrogant words he uttered in the Blue Lotus jarred Nicki back to reality. She swatted away his hand like a fly. "Watch it, boss. Don't get fresh with me. I'm nauseous enough." She rolled down her window despite the air-conditioning.

"You mean nauseated. Nauseous means you're the one making your stomach turn." He grinned like a cartoon cat right before he got steamrollered.

"You think you're pretty smart, huh?"

"Yep. I certainly hope I haven't been laboring under a misguided notion all these years." He threw back his head and laughed.

"You really know how to get on a person's nerves. My Maw—my grandmother used to say that to me. Her timing always took me by surprise."

"If she can catch you unawares, Nicolette, your grandmother sounds like a woman I'd like to meet."

Nicki knew he was just teasing her to make her forget her nervousness. "At least driving like a maniac got us to our destination quickly."

The yacht club marina opened before her like a playground for the rich and idle. Mrs. Galen's yacht was one of the largest in sight—no surprise there. Nicki tripped going up the gangplank to the *Queen Antoinette* and stuttered while being introduced to the captain and his crew of four.

"A pleasure to meet you, Miss Price," Captain Lucas said, doffing his cap. "A light lunch is ready in the stern, Mr. Galen. The chef arranged catering to be delivered due to our time frame. He hopes it meets your expectations." The captain bobbed his head as though addressing royalty.

"It will be fine. Thanks for accommodating my short notice."

Hunter led the way to the back of the boat, where lunch on the *Queen Antoinette* had no rival from any of the restaurants Nicki had favored in Natchez. They dined on chicken salad, fresh fruit, and warm baguettes under a huge umbrella. The glass-topped table had been set with linen, china, and crystal goblets. A nearby bouquet of lilies perfumed the air and added a further touch of loveliness to the day.

Hunter filled their goblets with sweet tea, which she usually drank by the quart. The boat idled behind a break wall until they finished eating and a crewmember cleared away the dishes. Then Hunter handed Nicki a life jacket and buckled one around his own waist, while several men hoisted huge white sails. A few minutes later the yacht heeled over and began cutting through the waves. Nicki felt glad for both the Dramamine and the life jacket.

"How can you go around barefoot? Isn't that deck surface hot on your feet?"

"Nope. I guess I'm used to it." He refilled tea glasses. "Shall I strap you in, Nicki? Are you afraid?"

"Only of you, Hunter," she murmured under her breath.

"You have doubts about me?" Removing his sunglasses, he locked gazes with her. "Do you really think I killed James?" His words, soft and melodic, held plenty of uncertainty.

"No, I don't, or I wouldn't be out here in the middle of a lake with you."

"Can you swim, *cherie*?"

"You betcha. Like a shark."

He scooted his chair back into the sunshine and replaced his shades. "I don't think a shark. Probably more like an angelfish or bottlenose dolphin. Perhaps a pufferbelly blowfish."

"I bet you just amuse the heck out of your girlfriend." Nicki immediately regretted bringing up the subject the moment she said the words. She'd never met the woman, probably never would, and preferred to keep their conversation professional.

His smile faded a tad. "Ashley appears to be happy enough. I am a lucky man."

"Tell me about your financial situation. Are you rich enough to absorb the losses caused by your late partner?"

Hunter sat up straight and frowned. "That's certainly getting right to the point."

"Well, we've come out here to discuss the case. So let's deal with that."

"You're right. I shouldn't keep secrets from my chief investigator. Right now, I don't know if I'm rich enough or not. The mess caused by James will doubtlessly create havoc. I need to talk to my accountant to gauge how much. I don't have full access to my money. It's held in a trust, originally to endow the arts of New Orleans, now diverted to various reconstruction projects, Habitat for Humanity, and other projects to restore the city to her former glory. I've been living off my salary and whatever income the trust generates."

"You can't get your hands on your inheritance? You're no spring chicken."

"This is how I set things up when I inherited my share of the estate. I don't need vast sums of money when many people around me struggle to keep a roof over their head." He stood and then began to pace in the limited deck space.

"That arrangement surprises me," she said, fascinated by how he morphed from a man of leisure to a prowling caged animal.

"Why? You didn't think rich people have humanitarian tendencies?"

"Can't say I've known enough rich folks to form an opinion. What does Miss Ashley think about your new financial status? I mean, is she used to living on a budget?" Nicki couldn't help herself. She was curious about the mysterious girlfriend of her employer.

"You don't know my Ashley. She's not exactly a woman accustomed to clipping supermarket coupons."

A miserable feeling reared its ugly head inside Nicki. "I've met women like her my whole life. More to the point, I've waited on them at the mall. They are all alike. They travel in packs like coyotes, never going anywhere alone. They giggle instead of laugh, condescend to clerks and waitresses, and make purchases without looking at the tags, as though price doesn't matter. After all, it's only money, right?" Nicki heard the contempt in her voice and knew she sounded envious.

He stopped and smiled at her, pity in his eyes. "I know that type too, but Ashley's not like that. She's really very nice. I think you'll like her when you meet her."

*Then you need to think again.* But instead of saying that, Nicki nodded her head and smiled back at him. "I look forward to it." She'd had enough of her pettiness for one day. Whatever his girlfriend was or wasn't, it was none of her business.

Hunter resumed his pacing. "She does like to spend money, no doubt about that. But her father, Philip Menard, is a self-made man. He's quite a success story. He grew up in what started out as a trapper's cabin on Lake Boudreaux. He earned every dime he has...and he has plenty now. He may have spoiled Ashley because she's an only child, but he knows the value of a dollar. I'm sure he taught her that lesson as well." Even as he said the words, Nicki had the impression he was hoping that was true.

She knew all about that. She practiced that type of logic on a regular basis. But for the moment, it was time to talk about something other than Ashley Menard, daughter of a swamper, who loved to spend money. "Why do you care so much about people you don't know? I'm talking about the charities you mentioned that benefit from your trust account."

"I'm sure you've written a check to charity, or thrown cash into a kettle, or put money in the collection plate at church. You don't see where the funds are going, but you take it on faith it will do some good."

She chuckled. "What I throw in the plate at church doesn't crimp my lifestyle."

"Maybe I believe somebody is keeping score." He pointed his finger at the cloudless blue sky.

"You can't buy your way into heaven, Hunter." She looked up, too, as though the pearly gates would suddenly become visible. Her eyes watered from the sun's intense glare until she lowered her gaze. "Besides, I didn't take you for a religious man."

"What did you take me for, Miss Price? A hedonistic misanthrope, debased beyond redemption?"

"I don't know what all that means, but I'll get back to you after I find my dictionary."

They both laughed at that—easy, relaxing laughter that smoothed away the hard edges from last night. Tension had accumulated from too much caffeine, too little sleep, and corporate books revealing things Hunter didn't want to know. Today the dark circles were gone from under his eyes. He looked as though a weight had been lifted, although nothing had changed. His partner was still dead and his fortune was not quite so vast anymore.

Suddenly, Hunter saw something out in the water. "Look there, Nicki! Come quick."

Scrambling to her feet, she approached the deck rail cautiously. Walking on an unsteady surface would take some adjustment time, but she spotted what he indicated. "Jumping dolphins!" she exclaimed. Her heart swelled with joy while her eyes filled with tears. She loved animals of all kinds, something that had distanced her from the hunters and trappers she'd grown up with.

"You're close. Breeching porpoises. Very rare in Pontchartrain. Dolphins are leaner, more plentiful, and have longer beaks. Porpoises are portly, have smaller mouths, and are less talkative. Did you know orcas are actually big dolphins?" Hunter leaned over the rail as though trying to get a better view.

"I did not, Jacques Cousteau, but I think I'm in love. I've only seen them on TV. They're beyond beautiful." Nicki felt as if her face might crack from grinning.

"I'll have the captain radio the Coast Guard. They'll have to be led back to sea by marine volunteers. Every now and then they get through one of the navigational canals."

Hunter went below while Nicki watched the creatures frolic and play until they disappeared from view. Her throat began to close with emotion as she worried about their welfare. She had to clear her throat twice when he rejoined her at the rail.

"Will they be okay until they find their way back to sea? Isn't this lake fresh water?"

"Not anymore. It's brackish, but they'll be fine until they're guided back. Have faith." He patted her hand.

She pulled back discretely. "Do your deep pockets fund any dolphin charities?" Her voice sounded alien to her own ears.

"Yep. I support the Clean Seas Foundation, Greenpeace, World Wildlife Fund, and protection for tortoise breeding habitats off the critical coastlines of Georgia, Alabama, Florida, and Mexico."

Nicki swallowed hard, understanding for the first time that great wealth could do more than buy fast cars and designer purses. It could preserve species, rebuild ruined cities, feed the hungry, and change people's lives—things poor people could only talk about. Yet the realization left her oddly annoyed.

"Good to hear that some of your dough is well spent. But we'd better head back in. I need to run some errands and then tackle your books again. I'm a working girl, not a lady of leisure." She softened her tone by saying, "Thanks for lunch and this lovely experience."

"You're very welcome. I'll tell the captain." Hunter headed for the pilothouse, leaving her staring out at the unbroken water.

This wasn't what she had planned. She didn't want to start liking this guy. She wanted to get him off the hook for murder for Nate's sake, not his. She wondered what Miss Ashley Menard thought about his tenderheartedness for wild creatures and their habitats.

Hunter's compassionate traits made him far more attractive than his silky hair or his well-developed muscles, but he was something Nicki couldn't have in a million years whether Ashley was in the picture or not.

# ELEVEN

*H*unter didn't go up to his apartment after dropping Nicki off at her car. With plenty of work to do, he headed downtown to his office. The police hadn't released the crime scene, but he could work in the outer office. He was eager to learn what financials on the office servers hadn't been uploaded to his laptop.

On the top floor, only a few junior brokers were at their desks, following up with potential clients interested in rebalancing their portfolios. His assistant had turned on the answering machine and taken the day off, along with the other employees, leaving Hunter with several unbroken hours to piece together an increasingly dismal economic picture.

"I'm surprised to find you at work today, in light of James's death." Ethan Galen's lilting accent floated into the room before he did.

"I wouldn't be if I wasn't a person of interest for a murder investigation. And I haven't been here all day. I took the *Queen Antoinette* out this morning to discuss the case with my investigator." Hunter barely glanced up from his computer monitor.

Ethan scanned the room before slouching into the opposite chair. "Really? I'd heard Nate was in jail again, that ne'er-do-well."

"He's out. I posted bail this morning. But I was with Nicki

Price, not Nate. Nicki is Nate's cousin." Hunter hit the printer button and leaned back in his chair.

Ethan frowned over the cluttered desktop, hating not being in the loop. "Nate's cousin Nicolette from rural Mississippi?" He pushed his sunglasses up into his hair. "You hired an underfed teenager to solve your partner's murder? Are you itching to go to jail, little brother? Or do you feel the experience will advance your already noble social conscience?"

Hunter ignored the jab. Ethan's favorite pastime was taunting him. "She's no longer underfed and no longer a teenager. Miss Price is a licensed investigator." He tried to sound more confident than he felt.

Ethan shook his head. "You need someone experienced, not a greenhorn without a clue as to how things work down here."

"I'm the one without a clue as to how things work." Hunter pushed a stack of printouts across his desk. "My partner *and friend* churned portfolios for years without our clients' knowledge. The sole purpose was to generate commissions for the firm, but mainly for himself. I could have found this out sooner if I had looked. Instead, my greenhorn investigator pointed it out last night at my dining room table."

"That's what Nowak was doing?" Ethan looked both angry and worried.

"We're way overextended at the bank, leveraged up to our teeth. But I think it even goes deeper than that. I'm trying to find out just how deep."

Hunter didn't like admitting to his brother how complacent he'd been with the business. He'd prided himself on the firm's outstanding reputation since he'd left Ethan's internship. Unfortunately, that reputation seemed to have been built on a house of cards. But he wouldn't let pride stand in his way of salvaging whatever goodwill remained with his clients.

"If you're talking fraud and corruption, I'm sure James covered his tracks. Don't be too hard on yourself, Hunter. It's easy to be hoodwinked in this business, and doubly so when that person is supposed to be your friend."

Hunter appreciated his brother's rationalizations, but he wouldn't have any of it. "I suspected something was fishy, Ethan. James was spending money like water, but I didn't want to confront him without concrete proof. I didn't want to jeopardize our friendship over minor blips in the cash flow. Now he's dead. If I had spoken to him about my concerns, maybe he wouldn't be."

Ethan opened his mouth to argue, but a knock on the door commanded their attention.

"Excuse me, gentlemen. Hope I'm not interrupting something important." Detective Russell Saville stood in the doorway. His sport coat was open, his shirt wrinkled, his hair uncombed. All in all, the detective looked as if he just rolled out of bed.

"Come in, Detective," said Hunter. "I was wondering when you'd pay another call. Are you here to slap on the cuffs since no other suspect has thrown themselves in your path?"

"They're goin' to like you in jail, Galen. You're a barrel of laughs besides being a pretty boy." Saville sauntered into the room, his gaze fixing on Ethan with interest.

Ethan looked from one adversary to the other and rose to his feet. "Ethan Galen." He extended his hand. "I assume you're the lead detective working on Nowak's death. Do you have new information on the case?"

"Whew, I'm just meeting one big man after another on this job. Lives of the rich and famous," drawled Saville. He shook Ethan's hand briefly and then slapped a piece of paper onto the desktop. "But, no. I'm here with an amended search warrant. This one includes your office computer, Galen. If you would be kind enough to step back—"

"I have a business to run, Saville," Hunter snapped. "And my clients' privacy needs to be respected."

"Not my problem. You should have considered that before you blew your partner away."

"I didn't blow anybody away. Like I told you, I had no reason to."

"That's not what your financial records are saying, bro. You had the oldest reason in the book—money. I'm no accountant, but your little company looks insolvent to me. You owe everybody in town, living or dead, money. The next check you write will probably bounce."

Hunter jumped to his feet, but Ethan managed to get in front of him. He held up his hand like a school crossing guard. "The Galen family has extensive holdings and interests with plenty of liquid capital, Detective. More than enough to cover any cash flow problems Galen-Nowak Investments might be experiencing. Our family doesn't usually shoot their way out of difficulties."

Hunter hated it when his brother did that—jumped in to fight his battles for him. He was no longer his protégé learning the ropes at Ethan's staid firm. He'd successfully managed corporate portfolios for years, making his clients tons of money despite the mess James had gotten them into.

"Ah, the elder Galen to the rescue," Saville said with a sneer. "Weren't you the big sponsor of last year's Mardi Gras? Got to be the Grand Marshall or Grand Poo-Bah or whatever. I saw you sitting on your float in the Rex Parade with your little boy tossing candy to the unwashed masses. Man, it's good to be you, no? King of the world? Or, at least, King of the Quarter."

Other than a slight flare of his nostrils and a narrowing of his focus, Ethan gave little indication he was even listening to Saville. But Hunter heard him loud and clear and his blood began to boil. Picking up the search warrant, he scanned it quickly. "Take what you came for and get out."

Saville walked to the window and peered down on the river and Algiers in the distance. "Your brother got me thinking about another theory of mine, the second oldest motive in the world— a woman. That is one fine-looking lady you have there, Hunter. Umm, umm." He smacked his lips. "Maybe you weren't providing everything she needed and she got herself a little love triangle going with your partner." Saville dragged out the word "love" like a country music singer. "And you found out about it."

"You dirty…" Hunter launched himself at Saville. Cop or no, he had taken all he planned to. Hunter grabbed Saville's jacket with his left hand and drew back his right.

Fortunately, Ethan had anticipated the response and caught hold of Hunter's arm. The punch went wild, missing its mark. Ethan wedged his body between the two men. "Don't, Hunter. You're smarter than this. He's baiting you so he can arrest you for assaulting an officer."

"What's the matter? Did I hit a soft spot, pretty boy?" Saville tugged down his sport coat, looking unhappy with Ethan's interference.

As though on cue, two uniformed officers appeared in the doorway. They had apparently been waiting in the outer office, hoping to witness Hunter's loss of control.

"Stay out of it, Ethan. This isn't your problem."

Ethan threw his body weight against his brother's chest, pushing him back from the detective. "You in jail becomes my problem. Settle down and stop making things worse. You and I are going to get some air." To Saville, he said, "Take what's listed on the warrant and get out."

Only the realization that Ethan was right kept Hunter from going after Saville again. It was obvious that this was exactly what the detective wanted. The brothers headed for the back stairwell away from the other brokers and cops. "Thanks," Hunter said as soon as he cooled off.

"What's the matter with you?" Ethan snapped as soon as the fire door closed. "Do you *want* to give him reason to throw you back in jail? This isn't like you, Hunter. You have always chosen the noncombatant way out."

"And look where that's gotten me. Ripped off by my partner, about to lose my company, and probably formally charged for something I didn't do." Hunter slapped his palm against the plastered concrete wall.

"Giving in to your temper won't help the situation. You were on the right track combing through the books. Your answer lies there, not punching out a New Orleans cop. Because you're innocent, law enforcement is supposed to be on your side."

"Oh, really? Someone ought to tell Saville that. And if he were tossing out innuendos about Cora instead of Ashley, you wouldn't be quite so calm and collected right now."

"*C'est vrai*, but you're not me."

"What does that mean? I'm not tough like you, not so powerful?"

Ethan raised his eyebrows. "I meant you're usually smarter about letting anger get the better of you. My temper hasn't always served me in the past. It's gotten in my way more times than I can count. You've always been the mild-mannered member of the family. What's changed?"

"Are you joking, Ethan? *Everything* has changed. My life is in turmoil and you expect me to be diplomatic?"

"I expect you to cooperate with the investigation and not antagonize the lead detective. Stop acting like you have something to hide when you don't."

Hunter sucked in a deep breath. "Maybe I do. Not about the murder, but I don't want the world to know the extent of James's duplicity. I can't afford to have every Galen-Nowak client march in and cash out their account. If Saville leaks information about the company's financial status to the press, I'm ruined."

"And you think assaulting him will secure his cooperation in that regard?"

Ethan's words were like gasoline on flame. He pivoted toward his brother, no longer able to suppress his frustration. "There is just no pleasing you, no way of living up to your expectations!"

"What are you talking about?" Ethan moved back from Hunter's wrath.

"It's always been like this between us."

"Hunter, you need to be more specific." Ethan seemed genuinely confused.

"A long time ago a bunch of thugs took away the basketball my friends were playing with. I negotiated with them for its return. If they let us finish our game, they could use the ball for the rest of the evening and the next day. They would have it most of the weekend."

Ethan furrowed his brow. "I don't recall the incident. How in the world is this relevant?"

"You were furious when I told you about my solution. You said sometimes a man must fight so the world doesn't think him a coward." Repeating the words still stung after all these years.

"I said that?"

"You did. You said I shouldn't have bargained with bullies. I should have fought for what was *right*." Hunter relaxed the fingers that had unwittingly curled into fists.

Ethan slicked his hair back from his face. "I vaguely remember that now. It was a stupid thing said by an immature adolescent, not a man. We were kids then. It has no bearing on anything happening now—"

"I've never forgotten your disappointment in me," interrupted Hunter, surprised by the admission.

Ethan placed a hand tentatively on his shoulder. "You should have forgotten it. I have nothing but respect for you and always have. Your ability to negotiate isn't a character weakness. It's a trait I admire. I was wrong back then, and I'm sorry I never told you that before. But please go home now and come back to your office tomorrow. You're innocent of this crime, Hunter. Saville can't hurt you unless you let him."

After a final squeeze to his brother's shoulder, Ethan crossed the parking lot, climbed into his car, and drove away. Hunter remained riveted to his spot for several more minutes, fighting to regain his composure.

He'd heard kind words and noble sentiments, but nothing had changed. Hunter was tired of negotiating, of peacemaking. *Sometimes a man must fight so the world doesn't think him a coward.* He was no longer a scrawny kid on the playground who had lost his basketball to thugs.

He was no coward. Someone had killed his partner. This was one fight he wouldn't walk away from.

# TWELVE

*N*icki stared at the wall a full five minutes before punching her mother's number in her phone. As much as she wanted to, as much as she needed to, calling Rose Price was never a simple chore on her to-do list. But with Christine at work and no place she needed to be, she sucked in a deep breath and took the plunge.

"Hello?"

"Mom? It's me, Nicki."

"Yes, dear, I recognize your voice. It hasn't been *that* long."

Hearing her mother's animated chuckle, Nicki began to relax.

"Are you all settled in at Christine's? Isn't it crowded in a trailer with two little kids running around?"

Her relaxation vanished. "Her kids are staying with Preston's mother due to a minor mishap with Children's Services, remember? I think I told you that Preston complained that the kids weren't being properly cared for. Christine flunked their impromptu inspection."

"That doesn't sound like a minor mishap to me or she would have them back by now. What kind of mother loses her children to a man like Preston Hall?"

"When Children's Services arrived she didn't have five days of food in her fridge and pantry. She hadn't been to the grocery store that week, but she would never let her kids go hungry. Now she must wait until after three unannounced visits."

"Did Christine get fired from her job or allow some trouble-maker to move in with her?"

With an image of Travis flickering through her mind, Nicki hesitated. She didn't want to lie, but also didn't want to give her mother ammo to use against her friend. "No, her new boyfriend doesn't live with her, and she works full-time at the coffee plant." Technically, both statements were true.

"Well, if you ask me—"

Knowing exactly where this road led, Nicki didn't let her finish. "Mom, I called to find out how *you* were, not to gossip about Christine. How do you feel with the new prescriptions?"

"Well, one pill makes me ravenous all day while the other causes nausea. So I can't eat more than half a sandwich or I'm in danger of not keeping it down. Not exactly my preference for losing weight."

"If that continues more than a week, call your doctor. And keep track of what does stay down, because he'll probably ask. How are you sleeping?" Nicki shifted restlessly on the sofa.

"I would sleep better if you weren't living in New Orleans." Rose emitted a huffy snort. "Every night the news reports another drive-by shooting or drug raid in the projects."

"On a Natchez television station? I can't believe they have nothing better to cover."

"Not on local TV. I subscribe to an electronic version of the *Times Picayune* so I can keep up with what's happening around you."

Nicki rolled her eyes at the idea of her mother stalking her via the Internet. "Every big city has crime. Wherever people are economically deprived, the crime rate goes up."

"I'm poor, but you don't see me manufacturing meth in my cellar."

"You don't have a cellar. You live in an apartment." Nicki took a long swig of diet cola.

"Don't get smart, missy. You know what I mean. How's your cousin? Nate needs to call Charlotte more. She worries about him the same way I worry about you."

"Funny you should ask. I was just talking with Nate yesterday after work. We were recalling old times when we were kids."

"Nicki, you're only twenty-five, not sixty."

"True, but when Nate started talking about Dad, it got me thinking."

All laughter, all affectionate banter ceased. Nicki checked the screen of her phone to see if the call had been dropped. Then her mother spoke.

"With plenty to learn on your new job, why on earth are you wasting time talking about your father?"

"Because I'm an investigator now, Mom. It's normal to be curious about what happened to him." Nicki struggled to remain calm.

"I don't know what else to tell you. Kermit went to the swamp with his pals and never came back. They were supposed to be fishing and turtle hunting—why, I don't know. Your father didn't even like turtle soup. Your uncles said he took the boat out after their card game broke up and must have fallen overboard. When people indulge in alcohol, bad things happen. I hope you haven't acquired the habit with all those fancy happy hours and boutique breweries on every corner." Rose never missed an opportunity to express her teetotaler viewpoint. Not that Nicki could blame her after years of living with an alcoholic husband.

"Don't worry, Mom. Soda and sweet tea remain my beverages of choice. But there must be more you're not telling me, and after all these years I deserve the truth."

"What on earth do you think I'm hiding?"

"Exactly who was there that night? If you're not hiding any-thing, then name names." Nicki mimicked her mother's brusque tone.

"For heaven's sake, Nicki. It was Kermit, your Uncle Charles and my two brothers, Eugene and Andre."

"No one else? Just the four of them?"

Rose breathed heavily into the mouthpiece. "I'll tell you who else, young lady, since you think I'm keeping something impor-tant from you. Your dad invited three men he'd met in a bar in Clay Creek to join them. They claimed to be brothers and were always flashing wads of money. I told him to steer clear of them since you can bet Saturday's supper they didn't come by that pile of cash honestly, but do you think your father listened to me?"

"I will assume that he didn't," said Nicki softly.

"No. Instead he said, 'Don't worry, Rosie. You'll have all the money you need for bills when I get home. A good chunk of the cash they flash around will be in my pocket come Sunday.'"

"Dad planned to rob those dangerous men?" Her father as a thief didn't fit the memory Nicki had of him building her a treehouse.

"No, not that. He planned to cheat them at cards. Kermit thought he was so clever. Nobody would ever figure out those full houses and flushes weren't just dumb luck. He always wore that silly alligator belt when he played poker. He said his twin cowgirls never let him down when he needed to make money."

"I don't remember any fancy belt."

"Because it's probably on the bottom of Henderson Lake in Louisiana. He bought it years earlier from some old Cajun who carved the buckle from a gator skull. It was atrocious if you ask me. Two gals with six-shooters standing back-to-back, wearing ten-gallon hats and spurs."

Nicki rubbed the bridge of her nose as a dull ache throbbed

behind her eyes. "Getting back to the men Dad planned to cheat, do you think one of them figured it out and killed him?"

"No, Nicolette. Uncle Eugene said that when they took their argument outside, Kermit gave them their money back, everything he had. Then those men came inside and your dad took off in a huff, furious his get-rich-quick scheme didn't work. The sheriff came to the cabin and looked around. Nothing inside or outside indicated it was anything but an accident on the waterway."

Silence spun out for several moments before Rose added, "Your Uncle Charles and my brothers had no reason to lie. They were fond of Kermit, just like everyone else—everyone who wasn't married to him. It was an accident, honey. Let it go. This isn't a mystery for you to solve, Nancy Drew. Concentrate on your new job. It should be enough of a challenge."

*Three brothers from Clay Creek were at the cabin too?* "Thanks for finally telling me the whole truth, Mom," she said. "I need to get some sleep, but I'll call you again soon." With her brain already five miles down the road, Nicki ended the call with a press of a button, even though she wouldn't be able to sleep for hours.

# THIRTEEN

The ringing of Nicki's phone interrupted her morning exercises. At least she could accomplish part of her normal routine without putting her fist through a window or whapping her head on the refrigerator. Even sit-ups were challenging because her feet had to slide under the couch and her torso wouldn't fit on the small square of indoor-outdoor carpeting. Wiping sweat from her eyes she said, "Hello?"

"Good morning, Nicolette. Hunter Galen."

His smooth, creamy voice didn't need identification. No other man she knew sounded like the male counterpart of a 1940s torch singer.

"Sure, I remember you. You signed the advance on my expense check. And the check didn't bounce. I'm in gravy."

He laughed good-naturedly. "Let's hope we find the killer before I go bankrupt. Are you busy? I'm driving out to St. James Parish to visit one of James's clients. I thought you might like to do some investigating. Maybe peek in his closets or listen in on his wife's telephone conversations."

Either the guy still had zero confidence in her abilities or everything was a big fat joke to him. The cops were convinced he murdered his partner, yet he still wore his happy face. "I've got nothing but time. You just saved me from jumping jacks that could put me into the hospital."

"I'll swing by Chalmette and pick you up, and then we'll jump on the freeway—"

"No!" she nearly shouted. "I mean, I need to come into the city anyway. I'll stop by your place. Be there in an hour." She hung up before he could argue. No way did she want him to drive out to Chalmette. She didn't want him to see where she lived. It would be impossible not to judge her by the neighborhood she called home.

Standing in a lukewarm shower, she considered what she'd gleaned from his company's books. Nowak bought and sold constantly to generate personal commissions, while the company's net worth had dwindled. If she considered every client who lost money under his management a suspect, her list ran to more than forty people. She wouldn't know which one to start with. Next she pondered what to wear to visit Hunter's client. St. James Parish sounded hot and buggy, so she selected a cool cotton dress and twisted her hair into a loose braid.

Less than an hour later she was climbing into Hunter's sporty Corvette. "I wasn't sure about the dress code for the occasion so I hope this outfit is okay."

"You look just fine," he said, barely glancing her way as they headed west out of the city.

Taking her cue from him, Nicki quietly studied her travel guide as they sped down the highway into the Acadiana parishes. According to the brochure, the French language and old-world traditions still dominated the Cajun culture.

"Are you going to tell me where we're headed?" she asked when they turned onto a parish road following the Mississippi River. Nicki stretched her arms over her head, loving the open expanse in a convertible.

"To see Mr. Robert Bissette."

"If we start making social calls to all of the clients your partner scammed, I'll have to pack a steamer trunk of multiseason clothes."

Hunter pulled down his sunglasses to stare at her before turning his attention back to the twisty road. A muscle tightened in his neck as his grip on the steering wheel tightened. "What do you mean by that?"

"You know exactly what I mean. Why didn't you keep an eye on him? I mean, if it was my company, I wouldn't have let him mess things up for so long."

"There you go again, saying whatever comes to mind. Can't you occasionally mince words, especially when you're spending the day with your boss?" A tic appeared in his cheek.

"I *am* mincing words, Hunter. I know he was your friend, but James took advantage of a lot of clients. Any one of them could have come after him."

Half a minute of reflection passed before he answered. "In the investment world, clients expect volatility in their returns. They don't reach for a gun if their portfolios take a nosedive. Besides, the definition of a partnership is two people splitting the work down the middle and trusting each other to operate for the good of both. I had no reason to believe James had gone this far off track."

"Off track is a major understatement. Robbery without a weapon would be more accurate."

Hunter leveled her a look that said she was on thin ice, but as usual, Nicki didn't change her tactics.

"Seriously, Hunter, if a punk goes into a mom-and-pop convenience store and robs the owner of sixty bucks at gunpoint, he'll get twenty years in the slammer. But some stockbroker can steal from his clients with relative impunity because there's no weapon of deadly force. *If* they get caught, they may have their wrists slapped."

"James wasn't stealing from our clients. He apparently made lots of unauthorized trades, which is called 'churning.' It's unethical but not illegal. He should have researched the investments he steered people into and matched their—" Hunter stopped mid-sentence and rolled his eyes. "I don't have time to teach you the investment world. You're here to investigate James's murder, and I would appreciate a tad of respect for my...dead...friend."

That put a damper on chitchat for the remainder of the drive.

Settling back against the soft leather, Nicki was soon amazed by the passing scenery. They had driven into an area where time had not only stood still but had improved upon the bygone era. The houses she glimpsed along the levee surpassed any Hollywood reconstruction of antebellum life. Mansions sat at the ends of oak-lined driveways with manicured lawns large enough to reenact a cavalry battle.

"You've got to be kidding me," she murmured softly. "People still live like this in the twenty-first century?"

Hunter followed her gaze, apparently accustomed to the sites. "Some do, but many of these old plantations are now museums owned by historical societies. They give tours and host weddings to pay for the expenses. Beautiful, yes, but nearly impossible to maintain as private residences these days."

"Beautiful doesn't begin to describe it. Six families could live in one and not get in each other's way." For a moment Nicki's heart clenched from the deprivation she grew up with and still struggled to overcome. It was easy not to be envious when everyone else was in the same financial situation, but witnessing the copious wealth these people probably took for granted made her teeth ache.

"Mr. Bissette lives in a house like these?"

"Not quite this big, but it's a lovely place. Personally, I prefer smaller, comfortable homes where I can find who I'm looking for." He laughed and ran a hand through his hair, his demeanor indicating he'd never coveted anything in his life.

Nicki struggled to tamp down her resentment. "Well, I sure didn't grow up in a place like this."

A few moments later Hunter turned onto a road that wandered through some beautiful old trees. Mr. Bissette's home may not have been a registered historical landmark, but its seclusion and coexistence with the environment appealed to Nicki more than the plantation mansions. They drove down the lane for two miles before the residence came into view. The house was Caribbean in architecture and sat on concrete pillars, ready for the Mississippi to overflow its banks. Wings and additions rambled off the main two-story section, as though added when the urge struck, yet the structure still possessed a cohesiveness that melded with, not battled against, its watery environment. A jungle of flowering plants surrounded the house, while bald cypress trees, live oaks, and swamp willows ringed the perimeter. Most of them dripped with Spanish moss. Morning glories and trumpet vines entwined porch rails and gutter boards. Windows were shuttered, French doors opened onto terraces, and balconies guaranteed family and guests were only a few steps from the morning sunshine or evening breeze.

"Nice, huh?" Hunter asked as he parked on the crushed shell turn-around. While she seemed mesmerized with the lovely home, he got out and went around the car to open her door for her.

"Nice is not the word." Nicki smoothed down her hair as they climbed the staircase. At least she'd worn a print sundress that wouldn't show nervous perspiration. She hid behind Hunter when he rang the bell.

Mr. Bissette, dressed in pressed slacks and a plaid shirt, appeared at the door. "Ah, Mr. Galen, thank you for making the trip. Do I have the pleasure of meeting your assistant at long last?"

"No, sir. This is Miss Nicolette Price, a private investigator from Natchez."

"How do you do, Miss Price?"

Instead of waiting for her reply, he turned and led them through several rooms, each more exquisite than the last. Unfortunately, Bissette walked too fast for Nicki to take in everything, but she spotted a fondness for African art, colorful textiles, and massive pieces of dark furniture. They exited the living room onto a terraced courtyard bathed in sunshine. The rambling wings of the house fully enclosed the flagstone courtyard and pool area.

"Please have a seat." Bissette pointed at an umbrella table and several chairs.

Nicki gawked left and right like a tourist on holiday before turning her gaze skyward. They were outdoors, but a net ceiling high overhead sealed out mosquitoes. Huge fans mounted in tree branches kept the humid air moving. "No need to douse yourself with insect repellent. What a great idea."

"Thank you, Miss Price." Bissette offered her an unfriendly smile before turning to Hunter. "I'm curious why you would bring an investigator to my home, Mr. Galen."

"Miss Price is helping me piece together Mr. Nowak's dealings with his clients...um, my clients now, sir."

Bissette's expression sweetened dramatically. "In that case, welcome to *Fenêtre sur l'Eau*. I am at your disposal."

"Thank you, sir." Nicki swallowed down her impulse to gush about the place. Instead, she noticed Hunter said nothing about her investigating James's murder.

"Shall we have refreshments?" asked Bissette.

As though on cue a butler in a starched white uniform appeared with a tray of Cokes and bottled water. Condensation dripped onto the tray's linen cloth.

While Nicki sipped from a bottle of water, Hunter opened the conversation with social formalities: how he regretted not keeping track of Bissette's portfolio himself. How unfortunate that the market hadn't rebounded since the recession of 2008. How some of the investments James chose may not have served the intended purpose.

Bissette listened patiently, nodding at appropriate intervals until Hunter finished. Then he launched into his view of the world. "My portfolio isn't down due to market corrections or even ill-timed trades by your partner." His drawl deepened as his agitation grew.

Nicki watched him sip something amber from a heavy crystal tumbler. Only alcohol was served in glasses like that, and it wasn't even eleven o'clock. Her hopes for a happy ending to the meeting dropped a notch.

"My portfolio is down because Nowak sold me a pack of worthless stocks of local companies that went bankrupt or should have thrown in the towel after the flood. Nowak assured me they were poised for a comeback after Katrina. What a pack of lies! Poised to make Nowak-Galen Investments a lot of money and nobody else." Bissette finished off the contents of his glass.

Nicki observed two things: First, when referring to the partnership, Bissette had reversed the order of names. And second, he possessed the ability to convey fury without yelling, cursing, or throwing things. That was unheard of in her neck of the woods. She had to admit it was an enviable trait. Only the heightened color of his face and neck betrayed his utter contempt. Nicki stole a glance at Hunter. He sat stiffly in his chair as though ready to face whatever music Bissette cued on the jukebox.

"If that's what our examination uncovers, I assure you I'll make this right."

"Have you heard of Ace Linen Supply over on Carondelet?" Bissette asked.

"Yes, sir. I was reviewing your portfolio in the wake of James's death." Hunter's grip tightened on his bottle of water. "They're a large commercial linen supply serving hotels and restaurants in the city, mainly tablecloths and napkins. Things that need to be pressed and starched."

Bissette grunted in agreement. "Nowak told me they were the *only* linen supply left in the city after Katrina. They had exclusive contracts all over town and were slated to make money hand over fist as tourism returned to the Quarter. He said some Houston businessman infused significant capital to get the place back on their feet. Once the tourists came back, the sky was the limit." Derision dripped from his words. "He didn't *ask* me, he *told* me I was getting in on the ground floor. A family business was going public, an IPO. I would be at the right place at the right time." Picking up his glass, Bissette glared upon discovering it empty. "Arnaud!" he called. "Bring the bottle, *s'il vous plaît.*"

A bottle of scotch appeared moments later, after which the white-haired Arnaud disappeared back into the house. Their host didn't offer the libation to them as he refreshed his tumbler.

Hunter said, "Please continue, Mr. Bissette."

"The offering was ten dollars a share. He said he would take me out at fifteen. He didn't. I called him. He said I should be patient and trust him. He assured me he would get me out at twenty, doubling my investment." Bissette clutched his glass with both hands like a lifeline, his left hand trembling. "When I returned from Europe, I read in the paper the price had hit thirty dollars per share." With great effort Bissette settled back in his chair. "Thirty dollars a share! I would have tripled my money. I called

Nowak and left a message on his machine telling him to sell my shares of Ace Supply. He never got back to me, but I assumed I was sitting on a barrelful of profits he had made in the sale. Nowak left me swinging in the breeze. I rode that stock up and back down again. Now it trades for under five dollars a share and I lost more than a million dollars. Tell me why I should have to keep tabs on a stock if I have a broker?"

"You shouldn't have to, sir."

"Now I either sell at a substantial loss or hold it until the next millennium to see if it recovers." Beads of perspiration formed on Bissette's forehead.

Nicki sat perfectly still, feeling a strange frisson of guilt even though she'd never heard of Galen-Nowak Investments when this took place.

Hunter rose to his feet. "I assure you, Mr. Bissette, if I find any malfeasance in the handling of James's account, any wrongdoing at all on his part, my company will reimburse your losses."

Nicki's mouth dropped open. Without batting an eyelash, Hunter just promised to make good on a million dollars. *My, my. The rich really are different.*

"Oh, you'll find malfeasance all right." Bissette spoke with a slight slur, the scotch having found its mark. "You won't even have to put your reading glasses on. Your partner was more than a bad broker, Mr. Galen. He was a thief. *Un voleur.*" Bissette stood and walked within inches of Hunter's face. Nicki could smell the alcohol on his breath from where she sat. "Besides not selling my shares to lock up profits, I never authorized that large of an investment in a local company barely hanging by a thread before the storm. He mentioned fifty thousand dollars and I agreed to *that*, not half a million dollars."

Nicki quickly pictured a number and then added zeroes to comprehend how much they were talking about.

"I call that more than malfeasance. I call him *un coquin*."

Hunter could probably get drunk on the fumes, but he stood his ground and slowly drew a business card from his wallet. "Here is my office number, my cell, and my home phone. Call me if you need to but know that I'll be devoting my full attention to this situation."

Bissette's face was growing darker by the moment. "Nowak was bad blood, *mon ami*. Don't mourn his passing. He was a thief." After his final summation, Bissette plucked the card from Hunter's fingers, turned on his heel, and marched into the house. "*Un voleur qui en vole un autre, le diable en rit*," he muttered in French.

Nicki and Hunter had no choice but to follow behind him inside. Considering Hunter's expression, she chose not to ask for a translation of their host's thoughts. Apparently, there would be no gracious offer of luncheon on the patio and no offers of bottled water for the drive back to New Orleans.

When Bissette turned down a hallway, Arnaud appeared in front of them. "I will see you out."

Nicki was growing giddy from the drama. Unfortunately, Bissette's dismissal curtailed any investigative work—no peeking into closets or eavesdropping on phone conversations. But as they exited the luxurious swamp house, she had an overwhelming feeling that repaying this client would be a wise thing to do.

Hunter started the car and they drove down the canopied driveway in a far more introspective mood than when they arrived. She waited until they reached the parish highway before expressing an opinion.

"Mr. Bissette seemed a bit irritated with James's job performance."

"You think this is funny, Nicolette? You find humor in your new line of work?" Hunter's butter-on-hot-shrimp tone turned icy.

Nicki regretted the comment as soon as the words left her

mouth. "I'm sorry. That didn't come out how I intended." She turned to face him, but his focus remained on the road, his eyes hidden behind his sunglasses.

"Apology accepted," he said after a moment. "That little chat with Bissette left us both out of sorts."

"Would you mind translating what he said about James?"

" 'When one thief steals from another, the devil laughs.' And there's more you need to know. While you napped on my dining room table, I checked into the Ace Linen Supply IPO. Do you know who owned the shares of stock that Nowak sold to Mr. Bissette and to a lot of other Galen-Nowak clients?"

"James Nowak?"

"*Oui*," he answered. Visiting the Acadiana parishes seemingly brought out the Galen family roots. "James, his brothers, and several cousins up in Baton Rouge. A little get-rich-quick scheme." Hunter stepped on the accelerator as the road straightened out. "They bought up the shares at the release and then resold those shares to investors led to the trough."

"I don't understand. How did James know the price would go that high?"

"Because he orchestrated the whole thing." Hunter slapped the wheel, his anger at a level to match Bissette's. "James created artificial demand by touting the stock to every client on our roster. Most of those he contacted bought in. Why wouldn't they? Why wouldn't they trust him? And he sold a lot of shares to clients without their knowledge. They didn't even know they were proud owners of Ace Linen Supply. Some clients give full control to their brokers. The stock was nearly worthless by yesterday's closing."

"So what I learned in economics class actually happens in real life," she said softly.

"He prods our clients to buy into Ace Linen, and the demand drives the price up. He spreads the word around town about this red-hot stock tip. More people buy in, driving the price even higher. He encourages clients to take a larger position. They shouldn't miss out. Eventually Nowak's family and friends unloaded all the shares they owned, making substantial profits. Once Nowak stops touting the stock, the simulated demand dries up. No new suckers? The price drops to a realistic value."

"Is that legal?"

Hunter exhaled a weary sigh. "No, the classic pump-and-dump boiler room scheme isn't legal. James broke at least half a dozen SEC regulations, besides felony fraud and embezzlement too. Maybe I'll go back tomorrow to talk to Bissette after he's had a chance to cool off."

"You should absolutely *not* do that. I get that you need to straighten this out, Hunter, but it should be in a safer place than here."

"What do you mean?" He pulled the Corvette onto the hard-packed gravel of a berm where there were no antebellum mansions or remote hideaways like the one they just left.

"Despite his gorgeous screened-in patio and pool area, Mr. Bissette is a dangerous man. He's hiding something." Nicki glanced at the road in the rearview mirror. "People don't live in the swamp because they love alligators and water moccasins. Surveillance cameras hidden in the trees registered our license plate and probably announced who was coming before we opened a car door. What do you know about your client?"

Hunter thought for a moment. "His grandfather made a fortune in the catfish industry. Then Robert took the money he inherited and invested it in Columbian coffee beans. He has since sold his foreign holdings and lives off investment income, a stream not as productive as it once was."

Nicki checked the mirror again as Hunter pulled back onto the pavement. "I'm willing to bet his Columbian investments weren't just in coffee. You should stay away from him. At least don't meet him out here. If men like Bissette get mad, they get even. James would have been better off ripping off the attorney general of the United States."

"That might be a stretch, Nicki. Bissette is retired now."

"If so, he has nothing to hide if the police check into where he was and what he was doing last Saturday night."

Hunter nodded. "Assuming Detective Saville can stop fixating on me long enough."

# FOURTEEN

The drive back from St. James Parish took considerably longer than the trip to the bayou because Hunter stayed on the road along the river. On a lark, they stopped at Oak Alley, an antebellum-plantation-turned-tourist-attraction, complete with costumed guides. After paying the admission, they wandered the manicured grounds but decided against the tour of the mansion. Nicki was astounded by the oak-lined driveway and the spectacular flower gardens. Viewing conspicuous wealth of bygone eras on the movie screen was one thing. Gawking at a place more impressive than the White House was something altogether different.

When they grew hungry, Hunter bought them shrimp gumbo and crab salad at the restaurant on the grounds. They dunked warm baguettes straight from the oven in their soup while uniformed school children marched two by two across the lawn. Nicki read aloud facts from a brochure, but Hunter seemed distracted during the meal. His partner's chicanery had to be a nightmare. How many clients had been scammed? After what happened at Mr. Bissette's, Hunter probably wouldn't get a good night's sleep for some time to come.

When Nicki asked if Galen ancestors lived in similar digs a hundred fifty years ago, his reply was curt and evasive. They owned a "place" out in Lafourche Parish that had been a land grant from Louis XV to his great-great-great granddaddy. She would have loved to hear why a French king would hand over a tract of land in the New World, but Hunter's tightly set mouth discouraged more questions. She let the matter drop, not eager to reveal that her ancestors lived in a four-room cabin without indoor plumbing, running water, or electricity until almost the twenty-first century. Papaw and Mamaw carried water from the spring, did laundry in a wringer washer on the porch, heated their home with a woodstove, and read by kerosene lamps until the 1970s. They no longer needed the outhouse, but electricity was supplied by a gas generator, which ran only a few hours a day.

On the drive back, Hunter kept a steady stream of blues queued on the CD player, rendering conversation impossible. Nicki rested her head against the seat and soaked up the mournful rhythms of B.B. King, John Lee Hooker, and Etta James.

It was dark by the time Hunter dropped Nicki off at her car and very late when she got back to the mobile home village. Fortunately, with Christine at work Nicki didn't need to be sociable. Unfortunately, the din of chaos in the neighborhood was at fever pitch. Apparently, everyone insisted on playing their TVs and sound systems at full blast. Between the revving cars and motorcycles, screaming babies, and arguments stemming from too many people confined in close quarters, Nicki would get little sleep that night. Her bones ached, her head pounded, and even her skin felt tired, but she lay in bed listening to the ticking of her clock add one more annoyance until the wee hours.

*You ain't living at Oak Alley, folks,* she thought as sirens in the distance rushed to another crime in progress.

Nicki awoke to a quiet trailer. She again struggled through her exercise routine in the cluttered living room. Wouldn't Christine find it easier to dust and run the sweeper if she would just throw half the junk into the trash?

Christine emerged from her bedroom at eleven o'clock, clear-eyed, in shorts, T-shirt, and sequined flip-flops. Her curly strawberry-blond hair hung across her back like a shawl. Without makeup, her freckles stood out against her pale skin. In fact, her arms and legs were blindingly white, as though she never left the house during daylight hours.

"You really need to get some sun," Nicki teased, pouring her a cup of coffee.

Christine looked down at her slim legs beneath the hem of her shorts. "You're right. I'll buy some fake spray-on tan at Walgreen's. I don't get to the beach anymore, not with my work schedule, and especially not with the kids gone." She took the cup and immediately downed half its contents.

Nicki noticed that the long acrylic nails she used to apply were gone. Her nails were short but clean. "Where are your old fingernails? You used to be able to weed-whack with those things."

"I got a write-up from my supervisor." Christine held up her hands for inspection. "I decided I needed the job more. Domestic court judges don't award children to unemployed parents." She chanted the phase with a singsong inflection. Apparently, she'd listened to the warning more than once. Christine gazed out the kitchen window into the yard, where overflowing trashcans waited for pickup. Her features were pinched with pain just talking about her children. Nicki knew that everything in her friend's life centered on the fact her kids had been taken away. And it would be no easy task to get them back.

Nicki's heart filled with compassion. Christine wasn't a bad person. She just made bad choices. Actually, she seldom made cognitive decisions. Instead, she reacted to whatever landed in her path on the spur of the moment. Nicki could easily be her. In fact, she had been *exactly* like her in high school until the day she chose to reinvent herself.

"Any good tales to tell about the case?" Christine's energy level had ratcheted up with the infusion of caffeine. "What's your new client like?" She positioned her hands on hips and stuck her elbows straight out. Christine considered her slimness her best feature, yet her figure looked scrawny, not chic. A few pounds would have done her a world of good.

Nicki refilled their mugs. "Hunter Galen isn't bad looking. Nice hair, nice clothes, *real* nice car. We drove out to Saint James Parish in his Corvette with the top down." She added extra *r*'s to Corvette and dragged "down" into two syllables for effect.

"Tell me everything and don't leave anything out. Don't worry about Travis coming back. We had a huge fight and I told him I didn't want to see him anymore."

Nicki tried to press her for details, but Christine only wanted to hear about yesterday's excursion to the Cajun bayou.

Nicki had been on the job as a professional investigator for all of two days, yet she couldn't remember enjoying herself more. Robert Bissette probably had corpses buried under every cypress tree, yet all she could remember was Hunter's hand on her knee, the smell of his aftershave, and his accent when he spoke her name. Even though she'd eaten crab salad hundreds of times, Nicki had loved every minute of lunch at Oak Alley.

"Hellooooo. Earth-to-Nicki. I think I lost you for a minute."

"Sorry, I was trying to remember details for the case. I should start taking notes."

"This Galen guy, is he rich or something? I saw his picture in the paper. He looks like Mr. Slick."

"Yeah, you could say he's rich. At least his family is. He's in a financial mess right now, though." In an instant, Nicki felt a stab of conscience. A licensed private investigator had an ethical code of confidentiality to uphold.

"I would use that to your advantage. If he has money, plan to get some for yourself. We ain't getting any younger, you know. I was twenty-five last month."

Nicki couldn't help smiling. It wasn't as if they were one step away from Medicare. "He has a girlfriend, Christine, and she's doubtlessly a rich and beautiful woman. I *work* for the guy, that's all."

"She ain't hooked him yet. You still have time to reel him in. Those wealthy types usually keep a wife at home and another one on the side once they're older, but this guy still looks young."

"And why would I go for such an arrangement?" Nicki didn't try to hide her indignation.

"Simmer down. It was just a joke. I know you're the church-on-Sunday, stay-chaste-till-married type."

"I remember you used to go with me on Sundays. Don't they have churches here in Chalmette?"

"Not since they took my kids away." Christine's mouth pulled into a frown. "Anyway, we were talking about you and this Galen guy. I suggest you turn on the charm. It might be nice still having money in the account after paying bills. Think about the nice apartment he must have, maybe even behind one of those fancy gates that opens with the push of a button."

It amazed Nicki what amenities rated high with people. "I've nothing against living large. That's why I went to college and got my degree, but I'm going to arrive there on my own." She winced at her sanctimoniousness tone.

Christine wasn't offended. "Who says you gotta quit your job? You could have the best of both worlds. I would love to work for your cousin too. Is he still single?"

The question caught Nicki off guard. A mental pairing of Christine Hall and Nate Price was too ludicrous to imagine. Nate had champagne tastes, whether he could afford them or not. "Yes, he's still single and still a big pain in the neck."

"Not more so than Travis. That creep said he'd make me sorry one of these days." Christine shivered. "The way I see it, you have one blue-ribbon opportunity here."

"And what would that be?" Nicki resumed her yoga stretches on the floor. She might as well finish exercising during her career assessment.

"Make yourself in-dee-spensable to this guy, especially since he's cute."

Nicki's laughter broke her concentration with the yoga pose. "Do you have a self-help DVD for this? No man has ever found me indispensable before."

"Sorry. Wish I could help you there."

Nicki switched to sit-ups. "That's all right. Since I'm not up to the challenge of competing with Hunter's girlfriend, maybe I'll just do my job."

"Okay, but wouldn't it be nice if the guy fell in love with you?"

Nicki sat up so fast she bumped her head on the coffee table. "You must be joking. Marrying the boss is the blue-ribbon opportunity you had in mind?" She rubbed her scalp gingerly.

"You're almost twenty-five too, Nic. Don't you want to get married and have children in this lifetime?"

Nicki took little time to decide. "Yeah, I'd like a couple kids someday, but I have plenty of hurdles to leap between now and then."

"If you wait too long your biological clock will run out of minutes. Do you think you'll have patience for a couple varmints in your sixties? Girl, that's the time for wearing purple hats and sitting in rockers on the porch."

Nicki smiled at the image. "Eating sweets and sipping cold lemonade?"

"You betcha. We'll finish off a bag of cookies every afternoon because we won't care how fat we get."

"They'd better not bankrupt Social Security." Nicki resumed her crunches.

"Man, you worry a lot. When did that start?" Christine plopped down on the floor and started doing sit-ups too, her legs shooting down the hallway.

"I suppose when my mom's health started going downhill. That's why I went to college so I wouldn't end up in a dead-end job."

As soon as the words were said, Nicki wanted to bite her tongue. Hunter was right. She did have a habit of saying exactly what was on her mind, and that didn't always come out as kind. "Sorry. That was mean and not what I intended."

"I know there's not a hateful bone in your body." Christine scrambled to her feet and reached down to pull Nicki up. The sit-ups hadn't turned out to be much fun. "And that's why you should marry Hunter Galen, grandson of the Grand Dame of the Garden District. You would be set for life."

"Grand Dame?" Nicki asked incredulously. "Where did you come up with that?"

She shrugged. "I do *read,* and that's what the newspapers called his grandmother. Just think, your little darlin's would get to wear the latest fashions and live in a big house with a yard. No generic cereals on your breakfast table. Private schools, a good college, maybe even a nanny." Christine's face glowed as though she'd won the lottery. "And you could go to the mall anytime you liked."

Nicki offered a tired smile for her friend. She knew Christine meant well, but there was no way Nicki could begin to describe what was wrong with her idea. Even if you set aside the moral ramifications of stealing someone's beau, she wanted to use her talents, not marry her way into a better economic future.

"I appreciate your worrying about me, but right now I need a shower." Nicki headed into the bathroom.

What she needed to do was get out of there. Despite Christine's generosity in letting her stay, Nicki needed to stand on her own two feet. It would be too easy to slip back into the low expectations of the path she'd once been on.

# FIFTEEN

*W*hat are you doing, Nicolette?" Hunter called down and then watched Nicki nearly jump out of her bright yellow sandals. She had parked behind his car in the narrow alley. In a denim skirt and yellow T-shirt, she looked rather cute. With a straw hat perched on her head and a tote bag advertising Aunt Sally's pralines on her shoulder, she also looked like the classic American tourist on vacation.

"Good grief, Hunter. You nearly scared the life out of me."

"How could I scare you? I live here." He leaned out the open window above her head. "But you can't leave your car hanging over the sidewalk like that. Traffic enforcement will give you a ticket or maybe tow you away, your being a habitual offender and all." For some reason, he loved to tease and bait her. Maybe because it wasn't something he indulged in with Ashley.

"Why are you watching the alley? I would think you have better things to do."

"I thought I heard someone breaking into my car. Did you plan to block me in and not tell me?"

"No, but I didn't think you would be at home. I've been driving around and couldn't find a place to park. If you were out with Ashley, I thought I could use your spot for a while."

"Ah, Saturday night in New Orleans. Everyone comes to town to party. Is that why you're here? Perhaps you wish to experience the dangerous, decadent lure of the French Quarter?" He studied her face, so young and innocent, so full of expectation.

"I would like to take a look around, maybe pick up a real estate magazine of available rentals."

"Is that how you spent your morning, checking out other places to live?"

"Only online. Also, I tried to find out everything I could about Robert Bissette. I didn't have much luck with that either. So here I am. I've never been on Bourbon Street or even in the Quarter."

"You're kidding, right? You live in Natchez, just three hours upriver, and you never came down for Mardi Gras?"

"Nope, and much unlike yourself, I almost never kid around."

"Here are my keys." He tossed down the ring. "Move my car over and park next to me. But if you chip the paint, I'll deduct it from your first check."

Nicki caught his keys easily. A few moments later he heard his car engine roar to life. He hoped she wouldn't press down too hard on the accelerator or she'd push over a two-hundred-year-old wall that had withstood Hurricanes Betsy, Camille, and Katrina. Hunter held his breath while she parked the two cars. Then Nicki squeezed out of her little Escort as though her spine were made of rubber. Not more than eight inches separated his car from hers.

"Ah, a perfect fit. You'll do well in the city. And as I have no plans for the evening, come on up. We'll start your tour of the Quarter off with something cold." He pulled in his head and closed the shutters before she could argue.

Hunter had no idea why he'd done that—invited Nate's cousin up for a drink as though he was the Welcome Wagon of New Orleans. He still had plenty of work examining James's portfolios if he wanted to see what trouble he was in. Besides, he'd gone barhopping down Bourbon Street more times than he cared to admit. That's why he was settling down and getting married. He never wanted to wake up bleary eyed with the taste of river sludge in his mouth again. Nicki probably had her own ideas of what constituted a good time. Ashley was always haranguing him to loosen up.

While waiting for her to discover the back stairs, Hunter poured two tall drinks. Soon he heard her shoes clattering on the metal gallery. Nicki walked through the French doors wearing gold hoop earrings, bright pink lipstick, and blue eye shadow. His heart clenched, remembering a commercial for disposable cameras to capture prom night.

"That is one hot car," she said. "Could I take it for a spin sometime? Maybe out to California?"

He handed her one of the drinks. "Not until you get me off the hook for murder."

"Fair enough. How's the accounting going? Are you ready to compare notes about what you found in the company's books?"

"Not yet. I need to review files to make sure no confidentiality issues are at stake. I know you're sworn to the PI code of secrecy, but my clients' privacy is essential. Anyway, we'll conduct no business tonight. You've come to town with a pretty dress on, so we're not talking about work."

"It's a skirt and top, not a dress."

Hunter pretended not to notice. "I stand corrected, Miss Price. Are you ready for Saturday night in the French Quarter? I hope you don't plan to earn any beads." He took a swallow of his bourbon.

Nicki sipped her drink and then grimaced. "What is this?"

"It's called the lazy man's mint julep. It's bourbon on the rocks with a splash of peppermint schnapps."

"It tastes awful. Could I have something else? And I heard

about getting beads on Bourbon Street. If I want beads, I'll just buy them at Target."

"Didn't your mama teach you never to say 'it tastes awful' to your host?"

Nicki momentarily covered her mouth with her fingers. Then she stood a bit straighter, smiled, and in a sweet Southern drawl said, "Excuse me, Mr. Galen, but may I trouble you for something else to sip? This beverage doesn't seem to suit my delicate constitution."

"That was perfect." Hunter took the glass from her. "What might sit better with your constitution, miss?" He emulated an exaggerated drawl too.

"Diet Coke would be lovely. I want to take in the sights, not become one."

When Hunter walked to his refrigerator for the soft drink, Nicki followed him. "Your hair is still dripping wet. How many showers do you take a day?"

He realized he hadn't finished drying his hair before sticking his head into the alley. "Two, at least." He poured her soft drink from a two-liter bottle. "See if this meets your expectations while I finish getting ready." He handed her the drink and left the kitchen. Somehow the country girl made him nervous and jumpy, as though this would be *his* first night in the Quarter instead of where he had been born.

A few minutes later he found her studying his paintings on the living room wall. "See anything you like?"

"Very much so. Are these by a member of your family?" She pointed at a signature in the corner of one canvass.

"My sister, Chloe. She has quite a gift. She recently graduated from Tulane and has been accepted into their graduate program. I think she wants to teach. There's not much else you can do with a master's in fine arts. You certainly don't need an advanced degree to put paint on canvas."

"The world will always need teachers." Nicki turned to face him. "She's a wonderful artist. Please give her my compliments on this piece. It makes me want to buy a rail pass and backpack through Europe."

Hunter gazed at the pastoral watercolor of mountains and a pristine village, complete with an old man tending his flock while a light burned in his farmhouse window. Simple, perfect, how life should be.

"Thank you. I will tell her. That painting has always been my favorite too." Turning his attention back on her, he asked, "Tell me how you lived less than two hundred miles away yet spent no weekends in the Big Easy with your friends. No spring break blowouts, no bachelorette parties, not even one Mardi Gras? Seems almost criminal to be so close yet never partake in the festivities."

"I worked to put myself through college and PI training. I had no help from my mother or athletic scholarships, and very little financial aid. That meant each weekend and every vacation I worked at the mall or waited on customers at a restaurant to pay my way." She sipped her cola, looking at him as though he were the naive one. "Don't get me wrong, Hunter. I'm not complaining. My education was more important than partying. Besides, I have a problem with people drinking themselves stupid on spring break. So in a nutshell, no time, no money, but no big deal." Nicki finished off the rest of her soft drink. "Any more questions?"

"I don't think so. That pretty much sums it up." He smiled because he couldn't think of anything else to do. He'd hit an unexpected nerve.

"Do I amuse you? Does Nicki-from-the-backwoods offer entertainment not available on pay-per-view?" She didn't look quite so young or innocent anymore.

"No, Nicolette, not in the way you think." Hunter chose his words carefully. "I would love to see things from your eyes, especially New Orleans. For three hundred years this city stayed pretty much the same. Then Katrina hit and now instead of making improvements, New Orleans is struggling to bring life back as it was. Fools probably got drunk and stupid on Bourbon Street back when men fought with swords and women wore corsets."

Nicki blushed. "You do have a way with words, boss."

"Everything is old here and hanging together with a gossamer thread." He met her eye. "You aren't bored with the world and everything in it. I envy that."

"In that case, you can show me around the city as long as your girlfriend doesn't mind your spending time with an employee. But for the record I don't imbibe, so no more of your lazy man cocktails or any other kind."

"Fine with me. My budget can use a break." Hunter winked and went for his wallet and a swig of mouthwash. Briefly he considered changing his silk shirt into something more casual. His new employee was making him concerned about matters he seldom worried about.

Soon he wasn't worried about anything at all.

Nicki took charge on their way down the back steps. "I picked up a tourist map and we're heading down Royal Street to Jackson Square." She unfolded the colorful brochure under a street lamp. "And we're not rushing or hurrying past anything."

She danced on the sidewalk, posed for a caricature sketch she paid for herself, and didn't pass a street musician's upturned hat without throwing in a dollar, but she paid no attention to the fortune-tellers with their crystal balls and flamboyant clothing.

"Don't you want your palm read to find out if you'll marry your old high school sweetheart and move to Mobile?" asked Hunter when they reached a corner.

"I didn't have a high school sweetheart. Besides, I think we should steer clear of fortune-tellers." She peered up at the filigree ironwork along the balconies of the Pontalba Buildings.

"Well, then. Would you like to look inside my church? My family has gone here for generations."

"You're Roman Catholic?"

"I am. I hope you didn't think only Southern Baptists go the heaven." He placed his hand over his heart.

Her complexion darkened. "Of course not. We're all judged individually."

When they stepped inside one of the oldest churches in the country, Nicki's eyes turned round as saucers. "Look at the carvings and stained glass!" They slipped into a back pew behind the tourists, the devout on bended knee, and those who came for cool relief from the heat. "What are those folks doing?" Nicki pointed at several women lighting candles.

"They're asking for intercession for someone sick, and maybe for the soul of a deceased loved one."

Nicki's brow furrowed with confusion. "Do you have to be Catholic to light a votive?"

"Of course not. Just put a buck in the box to help defray the cost."

Nicki grabbed a dollar out of her wallet and walked up to the rail looking more frightened than she had inside Robert Bissette's home. The moment her candle was glowing she hurried down the aisle and dragged him toward the door.

"I asked God to take some of Mom's pain away. Now I wish I put in a five."

Hunter pulled a fifty from his wallet and shoved it into the poor box on their way out. "All bases are covered."

"You'd better stop throwing your money around or you'll end up in debtor's prison. After all, time has stood still in New Orleans."

"At least it was fifty well spent. Where to now, tour guide?"

Nicki headed up an alley, home to a quaint bookstore and shuttered storefronts. On the next block she vetoed the voodoo shop but bought an overpriced flower from an elderly blind woman on the corner of Decatur and St. Ann.

"Ashley would demand proof of blindness before buying a flower from that woman," Hunter whispered once beyond the woman's hearing. He was only half joking.

"If she's faking it, then I'm only out five bucks. But what if she isn't and really needs our help? I'm not taking the chance." Nicki inhaled the scent of a long stemmed rose.

Hunter pondered that for a moment. Then he walked back and bought every one of her flowers. "When all my money's gone, I'll go home."

Nicki smiled behind her tourist map. "I hope you're not totally broke yet. We're on our way to the French Market." She took off at a trot while he struggled to keep up, looking like a deranged wedding planner with the massive bouquet.

Inside the market, Nicki handed a rose to every woman they encountered. If anyone asked, she explained they were the unofficial welcoming committee for New Orleans. Soon they met tourists from Alabama, Florida, and Georgia. Nicki chanted the LSU fight song with girls in head-to-toe purple and gave a high five to a kid from OSU with an appropriate O-H-I-O.

When an elderly couple said they hailed from Michigan, Nicki gave them two flowers. "This is to make up for the long winters you put up with," she explained.

When the grandmother hugged Nicki affectionately, Hunter yearned to do the same. Instead, when their roses ran out, he dragged her into Café du Monde for *café au lait* and sugary beignets. When Nicki excused herself to the ladies' room, he watched her walk away from him with bizarre wistfulness. *What is wrong with me?* She was the tourist, yet he wanted to ride the streetcar until their 24-hour-pass expired. After she returned to their table, they sat in the courtyard, sipping their coffee and watching an assortment of humanity pass by.

"Your city is beautiful, Hunter. True, it's old, but it's stately and classy. That's how I want to be when I'm sixty." Her face glowed. "Based on Nate's description, I thought I would hate it." She leaned over the tiny table. "But I may be falling in love."

He looked away as a flush climbed his neck. "I can almost guarantee you'll hate Bourbon Street, so we'll see that last. I insist you try the local cuisine before we run too far off track."

"Dutch treat, sir, and nothing expensive. I'm willing to eat from a street vendor. There's a cart on the next corner."

"We are *not* eating at a hot dog cart," he said flatly. Up to that point, she hadn't let him pay for anything but the flowers. She'd even insisted on paying for her coffee. "And I'm not accustomed to women paying their own way. I can't say I like it." Especially since he knew the state of her financial circumstances.

"Nobody ever died from eating at a pushcart."

"No, Nicolette. You agreed to let me to show you the city. I'm buying your dinner tonight and everything else or I'm taking you back to your double-parked car. Do we have a deal?"

Nicki glared at him over her powdered-sugar mustache. He glared back with equal determination. When she slanted her eyes, he did the same. She lifted her eyebrows and he matched the response.

"Shall we play a game of game of rock, paper, scissors next?" he asked.

"Okay, you win, but only because my face was starting to hurt. Remember, just good food and nothing pricey. Got that, *mon ami?*"

"In every language."

Hunter took her to Red Fish Grill, where they dined on crawfish etouffee, fried oysters, collard greens, and cornbread. Nicki marveled over every bite she ate, and they both cleaned their plates. Hunter savored each dish as though tasting it for the first time. He'd always loved the local cuisine, but at some point he'd stopped ordering his favorites. *Too rich, too spicy, too fattening*—Ashley's words rang in his ears. Ashley was entitled to her opinion, but why had he pulled away from foods he enjoyed?

After dinner they began their sojourn through the Quarter, avoiding Bourbon Street altogether. Instead on the edge of downtown, close to the river, they found a Cajun dance hall where the music was loud and the song lyrics in French. Instead of cloistered around the tables, everybody was up on their feet, dancing. Nicki started tapping her toe to the lively music before the hostess found them a small table against the wall.

"I love this place!" she exclaimed over a well-amplified fiddle.

"I thought you might," Hunter replied, and to the waitress he said, "Two Cokes please."

Nicki concentrated as the dancers two-stepped around the room. "I believe I can do that." She dragged him to the dance floor.

Before Hunter could refuse, they were moving around the room with couples of all ages. She stepped on his toes and he stepped on hers, yet no one seemed to notice how badly they danced. Suddenly, someone slipped a washboard over his head, and Hunter found himself accompanying the accordion and guitars with a pair of spoons. Nicki stamped her foot and cheered for him while taking pictures of his musical debut with her cell phone.

They both almost levitated from the floor with joy in that crowded dance hall where everyone smiled and no one tried to look sophisticated or chic. Soon he was spinning her around again as though they had danced together all their lives.

"If I lived in this town, I would come here every weekend to dance the night away." Breathless and flushed, Nicki waved her hand in front of her face as the band took a break.

"You do live in this town. Chalmette isn't that far away." Watching the exuberance vanish from her face, Hunter regretted mentioning her housing arrangements.

"I'm just staying there temporarily," she said with a shrug. "I don't know for how long."

"Should I help you find something else? Apartments are scarce, but I know a few restaurant owners who rent out upstairs rooms to select, quiet tenants."

"Select and quiet, that's me." Nicki shook her blond hair back from her face, her brown eyes flashing from the strobe lights. "But don't get ahead of yourself, boss. Nate might not hire me on a permanent basis. He won't need an assistant if he's headed to the slammer."

"Then we must make sure that doesn't happen."

She picked up her soft drink and took a sip. "And how do you propose we do that?"

"This is New Orleans. We throw money at every elected official who walks by the courthouse and then wait for the charges to be dropped."

"You wouldn't." She set the glass down with a thud.

"It's the classic New Orleans standing joke, Nicki. You really need to lighten up."

Grabbing his arm, she pulled him back toward the other dancers. "Laugh about this, Mr. Employer. If you're throwing money around, maybe it should go to keep *you* out of jail. I personally think prison will do Nate a world of good. But from what I hear, the person running your investigation doesn't know her behind from a beehive." She laughed all the way back to the dance floor and turned to face him. Just then, the band changed the tempo to a slow, melodic tune. It was the first break from their foot-stomping, hand-clapping, ear-deafening zydeco.

Hunter drew Nicki close and placed her hand on his shoulder. "I bet your grandmother, your *Mamaw*, taught you that line. It's a good one, but if it's true I'm in trouble."

"So you caught my down-home expression from the only person to love me with no strings attached." Her face was close with so many dancers surrounding them, her expression challenging him to take issue.

"I caught it and I love it. My siblings and I refer to our grandmother as *Grandmère*. Don't think we didn't take abuse over that expression. The French population, although plentiful in the western parishes, is rare in the Quarter these days. But I think everybody has a right to call their kin anything they want without fear of ridicule."

The corners of Nicki's mouth turned up, followed by an all-out grin. "I've been laboring under a false notion 'bout you, Mr. Galen. That's one more of Mamaw's favorites."

What happened next he hadn't meant to do. And it was a very bad idea because she worked for him.

Especially since he was almost engaged.

Hunter tipped up her chin and kissed her lightly on the mouth. The world stopped spinning for several delicious moments.

"Goodness, Hunter, I would have said my name for my grandmother sooner if I'd known how you'd react." Nicki dissolved into a fit of giggles while he dug his hands into his pockets like a schoolboy.

"So you don't disapprove?"

Nicki placed her hands on either side of his face, her fingers tangled through his hair, and she kissed him squarely on the mouth. "There, that's a kiss." She stepped back. "And we'll have no more of that nonsense, or I'll turn you in for sexual harassment. After all,

I work for you and you'll get into heaps of trouble with your girl-friend." She marched back to their table, picked up her straw hat and tote bag that miraculously hadn't been stolen, and headed for the door. "I have to get up early tomorrow, boss, so let's get going."

Hunter remained motionless on the dance floor. He'd been thunderstruck. Or lightning stuck. Or at least kissed by a woman who rocked him down to his Italian loafers. Kissing her had been a major mistake, but nevertheless something started to burn in his gut. Nicki was halfway to the door when he put tip money on the table and hurried after her. *What happened to my bravado and sophistication?*

"Wait up," he called, catching her as she reached the sidewalk. A light rain had started to fall. Hunter took hold of her arm so she wouldn't run off. "I have one more thing to show you." He held up his palms when she started to protest. "It's close by and won't take long. Please humor me."

"All right, but it had better not involve any more kissing. I have a reputation to maintain."

"No more, I promise."

They picked up their pace as the drizzle turned into a down-pour, arriving at the steps to the Alcazar damp but not soaked.

Nicki stared up at the eclectic Spanish-Moorish building. "Good grief, have we left the USA? This looks like the set from an old Humphrey Bogart movie." When the uniformed man swept open the door, she ran up the steps into the lobby.

"Here's looking at you, kid," Hunter murmured, his own enthusiasm growing.

The Alcazar's lobby was a two-story hexagon, with a polished mosaic floor, fireplace, and a fountain sprouting from a fishpond. Tiled steps led to upper balconies. Doors from the suites opened from these galleries to overlook the extraordinary indoor court-yard. In the lobby, potted plants separated areas for conversation or quiet reading. Classical music floated on the air while even the lighting was soft and subdued.

"This looks like a movie set! I expect Lauren Bacall or Katherine Hepburn to stroll down those stairs wearing Coco Chanel."

"I thought you'd like it. Take a peek in the lounge at the stained glass window over the bar. Louis C. Tiffany couldn't have done better himself." His hooked a thumb in the right direction. When Nicki took off through the swinging doors, Hunter headed to the reception desk. No way would he let her drive back to Chalmette tonight.

She joined him a few minutes later by the fountain, as excited as a child on Christmas morning. "What is this place? A hotel? Short-term apartments? They have bowls of peel-n-eat shrimp on ice in the bar *for free*. And I spotted the back garden. They have both a lily pond *and* a swimming pool. I would love to live here."

"This is a boutique hotel, and tonight it will be your home." Hunter held out an ornate, old-fashioned key.

Her expression turned wary. "What are you up to, Hunter? Is that a key to a room?" One hand perched on her hip. "If you think for one minute—"

"It's to your room, not mine." He pressed the key into her hand. "I'm going home and you aren't driving back to Chalmette late at night in the rain. Don't try to argue with me, Nicolette. You'll find a robe to sleep in on the back of the bathroom door. In the morning, coffee will be delivered to your room, and breakfast is served through those French doors. You can come by for your car tomorrow, but then take the rest of the day off. Give me a day on the books alone." Before she could argue, or before he lost his head and said something stupid, Hunter walked through the swinging doors. He didn't look back until he reached the sidewalk. Nicki was staring at the key in her hand as though unsure of its use. But there was definitely a smile on her pretty face.

# SIXTEEN

*I*f it hadn't been raining so hard, and if he hadn't been formulating a plan to keep Nicki from driving back to Chalmette, Hunter may have noticed the two women huddling under an umbrella across the street. They watched him enter the expensive hotel with Nicki, but unfortunately they left before he came out ten minutes later.

Particularly unfortunate because both women were friends of Ashley's. And one of the friends felt it her duty to inform Ashley of Hunter's indiscretion.

The woman had Ashley on the line within minutes, only too ready to dispense the news. After all, Ashley had been acting much too haughty since landing Hunter Galen.

"Ashley, got a minute? I have the most dreadful news to tell you." Justine wanted to draw out the drama for as long as possible.

"What could possibly be so important that couldn't wait for morning? I was sound asleep." Ashley didn't sound pleased to be in the news loop.

"You'll thank me when you hear this," continued Justine. "I'm in the Quarter with Suzanne blowing off a little steam. Guess who we saw going into the Alcazar not ten minutes ago?"

A short pause and then a much-put-upon sigh preceded

Ashley's peevish reply. "I can't possibly guess...Brad and Angelina? Why are you acting so juvenile?"

"Your boyfriend, that's who. Checking in with Miss PWT, who got all dolled up for her night on the town."

Ashley bolted upright. "Miss PWT? What on earth does that mean?"

"Well, Hunter's pretty date dresses like she has no money and she's Caucasian, so I'll let you figure out the rest." Justine and Suzanne broke into hoots and howls of laughter. "We gotta get out of this rain, but we'll stop by to commiserate tomorrow." They ended the call still laughing.

"Pretty, white..." Ashley jumped out of bed, fully awake. The hard plastic case on her cell phone almost crumpled between her fingers. It had to be that cousin of Nate Price's from Mississippi. How could Hunter possibly be attracted to her? Her stomach roiled with acid thinking about him with another woman. *A final fling before getting hitched? An act of kindness for someone new to town?*

Ashley's anger toward the love of her life faded. She needed to save some for the source of her troubles.

# SEVENTEEN

When Nicki arrived to retrieve her car the next morning, she stared up at Hunter's shuttered windows, perplexed as to what to do. Should she knock on his door and thank him for an evening in the loveliest hotel on earth? Waking up in that room was like waking up in paradise. Everything about the place screamed luxury, from the thick towels to the silky bed sheets to the dining room chef ready to make an omelet to your specifications. The orange juice was fresh squeezed, the bread warm from the oven, and the service impeccable.

Fortunately, Nicki spotted a note on her windshield tucked under the wiper blade, resolving her quandary. *Nicki, I had some errands to run. Drive home safely. I'll call later. Hunter.*

She jotted down a thank-you note, dropped it into his mailbox, and headed to Christine's trailer—an abode as far from the Alcazar on the comfort scale as you could find. Hunter's errands gave her time to ponder those kisses on the dance floor. What had that been about? And what was she going to do about it? Unfortunately, she had enjoyed them more than she cared to admit.

Once she was in her room, Nicki stayed only long enough to change her clothes before heading back outside to get back in her car. She had more to accomplish on her day off than contemplate her client. She would have loved to take Nate's and her mother's advice to let the sleeping dogs lie, but she couldn't. What kind of PI would she be if she didn't at least talk to her grandparents about her dad?

After her father disappeared and her mother couldn't pay the rent, they had moved from a quiet side street in Natchez to Red Haw, Mississippi, a town barely on local maps. Her mother had been laid off from her part-time job at the bakery. Food stamps, Aid to Dependent Children, and a pittance of Social Security only went so far, considering the cost of her mother's medications. Mamaw and Papaw had taken them in without a second thought, but Rose had found the adjustment to rustic living nearly impossible.

"Might as well live out on the prairie with the pioneers." If her mom said that once, she'd said it a thousand times. Nicki could still remember the tang of pine in the sheets and pillowcases. Cleaning house involved a broom, dustpan, and dust cloth. No wall-to-wall carpeting, no ceramic tile, and no granite counter-tops. But they always had plenty of food on the table, thanks to Papaw's dead shot with a rifle, luck with a fishing pole, and Mamaw's abundant garden.

Unlike her mother, Nicki had been happy growing up in the country. Everyone knew everyone at the small school she attended, and they all saw one another at church on Sundays. Life was slow paced yet sustaining. But Rose had found the isolation depressing, and her mother didn't need another reason to be depressed. When Rose finally landed another job five years later, they moved back to Natchez into subsidized housing. Mom seldom visited her parents anymore, and now that Nicki was on her way to Red Haw, she realized she didn't spend nearly enough time with them either.

As soon as she left southern Louisiana headed toward Mississippi, an ache began deep in her heart. Though she knew it was silly and had no foundation in reality, she experienced a sudden feeling of fear that her grandparents would die before she arrived, depriving her of a chance to say goodbye. But when she left the well-traveled interstate for the Mississippi back roads, she found new sources of distress that weren't a figment of her imagination: fields abandoned or neglected; sharecropper cabins that should have been knocked down inhabited by sour-faced mothers and barefoot children; broken fence posts, littered ditches, and utility poles papered with ancient ads for boiled peanuts. It seemed as though the world had moved on while this part of rural America remained trapped in a Steinbeck or Faulkner novel. Swallowing hard, Nicki tuned the radio to a gospel station and sang along, loud and off-key, as a way to improve her mood on a cool and rainy day.

On the rutted lane leading to her grandparents' home, she was struck by several incongruities. Vegetables grew in ruler-straight rows, while weed-free pansies and petunias encircled the house and bordered the pebble walkway. Yet rusty farm implements, a forlorn wheelbarrow, and an abandoned car still remained in the last spots they had been functional. Cracked window glass had been repaired with duct tape, and plastic sheeting covered a section of the roof. Of course, her grandparents existed on a small Social Security income, and trash pickup was expensive in rural areas.

Shaking off her critical appraisal, Nicki bounded out of the car. "Anybody home?" she crowed at the top of her lungs.

"Where else would we be, child?" Mamaw limped onto the porch and let the screen door slam behind her. A wide grin turned her papery skin into a roadmap of creases. "Come up here and let me see what the big city done to ya."

"I hope you don't mind my arriving unannounced, but I brought you something." Nicki pulled a large white box from the backseat.

"You don't need no invite, child. What you got there—dirty

clothes to wash? Maybe a litter of kittens?" Mamaw leaned over the rail, her gnarled hands gripping the post.

"Even better. I brought beignets, pecan pie, and sweet potato pie. *Mmm-mmm*." She rubbed her belly with a circular motion.

"Why would I need that stuff when I just baked a pan of corn-bread?" Mamaw asked, wrinkling her nose. Nevertheless she extracted a sugary beignet and took a bite before Nicki had a chance to sit down.

"Hey, there, sweet girl." Her grandfather walked into the kitchen, stiff and rumpled from his midday nap.

"Hi, Papaw! Look what I brought. Donuts and two kinds of pie." Nicki pushed the box across the table.

"You know I don't eat 'tween meals," he drawled as he pulled out a beignet.

"I thought this might be a rule-breaking sort of day." Nicki leaned back in her chair, trying to be subtle as her eyes perused the room. Everything looked the same. The same frayed dish towel hung on the exact same hook next to the dented stainless steel sink. *Nothing* had changed. Nicki half expected the wall calendar to be 1965 with ads for Bon Ami cleanser.

"How are you two getting on?" she asked, refocusing her attention on them. "Do you feel okay? Are there any errands I can run for you? How about a trip to Walmart? Do you need help with anything, Mamaw?" Nicki fired one question after another.

Her grandparents looked at each other and laughed. "We feel as good as we ought," Mamaw said with a shake of her head. "We don't need nothin' from town. And if I can't do a chore, it don't need doin' far as I'm concerned." She set a cold glass of sweet tea in front of Nicki without her having to ask for it. "Why don't you stop beatin' round the bush and tell me why you're here. It ain't my birthday, and you ain't lived in Orleans long 'nuff to get homesick."

Nicki drummed her fingers on the scarred table while choosing the best approach. "I want to know how my father died, but I can't get my mother to talk about it. It's like this big family secret, so I'm coming to you."

"What you want to know for? That was a long time ago, Nic'lette."

"Because I'm an adult and I have a right." She paused to take a sip from the striped plastic glass. "I understand Dad wasn't much of a provider or husband, but he was always nice to me and the only father I had."

"Your mama should have told you the truth long before this." Mamaw stared out the window at chickadees twittering in the bushes a long while before answering. "That weekend wasn't like the others. Your uncles usually spent more time chewing the fat 'bout nothin' but hunting or fishing."

"Half time they ain't got nothin' on their hooks," interjected Papaw. "What fish can you 'spect to catch like that?"

"Kermit invited a bad sort to come along." Mamaw's lips pulled into a thin line. "Things go wrong when fools start drinkin' and playing poker."

"Which of Dad's friends owned the cabin?"

Her grandmother squinted with a frown. "What you mean? Your Uncle Charles owned that cabin. That's why they went there."

"Uncle Charles?"

"Charles had that cabin for years till he caught the cancer and sold it to Andre."

"What about the men Dad invited? Mama said it was three brothers from Clay Creek." Nicki looked from one to the other, but they shook their head.

"Don't know 'bout them," said Mamaw. "You're the investigator now, missy. If you're so set on finding out, ask that sheriff who came out the next day. Maybe he filed a report. Get your hands on that interview and you'll have those names."

Nicki peered into her watery blue eyes and smiled. "Would you like to move to the big city for a spell? I could use you on my first case."

Mamaw reached over to pat her hand. "Be patient, honey, and you'll do fine. But if you get stuck, you can always come home for a visit."

# EIGHTEEN

"Hello, Miss Price? This is Naomi Prescott, Mr. Galen's assistant." The woman paused as though to let the information sink in.

Nicki struggled to sit up, her morning floor exercises thus complete. "Yes, Mrs. Prescott, how do you do?"

"Fine, dear, thank you. Mr. Galen asked me to call you." Her voice dripped with an accent unlike New Orleans, more like Savannah or Charleston, something Eastern Seaboard. "He would like you to meet him at a client's home to review documents."

"He told me he didn't need me today and that he wished to spend time on the books alone." Nicki shifted the phone to her other ear.

"Plans have changed. This must have just come up."

"Am I going out to Robert Bissette's again?"

There was a pause before she answered. "No, not Mr. Bissette's. The place is called *La Maison de Poisson*. The client's name is Michael Dennison, and he lives in Terrebonne Parish. Do you have paper and pencil? I'll give you the address and what directions I have, but you'll need to pick up a map. GPS may not work in that parish."

Nicki fumbled for a pen while the woman rattled off the

address. After she repeated it back, Mrs. Prescott clicked off as though in a big hurry. Nicki pictured all the phone lines lit up with clients wishing to buy or sell, or concerned about their investments with a murder investigation pending, but she knew switchboards like that only existed in the movies anymore.

"Terrebonne Parish? Why in the world couldn't you wait for me?" Nicki spoke to no one in particular. She would have to travel alone into the swamps, a place she wasn't particularly fond of. Visions of slimy creatures rising from the mist to surround her car while she studied a map flitted through her mind. If Hunter had waited they could have enjoyed the drive the way they did their trip to St. James Parish instead of wasting another tank of gas.

But she knew it wasn't fuel economy troubling her. Hunter was rapidly growing on her. His wit, charm, and gracious manners were quite appealing, but most of all it was the way he treated her. As though she mattered. As though she was a valuable asset instead of merely Nate's trainee.

*Miss Ashley Menard, whoever you are, you are one lucky chick.*

Nicki hurried to get ready because she had no intention of arriving in Terrebonne Parish when Hunter was ready to start back to the city. Then she dug out her map and examined it with a magnifying glass. Interstate 90 to Raceland, then hop on Route One. However, she suspected her parish map would be useless in finding the turnoff to *La Maison de Poisson.*

By the time Nicki was far out into the parish and looking for the road that would lead her to Michael Dennison's home, she found Mrs. Prescott's directions to be sketchier than those to the lost ark. After several wrong turns, quite a bit of backtracking, and asking directions from people whose English was barely decipherable, Nicki got lucky. A battered metal sign, attached to a rusty pipe with a single bolt, announced *Maison de Poisson*. A small red arrow pointed to the right.

"Oh, no," she moaned. The hand-painted sign indicated a narrow dirt road filled with potholes nearly large enough to swallow her car. A heavy rain would turn this driveway into a minefield of mini lakes. Hunter's client must crave privacy to put up with this every time he ran out for a quart of milk.

Nicki got out of her car and looked around. While she pondered a course of action, no vehicles passed by on the road. There was no mailbox or plastic tube for the newspaper.

She checked her cell phone for a message from Hunter. What she was hoping for was *"Where are you, darling? Hurry on up to the house. We're all ready to dive into a pitcher of lemonade and a bucket of crawfish."* But instead of a welcoming text, "No Service" blinked ominously in the message box.

After driving all the way to the bayou, she was standing like Chicken Little on the side of the road. Nicki sucked in a lungful of humid air and exhaled slowly. Her fear of swamps was personal and shouldn't interfere with her ability to do the job. She was Nicki Price, trained private investigator.

Dropping her phone into her purse, Nicki started the engine and inched slowly up the driveway. Many people would find the area beautiful. They would be glad that wild, natural areas still existed in a world where developers loved to drain swamps and put up another strip mall. Nicki may have felt that way too if her father's death in the swamp and how that horrible event had impacted her childhood wasn't closing around her now like kudzu.

With each turn in the road, with each successfully navigated pothole, she expected to see a Tara-like plantation mansion loom before her eyes, complete with double verandahs and a wide expanse of front lawn. Nicki imagined a home more palatial than

Bissette's *Fenêtre sur l'Eau*. Lunch would be ready to be served. Hunter would beckon with a smile and wave of his hand, having already soothed the nervous client. The ice tea would be sweet and strong, the cuisine served with style. Nicki would join the soirée and impress the boss with her resourcefulness in finding the place, besides her brilliant conversation skills.

*Boom!* A loud bang, followed by an ominous hissing, curtailed her daydream about lunch on the patio. The hissing sound meant only one thing—a flat tire. Nicki had suffered more than her share during her driving career. After scrambling from the car, her expectations were confirmed. The tire rested on its rim while something odd lay in the dirt beneath the flattened rubber. She'd driven over some sort of board, yet the wood wasn't dark with mildew like everything else in the swamp. This board was clean as a whistle. Nicki got back in the car and rolled it forward just enough to discover a strip of carpet tacking embedded in her tire.

With considerable effort she pried the strip loose. But instead of tacks, long and sturdy nails had ruined her scenic drive into the bayou. Someone had purposely hammered them into the row to ensure a blowout for the next hapless traveler. Wasn't it bad enough that bored teenagers bashed mailboxes from pickup trucks for amusement?

Muttering under her breath, Nicki grabbed her purse and headed up the driveway before her fears came home to roost. She didn't want to consider the strange sounds around her without the protection of her Escort. After all, how long could this drive-way be? Hunter and his rich client would soon appear and offer to put on the spare or maybe replace the ruined tire.

After another half mile, *La Maison de Poisson* came into view, but not the mansion with white pillars she had anticipated. It was a one-story, slat-board shack with a rusty corrugated roof. The porch leaned precariously to the right, while the front steps angled to the left. The house had the ambience of an amusement park fun house, but nothing about the situation struck Nicki as humorous.

Jagged glass shards clung to frames where windows once had been. The chimney had fallen in long ago, leaving a gaping hole in the roof for bats and bugs to come and go. Soda cans, beer bottles, discarded fishing nets, oil cans, broken lawn chairs, and everything imaginable from a man's getaway weekend littered the weedy yard. And "yard" would be stretching the definition— more like muddy high ground surrounded by swamp willows and moss-draped cypress trees. The driveway on which she stood looped around the cabin toward a channel's dark water.

Nicki shuddered and swallowed hard. It was obvious that no one had visited this place, let alone lived here, in quite some time. One of those mailbox-bashing brats probably found it funny to move the sign to the road leading to this hovel. Nicki stomped her espadrille in the dust. By the time she finally arrived at the client's home, Hunter probably would have given up and returned to New Orleans.

So much for the opportunity to enthrall them with witty conversation.

Starting back to her car, she planned to change the tire and get away from the tick-infested tall grass as soon as possible. But as she batted away a swarm of no-see-ums, Nicki noticed tracks in the dirt for the first time. These weren't from narrow economy tires like hers or the wide high-performance tires from Hunter's Corvette. These treads were made by one of those big, dual-axle pickups common on the country roads where she'd grown up. Queasiness settled in her stomach while perspiration ran down her temples. Suddenly, exasperation for phantom pranksters morphed into something more insidious. Considering how often it rained in the bayou, these tracks had been made recently.

Nicki began to run, heedless of muddy potholes. Hunter, his client, and lunch on the veranda were not nearly as important as feeling safe again. The sooner she changed the flat and left Terrebonne Parish, the better. She didn't slow down until she reached the final twist in the road. But the sight of her car did nothing to calm her anxiety. The doors on her Escort were open and the trunk lid was up. Nicki crept toward the back of the car. What choice did she have? Run headlong into the swamp and swim back to Orleans Parish?

Fortunately, no ax murderer, no bayou strangler, and no Freddie Kruger lurked behind the raised trunk lid.

But also no jack and no spare tire. And she was certain they were there the last time she looked. Nicki stood with hands on hips contemplating her options. As she waited for something brilliant to come to mind, she heard the sound of a vehicle approaching on the same road she was stuck in the middle of. Panic tightened her chest, choking off her air for several moments. Nicki braced her hands on the car and forced herself to breathe. Then, despite feeling light-headed, she turned and sprinted up the rutted washout as though an army of cutthroats were coming because that's what they sounded like.

Voices raised in a rebel yell reverberated through the dense undergrowth. The whooping, hollering, and horn blasting grew closer by the second, along with a radio tuned to a screechy hard rock station. Nicki also discerned a few obscenities aimed in her direction. For no apparent reason, these men were swearing at her and she had no clue why. Nor did she wish to find out.

She reached the cluttered yard of the shack panting like a dog. Her cotton top was plastered to her chest and a side stitch doubled her over with pain. Nothing around the cabin offered protection from the melee fast approaching. Her small car must have been little impediment because the truck was very close. With no alternative, Nicki circled around the shack and fought her way through the briars, trying not to consider what critters lived in the swamp's underbrush. Her goal became the boathouse sitting at water's edge—a boathouse if one stretched the definition. Thanks to Hurricanes Katrina and Rita, the shanty leaned to the side. Mossy stone steps led down to a rotted pier that extended into the waterway. Fishermen may have taken this path down to their boats in better days. Now they would break their necks for sure. Nicki couldn't imagine entering anything less appealing than the swamper's shack until she saw this boathouse. Yet visible through the filthy window was a lone pirogue.

How she wished she was licensed to carry and had brought along her Beretta 92, a semiautomatic 9mm. *I would fire off a few warning shots, and if they kept coming, I'd pick them off like Coke cans on a fence rail.* Of course, soda cans were the only objects she'd ever fired at, other than paper targets at the range.

Hidden behind thick vines entwining one of the boathouse's supports, Nicki watched a pickup skid to a stop in the yard. The cloud of dust kicked up by the truck obliterated her view of the thugs, but judging by the volume of shouting, there must be at least a hundred.

As Nicki's gut twisted into a knot, a young man stomped up the steps to the shack. "Where you at, woman?" he shouted. His booming voice carried through the cypress and tupelo trees.

*What could I have possibly done to infuriate total strangers?* The men sounded full of hate and rage as their shouting carried over the truck's blaring music.

"Where you at?" The first man yelled again. He sounded closer.

Nicki peeked from behind her post and spotted three men in dirty jeans and ball caps coming down the path toward the boathouse. They were muscular and mean looking, and one had a shotgun.

These weren't bored teenagers out to torment a tourist.

After hurriedly untying the pirogue with shaking fingers, Nicki scrambled in it, preferring her chances in the swamp to meeting those men face-to-face. The decrepit boat was coated with mildew, but she found a paddle on the wet bottom. Nicki wasted no time pushing off from the dock and into the waterway that connected the bayous like a road map. If she could get away from land she would be safe. No other boats were handy for her assailants to use.

"Where ya goin', missy?"

"Get back here so we can get better acquainted!"

"We got a littl' message for you."

Three distinctive voices called to her, but Nicki paddled with every ounce of strength she possessed. She glanced over her shoulder at the burly men standing shoulder to shoulder on the dock. Their shouts and expletives continued. When she reached the middle of the canal, a gunshot resounded in the trees on the other bank.

They were shooting at her.

They meant to kill her.

They didn't even know her, but apparently they would shoot a woman with no more pity than a muskrat for the stew pot.

Nicki's skin crawled as she stopped paddling and crouched down in the slimy vessel. She just knew she was going to die in her least favorite place on earth and be eaten by alligators, her remnants becoming shrimp or fish bait. Perhaps a turtle would savor the last mortal remains of Nicolette Price from Red Haw, Mississippi.

Another shot rang out, sending a cypress branch crashing down on shore. Two thoughts occurred to her while she huddled in the filthy boat: one, they were using solid shot loads, far more deadly than buckshot; and two, the falling branch indicated she'd drifted close to the bank, making it far easier for them.

But Nicki had another pressing problem to contend with. Her rescue craft was rapidly taking on water. She tried bailing with her cupped hands, but the pirogue was filling so fast it was useless. As she frantically bailed, a white glob floated to the surface of the dark water. *Putty!* Holes had been drilled and then filled with putty. She'd been a victim of that trick many years ago.

Nate had drilled holes in an old rowboat, filled the holes with soft putty, and then talked her into taking the boat for an excursion. He and his friends hid in the bushes until she reached the center of the pond, about which time the putty plugs popped loose. The boat quickly filled with water and sank. Nicki, wet and embarrassed, had to swim back to the group of boys on the shore. It took years before her cousins stopped teasing her about the incident.

But the ricochet of yet another gunshot meant these weren't immature kids pulling a prank. As the pirogue sank from beneath her to the dense, mysterious bottom of the canal, Nicki swam to the nearest solid mass. An old cypress lay uprooted and dying, its branches extending fifteen feet into the water. Covered with slippery moss and vines, the tree barely offered a handhold, but it effectively shielded her from view.

"What happened out there, missy? You go down like the *Titanic*?"

"That was the lamest escape attempt I ever saw."

"Swim on back to me, sugar. I got something to take your mind off that man in town."

Laughter and taunts echoed under the low branches, but at least they were mocking her now rather than shooting at her. Nicki clung to her tree and remained as quiet as possible. She tried to not let her feet touch the surface of the water. Visions of gators, snakes, and snapping crawfish came to mind as she fought down waves of nausea. Retching into the black water would be a dead giveaway to her location for gators, so Nicki fought back the impulse.

"I said get back here, woman!" the most venomous voice shouted, followed by another shotgun blast not far above her head. Leaves and debris rained down into her hair.

Nicki laid her face against the lichen-encrusted bark and started to cry. Tears streamed down her cheeks, and she prayed every prayer she had ever been taught. After a while she could only whisper over and over, "Please, God, help me."

For an hour, maybe two, the men milled around the boat-house, shouting at her, at each other, or maybe just making a racket for no reason. Nicki lost track of time as her arms and legs grew numb. It seemed each time she gingerly shifted position to gain a better grip on the cypress someone took a shot at her. At least none of the creeps wished to ruin their alligator skin boots by coming after her into the murky water. The scratches on her face began to swell and hurt, while mosquitoes feasted on every part of her exposed flesh. She shuddered to think what lurked beneath the water level. She knew at some point she would have to enter it again if she were ever to get off that tree.

Eventually she heard the pickup start up again and drive off. Could she trust that they all left and someone wasn't just wait-ing for her to come out from behind her shelter and make herself an easier target? She waited as the other bank finally grew silent. There were no further insults or shouted obscenities, no blaring hard rock music. Other than birdcalls and the insistent buzzing of mosquitoes, Nicki heard nothing at all.

Once darkness had fallen, Nicki slipped from her log into the water and waded to shore, except that her destination turned out to be a raised hillock surrounded by more water and dense veg-etation. The land mass was nothing more than a thick, floating crust that trembled beneath her body weight. Seeing a pair of shiny yellow eyes watching her from the weeds, Nicki started to cry again. Salty tears streamed down her face with the realization she had nowhere to go but into the swamp.

Quietly, carefully, she half waded, half swam back to the dock, praying not to encounter either a poisonous copperhead or a hungry alligator. Once she was out of the black water, she crept from one tree trunk to the next toward the camp. She scanned the area for signs of the men, but nothing moved in the weed-choked yard. The truck, the men, and the nightmare appeared to be gone.

Nicki sat down on the dock's bottom step to assess her sorry condition. She was coated with black mud and green slime, and she smelled awful. Her limbs ached, and her bites and scratches itched and hurt simultaneously, but she was alive. Before she had a chance to grow giddy from her good fortune, the step broke through, sending her downward. Nicki scraped an elbow and a knee and banged her chin hard. Once she regained her footing with solid land beneath her feet, she headed straight to the shack. She felt braver now that her tormentors were gone.

But now she faced a new worry. No streetlights illuminated the path because she was still in the swamp—an unnerving place with or without the good old boys. Her stomach growled, her throat tightened, and her legs felt like rubber as she walked. There was no way could she navigate the long driveway to the highway and then get to the nearest town in total darkness.

Tears streamed down her face as Nicki climbed the steps and entered the shack. The hovel was missing several floorboards, so snakes could slither up at will. She stepped carefully, testing each board before shifting her weight forward. A visual of herself breaking through the floor and wedging herself half inside the cabin and half in the stagnant water below flitted across her mind. She inched her way toward the sturdiest looking part of the room and sank down against the wall.

Vines had grown in through the broken windows, between the floor boards, across the windowsills, and then wrapped around everything upright in the room. Nothing prevented any bug, reptile, amphibian, or mammal from reaching her if they set their mind to it.

This shack would be her hospitality suite for the evening. There would be no turndown service, no mint on the pillow, and no complimentary breakfast in the morning, along with a copy of *USA Today*. The prospect of spending the night there frightened her as much as the gun-toting hooligans. Maybe even more.

Nicki sat utterly motionless as night arrived, bringing with it the sounds of hoot owls, nightjars, and whippoorwills. After several hours, a full moon rose over the black water, offering additional ghoulish special effects. Then a thick cloud crossed the moon's face, blotting out even the small amount of illumination it had given her. Just when she thought things couldn't get any worse, she was wrong. As Nicki curled into a fetal position and tried to sleep, it started to rain. A cold, unrelenting, merciless rain.

# NINETEEN

*H*unter spent Monday and most of Tuesday reassuring corporate clients that recent events wouldn't affect investment strategies already in place. Word traveled fast in the business world, especially as many clients came to his firm by word-of-mouth at the country club or at children's soccer matches. Fortunately, few clients jumped ship to other investment houses. Apparently one dead partner and the other suspected of murder didn't negate suitability as a financial advisor. Performance was king, and Hunter's performance had beaten all indices for the past year. James's clients were another story. Ironing out those considerable wrinkles would probably drag on for weeks.

But Hunter had something else on his mind other than money at the moment, something that had been bothering him since Saturday night. What in the world moved him to kiss Nicki? For one thing, she was Nate's cousin. For another, she worked for him and he took issues such as sexual harassment seriously.

Then there was the matter of Ashley. He was practically engaged to another woman, so what did that make him? A bad cliché of a sleazy bridegroom who couldn't handle restricting himself to one woman? Or maybe the groom-to-be acted out because he feared taking the big plunge?

Hunter knew he was neither promiscuous nor afraid to get married. But something had prompted him to kiss sweet Nicki in the dance hall, and he couldn't lay the blame on alcohol. The "why" would remain a mystery, but in the meantime he owed her an apology for his behavior. And it must never happen again.

The ring of his cell phone pulled his attention from the client roster and his personal remonstrations.

"Hey, little brother, are you still speaking to me? Or shall I clean the dueling pistols for a dawn rendezvous on the levee?"

Ethan. Always with a flare for the dramatic.

"There's been enough gunplay for a while," said Hunter.

There was a sharp intake of air, and then Ethan said, "I'm sorry. That was a tasteless thing to say. I'm actually calling because Cora and I are hosting a get-together tonight. We hope you and Ashley could join us. Cora has already talked to Ashley about some fund-raising matter, and she's all for it. Why don't you two swing by around seven thirty?"

Hunter bristled like a cornered cat. Why had Ashley been asked *first* instead of Ethan checking with his brother to see if he had a previous business engagement? He still had clients to entertain, and that often meant dinner or cocktails, especially when many tail feathers had been ruffled by James. Then Hunter remembered his disloyal, spur-of-the-moment kiss and decided not to disappoint Ashley. She did love a party and was so good at them. Seldom did another partygoer look more beautiful, dress more chicly, or have a better time.

"That sounds great, Ethan. Ashley and I will see you then."

"A sport coat will be fine. No tux or tails." With his chore complete, Ethan hung up.

*Sport coat?* Why couldn't everyone just wear jeans like at other parties? Ethan always had to maintain society's standards. Someone needed to tell his brother this was the twenty-first century.

~ᴖ

On his way to the Garden District, Hunter did a little soul-searching. It had been several days since he'd seen Ashley, yet he hadn't spent much time missing her. The sooner he forgot about that misguided kiss, the better off he would be.

Ashley was ready when Hunter picked her up at her father's home. She looked spectacular in a silky dress in deep green with very high heels, an emerald choker, and matching earrings. The jewelry had been twenty-first birthday gifts from her parents shortly before her mother's death. Since her passing, Ashley has spent so much time at her dad's she might as well give up her apartment.

"You look beautiful," he said, running his hands over her bare shoulders. "Beautiful, rich, and spoiled."

"And I hope to grow even more so of all three, sweet prince." Ashley batted her long eyelashes as she shook away his embrace. "Please don't mess up my hair. I have it sprayed to look perfectly natural."

Hunter let the contradiction in terms pass on the drive to the Galen ancestral home. The Menards lived only a few blocks from Chestnut Street, home to Ethan and Cora, but Hunter kept the convertible top up so that not a single hair would get mussed during the short drive.

Valets hired by Ethan opened their doors at the front gate. His car would be parked around back instead of down the block with the others. Hunter let his gaze travel up the four-story mansion. How he loved this house. West Indian in style with iron galleries, a third-floor ballroom, and elegant gardens with wisteria arbors, a secluded gazebo, and a goldfish pond. Although damaged during Katrina, repairs had restored the house to its time-honored beauty. *Grandmère* still lived in her first-floor suite when not traveling and continued to work among the flowers. Beautiful things bloomed almost year round, often competing in brilliance of color and fragrance.

They took the flagstone walkway around the mansion to the backyard. Ashley seemed more vivacious than usual as she clutched his hand. When the path opened into the courtyard, they both stopped in their tracks.

"Oh, my," she murmured.

The terrace had been transformed into a world usually seen only in fairy tales. Thousands of tiny lights were strung through the branches of two-hundred-year-old trees. A dozen tables set with silver, long-stemmed crystal, and bouquets of magnolia waited for the guests. In the center of each table candles burned in hurricane globes, while sprigs of ivy draped over the linens to the flagstones. Other tables had been set on the manicured lawn, a step below the terrace, while a platform dance floor and covered bandstand were ready for revelers.

"A few people for a *little* get-together?" Hunter muttered under his breath.

"Oh, don't be a party pooper, darling," Ashley cooed, her blue eyes sparkling with mischief.

As though on cue, musicians rose to their feet and broke into a rendition of "I Will Always Love You." Dozens of people poured from the house onto the terrace. Children emerged from every shrub and potted plant, and even a few guests jumped from behind trees.

"Surprise!"

"Good grief!" and "Oh, goody!" were Hunter's and Ashley's respective responses.

Ashley ran to embrace her father. Philip Menard had emerged from behind a live oak tree. He kissed her forehead with loving affection. Hunter was soon surrounded by his mother, Kenneth

Douglas—her apparent beau—Cora, Ethan, and their son, Gabriel.

"Surprise!" Chloe and Aaron, punctuality not their particular virtue, bounded up the path from the street. Chloe squeezed Hunter's midsection tightly. "Tonight's the big night, eh, brother? There will be no backing down now after this Galen family extravaganza."

Before he could ask what Chloe meant by that, Aaron grabbed him in a man-hug. Then Ethan reached his side, clutching three icy beers that he quickly distributed. "A toast to bachelorhood and your dwindling days of freedom!"

As Ashley was joyously whisked away by her girlfriends, Hunter remembered Nicki's words: *They travel in packs like coyotes, never going anywhere alone.* "Drink up, drink up!" Ethan demanded. "You'll need it for strength and fortification." Aaron and Ethan downed their beers in a postcollege chugging fashion, but Hunter took only a small sip. Something told him he would need his full faculties tonight.

When a white-coated waiter appeared to relieve them of the bottles, Ethan dragged Hunter toward the band's podium. With a sinking feeling, Hunter knew what was about to happen. To confirm his suspicions, Ashley's pals circled behind her, maneuvering her toward the center of the terrace.

The always-dapper Ethan took the microphone from the bandleader. "Friends, relatives, countrymen, New Orleanians, outlanders, tourists, ruffians..."

"Get on with it, Galen!" Philip called from his position near the oak. "Or do I have to get my shotgun?"

The eager crowd surged forward like onlookers at a car wreck. "Patience, Phil. These are Hunter's waning moments as a free man," said Ethan. "Let's not hasten the pony cart to the gallows so quickly." The men laughed and the women emitted catcalls, while Hunter felt his heart drop into his gut.

"I have invited y'all to our home tonight to witness history in the making. My younger brother has a question for his lovely girlfriend, Miss Ashley Menard."

With the mention of her name, Ashley's friends burst into shouts and applause as though she had won another pageant. Ashley's pale porcelain skin glowed rosy pink.

Ethan paused to allow the women time to settle down before continuing. "Hunter, brave both in battle and investment banking, needs a little courage. So we have aged bourbon, a keg of beer, friends old and new, and plenty of shotgun shells. What do you say we get the man up here?"

The band struck up the chorus of "For He's a Jolly Good Fellow."

Everyone clapped and beamed with unbridled enthusiasm.

Everyone but Hunter, that is. If Philip had actually produced a shotgun, Hunter would have been tempted to use it on his brother. How did Ethan dare presume he needed help with proposing to Ashley? He'd purchased the ring and they had decided on a honeymoon destination. He was simply waiting for the right moment to make it official. Ashley hadn't pressured him to set a date, yet his brother decided to meddle into something that was none of his business. As much as Ethan resented their father controlling the family with an iron hand, he'd turned into the man after his death.

Hunter scanned the assembled guests. Ashley's father had a full tumbler in hand despite having chronic liver problems. Clotilde waved like a sightseer from a passing riverboat. Chloe wagged her hands behind her ears with juvenile idiocy. Cora smiled back with subtle pity. Nate lifted his beer stein in salute.

Everyone was looking at him to say something.

So he would tell them to eat heartily from the platters of food covering the tables under the trees, drink libations with abandon, dance and sing and have a great time. Everyone could stay until the wee hours, and then he would pay for taxis to get them home safely. But he would propose to his fiancée when he was ready. He and Ashley were old enough to set their own terms and not fall under pressure from either family.

Then he met Ashley's gaze. With her startling blue eyes glassy with tears, she glowed with expectation and anticipation. Not for one moment did she suspect the thoughts crossing his mind. How could he embarrass her in front of her friends and family?

How could he possibly disappoint her?

Hunter reached for her hand as she hurried up the steps to the platform. Once her fingers touched his, he dropped to one knee and uttered the words that everyone in the backyard was expecting.

"Ashley, will you marry me?"

It hadn't been difficult. And from the look on her flushed face, he had his answer before she said, "I will, sweet Hunter."

Family and friends clapped and shouted. The band started playing "Everlasting Love" while waiters materialized with trays of flutes filled with champagne. Men surrounded Philip and pounded his back with congratulations as though he'd accomplished some great feat. Little girls whom Hunter didn't recognize threw confetti into the air. All that was missing was a flock of white doves released into the night air.

*Good grief. If they went to this much trouble for the engagement party, I can't wait to see what tricks lie in store for the wedding.*

Ashley looked radiantly happy as Clotilde enfolded her in a warm embrace. She also did not look surprised.

Something told Hunter this hadn't been quite the bombshell for her that it was for him. Hence the stunning new dress, the perfect hair, and the emeralds that usually stayed in the Menard safe. He felt a bit like a dolt. And he didn't like the feeling one bit.

Did men throughout the ages often feel as if their grand plans had been orchestrated by others well in advance?

Soon he was enveloped by the crowd and pulled toward the buffet table. A toast to eternal happiness and then a dance with one of the newly announced bridesmaids. Funny how eight, specially selected women were all present at Ethan and Cora's little get-together.

Hunter ate some fried oysters and sweet potato pie, behaving like the good sport everyone knew him to be. He drank a shot of bourbon with his brother and Nate, while Ashley toasted her friends with champagne. Then he requested a glass of iced tea from a waiter. Getting drunk wasn't his style and never had been. And he refused to make an exception just because he'd been maneuvered like a chess piece.

He had just joined *Daddy* Menard at the dessert table when he spotted someone skinny and forlorn under the arch to the terrace. Nicki, wearing capris, T-shirt, and sneakers. And she looked as mad as a hornet. He scanned the crowd for Nate but didn't see him. So Hunter excused himself from Mr. Menard and went to greet the late arrival to the party.

"Good evening, Miss Price. Have you come to offer congratulations to me or your sympathies to Ashley?" He smiled at her in welcome and then noticed the cuts and scratches on her forehead and cheeks. Further inspection showed that they also crisscrossed her neck, arms, and legs. A nasty bruise marred her jawline, while at least a dozen welts from bites stood in stark contrast against her freckled skin. "What happened to you?" he demanded.

"What happened to *you* yesterday?" Nicki snapped, huffing out her breath in exasperation. "Someone was trying to kill me in the swamp. Was that your idea of a *joke*, Hunter? Because it wasn't very funny!" Her cheeks flamed with anger and indignation as her voice drew the stares of several curious partygoers.

"What are you talking about? I tried calling you yesterday, but your phone was turned off. *Who* tried to kill you, and why were you in the swamp?" Hunter scratched his head at a loss as to what he should do. He wanted to console her but didn't quite know how.

Nicki gritted her teeth before responding. "First, the three men chasing me didn't properly introduce themselves before firing a shotgun in my direction. Second, I went out to the swamp because *you* said to meet you there, to see some client named Michael Dennison." She crossed her arms over her chest as she began to notice people creeping closer.

"Mr. Dennison lives in Gretna, not in the swamp, Nicki. I don't know what you're talking about. Please, sit down. Let me get you something to drink and then we'll get to the bottom of this."

But before he had taken two steps toward the refreshment table, Ethan arrived with Nate on his heels. Both men began pelting Nicki with questions. Ethan demanded to know if someone on the premises was in some way responsible for her appearance. Nate, already frightened by his cousin's physical condition, grew incensed as he pieced together the fragments of her tale.

But the true fly in the ointment was Ashley. Hunter's new fiancée slipped to the front of the fracas and peered down at Nicki. "Who might you be?" she asked. The wrinkle of her nose betrayed disdain for Nicki's choice of outfits. "We're in the middle of an engagement party. If you're with the caterer's cleaning crew, please wait at the back gate until you're needed." Though her words were rude, her tone could be described by some as sweet.

But if Nicki's expression were any indication, Ashley's question just created an enemy for life.

# TWENTY

When she awoke the next morning, Nicki never had felt worse in her life. Painful cuts, inflamed scratches, and itchy bug bites added discomfort to her sore feet and strained muscles. Her stomach felt queasy, and a headache pounded between her eyes. She shuddered to think about what nasty things lived in the stagnant black water that had entered her bloodstream at every break in the skin.

But her physical ailments paled in comparison to her emotional state. What a fool she had been. One kiss on a crowded dance floor had her imagining life with Hunter. How pathetic was that? No doubt it had been a sympathy kiss for the socially deprived out-of-towner. She knew he had a girlfriend, so why had his formal engagement party caused so much heartache?

Maybe because Ashley was a combination of every mean girl she'd ever met.

Hunter deserved better. But how could she convince a man that a rich, long-legged, perfect-skinned woman who dressed like a fashion model was totally wrong for him? Perhaps Nicki's Keds, denim capris, and T-shirt had been a bad wardrobe choice for crashing a boss's engagement party, but when Nate's message on her voice mail indicated where he would be, off she went to the Garden District. In the aftermath of her horrible ordeal, she never gave a thought that she would walk into a mansion owned by Hunter's grandmother. She could handle a snobby tea party, maybe even a cocktail soirée with those silly little sandwiches, but now she regretted blundering into Hunter's private affairs.

Nicki nibbled on dry toast before swallowing a mouthful of coffee and then her pride. She needed to call Hunter before she lost her nerve. But then her phone rang. "Hello?"

"Hey, Nic. Just checking to make sure you're okay." Nate's voice was tender.

"Other than making a queen-sized fool of myself in front of our paying client, I'm fine." She slumped into a chair.

"I'm more concerned with your physical condition. Want me to take you to the clinic to have those scratches checked out?"

"Dying alone of African sleeping sickness or typhoid fever in my friend's trailer is the least of my worries. That may spare me my eventual destiny of mortal humiliation."

"You've survived embarrassment before. Besides you won't die alone—your favorite cousin will be there until the brutal end."

The mental image made her smile. "Good to know. I was comparing my circle of pals to Hunter and Ashley's and came up a hundred or two short."

"Even without me and Christine, you're not alone and never have been. You've felt confused and overwhelmed since coming to town. That's normal for a country girl in the big city, but people with faith as deep as yours don't need lots of friends or even a loving family. They already have exactly what they need to live a contented life."

Nicki reflected before replying. "Wow, just when I all but give up on you, you spout wisdom like a sage."

"Anything else you want to know?" Nate chuckled.

"Yeah. How should I apologize to Hunter?"

"Short and sweet and don't grovel, not after what you've gone through."

"Thanks, cousin." She said goodbye and ended the call with Nate. Before she lost her nerve, she found Hunter's number in her contacts list and selected it.

Perhaps his voice mail would pick up and she could dodge a bullet. But no such luck. He answered on the second ring.

"Hunter, I owe you an apology—for crashing your engagement party and for accusing you of trying to murder me in the bayou. When Mrs. Prescott called, I was suspicious. But then I put my first instinct out of mind and went out there anyway. A good private investigator should always go with her gut feeling." Inhaling a breath, she waited to be fired.

"On the first count, you didn't crash," he said in a soft drawl. "The engagement party was a surprise courtesy of my family. Had I known about it beforehand, I would have invited you personally. On the second count, no apology is necessary. Spending the night in the swamp after being chased by thugs with shotguns would make anyone upset. And I don't agree that those men were out terrorizing simply for a good time. That's why we're driving back there today and we'll retrace your steps. Someone tried to kill you, Nicki. Someone may think you're close to finding James's killer. Come to the Quarter as fast as you can. I'm eager to get out there."

He hung up before she could explain she wasn't going back to that blighted, mosquito-filled, snake-infested world. The bayou had never appealed to her. After her father died, she would sooner cross the Sahara Desert on a one-hump camel than spend time there. But how could she refuse? And how could she admit to Hunter she was no closer to finding Nowak's killer than the day he hired her?

Sighing, she swallowed some ibuprofen, tied her hair into a

ponytail, and gingerly sprayed bug repellant on all exposed skin surfaces. Then she grabbed a bottle of water and her keys and drove to Hunter's Rue Royale apartment. Before she found parking on the street, he came down and said she could have his spot. After he had backed out his Corvette, Nicki pulled into his parking space and then hopped in his car. With unusually heavy traffic demanding his attention, she focused on the roadmap and passing landmarks. This time she had no trouble finding the dirt road leading to *La Maison de Poisson*.

"You thought *this* was the driveway to the home of a client?" Hunter stopped at the rusty sign hanging precariously by its single bolt. "*La Maison de Poisson* just means fishing camp in French, Nicki."

"Unfortunately, I took Spanish in school. I thought the name sounded pretty and rather romantic."

"And the badly potholed surface is simply a ruse to keep solicitors at bay?" He flashed a smile at her, the first she'd seen that day.

"Something like that," she mumbled, feeling dumber by the minute.

"Tell me again everything that happened. Leave out no details." He drove down the road very slowly, watching for strips of carpet tacks and other booby traps she'd warned him of.

Nicki recounted her saga, describing the thugs, the truck, and their weaponry. But she couldn't describe the sheer, paralyzing fear she'd experienced even if she tried.

"What happened the next morning? How did you get back to New Orleans?" Hunter's focus shifted from one side of the road to the other.

"After a sleepless night in the shack, I walked back to my car. Those creeps had pushed my Escort into the weeds so they could pass it with their truck. At least they didn't wreck it. When I reached the road, I started walking back in the direction I had come. But in less than half a mile, I saw my spare tire and jack lying off to the side. If I wasn't such an observant, trained investigator, I may not have spotted them." She glanced over for his reaction. He was trying hard not to laugh.

"They threw my stuff in the ditch just to be mean. Anyway, I carried the jack and rolled the spare back to my car and changed the flat."

"You didn't," he said, incredulous. "All by yourself?"

"Sure enough. I am no shrinking violet." Nicki couldn't tell if he was mocking her or truly impressed.

"I'll keep that in mind." Grinning from ear to ear, Hunter parked the Corvette in the sparse gravel in the turn-around.

Without the torrential rain, the eerie mist, the night sounds, and the wind rattling the metal roof, the place looked far less ominous. "Funny how bright sunshine and singing birds keep the ghosts and vampires away."

Hunter crisscrossed the area, photographing tire treads and gathering discarded beer cans. He picked up discarded shotgun casings carefully, placing them in individual zippered bags. Nicki should have been doing that, but she stayed in the car gathering her courage. *What kind of PI allows the client to collect evidence?* Many private investigators hired on as bodyguards instead of needing one themselves.

Hunter approached her side of the car. "You're right about the truck—dual axle, monster tires, probably an F-350. Let's head down to the bayou."

With shame finally getting the better of her, Nicki jumped out to follow. "Hold up there, Hunter. Let me lead the way since I've been here before."

The moment he reached the dock, he dropped to his hands and knees to inspect the top step. "This board has been sawed, Nicki. It was sabotaged."

"I've never heard anyone use the word 'sabotage' before except in movies."

"And look up there." Hunter pointed at a fresh gouge in the cypress trunk. "You're right. They used solid loads, but they were aiming at least six feet over your head."

"They weren't aiming at me here. I was already out on the water. They must have been shooting in the air."

Nicki then led the way to the waterway where they stood on the shady bank and stared at the still water. No animals crept along the bank; no birds called to each other in the trees. And there was no sign of the ill-fated pirogue that initiated her uncomfortable night in the shack.

"Where did the boat sink?" he asked, as though reading her mind.

"Out maybe fifty feet into the canal, close to that fallen tree."

"Shall we swim out, dive down, and haul her to the surface?" he asked.

"Absolutely not!" Nicki turned on her heel and headed back to the overgrown backyard. She could feel the symptoms of a panic attack change her heart rate, respiration, and body temperature. No way could she allow Hunter to see how the swamp affected her.

"That was a joke, Nicolette." Hunter caught up with her as she cut a wide swath around the cabin.

"I wasn't taking any chances." Panting, she stopped under a moss-shrouded oak. "The sooner I'm away from here the better. Okay, some punks tried to scare me, not kill me. Apparently they succeeded."

Hunter took hold of her arm with a strong grip. "Take a breath. Slowly, now. That's better. We need to get to the bottom of this. Those punks didn't pick you out randomly as their victim. Someone who knows you work for me sent you here."

Nicki peered up into his face, forcing herself to breathe deeply. "That occurred to me, but I'd rather not dwell on it. What did your assistant say when you questioned her? She's the one who sent me on this wild goose chase."

Hunter shrugged. Deep squint lines around his eyes revealed how often he forgot his sunglasses. "Someone left a message for her on the office answering machine. It said I was trying to get a hold of you and that she should keep trying. And when she did...well, you know the rest."

"She didn't find that strange?"

"She didn't, but I do. Naomi didn't recognize the voice and, unfortunately, she erased the message. She's very upset about the whole matter. She was at Ethan's party yesterday when you arrived and saw the end result of her bogus instructions."

"Did she think I should have waited at the back gate too?" Nicki knew that sounded petty and childish, but Ashley had scratched her soft underbelly.

Hunter walked her back to his car and opened the door for her. "Ashley regrets the misunderstanding and asked me to pass along her apology. She didn't know you worked for Nate."

"So your fiancée is only rude and condescending to the *real* catering staff," she said as she sat down huffily on the seat.

Hunter lifted an eyebrow. "Ashley was a little high-strung last night. Normally she's nice to everybody."

Nicki stared silently through the windshield until she was able to readjust her attitude. Then she turned to him and said, "I'm sorry, Hunter. I'm sure she is or you wouldn't be marrying her."

"The whole evening caught me a bit off guard too."

"You hadn't asked her to marry you before last night?"

"Not in so many words."

"Pul-leaze. I'm sure your family didn't *imagine* your intentions." Her sweet voice disappeared, replaced by a rather catty tone.

"Of course not. Our relationship was serious. But I didn't like people taking matters into their own hands. I should have been able to propose when I was ready."

Something told Nicki it was more than his pushy family or her nosiness that raised his hackles. "All right, enough of me asking questions that are none of my business. What do you say we leave the charming fishing camp and I buy you a burger and fries at Mickey D's for lunch? I say an employee celebration is in order." Nicki snapped on her seatbelt.

"Sounds lovely, but I need to check out the cabin first. You stay in the car."

"Wait! Please don't go in there." Alarm crawled up her spine. Visions of every teenage horror movie she'd ever seen returned despite the sunshine and blue sky. "Hunter...let's just get out of here."

He gazed at her, his face filled with compassion. "Easy, Nicki. The bad guys are long gone. There's nothing inside but spiders. Take deep breaths till I get back."

"There could be poisonous copperheads! Or the floorboards could give way and a fifteen-foot bull alligator will make your leg his lunch. Or—"

Hunter turned around on the bottom step. "Are you packing heat? Did your permit-to-carry arrive in the mail? If so, draw your weapon and defend your client 'cause I'm goin' in." He turned back to the door and with a flourish threw it open and disappeared inside.

He was making sport of her. Hunter really knew how to get under a gal's skin, yet she couldn't blame him. Nicki opened her door and stepped out, but she still couldn't follow him into that horrible place. Anxiety continued to claw at her consciousness. Feeling faint and mildly sick to her stomach, she slouched back into the car. Gritting her teeth, Nicki closed her eyes and prayed she wouldn't have to retrieve a partially eaten body. Fortunately, she didn't have long to wait.

Hunter's blond head soon emerged from the doorway. "I talked the gator into Bob's Crab Shack for the all-you-can-eat buffet instead of my leg." He laughed all the way across the yard.

"Very funny. I have half a mind to leave you here." From the passenger seat, Nicki turned the key in the ignition, causing the powerful engine to roar to life.

Hunter slipped in behind the wheel and put on his sunglasses, his face becoming unreadable. "I didn't see any evidence in the cabin. You really don't like it in the swamp, do you? Even without people shooting at you."

"I grew up in the country, remember? I had a belly full. Now I'm enchanted with concrete, neon lights, and traffic jams."

"I suspect there's more to it than that." He patted her knee and then turned the car around in the grass.

The touch lasted only a moment, but it was enough to send her blood pressure skyrocketing again. "Please, let's talk about something else." In her side mirror Nicki watched the shack disappear. *Good riddance.*

Hunter drove slowly, watching both sides of the drive. Once they were back on the parish road headed toward civilization, he settled back against the leather seat. "Ashley really is a nice person. She didn't mean anything by mistaking you for cleaning help."

"Are you trying to convince me or yourself?"

"Excuse me?" He pulled his sunglasses down with one finger and gave her a very direct look.

"I know I work for you, Hunter, and I should mind my manners—"

"Besides respecting your elders," he added.

"And let's not forget 'Don't bite the hand that feeds you.'"

"Ah, one of my favorites. But by all means, Nicki, speak your mind. Forget that your Christmas bonus hangs by one slender thread, along with employer paid health care." His laughter filled the car.

Ignoring her intuition that said to keep her mouth shut, she forged on. "I believe Miss Menard was sorry she insulted me, but only because I *do* actually work for you. If I had been with the caterers and had mistakenly interrupted the party, she wouldn't think twice about being rude and unkind. She took one look at me and instantly felt I didn't belong there."

Hunter said nothing for the longest half minute of her life. Then he spoke. "Sounds like you're carrying around a load of resentment from the past. It's true that people often draw conclusions based on clothes, but why is your nose so out of joint? You're just starting out in your career. Someday you'll be able to dress however you like or maybe you'll stop putting so much importance on other people's opinions." His voice was tender, soothing.

"I don't disagree with you. Of course you're right. But why is it no matter how high you climb, people never forget where you started? Look at the pop stars. They're filthy rich, but tabloid TV never lets them live down their humble beginnings."

"First off, stop watching bad TV. And maybe it's the stars' behavior that makes them tabloid fodder, not their background or lineage. If they act without considering the consequences, they become easy targets. Rich or poor, people who behave with dignity will be treated with respect."

Nicki had nothing to say to that. She sat back and watched the watery scenery fly by. When the lump in her throat finally dissolved, she regained her voice along with her composure. "How did you get so smart, Hunter?"

"From eating Quarter Pounders with fries. You said you're buying, so dig out your wallet. We're only twelve miles from the next town."

Nicki pulled her purse from the floor to her lap. "Forget what I said about Ashley. I was just envious about her cool clothes. You're one lucky man."

"I forgive you. After what you endured in the swamp, anybody else would need major PTSD counseling." Hunter's smile caused Nicki's breath to catch in her chest, and it had nothing to do with panic attacks.

Too bad the guy was already engaged. Otherwise, she was halfway to falling in love.

# TWENTY-ONE

*H*unter arrived home to his Rue Royale apartment with more questions than answers. They were no closer to figuring out who killed James, and now someone was trying to hurt Nicki. The flat tire and stolen spare may have been pranks, but rigging the boat and shooting at her were dangerous games to play. They had no way of knowing whether she could swim and aiming high didn't always work out as planned. And plenty of things could go wrong in a rotted shack in the middle of the night after they had left her stranded.

By the time he dropped Nicki at her car and climbed the steps to his apartment, he was ready for a cold beverage, a couple of aspirin, and an early bedtime. But what he found was Ashley cooking in the kitchen, or at least reheating dinner. Dressed in a long skirt and summer top, she looked tanned and radiant.

"Good evening, Hunter," she drawled. "I was going to throw my dinner down the disposal if you didn't get home soon." A brilliant smile accompanied her gentle chastisement.

After she had turned back to the stove, Hunter quietly stuffed the bag of evidence he'd brought in from the car under the sink and then pecked her cheek. "I didn't know you were coming over.

I would have called to say when I'd be back." He reached into the refrigerator for a Coke.

"You put that back. I brought red wine to go with my roast beef and mashed potatoes."

Hunter had spotted multiple takeout containers sticking out of the trash can but decided not to comment. He wasn't marrying her for her culinary abilities. He wasn't exactly sure why he was marrying her, other than she was pretty and sweet and his family liked her. And it was the right thing to do considering how long they had dated.

He shook off the doubts he figured every prospective groom faced and put the soda back. "Everything smells wonderful, Ash." He dug in the drawer for the corkscrew.

"Try just a bite of this." Leaning in close, she fed him a forkful of beef. "Since I'm about to become your wife, I decided to become domestic."

"It tastes delicious." Hunter opened the wine and poured them each a glass. His thoughts, however, drifted to Nicki instead of the meal Ashley was placing on the table. *How can I relax when some psycho may be trying to finish what he started in the swamp?*

"Where did you go today? Even Naomi didn't know where you were."

Hunter's attention snapped back to Ashley. He was feeling strangely disloyal. "I drove out to Terrebonne Parish with Miss Price."

"Terrebonne Parish? Why, it's been ages since I've been out there, not since Katrina. Is there any dry ground left?"

"Plenty. They have recovered nicely. Do you remember meeting my investigator?" He handed her a glass of wine.

"Of course I do." Ashley dried her hands on a towel and tossed it next to the sink. "She was that skinny, stringy-haired gal I thought had come to pack up the rented china. If a person plans to crash a party, they should at least dress like the other guests." Her laughter contained a brittle edge.

"If I had known about the party, I would have invited her. Nicki works for Nate Price, so indirectly she works for me. She's trying to find James's killer and clear my name."

"Lighten up, Hunter. That was a little joke. My, you are tense tonight. You've been tense a lot lately. That's why your family wanted to surprise us, to spare us worry over inconsequential details."

"James's murder has become an inconsequential detail?"

Ashley took a sip of wine and wrapped her arm around his waist. "In a way, yes. Last night was special for us—a celebration of our future. Can't we forget about James's tiresome murder and the investigation for one night?" She waved her hand over the table like a game show hostess. "Let's eat before everything gets cold."

Hunter settled onto his chair a little stiffly. "I didn't know that you found James tiresome."

"You never really asked, did you?" She fluttered her long lashes. "I hate to speak ill of the dead, but I never could understand your loyalty to him." She brushed a silky strand of hair from her face. "It's not as though his family was connected to yours. He was just your college roommate for a few years. He was a user, a manipulator. Really, Hunter, you should have left him in your dust ages ago." Ashley cut her roast beef into small pieces and daintily chewed a bite.

Hunter stared at her over his wineglass. This was an unexpected revelation. She and James had appeared to get along in the past. In fact, Ashley often arranged double dates with James and whoever he was seeing.

"He was my friend. I wouldn't have called him a user." He took a scoop of lumpy mashed potatoes, noticing as he did so that the mood music she had put on the CD player was grating on his nerves.

"Because you didn't know him very well, darling. You were blind to that side of him."

The potatoes stuck to the roof of his mouth. Hunter tried to wash them down with wine but nearly choked. "Did you make any sweet tea?" Following an affirmative nod, he went to the refrigerator for a glass. "I would love to know how you were able to form this opinion. Apparently, the guy I had known for years was able to delude me with no difficulty."

Ashley finished chewing and swallowed. Then she sipped wine and wiped her mouth on the napkin. Finally, she focused her attention on him. *Everything* about her seemed precisely orchestrated, even the moisture welling in the corners of her luminous eyes. "Oh, Hunter, let's not spoil the evening—our first dinner as an engaged couple. I so wanted tonight to be special." A tear slipped from beneath her lashes. "I would rather not reveal the truth about your friend." Her tone turned particularly sorrowful.

Hunter gulped his iced tea and set down the glass. "You have my full attention. I think it's time I know what *you* know about my business partner."

Ashley was acting as though this were a dramatic performance. At any moment, a director might step from the wings and yell *cut*. "Please don't be upset, but James was no gentleman." She refilled her wineglass from the bottle, something she never did on her own.

If Hunter didn't have a splitting headache from the hot sun in the bayou, if his best friend wouldn't soon be moldering in his crypt in Metairie Cemetery, if someone hadn't tried to harm Nicki yesterday, he may have found her choice of words laughable. "Not many men are these days, Ashley. Would you stop being so cryptic and just say what's on your mind?"

Apparently she didn't like his directness. Her pert nose turned up and her eyes narrowed. "Your noble frat brother found something out about me—something I'm not proud of—and he tormented me endlessly about it. He wouldn't let me forget a mistake I made after college. He threw it in my face every chance he got just to embarrass me." Her haughty tone dropped to the barest whisper by the end of the sentence. She lowered her head and stared at her flowery skirt.

Silence spun out between them. Street sounds ebbed, the music usually audible from Bourbon Street fading to an occasional drumbeat. This was the last thing he expected from sweet Miss Louisiana.

"Hunter, please say something. You're frightening me." Ashley peered up, her face awash with misery.

He rose, walked to her side of the table, and then pulled out a chair next to hers. "Tell me your secret. I'm sure it's not as bad as you're making this into."

"Are you sure?"

"Yes." He slipped an arm around her shoulders.

After an exaggerated sigh, she began. "Three of my sorority sisters and I spent the summer after graduation in Atlanta at a condo that Megan's parents owned. We wanted to have some fun after four boring years of college and before we settled into careers and got married. Everything we were expected to do." She took a swallow of wine.

"You met James in Atlanta?"

"No, I never actually ran into him, but somehow he found out how we entertained ourselves that summer." She glanced at his face. "And James never let me forget my foolishness."

Hunter grew irritated with her evasiveness. Why couldn't she just spit it out, even if she and her friends had been paid assassins for the mob? But he had a feeling their cottage industry involved her considerable feminine charms rather than firearms. "What exactly did you do that summer?"

"I...*we* worked for an exclusive Buckhead escort service, catering to international businessmen." A note of pride etched her words.

"You were a *hooker*, Ashley?" He tried not to sound shocked and judgmental but failed. This was his fiancée, a former homecoming queen, runner-up to Miss Louisiana, and Daddy's little girl. A bad taste rose in his mouth from the pit of his stomach.

"No, not a prostitute! Some escort services provide *escorts*, plain and simple. Travelers, usually older men, wish to dine with attractive women who can make conversation for a few hours of companionship while they are far from home."

Only Ashley Menard could make her first *career* sound like Atlanta's Welcome Wagon for lonely businessmen. He swallowed his anger along with the bile in his throat. "So you were paid to have dinner and make polite conversation?"

"Yes, that's right. It wasn't sexual. We were paid three hundred dollars to eat at fabulous restaurants and be...nice to them."

"It sounds dangerous. You could have been raped or killed. Then someone with diplomatic immunity could have gotten on the next plane home." Hunter fought to control his temper, not wishing to admit what he thought about her vocation.

Ashley shook her silky mane of hair. "We carried a device for security. All we had to do was push a button if the gentleman got fresh. An alarm would sound and the authorities would be alerted."

"You describe these customers as gentlemen, but you excluded James from the category because he found out about it?"

"Oh, darling. I know how tacky this whole thing sounds. I'm truly mortified by my behavior." Several tears ran down her perfect complexion. "We were so ashamed by the end of summer we took a pledge never to reveal what we did to anyone. My friends are all wives and mothers now; one's even a pediatrician. Everyone regrets working for that service. It was just a lark—an easy way to make money. We were young and didn't think how it could damage a girl's reputation." Ashley reached for his hand, her voice dropping to a whisper. "I would do anything to erase that summer, to change the past, but I can't." Her composure faltered as she collapsed into uncontrollable tears. "Can you...ever forgive me?"

What could he say? The mental picture of her batting her eye-lashes while hanging on to every word from some lecherous man filled Hunter's mind. A wave of fury and jealousy stiffened his spine and bunched his hands into fists. But all this had happened a long time before he met her, when she had been young and foolish.

He didn't exactly savor every action during his youth either.

If he loved her, it was for better or for worse.

If he loved her, he had to forgive her. Isn't that what he'd been taught at Cathedral Academy?

Hunter stared at his fiancée, feeling pity along with estrange-ment, compassion but also detachment. It felt as if he'd woken up with a total stranger without a clue as to how he got there. He cleared his throat and said, "Of course, I forgive you. You made a mistake. Everyone make mistakes while growing up."

"Thank you, Hunter." Ashley threw her arms around his neck. "Promise me you'll never bring up this horrible subject. I couldn't bear to ever talk about it again." Her hug cut off his oxygen.

"I promise. It's already forgotten." It was a stupid thing to say, but a better reply eluded him.

"And you won't say anything to my father?" Ashley leaned back to study his face. Her makeup was streaked. "Daddy would kill me if he knew what I had done."

"Your father loves you."

"I know that, but he's old fashioned. He would never understand."

He had to agree with her there. Philip would track down every former client and wring their necks for sullying his only daughter's virtue. "I promise I won't say anything to him."

Ashley exhaled a great breath of air, visibly relaxing before his eyes. "Let's forget this silly dinner." She carried their plates to the sink. "I couldn't eat another bite. Let's go to the yacht with a bottle of cabernet and take the boat out to watch the moon rise. We need to forget all this unpleasantness. I'll go wash my face and freshen my makeup." She picked up her purse and headed for the bathroom.

There was no more mention of James Nowak or his role in her secret past. The matter had been swept under the rug like a dust bunny. Hunter exhaled a weary sigh of frustration. The last thing he wanted to do was fight traffic all the way to the marina while consoling Ashley in her current state. But he had no believable excuse at hand to get out of it.

They would go sailing after red wine, sweet tea, and bad takeout food, along with the bombshell he was marrying a former call girl. His stomach churned with indigestion already. With any luck, he would be swept overboard or die of seasickness.

# TWENTY-TWO

*N*icki finished her morning exercises and then jogged down to the row of mailboxes at the entrance to the trailer park. Unfortunately, Christine's mailman only seemed to deliver flyers, catalogs, and final-notice bills. No cards or letters for her from Natchez...and no license to carry a firearm. She'd scored high marks on the exam, and the background check wouldn't have found skeletons in her closet. Yet by the time her permit arrived, everyone else would be using laser guns.

After checking email, she decided to google the deceased James Nowak. Perhaps sifting through the man's past would yield a clue to his murder. All Hunter's records had revealed was that most of his clients had motive. Almost all who had portfolios under his control had lost a ton of money. If churning a client's portfolio for personal gain created killers, Nicki's list of suspects stretched three pages long.

*"Someone may think you're close to finding James's killer."*

What a joke that was. Hunter's words had made her feel guilty about cashing her first paycheck, but that was about to change. Nicki refilled her coffee cup and studied the Internet's first reference on Nowak. By the time she finished, she would know him better than the back of her hand.

Hours later Nicki's back hurt, her eyes were watering, and her neck had developed a painful crick. But James Nowak's life had opened before her in all its excessive glory. He had one DUI, three civil judgments against him involving back rent, an unpaid store charge, and an IRS lien that was subsequently discharged by a third party. Not exactly the credentials she would want in a financial advisor, but with only one hundred forty-two dollars in her checking account, she needn't worry. More enlightening was the pile of negative information about the company Nowak interned with after college.

The résumé of Wellert Securities read like a how-to manual of corporate greed and corruption for the 1990s: multiple security violations, imposed sanctions stemming from alleged insider trading, and accounting malfeasance. Even the vice squad had raided a company party for pandering. Apparently, the brokers invited a group of working girls to a bash who definitely weren't from the clerical pool.

*Tsk, tsk. Atlanta must be a great place to be young, rich, and male.* James Nowak had lived on the edge, but since two years ago he remained on the right side of the law. Maybe he wheeled-and-dealed, but after partnering with Hunter, he hadn't gotten as much as a speeding ticket with his shiny green Corvette. Until recently, that is. Something had changed. And someone hated him enough to shoot him.

Hearing Christine's car under the kitchen window, Nicki closed down her laptop and packed up her notes. Her roommate loved to read over her shoulder and ask endless questions no matter how many times she cited client confidentiality. Nicki appreciated Christine's generosity, but constant updates on TV shows and magazine exposés were growing tiresome. After greeting her friend, Nicki grabbed a Coke and her laptop, and headed for the door.

"Leaving already?" asked Christine. "I thought we could send out for pizza."

"I'll take a rain check. Gotta pick up my new tire and get the spare back in the trunk." Nicki didn't mention that Hunter had insisted on buying the tire. He considered the flat his assistant's fault. Nicki considered it evidence of her gullibility. But Christine would consider it proof of Hunter's attraction for her. Whichever conclusion you drew, if she never set foot in the Cajun parishes again, it was fine with her.

Once her new tire was installed, Nicki left the repair shop with more time on her hands than she had anticipated. She contemplated another stroll through the French Quarter. A streetcar ride to the campuses of Tulane and Loyola? Maybe a group tour of the Garden District that included the famous Lafayette Cemetery? She had been so mad the night of Hunter's party that she'd missed the area's extraordinary architecture.

Unfortunately, Nicki was a creature of habit, or maybe a moth drawn helplessly to flame, but nothing could tamp down her frisson of anticipation as she headed to Hunter's apartment. The man affected her in dangerous ways. Everything about him intrigued her. Their backgrounds and lifestyles couldn't be more different. He drank Dom Perignon; she drank sweetened sun tea. He visited Paris for bachelor parties and skied in Zurich every winter. Her sole trip away from home was the Nascar races in Talladega with her Papaw. Was that it? She was curious about a life unlike hers? Too bad his fiancée out-matched her in every category.

Nicki squeezed her car next to his in the alley, tugged her hair loose from its ponytail, and rang the bell. She tried not to hold her breath.

Hunter opened the door in ripped jeans and a faded T-shirt. He gave her a thin smile. "Come in, Nicolette. I would appreciate some diversion." Deep creases ringed his eyes, while his previously glowing tan had faded to a dull pallor.

"You look terrible, boss. What happened?" She didn't add that even on bad days he still looked handsome. Nicki set her bag on the foyer table and pulled out her laptop.

"Didn't sleep well last night. What have you found out?" He loomed over her shoulder while she searched for the correct program. Although similar to her roommate's habit, Hunter's aftershave smelled much better than Christine's perfume.

"I've been checking Nowak's background, trying to come at this from another angle." Nicki moved into the living room but stopped short. Every piece of furniture had been pushed away from the walls, the rugs had been rolled up and stood on end, and a tiny, ebony-skinned woman was zealously dustmopping the floor. "I'm sorry. I didn't know you had company."

The woman arched an eyebrow and switched off the sweeper. "Who are you?"

"Nicolette Price, ma'am. I'm Mr. Galen's private investigator." Smiling warmly, Nicki offered her hand.

"Nicki, this is Mrs. Peteriere," said Hunter. "Our beloved Jeanette is *Grandmère's* friend and former housekeeper."

While shaking Nicki's hand, the woman glared at Hunter. "*Former?* What do you mean by that, young man? I haven't been fired." Before Hunter could answer, she turned her attention back to Nicki. "Do you know *Monsieur* Nathan Price?"

"I do. He's my cousin and mentor."

Mrs. Peteriere shook her tiny head. "He's a worthless bum and a bad influence on people's behavior."

"Yes, ma'am. I totally agree. He was a thorn in my foot while growing up."

A smile spread across Jeanette's deeply lined face. "You should pick a new mentor, *O'lette*." Her grin widened, revealing one prominent gold tooth.

It took Nicki a moment to realize that the word Jeanette had just used was her shortening "Nicolette." She thought it was lovely and smiled in return. "I'll put that on my to-do list, ma'am."

Hunter cleared his throat. "Thank you, Jeanette. Nicki, why don't we work in the kitchen? Jeanette has already finished in there. She insists on cleaning my apartment once a month, even though I take care of things on a regular basis."

"*Harrumph*. Men never move anything. They would dust around an elephant rather than ask him to move."

Hunter held open the swinging doors. "Before you report me to the labor authorities, Jeanette is officially retired and collects a pension in addition to medical benefits. Yet nothing will stop her. Someday she will rise from her eternal rest on All Saint's Day to whitewash her own crypt. But we love her and she loves us."

The elderly housekeeper snickered as she went back to her work.

"Your family is lucky to have her," Nicki said as the door swung shut.

"That we are, Nicolette. That we are." Hunter gazed straight into her eyes as he replied. He had a way of doing that that caused the bottom to fall from her stomach.

"May I have something to drink?"

"Of course. I have iced tea, soft drinks, and hemlock juice." He took down two glasses from the cupboard, along with an amber bottle of something homemade.

"I'll take a diet soda if you have one. That looks dangerous, whatever it is."

Hunter peered at the tiny lettering on the label. "It's supposed to be sassafras tea that Jeanette made, but I'm afraid to try it." He placed the bottle on the windowsill and pulled two cans of Diet Coke from the refrigerator. His every movement was slow and deliberate.

"What is wrong with you, Hunter?"

"I have a lot on my mind." He stretched his neck from side to side. "Tell me what you uncovered about James."

"He had troubles with the IRS, SEC, and the local police. And he worked for an unusual firm during his internship in Atlanta. Hookers were regularly invited to their business meetings. I wonder what they did with the female brokers while this was happening. Send them out on a beer run?"

Hunter stared at her, his fingers tightening around the can enough to dent the aluminum. "That company was a sexist pack of good old boys that didn't hire women brokers back then." A muscle jumped in his neck. "You read about hookers being arrested at Wellert Securities?"

"Yep. Police reports are public record. Sounds like a different way of doing business than what would be acceptable at Galen-Nowak Investments."

He slouched onto a kitchen chair, looking desolate.

"Hunter, you shouldn't take it so hard. I mean, it was bad, yes, but—"

"I learned things about Ashley yesterday that I didn't like. I can't seem to think about anything else."

The apartment suddenly turned quiet. No vacuum sounds emanated from the other room, no noise from boisterous tourists filtered through the window. Even the wall clock failed to tick.

Nicki desperately wanted to ask: *What did Ashley do? What did she say? Will you still marry her?*

"I'm sorry to hear that," she said softly instead. "The course of true love never runs straight...or something like that."

"*C'est vrai*, Nicolette. I don't know why I'm troubling you with my personal problems." Exhaling a sigh, Hunter shook his head. "Do you think James's death is somehow tied to Wellert Securities? That was a long time ago."

"I'm not sure, but he definitely could have learned a few unsavory tricks during his internship. Wellert was investigated many times for unscrupulous trading practices." She crossed the kitchen to the window, needing more space between them.

"True, but isn't it more logical to look for suspects among those who lost money now? Those other incidents happened years ago. We should be able to narrow it down to a few dozen."

He sounded at the end of his rope. He reached for a bottle of bourbon from the shelf, but Nicki pulled it from his fingers. "Seriously, Hunter? This has to be about more than a fight with Ashley. Every engaged couple has spats."

"Have you even been engaged, Nicki? Did a guy ask to marry you after you just finished kissing somebody else on the dance floor?"

Nicki's heart pressed against her ribcage. He was talking about her, about them, about a kiss she thought he'd forgotten about. "No, but one kiss—even two—shouldn't change the future if you love her."

*If you love her.* There it was, the elephant in the room that Mrs. Peteriere accused him of cleaning around. Nicki didn't dare breathe.

Hunter stared out the window, where a gentle rain beat against the pane. "You're right. Kissing you could have been a regrettable misjudgment caused by alcohol, cold feet, or garden variety stupidity." A flash of lightning and a rumble of thunder heightened the tension in the room, adding drama no one needed.

"But I wasn't drunk. I'm not usually stupid. And I don't regret kissing you." Hunter crossed his arms over his chest.

"What motivated you?" Nicki tried to sound like a casual observer merely gathering facts without prejudice.

"I don't know. But I'm not in love with Ashley."

"Then why would you ask her to marry you?"

"Strike my earlier comment about not being stupid. I proposed because I didn't want to disappoint her or embarrass her or hurt her feelings. And why wouldn't I marry her? She's pretty, kind to small animals, works hard at her chosen career, and almost everybody likes her. I did what I've done my entire life—took the easy way out. I got caught up in the current and allowed choices to be made for me."

Nicki felt conflicted. "Marry her or don't marry her. It's up to you, but your decision has nothing to do with me. Those kisses were due to momentary insanity. We have no future, Hunter, because the only thing we have in common is this case."

"I know that, and I plan to take care of this. My cowardly people-pleasing is what led to this mess. If I hadn't been so busy avoiding confrontation, James might still be alive."

She shook her head vigorously. "You're responsible for this mess with Ashley, but Nowak's death is on him. He built a house of cards that came crashing down on top of him."

Hunter forced a thin, patient smile. "I'm not sure how you are around puppies and kittens, but you are a nice person, Miss Price."

"Yeah? Well, I'm not getting paid to be nice. And because you're distracted with love life problems, I'll work on the case in the den. I want to check if any of Nowak's clients from Wellert Securities followed him to your company. There might be a connection there." She almost ran from the kitchen. No way could he see how much his confession had upset her.

Discovering that she cared about Hunter came as no surprise.

Discovering how deep those feelings went scared Nicki to the bone.

# TWENTY-THREE

*H*unter watched Nicki leave the kitchen. It was obviously she couldn't wait to get away from him. She had a job to do and didn't need his personal dilemmas. But as she pushed through the swinging door, she ran smack into an unsmiling Ashley.

"Excuse me," Nicki said, holding the door open with her hip.

"Oh, hello," Ashley drawled. "You're the new investigator." She stared down her tiny nose. It wasn't a gesture Hunter admired. "Nicole Price, right?"

"Yes. No. I mean, it's Nicolette, not Nicole."

Ashley's brow furrowed. "Nicorette? You were named after a stop smoking gum?" She giggled with amusement.

Giving Nicki no chance to reply, Jeanette pushed in between the two women. "Mr. Galan's busy working now, Miz Menard. You come back later. Wait till he calls you."

"I'll do no such thing. I'm here now." Ashley didn't sound pleased. "And I will talk to my fiancé whenever I desire. Don't you have some cleaning to do?" Her gaze held nothing but contempt for the diminutive housekeeper.

"It'll keep. A lady shouldn't push her way into things not her business." Jeanette spoke in a low voice, but every word was audible.

"What?" Ashley squawked. "I don't think it's a maid's prerogative to decide what constitutes ladylike behavior." The two women faced off like bulldogs on opposite sides of a fence.

"While you two sort this out, I'm going to work quietly in the other room." Nicki squeezed through the doorway as the other women continued to glare at each other.

"Good idea, Nicorette," said Ashley, her focus never leaving Jeanette.

Hunter knew it was time to intervene. Maybe with his well-honed skills of mediation and negotiation he could prevent a bloodbath in his kitchen. "Her name is Nicolette, Ashley," he said, his tone encouraging no argument. "She works for me and we have much to do."

Ashley pivoted to face him. "For heaven's sake, Hunter, you're working in your kitchen, not chairing an annual board meeting. And why don't you ever go to the office anymore?"

"Because I feel it's more important to clear my name of James's murder and calm my clients' fears so they don't bolt. Both of those are better accomplished from home. Furthermore, Mrs. Peteriere is *not* my maid. I have no maid. You should know that by now."

Suddenly, Ashley morphed before his eyes. She shrugged her shoulders as though confused. "Darling, why are you getting so mad? I know she's your grandmother's maid. But the point is I shouldn't be denied access to you by the hired help."

Jeanette marched toward the sink and began washing the two glasses there. She muttered a string of French phrases as she ran the water.

"Jeanette didn't deny you access. She simply indicated I was busy with something important." Hunter tried his best to control his temper.

Ashley's nostrils flared. "What could possibly be so important with Nate's cousin? Didn't she get her PI license from some online correspondence course? You need Nate back on the case to avoid going to prison."

Hunter pulled Ashley into the kitchen, letting the door swing shut. "What's the matter with you? She could still be in the dining room and might have heard you."

"Oh, pooh, I was just joking. Lighten up." Pulling from his grasp, she flounced across the room. "Do you have any diet soda?" Her words drifted from the refrigerator's interior. "Seriously, wouldn't you do better with an experienced investigator rather than a backwoods farm girl?"

A coffee cup Jeanette was washing slipped from her fingers and shattered in the sink. Hunter felt close to the boiling point. "Jeanette, would you please leave those dishes for now? I would like to talk to Miss Menard."

"You go ahead, Mr. Galen. I'll just close my ears. I need to clean up these sharp pieces before someone's throat gets cut."

"See what I mean?" Ashley whined. "She's incorrigible. Jeanette refuses to do what she's told, and now she has broken another coffee mug. I thought sixty-five was the mandatory retirement age in this country. Why must we have someone who won't take orders working here?"

Hunter closed his eyes. He pretended just for a moment he was someplace else instead of captive in his own apartment with three difficult women.

His father never had these problems.

His brother, Ethan, didn't have these problems.

But he had only himself to blame. In his misguided attempt to make everyone happy, he made no one happy, especially not himself. He had gone out of his way to avoid confrontation and ended up with an intolerable life. And only he could take back control.

"Jeanette, please take Miss Price the can of soda she requested.

She's probably in the den. Why don't you remain there with her? I wish to speak to Miss Menard *in private*."

"*Oui, monsieur*." Jeanette picked up the soft drink and left the room.

"Thank goodness," said Ashley. "I thought we would need a crowbar to get her out of here." She crossed her arms over her impeccable silk suit.

Visions of Ashley entertaining rich old men, fawning and cooing over cocktails, flashed through Hunter's mind like a movie clip. But his anger had nothing to do with her postcollege behavior. He could forgive foolish mistakes made while someone was young, but he couldn't abide with rude and arrogant behavior by adults. "We need to talk."

But Ashley began rummaging in his pantry. "Did that Miss Price take the last diet soda? I don't see any other six-packs." With narrowed eyes and a hard-set jaw, she resembled a hawk spotting something tasty in a bean field.

"Ashley, please sit down." A headache throbbed behind his eyes as the woman he had recently asked to marry him turned into a stranger.

"Oh, Hunter, can't we just put this behind us and get out of here? You've been working too hard. We'll have an early dinner at Jerome's and take the yacht out for a sail. I'll call the captain and crew. Would you like that?"

"No, I would not. You haven't listened to a word I've said and you haven't for a long time. But you're going to listen now." Hunter was one notch away from shouting.

Chastised, she closed the pantry door and sat primly on a chair. "I'm all ears."

"I don't like how you treat Mrs. Peteriere or Miss Price and a lot of other people you encounter. If you feel someone is socially beneath you, you're not very nice to them. And that must change."

"You're absolutely right. I've been under so much stress lately.

If I promise to do better, will you forgive me?" She turned up her blue eyes and moistened her lips with her tongue.

"No, Ashley. I'm serious this time. I tried discussing this before, but you always shrug it off." Hunter straightened his back. Postponing the inevitable would only make matters worse. "You have many admirable qualities. You are a beautiful, accomplished woman, and any man would be proud to make you his wife, but in many ways we are incompatible. We need to take a break from each other and think things through carefully."

Ashley seemed flabbergasted by his decision. "What about our engagement? The announcement will appear in Saturday's society pages. What about the lovely party our families threw for us? We couldn't possibly disappoint everyone after they went to so much trouble." She rose to her feet regally, like a queen. "I will apologize to Jeanette. I know I should make allowances for the elderly. And I promise to be nice to your investigator, but let's not overreact to a minor disagreement. Every engaged couple has them."

Hunter felt worse than at any point in his life. Ashley didn't get it. She thought this was how people acted in a relationship— like actors on a stage playing their roles for an appreciative audience. "I'm sorry my family went ahead with the party without checking with me first. They had no right to take the decision out of our hands."

She looked at him in shock and then in dismay. Sniffing delicately, she went to the counter to tear off a paper towel from the hanging roll. Then she softly dabbed her eyes with it. "You mean you would have *stopped* them had you known?" Her tone indicated disbelief in the possibility.

"Yes, I would have. I thought things between us were moving too fast. I had little control of your...agenda." Hunter shook his head, feeling lower than a snake in the grass. "I'm sorry, Ashley, but we need to step back and take a good look at our relationship."

He let several seconds pass before adding, "Because I'm not the right man for you."

She shook her head, sending her long hair flying. "No, you're angry because I was rude to Jeanette. I shouldn't have acted that way. I know she has been with your family since before you were born. Everyone else is so fond of her. Besides I was taught to respect my elders." Ashley pursed her lips and blew out her frustration. "We'll let the announcement run in Saturday's paper as planned. Then I'll go up to Baton Rouge for a week. We'll take a breather from each other and I can do some shopping." Her eyes lit as the plan to save her world took shape. "By the time I get back, this spat will be forgotten. You'll be glad to see me." She placed a well-manicured hand against his chest, while a mega-watt smile bloomed across her lovely face. "And, of course, I'll apologize to Jeanette on my way out.

Hunter removed her hand from his shirt. "No, Miss Menard. You'll call the *Times* and cancel the announcement. We can talk more when you get back from Baton Rouge, but I won't change my mind. Put whatever spin you want on this because I have no desire to embarrass you. Tell everyone the breakup was your idea—the strain of James's murder was too much. You couldn't possibly proceed with wedding plans while I'm a murder suspect."

"You can't *possibly* be serious."

Hunter walked to the window overlooking the garden. The dismal weather precisely matched his mood. "I don't care if you tell people the wedding's off because I am a murderer. Let's just stop before any more arrangements are made for us."

Ashley wilted before his eyes, her face as white as a sheet as she finally realized she wasn't going to get her way. "Very well, Hunter. We'll say no more about this for now. I'll do as you say and call the papers."

Hunter pitied her, not for the broken engagement—she

would find a richer, taller, better-looking replacement by the end of summer—but because this could be the first time someone had ever said no to her. "Eventually you'll agree we made the right decision," he said as gently as possible.

Ashley arched her neck and lifted her chin as a spark of her formidable spirit returned. "No. I think you're making a mistake. A big mistake." With that she marched out of the kitchen, through the dining room, and out the front door. She didn't look back. And she also didn't bother to apologize to Jeanette.

# TWENTY-FOUR

trange how life worked out. You finally got what you think you wanted, and suddenly, what you wanted changed. Nicki felt no overwhelming joy when Ashley left the apartment, her face fraught with pain. The woman no longer looked imposing in her expensive heels and designer suit. Nicki felt pity for her until Ashley cast a withering glance over her shoulder on her way out the front door. She focused her wrath first on Mrs. Peteriere and then on her.

What had Hunter seen in that scrawny scarecrow? How could he put up with such an overbearing attitude? Why couldn't he date a nice person for a change? A person like her, for instance. Not that a man like him would look twice at someone with six-dollar haircuts and who ordered food off the value menu. Exhaling a weary sigh, Nicki locked eyes with Mrs. Peteriere. The woman was staring at her curiously, her vacuum cleaner forgotten.

"You just gonna sit there, *O'lette*?"

"I have gone over Mr. Galen's books until I can practically recite them chapter and verse. I'm not discovering anything I hadn't already considered about Mr. Nowak."

Mrs. Peteriere clucked her tongue and muttered something in French. "I'm not talking about your job." She shook her tiny silvery head.

Nicki closed the lid of her laptop, uncertain what to do. She'd watched the semiretired housekeeper open the kitchen door an inch so she could eavesdrop and smirk over some overheard exchange. Now she had been dusting a small Chinese vase for five full minutes. But brave, industrious Nicolette Price couldn't possibly ask her what happened or what she found so amusing. It was her job to find a client with a motive to kill James Nowak better than Hunter Galen's. "Then what are you talking about, Mrs. Peteriere?"

"They are kaput, he and Miz Menard," Mrs. Peteriere whispered, dipping her head toward the closed door. "Perhaps *Monsieur* Galen needs a shoulder to cry on."

Nicki's jaw dropped open. "Then perhaps you can call his parish priest. I don't know anything about salving wounded souls."

Mrs. Peteriere clucked her tongue a second time. "You are *nothing* like your cousin."

"Thank you. I consider that a compliment. My cousin would try the patience of a saint." Nicki tucked her laptop into her tote bag, giving up on work for the moment.

When she glanced up, Mrs. Peteriere was staring at her. "Maybe I can fix something to eat for you two. Serve it out on the terrace. Very nice out there, you'll see." Her papery skin crinkled into a web of fine lines with her grin.

"I'm sure the terrace is lovely, but I'm leaving. Thank you for your offer of lunch. Please ask Mr. Galen to call me later tonight." Nicki picked up her purse and bag.

"What's your big hurry?

"He needs time alone. But it was nice to meet you, Mrs. Peteriere. And you're right about men not moving things when they clean." Nicki bobbed her head at the elderly woman and hurried toward the door. The elegant suite of rooms suddenly felt cramped and confining, as though the walls had moved inward.

"You know what they say about opportunities, *O'lette*."

Nicki heard the woman's words follow her down the metal stairs to ground level. Good grief, she was a full-service employee—cooking, cleaning, and unlimited, unsolicited advice. Martha Stewart and Dr. Phil rolled into one.

*And I have trouble holding down one job at a time.*

Nicki lengthened her stride once she reached the sidewalk. The rain had stopped and the breeze felt cool on her flushed face. It would have been nice to share a quiet dinner with Hunter. Something told her Mrs. Peteriere was a better cook than Christine or herself, for that matter. They could have compared notes on the case, and maybe even tried that kissing business they had started in the dance hall. Nicki's thoughts drifted into never-never-land until she sensed someone following behind her. The French Quarter wasn't a good place to wander around daydreaming.

Nicki ducked into the next shop, stepping from the sidewalk's flow of humanity.

A tall man with wavy hair and oily skin stopped short in the open doorway. "Nicki Price?" he asked with a melodic drawl.

When he reached inside his jacket, she shouted, "Hold it right there, buddy!" She pretended to go for her own weapon under her cotton blazer.

"Easy there, lady. I'm Detective Russ Saville, NOPD." He flashed a badge. "You been watchin' too many old cop shows."

"Can't be too careful these days," she said. When he covered his shield, Nicki spotted a shoulder holster.

"I just want to ask you a few questions about your new best friend, Hunter Galen." Saville's smile was reminiscent of a used car salesman trying to sell a vehicle pulled from the muck of Katrina.

"I don't think so. I'm late for an appointment."

Nicki tried to step past him, but with his size and agility, the detective easily blocked her path. "You're still waiting on your concealed carry permit, no? You don't want me to file a complaint with the commission that you're uncooperative with law enforcement, do you, sugar?"

"I'm not being uncooperative, Detective. I just don't know anything. There's a big difference. And my name's not 'sugar.'" Nicki straightened her back to increase her height.

"You'd be surprised what you might know. Let's go somewhere we can talk." Saville took hold of her upper arm and practically dragged her from the doorway.

Nicki tugged free from his grasp but followed him into the alley nevertheless. She decided it would be good to know what the cops thought they had on Hunter. "What can I do for you? I'm curious as to why you like Hunter for Nowak's murder so much. Plenty of clients have motive."

"That's much better, Jessica Fletcher from Natchez." Saville laughed down at her. "It pays to stay friendly with law enforcement when you're a PI. You never know when you may need a real cop to rescue you."

Nicki's revulsion notched up a level. "I don't mind talking as long as we're trading information."

"All right. Tell me why a nice girl like you wants to work in the Big Easy? You think you can step into your cousin's shoes now that his license is gonna be yanked?" He scratched the stubble on his chin. "Nate Price has been on the Galen payroll for years, even though he hasn't done an honest day's work since old man Galen went to his crypt in Lafayette Cemetery. Is he pulling your strings like some puppeteer?"

"A puppet doesn't have strings, Detective. You're thinking of a marionette. And nobody pulls mine. I came to New Orleans to work for him. Now I work for Mr. Galen. I'm a licensed investigator who's looking into his partner's murder and whatever scams Mr. Nowak may have been involved with." Nicki could have kicked herself. There was no reason to tell the cops that James stole from his clients.

"I don't give a hoot how many people Nowak ripped off—that's the feds' business. I know who killed the guy—Hunter Galen—and you're going to help me prove it." Saville's lips pulled back to reveal yellowed teeth when he laughed again. Someone needed to tell him about smoker's toothpaste.

"Why would I help you?" Nicki hefted her tote bag higher on her shoulder. "I just told you I work for the man you're trying to hang this on."

He took his time lighting a cigarette. "Let me count the ways. First, do you have a Louisiana license? You ain't in Mississippi anymore where they give anybody one. So I could run you out of town on the next barge headed upriver. Or I can arrest you for obstruction of justice and hold you for questioning for twenty-four hours. Maybe a couple nights in lockup will change your mind about our fair city. Of course, none of this will look good to the review board, you being from the most recent graduation class and all." He exhaled smoke in her direction.

Nicki moved upwind and changed her tack. "I *am* licensed in your fair state, so why are you so worried about me? I'm just doing my job and earning a paycheck. If you have the necessary evidence to convict Hunter, you have nothing to worry about from me." Nicki smiled as sweetly as she could considering the cigarette smoke.

Saville leaned so close they were almost nose-to-nose. "Do I look worried to you?"

Nicki had the distinct impression he'd changed shirts without bothering to shower first. She took a step back. "Not especially, but we've only just met. And since you're not worried, you've got no reason to run me out of town."

"Maybe you're just getting on people's nerves, burrowing under their skin like a chigger. I see you following Galen around like a groupie. Is that what you are, sugar, a Galen groupie?"

"It's your turn, Detective Saville. What motive does Hunter have to kill his partner? Or doesn't motive count much in the state of Louisiana?"

"Oh, Galen had plenty of motive. He probably found out his sweet little girlfriend was seeing his partner behind his back. Can't say I'd blame the woman much. Miss Menard paid Nowak a social call that afternoon. Or haven't you gotten that far in your *investigation*?"

Nicki swallowed hard. She hadn't known about Ashley's visit. There had been no mention on Nowak's day planner or on Naomi's calendar. "There could be all kinds of reasons why Ashley went to see him. They were friends."

"Man, I wish my friends looked like that. I'd cancel the rest of my appointments." He ran a hand through his hair. "Yeah, I know all about Nowak's scams. He was running the partnership into the ground while skimming profits to his own bank account." He shook his head and a lock of hair fell across his greasy forehead.

She sighed. "All right. Nowak was up to no-good that Hunter would have to make right. But he and his family are rich. They have plenty of eggs in their basket. They're not going to kill somebody over a couple of mil."

"Money ain't everything to men like Galen. They got their reputation and the family name to worry about. Nowak pissed off every client they had, but it's Galen's name that would take the trouncing. Mama don't want the muckety-mucks saying her little boy was nothing but a thief in a thousand-dollar suit. Family status—that's something you probably don't know nothing about. Ain't that right, country girl? They got a debutante ball out in Jefferson County, Mississippi?"

Nicki didn't like it that the detective had checked on her

background, but she refused to let it show. "Sure, we have a cotil-lion. It's the weekend after the women's mud wrestling cham-pionship. Winners of both events ride front and center in the Memorial Day parade. Why don't you come up that weekend? I'd bet it's just your style."

He smiled, slow and easy. "Because I'm having too much fun down here. I think I've got you figured out, Nicolette Price. You came on down to your first real job with an expense account and a smooth-as-silk boss. You're just sittin' in high cotton now, aren't you, country girl?"

"What are you talking about?" Nicki's right hand bunched into a fist as though punching him in the face might be a possibility.

"You think that if you solve the case and get Mr. Deep Pock-ets off for his partner's murder, then old Hunter will fall madly in love with you." He shook his head sadly. "You must not have seen your competition. That Miz Menard is the total package—pretty face, hot body, and pleasin' personality." Saville sneered at a homeless man digging around in a trash can before refocusing on her. "You know what I'm talkin' about? Then you throw in the added bonus of her daddy's money, and I say Miz Menard sweeps the series. What you got goin' for you, Nicki? A dead shot with a squirrel rifle? You can cook up a mean pot of roadkill stew with some sweet cornbread?" He laughed once more with little amuse-ment before a hint of pity crept into his expression. "Rich peo-ple—they marry their own kind."

Nicki's complexion turned the color of boiled lobster at serv-ing time. "I told you, Detective. My interest is purely professional."

"Sure, I understand, but let me give you a little advice anyway. You're pretty enough for cruising the Winn Dixie parking lot on a Saturday night in upstate Mississippi, but old lady Galen ain't inviting you to no tea party in the Garden District. So don't jeop-ardize that PI license you worked so hard for. Galen did it. That I am sure of. He whacked his partner and thinks he's rich enough to get away with it. If you do anything stupid—withhold evidence or cover his tracks—you'll end up in jail too." Pulling a business card from his pocket, he held it up in front of her. "Don't get in my way, Nicki Price. I'm bringing Hunter Galen down, and it don't make no never-mind to me if you go down with him or not." He stuck the card in her shirt pocket and strolled toward the street.

She remained rooted where she was standing until the homeless man foraging in the trash bins made her more nervous than the arrogant cop. When she exited the alley, Saville was nowhere in sight, but one thing was crystal clear. The man was bound and determined to pin the murder on Hunter. And his desire went deeper than pride in his job. Detective Saville hated Hunter, so he wouldn't be looking for the real killer any time soon. The suggestion of planted evidence and covering up tracks had been on *his mind,* not hers.

Nicki didn't appreciate his unfavorable comparison between her and Ashley, but that didn't matter now. She had a job to do. Hunter had a very real enemy—one sworn to protect and serve. His enemy wore a fully loaded Glock with an extra clip in his pocket. It looked as if she might earn her paycheck after all.

# TWENTY-FIVE

$\mathcal{A}$lthough this was the twenty-first century and she was a licensed private investigator with access to all kinds of law enforcement databases, Nicki decided to visit St. Landry Parish the very next morning to obtain the sheriff's report of her father's disappearance. No phone call, fax machine, or email request felt right for something so personal.

Last night she'd met Nate for dinner so she could bring him up to speed on the case. Hunter had called during the meal to say that because he would probably need her on Saturday, she was free to do as she pleased on Friday.

She took Route 10 to Lafayette and then opted for the scenic route to the city of Opelousas. Along the way she spotted several antebellum mansions, as well as many tiny homes on postage-stamp lots. Residents' possessions—effluvia from sports and hobbies—spilled over into yards and driveways as though it didn't rain on a regular basis. Stuff was everywhere, yet none of it looked new or worth much. People of all ages lounged on porches, tinkered on cars, and played on rusty jungle gyms. *What is the unemployment rate in this part of Louisiana?* she wondered, considering that everyone seemed to be home on a midweek day.

In a perverse way Nicki was heartened by the snapshot of

poverty and hardship, comforted that she wasn't the only one who hailed from modest roots. Working for a wealthy man and living in a city where tourists bought hundred-dollar breakfasts and overpriced foo-foo drinks had skewed her perspective. Far more Americans lived like these families than Hunter's rich friends in the Garden District.

Once Nicki reached the charming parish seat, she easily found the sheriff's department. The friendly woman at the counter, Sophie Godrey, called her "honey" at least six times during their brief conversation. Once Nicki had showed her ID and provided what information she had regarding dates and locations, the dispatcher searched databases.

"Uh-oh," she said. "Unless you have a court order, I'm afraid I can't help you. This is still an open case. Because no charges were filed, nothing is public record." Her expression was sympathetic.

"Who would have access to the report?"

"The DA, our homicide detectives, of course, and any member of law enforcement with proper identification."

"I see." Nicki tried to shake off her disappointment. "May I speak with one of your homicide detectives, ma'am?"

"None of them are here. I don't expect any in the office until after lunch."

Nicki glanced at the clock on the wall. It wasn't even ten yet. "Could you make a copy of my PI license and give it to him or her along with my request? I will be back this afternoon to speak with one of them."

"I'll do my best, honey. Can't make any promises."

Nicki passed the time at the library. The librarian directed her to the sole computer capable of accessing newspapers from the past. Because most patrons surfed the Internet or downloaded games, the library's archives weren't available at all terminals. For two hours Nicki scanned stories about road repair fiascos, fund-raising misappropriations, convenience store robberies, and political backstabbing, but she found no mention of a Mississippi resident missing in the swamp. Perhaps a husband disappearing into thin air—or dark water—wasn't as newsworthy as a PTA mom paying her cable bill with cookie sale profits.

When her stomach growled loud enough to be heard, Nicki drove to the café recommended by Mrs. Godrey. While nibbling on a shrimp po'boy, Nicki studied a brochure from the tourist rack. The Atchafalaya National Wildlife Refuge—home to bobcats, muskrats, minks, alligators, and eighty-five species of fish—was a small part of a huge basin of swamps, lakes, and bayous flowing toward the Gulf of Mexico. One and a half million acres to be exact. *How will I ever be able to find the last person to see my father alive?* Staggered by the size of the playground for hunters and fishermen, Nicki forced herself to focus. Her Aunt Charlotte knew the exact location of the cabin. Once she had a copy of the police report, she would have every name she needed to find answers.

Tucking the brochure into her purse, Nicki returned to the sheriff's department and was promptly interrogated as to what she had for lunch. Perhaps Mrs. Godrey thought she said food critic instead of PI from New Orleans. After Nicki finished her restaurant review she was told that none of the detectives were in the office. She could either wait or come back tomorrow. Nicki headed to the bench along the wall and settled back.

Two hours later, when she'd begun to doze with her head against the hard wall, Mrs. Godrey shook her shoulder. "You may read this here but not take it with you. Detective Brown has no further information for you." The woman handed Nicki a manila folder and returned to her post.

With shaking hands Nicki opened the folder and gazed on the September 1998 report filed by Sheriff Tom Latanier.

The cabin was owned by Charles Price, permanent address Natchez, Mississippi. Witnesses interviewed had been playing poker and drinking on Friday when an argument ensued between Kermit Price and Theodore "Junior" Cheval. Kermit Price left the cabin in a homemade canoe at approximately midnight after reportedly surrendering his winnings to Junior Cheval of Clay Creek, Mississippi. Mr. Price did not return during the period the cabin remained occupied. At approximately six p.m., Charles Price called the St. Landry Sheriff's Department. Responding to call were Sheriff Tom Latanier, and Officers Roulish and McDuff. Witnesses interviewed the night of Saturday, September 13, reported hearing no gunshots in the general vicinity. Officer Roulish tested the cabin's occupants' hands for gunshot residue. Negative. Eleven firearms were collected from the premises, none recently discharged. The fishing dock, bank of unnamed canal, and back porch were all negative for blood residue. No evidence of foul play inside the cabin or surrounding perimeter. Mr. Price's body was later discovered by the St. Martin Parish Sheriff's Department on Thursday, September 18, where it was then transferred to the St. Martin Medical Examiner. Coroner's report attached.

Nothing on the page was particularly helpful except for the names and addresses of the six witnesses. The report had been signed by Sheriff Latanier, St. Landry Parish, and dated November 1998. Conclusion: Insufficient evidence at this time to continue homicide investigation.

*A cold case, not accidental death?* Nicki flipped to the next sheet, a coroner's report dated ten days after the Saturday disappearance.

She skimmed the facts while spicy shrimp churned in her belly. Apparently her father's corpse had been devoured by fish, crabs, and alligators, in addition to normal decomposition in heavily vegetated water. But one detail grabbed her attention from the clinical findings.

> Skull indentation consistent with a single gunshot wound to the head, type of weapon and caliber of bullet unknown. Inconclusive cause of death, possible self-inflicted, probable homicide.

Nicki took another look at the list of witnesses. Charles Price. Andre Martin. Eugene Martin. Terrence Cheval. Theodore Cheval. Louis Cheval. Her three uncles and the mysterious three brothers from Clay Creek. Most likely one of those men was a killer. Her father hadn't stormed off in a pirogue after being robbed of ill-gotten winnings. Someone had shot him in the head and dumped his body in the swamp.

Back at the counter, the helpful Mrs. Godrey explained that Sheriff Latanier had retired eleven years ago. "I'd just started with the department," she said. "But the town threw quite a shindig, including a full seafood buffet—shrimp, crab, oysters, fried catfish—you name it. Sheriff Latanier even drank a Budweiser that night, and everybody knew he was a teetotaler." She shook her head as though still shocked by the incongruity.

Nicki clucked her tongue appropriately. "Sounds like a wonderful retirement party. Everyone must have loved and respected him. Could I please have his address or perhaps a phone number?"

Mrs. Godrey quickly sobered. "Oh, no, honey. We don't release our officers' personal information whether retired or currently on payroll. It's department policy." She leaned across the desk. "Too many folks with axes to grind, if you know what I mean."

Nicki kept her initial thought to herself. *But you saw I had no outstanding warrants.* "Could you at least give the sheriff my contact information? With all due respect, I'd like to talk to him either by phone or in person." Nicki placed her business card on the counter.

"I suppose there's no harm in that." Picking up the card, Mrs. Godrey bestowed one final toothy grin. "Have a safe trip back to New Orleans, honey. And thanks for visiting St. Landry Parish. Tell all your friends to come see us in Opelousas. We love company."

# TWENTY-SIX

After several hours of poring over client records, Hunter filled his travel mug with black coffee and headed for the door on a gorgeous Saturday morning. Although James had a gift for picking loser stocks, Hunter found little in the last two years that could have gotten him killed, other than the Ace Linen Supply scam. His assistant, who refused to speak ill of the dead, could shed no new light on the subject. Naomi had always had a soft spot for James.

Hunter headed toward James's home, hoping to find something that wasn't in the firm's records. He wasn't accomplishing anything at his place other than contemplating the enigmatic Nicki or mulling over his breakup with Ashley.

He knew he'd made the right decision in that area. Ashley was a wonderful woman in many ways but not the person he yearned to spend his life with, even without the recent revelations of her postcollege cottage industry. Although he didn't like the idea of her socializing for pay, he liked her insincerity even less. More than once he got the notion that what she said and what she felt weren't remotely related.

Ashley was a people-pleaser as long as they fit into her agenda, unlike Nicki, who said whatever popped into her mind without considering the consequences.

Nicki. Honest, driven, so motivated to rise above her modest circumstances and make something of herself. So different from Ashley.

So different from himself. He'd never had to struggle for anything in his life. His parents had paved an easy path for him and his siblings.

Nicki's face flitted through his mind—her silky hair, her voice, her scent of Ivory soap and raspberry shampoo. She wasn't his type, so why did he find himself thinking about her forty times a day?

Because the partners had keys to each other's home in case of emergencies, Hunter let himself into James's townhouse. A sudden death often left behind a sad, surreal world. A Grisham novel lay facedown on his coffee table, its spine cracked. Mugs sat in the sink, the coffee dried to a dark residue in the bottom. The *Times* sports section had been folded back to an article on the NBA draft. A forlorn ficus tree, desperate for water, had dropped half its leaves on the carpet. The air smelled stale and musty, akin to unused closets and poorly ventilated attics. James's parents hadn't been here yet to clean out his home, an understandably impossible task in their state of early grief.

Hunter switched on the AC, threw out the accumulated junk mail, watered the ficus, and headed for the den. He prayed James hadn't changed the passwords on his computer. His prayer was answered.

Both partners downloaded office files to their laptops so they could handle exchange requests at home. Because their clients were active investors, Galen-Nowak brokers were available twenty-four seven. After several wrong turns and missteps, a spreadsheet of James's clients bloomed across the screen, with one unsettling difference. These financial statements bore no resemblance to the spreadsheets Hunter had studied all week.

He pulled the printouts from his briefcase and began to

compare. As his focus flitted between his papers and the monitor, a bad feeling grew in the pit of his belly. None of the individual account balances matched. They didn't even come close. As Hunter studied each client's monthly activity, a pattern emerged—a pattern of deception, subterfuge, and outright theft. Each month James selected one or two clients whose assets exceeded a million dollars to be his personal banker. He siphoned money from their account and deposited it into his own. Then he made investments in his own name, besides using the money to augment his lavish lifestyle. If the stocks he picked gained value, he returned the original "borrowed" amount and kept the profits. If they lost value, *c'est la vie*. He returned whatever was left after thirty days. Either way he generated a phony statement on his laptop and printed it to mail to the client—one that didn't match the one on file at Galen-Nowak Investments.

James had been leading a double life that enriched himself, not his clients. If any of them had figured out his scam, they would have been furious. And that sounded like motive for murder. Hunter printed copies of the phony accounting records with growing anxiety. Last month three clients received statements indicating substantial losses due to his machinations. Among those who had lost more than a hundred thousand dollars was a familiar name: Philip Menard.

*By the way, Papa Menard, besides causing your only daughter to lose face with her catty girlfriends, I just discovered my business partner has been using your account as his own personal ATM.*

What a mess. Packing up the computer printouts from James's laptop, Hunter scrolled through his contact list on his phone and selected Nicki's number. Her training in forensic accounting would enable her to create an accurate record of James's thievery. If Hunter aimed to do right by his clients, he needed to know the complete picture.

"Nicki, where are you?" he asked when she picked up. "Can you meet me in the Quarter? I have papers to give you along with James's computer. I need your help." He heard her suck in a gulp of air.

"What have you found out?"

"I don't want to discuss this on the phone. Meet me at Lafitte's Blacksmith Shop Bar, corner of Bourbon and St. Phillip."

"You want me to meet you in a *bar*? Why can't I come back to your apartment?"

"Because Jeanette is there, and no one will know me or you in Lafitte's." He ended the call. Despite their short acquaintance, he knew she would ask a dozen questions, and he couldn't spare the time.

Hunter drove back to the French Quarter, the crowds still sparse due to the time of day. What visitors were in town were either snoozing in their hotel rooms or grabbing a late lunch. As expected, Nicki wasn't smiling when he found her in the oldest bar in the United States. "This place gives me the willies," she whispered. "I refuse to pour my Coke into a glass. It's so dark in here."

"They wash their glassware, Nicki. That's not what we need to fear."

"Where have you been? What have you found out?"

Hunter ordered a Coke and then provided a bare bones explanation to fill the gap since she'd left his apartment two days earlier. She gazed at him with an expression of disbelief and amazement as he described James's method of personal betterment.

"That's unbelievable," she said. "How much do you think he stole?"

"That exact figure is what you're going to find out. I'm guessing at least a mil."

"A million dollars!" Her voice carried across the room, drawing the attention of several patrons. Nicki covered her mouth with her hand.

"Depends on how long he's been doing this. It could be quite a bit more."

Nicki's expression changed to disgust. "I don't get it. Nowak robs a million from rich folks using his personal charm and a computer, and he probably would have received probation and restitution."

Hunter swiveled to face her, irritated yet not wholly in dis-agreement. "May I remind you that someone *killed* him, proba-bly over his scam? So I would say he got capital punishment for his crime."

Her face scrunched with shame. "I'm sorry, Hunter. Really. Maybe I'm just envious because obviously my personal charm wouldn't amass enough money for a streetcar ride."

"Apology accepted...and charm is highly overrated. Now, if you'll excuse me, I have a long drive ahead of me—"

"Wherever you're going, I'm going with you. It's safer if we stick together."

He smiled at her earnestness, as though they were tourists ven-turing into a cemetery after dark. "I need to stop at home and pack an overnight bag and then drive out to the Menards'. Not their house in the Garden District but their rustic retreat out in the country."

"I'm your private investigator. You're not going there alone."

Hunter pushed James's laptop and his file folders across the scarred table. "You have work to do, Nicki. I need an accurate record of everything James did off the radar. I'm sure the reason he was killed is in there. That may also be why you were lured into the bayou."

"All the more reason you shouldn't go solo." She picked up the laptop but rose to her feet. Her determination reminded him of

Chloe while losing an argument with their mother. *Remain stead-fast, even when all you're holding is a pair of threes in a poker game.*

"Listen to me carefully. One of the clients he ripped off last month was Philip Menard." Hunter watched her face pale considerably.

"Ashley's *dad*? James ripped off your fiancée's father? Why would he do such a thing?" Nicki's brown eyes rounded with confusion.

"Philip may not even know, but I need to talk to him."

"Then for sure I'm going with you, boss!" She slapped a five-dollar bill down for her Coke and quickly gathered the file folders.

He clamped a hand on her wrist. "No, Nicki. Mr. Menard may not know he's been scammed, but I'm sure by now that he's heard about his daughter's broken engagement and—"

"That has nothing to do with me! I work for you and this is my job."

Hunter waited until she looked him in the eye before replying. "Ashley may have the misguided notion *you* had something to do with our breakup."

Lafitte's grew deathly quiet. *Where are all the boisterous drunks when you need them?*

"Did I? Did your decision to end it have anything to do with me?"

"Are you asking me if I find you attractive?" Hunter released her arm as silence continued to spin out in the room. "I do, but I broke up with Ashley for my own reasons. And I'm not prepared to discuss those reasons with you or Philip or anyone else." He tapped his fingernail on the laptop and then wrote something down on a Post-it Note. "Here is James's password. Work up financial profiles for each of his clients and I'll call you later. Thanks, Nicki."

Hunter walked out into the sunshine on Bourbon Street with his investigator close on his heels.

"That's good to know, boss," she called, hefting the computer bag onto her shoulder. "Don't change your life with me in mind because I'm just here for the paycheck, good medical benefits, and experience to put on my résumé. I'll get you out of the hot water you're in and move on to the next client."

When Hunter stopped short at the corner, Nicki almost collided into him. "Understood, Miss Price. And we haven't even discussed accrued vacation time or a retirement account." He laughed as a blush spread up her cheeks.

"Where does Mr. Menard live? Just in case you never make it back to New Orleans and I have to call the authorities."

Hunter considered his options. He didn't like the idea of Nicki coming to the Menard country home, not after what happened in the swamp, but to deny her the information showed a lack of trust.

He released a weary sigh. "Their home is out in Terrebonne on the southern end of Lake Boudreaux. But I need you in town. For all I know, Ashley might be visiting her dad and that would make things uncomfortable." Hunter doubted Ashley would lick her wounds at her father's rustic retreat. The bars, restaurants, and shopping malls of Baton Rouge would infinitely better suit her style, but Philip had a mean streak. Hunter didn't want his wrath directed at Nicki if Ashley had implicated her as a home wrecker.

"Fine, Hunter. You're the boss."

He made sure she climbed into her Escort and drove away before heading to his own car. Back at home, he threw some clothes, his shaving kit, and the two versions of the Menard account statement into an overnight bag. He avoided Jeanette's bewildering scowls along with the blinking light on his answering machine and left the city. Although the swamp would be hot, humid, and buggy, the crowded streets of New Orleans had a way of closing in around you.

Out at the Menard family home on Lake Boudreaux, Hunter

found Philip as he thought he would—not in the best of moods. A uniformed butler showed Hunter to the paneled den. No one else living in the bayou would insist that household staff wear livery but Ashley's family. Several hunting prints decorated the walls, while a vintage muzzleloader hung over the seldom-used fireplace. An oak gun cabinet displayed an impressive collection of contemporary lethal weapons. Menard was bent over open ledgers and a stack of bills.

When Hunter spotted Galen letterhead at the top of the pile, he swallowed down a golf-ball-sized lump. "Good afternoon, Mr. Menard. I see you're going over your accounts. That's why I'm here." Hunter extended his hand in greeting.

Menard looked up at his guest from under his reading glasses and shook with little enthusiasm. "*That's* why you're here, boy? I would think you'd have more pressing matters to discuss with me, such as whatever is going on between you and my daughter."

At thirty years old, Hunter didn't appreciate being referred to as "boy" and enjoyed discussing his personal relationships even less. It wasn't as though he and Ashley were underage teenagers in trouble, facing the music with Daddy. "I see Ashley has mentioned we're taking a break from each other. Things have been tense since James's murder. And you and my family didn't help matters by orchestrating that party behind our backs."

"I didn't go behind my daughter's back. She was all for the idea. You're the one with *issues*, Hunter. Isn't that what they call cold feet these days?" His tone had softened quite a bit, apparently opting for the honey-instead-of-vinegar approach.

Hunter inhaled a deep breath. No way would he discuss character flaws with someone's father, but it was hard to say "stay out of my personal business" when he owed the man hundreds of thousands of dollars thanks to James's schemes. "Ashley and I will reach a decision about our future when she returns from Baton

Rouge, sir. I'm here today about the management of your investment portfolio. I've discovered a substantial inaccuracy in your statement, but I assure you I intend to straighten this out."

*Substantial inaccuracy in your statement?* He was starting to sound like a corporate spin-doctor. Yet a sense of misguided loyalty prevented him from calling James an outright thief.

Surprisingly, Menard just laughed. "Substantial inaccuracy, Hunter? Yes, I'd agree with that. You should have kept your partner on a short leash. Either that guy was the stupidest stockbroker in Louisiana or he was up to something illegal. Which do you suppose it was?" Menard leaned back in his upholstered chair, interlocking his fingers across his substantial midsection and narrowing his eyes.

"I suspect the former, but James is dead. There's no sense getting into the legal or ethical implications. You have my word I'll make right whatever losses were unjustified even if it takes me years." Hunter shifted his weight from one foot to the other. Menard hadn't asked him to sit down. He felt like a schoolboy in the headmaster's office, but he deserved as much for not spotting this scam long ago.

With a snort Menard pulled a crystal decanter of something amber and a glass from his desk drawer. "Care for a drink, Galen?" Suddenly he sounded downright hospitable.

"No, thank you, sir." Hunter watched him pour a hefty portion.

"Did you know Nowak was a gambler? I don't mean playing a few slots on the riverboat or penny-ante cards on somebody's back porch. I mean high stakes poker—thousand-dollar buy-ins, five- and six-figure pots. I saw him once in a private suite on the *Cajun Queen.*" He paused a moment to let this sink in. "And he wasn't winning."

Hunter's heart pounded against his chest wall. *James stole hundreds of thousands of dollars to gamble with?* Hunter's loyalty toward his friend slipped a few notches. "I didn't know he was a gambler. That explains a lot, but it doesn't change what I need to do."

"That's not the mess you gotta make right, boy." Menard sat up, his feet landing on the den's Oriental rug with a thump. "I don't like being duped by your partner, but my finances will recover. Money ain't everything. I can survive without the money that crook stole, but I can't stand hearing my little girl cry." Menard squinted, his eyes bleary after years of hard drinking. "It makes my blood boil. Someday you'll understand when you're a father."

"Sir, you'll have to trust us—"

"No!" he shouted. He struggled to his feet, knocking a stack of bills onto the floor. "My Ashley has her heart set on marrying you. You will do the right thing by my daughter!" His threat echoed against the tin ceiling and then silence fell like a final curtain.

"Mr. Menard, you have every right to be angry. I was lackadaisical and too trusting of my partner, who ended up scamming thousands of dollars." Hunter enunciated each word carefully. "I take personal responsibility for James's actions in Galen-Nowak Investments, but I *will not* be coerced into a marriage with a woman I apparently barely know. There isn't enough money in all of Switzerland or bourbon in your desk drawer to make me marry Ashley now."

# TWENTY-SEVEN

*P*erspiration dampened the back of Nicki's shirt, but she opted against running the car's air-conditioning. She hated to waste any gasoline at the current prices. Besides, the less attention she drew to herself during the first official stakeout of her career the better.

She peered out the dusty car windows at the structure visible between twin oak trees. She was back in the swamp again—her least favorite place in the world—at the hottest time of day. Her legs beneath her shorts felt glued to the vinyl upholstery, but she couldn't let Hunter drive to the Menards' Terrebonne Parish home by himself, not with Nowak's killer still at large. If Hunter wasn't the killer, then the real killer could have Hunter next on his list.

And Hunter was no killer.

So Nicki had hurried back to Christine's trailer, thrown a change of clothes, pepper spray, insect repellant, and a flashlight into her duffel bag, and grabbed a couple bottles of water and a bag of chips on her way out the door. She was willing to return to the bayou to keep Hunter safe, but she wouldn't go unprepared. She ended up near his apartment just as he pulled the Corvette onto the street. Trailing him at a safe distance wasn't easy, but at least heavy afternoon traffic kept him from getting too far ahead of her. Despite her reluctance to follow too closely, she managed to keep the Corvette within view all the way to the country home and roots of Ashley Menard. And apparently no gun-toting assassin had followed them to Terrebonne.

The Menard weekend retreat was just a two-story house with tile roof, wraparound front porch, and a gravel turnaround that encircled overgrown palmetto trees. Then again, Nicki's birthplace outside of Natchez wasn't much to look at either. According to Hunter, Mr. Menard used this home only for hunting or fishing with his cronies. Ashley refused to stay there after her mother died, but the true reason had more to do with no malls within easy distance than painful memories.

Nicki didn't like Ashley, but she would keep her opinion to herself because Hunter probably harbored lingering feelings for the woman.

Nicki swatted a mosquito that evidently hadn't read about her bug repellant's effectiveness and opened her second bottle of water. Fortunately, Hunter's blond head appeared on the front porch before she needed to use the woods as a restroom facility. Sporting no bruises or bloody wounds after his visit with Mr. Menard, Hunter walked quickly to his Corvette. Nicki started her car and then backed it under some low-hanging tree limbs, hoping the lush Spanish moss would conceal her identity. No need to reveal herself now since her first stakeout was a complete success. If Hunter looked in her direction, he would think it was just another abandoned car along the roadside, all too common in southern Louisiana.

The Corvette barreled down the driveway and turned onto the highway in a cloud of dust. While Nicki waited for him to disappear around the bend, she felt her rear car wheels shifting on the soft ground. Her heart sank too, as she imagined her compact swallowed up by a gaping black hole, the counterpart of quicksand in old TV Westerns. She scrambled out to assess the damage and sighed with relief. One wheel had sunk only a few inches. With any luck she wouldn't need a tow truck. Nicki got back in, shifted into low gear, and tried to pull forward. The car advanced a few inches and then stopped, spinning both rear tires now into a deeper indentation. She turned the wheel slightly to the left for an attempt and then to the right. Each time the car almost broke free but then slid back into the original rut. Nicki climbed out again and slammed the door.

"Need a little help there, missy?" asked a disembodied voice.

Startled, Nicki stepped back into a puddle of water, coating her sneakers with dark muck. She glared up into a familiar face. "Hunter Galen, what are you doing here?"

"I was about to ask you the same question, Miss Price. I had business in Terrebonne. Weren't you told to stay in New Orleans?"

"Well...yes, but I was afraid something bad might happen to you. Anyway, how did you know I was here? I saw you drive away without a glance in my direction."

"When you didn't jump back on my tail, I decided to see what happened." He sauntered into the tall weeds to where she stood, smelling spicy and fresh, totally contrary to the humid afternoon.

"Jump back on your tail?" Her first real accomplishment since barging into her cousin's office vanished. "When did you realize I was following you? When I turned off Highway 1 onto this road?"

Hunter's smile deepened his dimples. "It was a little before that...when I turned off Royale onto Canal."

Nicki slapped her open palm on the trunk of her car. "While we were still in the Quarter? You're not serious."

"I certainly wouldn't have driven that slow if I weren't trying to make it easy on you. My foot was cramping from hitting the brake so often." His laughter caused several birds to abandon their overhead perches. "But let's get you away from standing water. Have you forgotten what I told you about snakes in the swamp?" He reached out for her.

With her right foot still mired in the dank water she accepted his hand. The touch of his fingers sent her already heightened body temperature into triple digits. "There are speed limits in this state. But since you were noble enough to return for me, how about a push back to the driveway?"

Hunter inspected all four wheels and shook his head. "I can't believe you pulled this far off the road. You grew up in the Mississippi delta, not in upstate Idaho. If a car sits on soft ground, the wheels start to sink immediately. Everybody knows that."

Fighting the urge to scream, Nicki pasted a smile on her face. Hunter was her boss and she certainly needed him at the moment. "Thank you, Mr. Galen, for the timely reminder. But if you don't mind, could we do something before Mr. Menard decides to run to the market?"

"Let me do some snake-chasing first. You wait in the driver's seat." Hunter picked up a stout branch and then beat the weeds behind the car. Then he positioned both palms on the bumper, avoiding the rut of stagnant water. "All right, Nicki. Just give it a little gas when you shift into drive. I'm ready at this end."

She revved the engine, put it in gear, and pressed down on the accelerator. The wheels spun for a moment and then caught. The car lurched forward onto the Menard driveway. She offered a thumbs-up of sheer joy until she caught sight of Hunter in her rearview mirror. He approached her with a dark stripe of muck down his white polo shirt and tan chinos. Several strands of swamp grass clung to his clothes like accessories, while speckles of mud dotted his suntanned cheeks and nose.

He leaned in through the open passenger window. "Someday

over cold drinks, we'll discuss the difference between 'a little gas' and 'pedal to the floorboard.' But right now, why don't you drive me back to my car?" Without waiting for an answer he climbed in, careful not to touch her upholstery with his dirty hands.

Nicki handed him a pop-up container of wipes she kept beneath the seat. "I knew these would come in handy one day." He shot her an exasperated look, but he didn't yell or curse or display the reaction she'd come to expect from men.

"I'm really sorry, Hunter," she said softly. "I didn't spin my wheels on purpose."

"I know that. But to make up for ruining my shirt, you'll have to follow me to St. Martinville."

Nicki narrowed her gaze at him. "Isn't St. Martinville still in the Cajun parishes? That's definitely not my comfort zone. So if it's just the same, I'll head back to the city and start on those files."

"It's *not* just the same. You trailed me to protect me, right? So do your job, Miss Price. After I finished with Mr. Menard, I'd planned to head to my aunt's for a weekend party. Because there could be an assortment of desperadoes there, I may need you." He winked. Even coated with swamp mud, Hunter managed to look handsome.

But Nicki shook off her attraction to him. "No way, Jose. I'm not dressed for a Galen society affair. I brought only jeans and another T-shirt."

"Jeans will be fine, and if you don't come you're fired. Any more questions, Nicolette?" he asked, his face impossible to read.

"None whatsoever, but I'm still on the clock." She stopped next to his car on the berm of the highway.

"Understood." Hunter climbed out, taking the container of wipes with him.

Nicki held her breath until he got in his own car. Actually, she had plenty of questions about meeting more members of the

Galen family. Even if this wasn't a black-tie event, how would he explain *her* within days of breaking up with his fiancée? What if Ashley showed up in a desperate attempt to win him back? Nicki stewed all the way to St. Martinville.

The western part of the parish was still rural but didn't seem as remote as either the fishing camp she'd been lured to or the Menard place. Flocks of egrets and cranes filled the skies over crystal-blue lakes and waterways. The landscape appeared wider, more open, and less harsh as they neared the home of his aunt. Trying to picture the sister of Etienne Galen, Sr., Nicki imagined a tall, severe woman with an angular face and couture clothes. But instead a very round woman barely five feet tall with graying hair, cropped jeans, and a baggy shirt greeted them at the front door.

"Good grief! What happened to you, Hunter?" The woman scanned him from head to toe. Nicki had almost forgotten his appearance by the time they arrived at the rambling old farmhouse set far back from the road. A variety of vehicles were lined up in neat rows across the front lawn from battered pickups to conservative minivans.

"Hello, Aunt Donna. We had a little mishap along the way." Hunter stretched out his arms, but she avoided his hug.

"Let's postpone that for later." Instead, Aunt Donna immediately threw her meaty arm around Nicki and squeezed. "Why, it's 'bout time you came to our neck of the woods and got to know the rest of Hunter's kin."

"Thank you, ma'am. It's kind of you to welcome me since I'm just an employee of Mr. Galen's." Nicki gently extracted herself from the embrace.

"Are you on the job right now?" Donna's brow furrowed in confusion.

When Nicki glanced at Hunter, he stepped back and crossed his arms over his mud-spattered shirt. *No help from that quarter.*

"Yes, ma'am. I'm serving as his bodyguard today."

Donna broke into uproarious laughter. "Who are you protecting him from? His ill-mannered cousins during a volleyball game? From the looks of his shirt, the trouble was on your way here."

"It was nothing Miss Price couldn't handle." Hunter uncrossed his arms to pat her on the back like his favorite pet dog.

His aunt eyed her suspiciously. "Okay, as long as you promise not to shoot my sons, come on in." Grabbing them both by the arm, Donna pulled them into her crowded home. People of all ages and sizes were working industriously—dusting, cleaning shrimp at the kitchen sink, and paring potatoes in front of the TV, while a man on a stepladder replaced the screen in the patio door.

With hands perched on hips, Donna gestured toward her helpers. "Look around. We don't allow bad people here in St. Martin Parish. We make them stay in Orleans. Miss Price, you go on up to the guest room at the end of the hall. I see you've come for some fun." She pointed at the bag hanging from Nicki's shoulder. "My nephew has some explaining to do, but he'll holler up if he needs any emergency protection." Her laughter filled the already noisy room.

When Hunter was dragged to another part of the house, Nicki had no recourse but to climb the stairs and find the empty guest room. She washed her face and hands, brushed out her hair, and then settled in a rocking chair by an open window. Below on the wide expanse of lawn, teenagers streamed in and out of a barn carrying bags of ice and cases of soft drinks. An outdoor kitchen had been set up on the patio under a plastic canopy with several grills heaped with charcoal, while giant steamers rested on tripods above propane burners. Streamers, party lights, and balloons had been strung between the trees and from the house to the barn. Everyone she saw wore shorts and flip-flops, without a tie, dinner jacket, or uniformed waiter in sight. Watching the party come together, Nicki felt vaguely homesick despite the fact her family never entertained with this kind of energy.

"In case you're curious, my mother and grandmother won't be at tonight's festivities."

Nicki nearly hit the ceiling with surprise. "Don't sneak up on people like that!" she snapped before remembering her manners. She looked up to see Hunter leaning his shoulder against the door frame. Shaking her head, she tried to remember she was his guest and should behave accordingly. "I mean, I beg your pardon?"

"I said my mother and grandmother won't be attending this evening, although I'm sure they were invited. They came once in clothes bought for the occasion, which they never wore again." Hunter strolled across the room to the window. "But my sister may show up. Chloe loves to dance."

"There will be dancing tonight?" Nicki scrambled to her feet.

"Yup. We'll have a jazz-and-blues combo on the dock under the stars and real Cajun music in the barn. Something for everyone."

"I thought you said your family wasn't Cajun."

"We're not, but most of Aunt Donna's neighbors are. So you can count on plenty of good eats. And if you happen to hate steamed crawfish and spicy barbeque, at least you'll be 'on the clock.'" Hunter flopped down on the bed's colorful quilt and put his hands behind his head, apparently at ease anywhere in the house.

Nicki didn't share his calm tranquility. "Did your aunt ask about Ashley?" She lowered herself to the rocking chair again.

"She did."

Nicki waited a polite interval and then demanded, "Stop stalling. How did you explain the situation?"

"I told her the truth. Ashley and I parted ways because of irreconcilable differences."

"What did she say?" Nicki got up and paced the carpet like a caged animal, the temperature in the room growing oppressively warm.

"Will you stop worrying? My aunt said better now than after she shelled out for both a shower and wedding gift. Donna is rather frugal with her money."

Nicki watched for any sign he was teasing before releasing her breath with a *whoosh.* "That worked out well." She plopped down on the blanket chest.

Hunter swung his legs off the bed and stood. A moment later he was sitting next to her. "What are you afraid of, Nicki? Why do you think only bad things happen in life? It seems as though you're always waiting for the ax to fall."

"Is that how it appears? You could be right, but this isn't about me. I thought severing an engagement might cause problems in your family." His close proximity affected her in mysterious ways.

"Not for me. And I made sure Ashley didn't lose face with her friends. I have no desire to cause her pain. My family doesn't sit around questioning people's decisions. Even if I told Donna I broke up because another woman caught my eye, she wouldn't judge me harshly. Things like that happen in life." Hunter trailed a finger across her kneecap, the sensation tickling her funny bone.

"Stop that." Nicki slapped his hand away. "Don't you think you should take a shower, boss? That shirt is starting to smell."

He rose with the sleekness of a cat. "Good idea. You, Miss Price, will meet me in exactly twenty minutes on the boat dock. If you walk out the back door, someone will point you in the right direction."

"I saw it from my window. It's been strung with colored lights."

"Perfect. You and I are taking an airboat ride." Hunter headed for the door.

"I would prefer—"

He cut off her protest with a shake of his head. "No arguments and no excuses. This ain't *La Maison de Poisson* or growing up back home with Nate. My relatives don't drill holes in pirogues and fill them with putty. You are safe with my family, just like I'm safe with you as my bodyguard. Agreed?"

She hated the thought of going deeper into the bayou but then remembered Jeanette's words: *You know what they say about opportunities, O'lette.* "Very well. I'm placing my life in your hands."

"Splendid. We won't go far. I wouldn't want to miss the dinner bell." He disappeared down the hallway without a backward glance.

Nicki focused on the motionless waterway beyond Donna's sloping backyard. Her boss wanted her to return to the swamp, where she'd spent the worst night of her life. Yet somehow she felt safe with him. Hunter carried no weapons and was only average-sized at best, yet he possessed more confidence than Goliath with a grenade launcher.

Nicki had two choices. She could stay on dry ground and look like a coward, undeserving of his trust and the generous paycheck she was paid, or she could take her courage in both hands, swallow a few antacids, and show up ready to do her job. She yearned for Hunter's approval, something she'd never sought from a man in her life. Her chance for a future with him might be one notch above none, but she wanted that one chance.

Grabbing her overnight bag, Nicki headed for the bathroom ready to face the swamp monsters head-on. Twenty minutes later, she was clinging to the seat of an airboat as it rocketed across a wide expanse of water. Hunter opened the engine to full throttle, making conversation, sightseeing, or anything other than hanging on for dear life impossible. But once they had turned down a narrow waterway and he slowed to a gentler pace, Nicki settled back to watch the passing scenery.

Life was abundant in the watery landscape. Hawks and vultures soared on air currents, ducks and geese bobbed on waves, and egrets and great blue herons fished in the shallows close to shore. Uncountable species of insects darted above the water, while fish, snakes, and nutria lurked unseen. Only an occasional ripple revealed their furtive movements beneath the surface. Thick vegetation encroached from all sides. Trumpet vines filled with orange blooms and purple morning glories hung from the overhead canopy. Cupping her hands, Nicki scooped up some water to inspect. Three types of plant life floated in her palms.

Hunter leaned over her shoulder to see. "Looks like duck weed, invasive Slovenia, and floating lettuce. But do me a favor and keep your hands in the boat. Gators live in this bayou, and I would hate for one to spoil the party with his afternoon snack. If you lose a finger or hand, I'll never get you back to my favorite place on earth."

"I fear creepy men with shotguns more than alligators, but I'll keep my hands out of the water. What are those flowers?" Nicki pointed at clumps of floating blooms.

"Those are invasive water hyacinths. Think of them as kudzu on the water. They fill the canals, depleting the oxygen and killing the fish. They form such thick mats that fishermen have become tangled up and drowned after falling overboard. Pretty but deadly, just like all females." Hunter pulled down his sunglasses and winked.

"In that case, put on your life jacket, boss. We're all alone out here." Nicki closed her eyes and breathed deeply. The humid air felt cooler than it was at the house and smelled sweeter than at the fishing camp. The drone of insects and birdsong lulled her into drowsiness as they cruised up and down coves and inlets. Around every corner lay another discovery in the ageless, unpredictable ecosystem.

"Quick, Nicki. Look there."

Turning her head, she saw six box turtles uniformly spaced on a fallen cypress log, contentedly sunning their shells in the dappled light. "Someone ought to warn them about deadly UVA and UVB rays. They can be so aging to reptile skin."

"And they thought they only had hungry gators to contend with." Hunter eased up on the throttle.

Ten minutes later a majestic bald eagle soared over a wide stretch of bayou, waiting for lunch to approach the surface. The patient eagle soon carried off a writhing fish to its fate. "Our timing couldn't have been better with that nature show," Nicki whispered with reverential awe.

"What do you think about the swamp now that you're not being chased, shot at, half drowned, or stranded overnight in a falling-down shack?" Hunter asked with a smile.

"There is beauty here, no doubt about it, but it's hard for me to relax." Nicki pulled on a handful of bull rushes as they drooped over the boat. "Something bad happened in the bayou to someone I loved. It was long ago, but I can't forget it." She stared down into the dark water.

Hunter killed the engine and let the airboat drift with the current. "Care to talk about it? Maybe it would help."

"I don't think so, but I might as well finish what I started." Nicki raked her fingers through her hair, working out some windblown tangles while she contemplated how much to reveal. "My father died after a poker game in a trapper's shack. He told my mother and me he would be hunting and fishing for the weekend. Apparently, someone accused my dad of cheating at cards and followed him out to the water. Nobody knew exactly how far the argument went or what happened to my dad, but he disappeared that night, and two days later everyone went home to their families as if it never happened. A fisherman found his body days later, but gators had eaten most of him for dinner. By the time the sheriff got word to my mother, she was sick with worry." Nicki arched her back against the metal seat. "Mom hasn't been the same since. He may not have been a good dad, but he was the only one I had. Now when I'm near a swamp I think about those men throwing him in like nothing more than roadkill."

They both sat quietly, watching mist rise among the cypress knees. Then Nicki made a serious mistake. She looked into Hunter's face and found it filled with compassion, not pity, and love...or the closest she had ever come to love.

"I'm sorry you experienced such tragedy so young." He wrapped a strong arm around her shoulders. "I would pay any price to wipe away that memory."

When Hunter pulled her into his arms, Nicki lost her fragile semblance of control. She cried for her dead father and for the lost innocence of childhood. She sobbed into his shirt, and when she finally stopped crying, she realized he'd been right. She did feel better.

Hunter kissed her forehead, her nose, and hovered above her lips until she thought she would lose her mind. Then he kissed her with passion she'd never experienced in Natchez or anywhere else. For a few moments, Nicki forgot he was her employer and he had just broken up with his fiancée, and that some people thought him a murderer. She enjoyed feeling desirable for the first time in her life.

"Whew." She pulled away from him long moments later and scooted across the seat. "That's enough sad stories and the mischief they apparently inspire. Today I was officially invited to a Galen party and I don't plan to mess this up. Your little tour of the swamp worked wonders, but please take me back to your Aunt Donna's. I want to wash my face, comb my hair, and put on my party shoes. I plan to dance the night away."

"That's what I like to hear!" Hunter opened the controls to full throttle and the airboat roared to life.

Nicki clung to her seat, but for a change she wasn't afraid. Instead, she hoped this night in the bayou—her formerly least-favorite place on earth—would never end.

# TWENTY-EIGHT

*H*unter sipped lemonade as he tried to listen to his cousins' tales of victory on the gridiron or the baseball diamond. He asked appropriate questions at the appropriate time, but his mind kept wandering back to Nicki and her grim tale of backwoods violence. He had read about such things in local papers, but he never met the victim of such an ignorant, senseless crime.

Of course, he'd never met anyone quite like Nicolette Price before. What you saw was what you got. She wasn't one to soften the rough edges to preserve her image. It was no myth that many Southern women ate before going out to preserve the impression they ate like sparrows. It was also true many women put on makeup to weed the garden. But image was the least of Nicki's concerns. Hunter found her honesty and lack of artifice almost as appealing as her great legs and stunning smile.

He glanced back at the house for the tenth time. *What is taking her so long to change and brush her hair?* Just when he decided to break down the guest room door, he spotted her carrying a platter of meat out to the grill with Aunt Donna on her heels with bowls of potato salad. So like Donna to commandeer any passerby and put them to work. And so like Nicki to pitch in and help without being asked.

Ashley would have sweetly agreed but then grumbled end-lessly to her friends later. Funny how he didn't miss her. Hunter felt only a sense of relief, as though he had dodged a bullet, but he also knew this was all his fault. Ashley may have connived and manipulated, but he hadn't been oblivious to what was happen-ing. He went willingly down the path to matrimony—a good match, *Grandmère* had called it—two families of equal social standing united to preserve wealth for future generations. Ugh. No matter how times changed, some things stayed the same.

Hunter excused himself from the conversation about the LSU Tigers and tracked Nicki back to the kitchen. In acid-washed jeans and a mint-green top, with her hair caught in a butterfly clip, she looked gorgeous. "I'm looking for my favorite employee," he announced, stepping through the doorway. "I need to make sure she's not napping in the hayloft."

"Hi, Hunter. Your aunt found me first." Nicki's brown eyes sparkled, and her cheeks still glowed from the afternoon boat ride.

Donna gave him a sly wink. "Go on, Nicki. You've helped enough to earn your supper. Time for you to guard my nephew's body." She pushed Nicki toward the door, while her kitchen help-ers hooted uproariously.

"Well...if you're sure you don't need me." Nicki laid her apron on the counter and followed Hunter outside.

"Aunt Donna does stand-up comedy on open-mike night in Lafayette," he murmured under his breath.

"I would love to go some time."

"Hey, Hunter." Donna called through the kitchen window. "I don't know what the last one was like, but this one's a keeper."

Nicki blushed a little. "Wow, she's really nice. Can I have her?"

"Maybe someday I'll share."

Nicki's cheeks turned an even brighter pink. "Hunter, I didn't mean to imply—"

"I know you didn't. Will you please relax? I want you to take one evening off from worrying." He reached for her hand. "Tomorrow global warming, famine in sub-Saharan Africa, the devaluation of the yen, and world peace can be your concern, but tonight I want you to just have a good time."

Suddenly a horde of people converged from the parking area. The new arrivals carried covered casseroles and coolers of cold drinks, while their kids ran toward tree swings and yard games with boundless energy. "Was anyone who lives in a thirty-mile radius not invited?" she asked. "Considering the grills, steamers, and what's being baked in the kitchen, there will be enough food to feed the whole parish."

"I believe Donna excluded a few atheists. She has a hard time dealing with them. But don't change the subject. What about my proposition?"

"All right, you have a deal. For one night I promise not to worry about anything—past, present, or future."

"With that settled, would you like to dance?" Hunter bowed from the waist. The first twangs from guitars and fiddles drifted on the air as musicians tuned their instruments.

"Not yet. Let's eat before we dance. I'm starving."

"Dinner it is. Lead the way, but be prepared for anything."

Nicki slipped into the buffet line oblivious that the queue wrapped around the garden shed. When Hunter fell in behind her, a burly neighbor took exception.

"No cuts, Galen. You need to get yourself to the end of the line, but the pretty woman can stay."

"It's okay." Nicki dipped one shoulder seductively and batted her lashes. "He's with me."

The man hooted and swept the ball cap from his shaved head. "Anything you say, darlin'."

Nicki smiled at the neighbor's wife, picked up two plates, and handed Hunter one. "Better stay close," she warned. "This looks like an ornery crowd to me."

"And they're still sober as judges," Hunter whispered in her ear. "Bringing a bodyguard wasn't a bad idea."

They loaded grilled chicken, *boudin*, corn on the cob, and squares of cornbread onto their plates. When Nicki looked at his selections, she shook her head. "I suggest you eat heartier than that, boss. You and I will be dancing till dawn."

"Have no fear. The best is yet to come." At the end of the line one of Donna's helpers hung a plastic bucket brimming with steamed shrimp and crawfish over Hunter's arm and offered another one to Nicki. Butter melting over the contents mingled with the pungent broth.

She shook her head. "None for me. I'll sample some of his and come back if we need more."

Hunter found them a table in the shade and went for soft drinks. By the time he got back, children had surrounded Nicki. Apparently, she had asked how to eat crawfish and ended up with several young volunteers eager to demonstrate.

Hunter watched her savor both the food and the children's attention. No picking listlessly at a broiled fish filet. No large green salad sans dressing. Nicki stirred hot sauce into her coleslaw, coated her corn with butter, and licked shrimp seasoning from her fingers. She ate everything on her plate and then sent a precocious eight-year-old to fetch a brownie.

"I'm surprised a Mississippi delta girl didn't know how to eat crawdads." He waited until all of the kids left to raid the dessert table.

"Oh, I knew, but I saw them studying me when I sat down. I thought it would be a good way to make new friends."

"Worked like a charm." Hunter sopped up the last of his red beans and rice with a piece of cornbread.

"These definitely were some great vittles," she said, tapping her finger on her chin. "Or should I say the Galen cuisine was superb as usual? And no one seems to care that I'm here, or that you had the shortest engagement in recorded history."

"I told you they wouldn't."

Nicki glanced at him with a huge smile and glowing eyes. "Ready to retire to the party barn and do some dancin'?"

"Fill in your dance card with nothing but my name, missy." Hunter cleared their plates and then offered his elbow.

But instead she took hold of his hand. "This is only for your protection. There could be troublemakers inside." She nodded toward the barn, where people milled in the open doorway and yellow light streamed from the upper story windows.

"I've never felt safer facing a horde of rowdy relatives."

They squeezed inside and found standing room by a support beam. Hunter stood behind her and put his arms around her shoulders. The upbeat Cajun tempo soon got their toes tapping. Dancers of all ages whirled around the floor.

"I take it no farm animals live in here between your aunt's parties." Nicki pointed at the polished hardwood floor.

"Not for the last hundred years, *O'lette.*" Hunter rested his chin on the top of her head, inhaling the raspberry fragrance of her shampoo. "I like the name Jeanette called you. I'm going to use it from now on."

"Tonight you can call me anything you want. I just hope the veterans don't trample novices into the sawdust." Her focus was on the dance floor, where everyone two-stepped around the room at a brisk pace. "I believe I'm ready to give it a try. If I procrastinate too long, I'll stay a wallflower all night." Nicki pulled him into the stream of dancers.

"We have nothing to fear but fear itself." Hunter put a hand at the small of her back, grabbed her other hand, and led the best two-step of his life. At times they squashed each other's feet and bumped into other dancers, but they soon got the hang of it. They ended up dancing for hours and laughing almost as long. Hunter had never enjoyed himself so much.

Finally the tempo slowed as the lead singer wailed a mournful ballad. Hunter drew Nicki into his arms, holding her close to his chest.

"Any idea what the song is about?" she asked. "I forgot my French dictionary again, but he sounds so miserable I'm ready to cry."

"I'm not fluent like the rest of my family, but I believe the singer is brokenhearted because his lady won't take him seriously. She treats him like any other work cohort."

"Is that right?" Nicki glanced back at the middle-aged Cajun crooning into the microphone. "Funny how personal problems sound more interesting in another language."

"You mock the singer's distress?" Hunter picked her up and swung her around in a circle.

"Put me down! If my feet knock someone unconscious, I'll end up having to flee for my life."

"You broke your promise." Hunter set her down on the floor.

"And what promise would that be?" She turned her face up.

"You weren't supposed to worry about anything tonight."

"True, but I'm not really worried about knocking someone out. And I wasn't mocking that French guy, even though I doubt that's what he was saying." As the song ended and another fast tune began, dancers entering the dance floor jostled them from all sides.

"Let's get some fresh air," Hunter said over the music.

"Good idea." Nicki led the way through the crowd. "Do you know all of these people?"

"Nope, but there's only one person I'd like to know better right now." Hunter hoped that didn't sound as idiotic to her as it did to him. His well of smooth things to say had unfortunately run dry.

They walked to the weathered boat dock, where a teenaged couple stood hand in hand. When they approached, the young pair slipped down a path known only to them. Hunter took hold of Nicki's hand, afraid she might bolt as well. Before them, the wide bayou stretched dark and mysterious. Moonlight reflected off the glassy surface, and the ever-present mist hung close to the shoreline.

"Look there." Hunter pointed at an alligator swimming less than fifteen feet from the shore. The tip of his snout and bulging eyes moved soundlessly through the water. Dragonflies fearlessly skittered in and out of his path.

Nicki craned her neck. "Now I understand why people don't swim in the bayou."

"Does the sight of them upset you?" Hunter kissed the back of her fingers as the ancient creature glided away to its nest.

"Not really. It was a man who killed my dad, not an animal. Only humans are capable of unmitigated cruelty. The gator does only what comes naturally. Do you suppose that was a male or female?"

"You and I aren't able to tell, but somehow gators seem to know." Hunter lifted his eyebrows.

"Do you think some have a particularly curvaceous arrangement of scales?"

"Mother Nature has methods to make sure creatures find the perfect mate." Hunter wrapped an arm around her waist.

Nicki turned within his embrace. "I believe in God's handiwork, not some green lady on TV commercials invented by an ad agency. And I do take you seriously, Hunter. You're not just a work cohort to me."

Her sincerity melted his heart. He leaned in for a kiss, but she placed her finger on his lips.

"Listen. Do you hear that?"

Hunter cocked his head but heard nothing but music from the barn and kids playing hide-and-seek. "Nope."

"*Shhh.* Close your eyes and listen."

Hunter complied and soon heard a cacophony of chirps, hoots, croaks, and the drone of a million insects beating their wings. "I'll bet you didn't expect it to be so noisy."

"Noisy, yes, but the swamp is growing on me. I never thought I would say that." A smile turned up the corners of her mouth. "In Natchez the heat and humidity feel oppressive, but here it somehow feels nurturing, like being in a protective womb."

Hunter laughed. "As long as you're wearing Eau de Bayou. That's what country folk call insect repellant."

"Bugs don't bother me. Your aunt's home is so beautiful."

"More so this weekend than I'd noticed in the past." Hunter bent his head and kissed her. When she didn't pull away, he kissed her again—longer, slower, deeper.

"You think I'm beautiful?" she asked a little breathlessly when the kiss ended.

"Absolutely. You think I would smooch with just anybody?" He ran his fingertips down her cheek.

"I'm nothing like Ashley. Your former fiancée is so...sophisticated, whereas I've been known to wear white shoes after Labor Day, eat with the wrong fork, and buy my underwear in multipacks."

Hunter clutched his chest. "No kidding? I buy my underwear in multipacks too. It sounds like we're perfect for each other."

Nicki focused under the trees, where two armadillos foraged for discarded food scraps in the growing darkness. "We're hardly perfect and you know it." Her voice was the barest whisper.

He turned her face with one finger, their mouths inches apart. "We're as perfect as you let us be, *O'lette*. It's up to you. There is no Ashley anymore. It's just you and me, if you find me remotely tolerable." He wanted to kiss her again more than draw his next breath of air, but he didn't want to scare her off.

"I almost slipped up and worried about the future," she said, and then she pressed her soft lips to his.

Hunter pulled her close and kissed her as though this was their last night on earth. He wouldn't worry either, not about rebound relationships, professional decorum, or anything else. He knew what he wanted, and it was Nicki.

After several exquisite minutes, she stepped back and cleared her throat. "Wow, must be something in the air tonight."

"Are you ready to do more dancing? We could try the blues combo on the fishing dock."

"Although the spirit is willing, my legs and feet are not. I'm exhausted. Could you walk me to the house?" She hooked her arm through his.

"I had a feeling the dancing-till-dawn promise was a smoke screen."

They quietly slipped into the laundry room and headed up the stairs. None of his family remained in the kitchen washing dishes or refilling ice buckets.

Nicki paused at the top of the steps. "I don't remember which room your aunt assigned me. All of the closed doors look the same."

"Probably that one." Hunter pointed at the last room on the left.

"Do you think people are already asleep?" she asked as they tip-toed down the hall. "The house seems too quiet considering the constant chaos all day long."

"Some certainly are. Everyone is welcome at parties in the bayou, from newborn babies to age one hundred and five. No adult receptions, none of those show-your-invitation-at-the-door events. Guests eat and sleep, arrive and depart on their own schedules."

"What about the atheists?" she whispered.

"I believe I spotted a pair near the punch bowl. Donna must be softening up." Hunter leaned over and kissed her.

Suddenly three teenaged girls came loudly up the steps and invaded their private world. Nicki pushed Hunter away as he scowled at the trio. "Settle down, you hooligans."

"Hey, cousin, what's happening?" asked a girl Nicki remembered as Adeline. Her friends broke into a fit of giggles as they piled into the opposite room.

Rolling his eyes, Hunter tried to pick up where he'd left off, but the fragile moment had been lost. Nicki patted down her clothes and hair, which hadn't been remotely mussed.

"Don't worry, your reputation is safe. They won't tell anybody about us. They're Galens." Hunter reached behind her and turned the doorknob of her room.

Nicki raised her hands to fend him off, holding her ground like a statue. "That's enough kissing. Lock your door, say your prayers, and hope for the best. I'm off duty and so tired I wouldn't hear if giants storm the place."

"Good night, *O'lette*. I'll see you at breakfast." He kissed her forehead and started down the hallway.

"Hunter? Thank you."

"For what?" He whispered in case the teenagers were listening.

"For not being mad when I followed you, for bringing me to the party, and for being so nice."

She looked so earnest he thought his heart would break. "You're an easy person to be nice to, Miss Price."

After she smiled sweetly at him and then closed her door, Hunter walked to the second-floor screened porch where he would sleep. One of his cousins from Lafayette was already snoring up a storm. Hunter thought he would toss and turn for hours about whether he should date Nicki this soon after his breakup. Stripping to his boxers, he stretched out on the metal twin bed and listened to night sounds in the swamp. An hour or two later the music and revelry dwindled in the barn. Car doors slammed and friends called good night, leaving only the mercury vapor light emitting a low, steady hum.

Hunter felt oddly content despite the fact a murderer was still at large and Philip had issued a serious ultimatum. Nicki thought he was a great guy.

He shut his eyes and slept like a baby.

# TWENTY-NINE

Nicki parted ways with Hunter after an early breakfast Sunday morning, saying she needed to visit kinfolk.

Despite her aversion to watery environs, she wanted to drive straight to the cabin formerly owned by her Uncle Charles, now owned by her Uncle Andre, though not because she thought evidence overlooked by trained deputies and forensic experts seventeen years ago still existed under a palmetto frond. For the sake of needed closure, Nicki wanted to see firsthand the place her father had dealt his last hand of marked cards, but her acute survival instinct soon kicked in. She knew approaching a trapper's cabin unannounced and uninvited wouldn't be a good idea, so she called her mother for Andre and Rita Martin's home address and plotted her course for the fastest route.

She'd lost touch with this particular aunt and uncle over the years, the cost of stamps and the expansive list of Price and Martin relatives limiting her Christmas card list. Her mother hadn't talked to her brother in months over some sibling disagreement as to whose turn it was to spring for a tank of gas. Uncle Andre lived in Louisiana—West Feliciana Parish, to be exact. His house wasn't in the expansive Atchafalaya River basin, but at least it was closer to New Orleans than Natchez. After all, Nicki had her own tank of gas to worry about. She wouldn't be on Hunter Galen's expense account for this pleasurable country drive.

Although Nicki had called ahead and left a message on their answering machine, the Martins didn't seem overjoyed to see Rose's only daughter.

"Would you like to come in?" Aunt Rita asked after uncomfortable moments of hesitation at the front door.

"Yes, ma'am, I would. Mama sends her love to you both." Nicki handed her a tin of cookies she'd bought at a drug store along the interstate. *Add six bucks for shortbread to the price of a tank of gas.*

"Your message said you needed to talk to Andre. He'll be right down. He was cutting grass after Mass this mornin' and needed another shower if we were having company." Rita pointed out the window at the freshly mown lawn. "Your uncle sets great store by his yard."

"I noticed how nice it looked when I drove up." Nicki hoped her little white lie didn't set a precedent for the afternoon.

"Why don't you sit on the couch?" Rita perched on the edge of a chair. "The last time we talked to Rose she said you were in school, some kind of police academy." Her aunt seemed to search for appropriate topics of chitchat.

"Yes, ma'am. I recently graduated as a licensed private investigator." Nicki glanced toward the stairs, hoping Uncle Andre didn't indulge in long showers. "I work for Nate in New Orleans now."

"Oh, my...New Orleans," she drawled. "Did Charlotte's boy ever get married? So good looking, that one, and such a charmer! I had hoped to fix Nate up with my hairdresser's girl, Corrine."

Usually Nicki wouldn't agree with Rita's such-a-charmer assessment regarding her cousin Nate, but as her uncle padded barefoot into the room, she nodded her head politely. "He's single, so there's still hope for Corrine."

"What's this about, Nicolette?" Andre didn't waste time with pleasantries. "Rose called me and said you wanted to know 'bout the night your dad disappeared."

"Good to see you again, Uncle Andre. Yes, I'd like to ask you a few questions if you don't mind." Nicki scooted to the edge of the low sofa.

"What for? That was twenty years ago."

"Seventeen, to be exact. I'm just curious as to how my father died." She placed special emphasis on the word "father."

Andre muttered a vulgar word with a scowl. "Your *father* wasn't worth half a minute of your time, niece."

Aunt Rita scrambled to her feet. "Why don't I get us some iced tea?" She bolted from the room before anyone could respond yea or nay.

"You're certainly entitled to an opinion, but he was my dad." Nicki struggled to control her temper.

"Yeah, I get that, but Kermit was no good." Andre lifted his chin, as though he had a God-given right to judge his fellow man.

"Be that as it may—"

He didn't allow her to finish. "Don't go pokin' around in things you don't understand. Let the past stay buried."

"I have a right to make my own decisions, Uncle Andre."

"Kermit may have had a soft spot for you, but he beat your mama, Nicki. He beat Rose for no reason a'tal because he was a mean drunk. What's more, he was dealin' from the bottom of the deck that night in the swamp. Kermit tried to win big by cheatin' those fellas from Clay Creek."

"I saw the coroner's report." Nicki jumped up, no longer concerned about her temper. "My father was shot and dumped in the bayou. Even if he was a wife beater and cheat, he didn't deserve that."

Aunt Rita flinched as she returned with a tray of drinks. "Anyone ready for something cool?"

Andre ignored the suggestion. "I was there, young lady. If there had been gunfire, I would have heard it. Your daddy got mad because he got caught in a crooked game. That's why he took the pirogue out. If Kermit got himself murdered, it was someplace else. He probably paddled to the next bar down the bayou."

"No shots?" Nicki glanced over at her poor aunt, standing there with full tray. She took a glass of tea and turned her attention back on her uncle.

"None, and believe me, Eugene and Charles and me were listening. We had a bad feelin' from the minute those Cheval brothers showed up. We heard nothing when Terrence and Junior followed Kermit outside. Pretty soon Junior strolled back inside. He said he'd had it out with Kermit and your dad took off in the pirogue. Junior told Terrence to go after Kermit and get back what he stole, but Terrence came back not fifteen minutes later soaking wet. The older of Charles's pirogues had a leak. Terrence was furious but couldn't do a thing about it. We all went to bed soon after that."

"Was my dad wearing his alligator belt that night—the one with the two cowgirls carved on the buckle?" Nicki took a long sip of weak tea.

Andre's forehead furrowed as he thought a moment. "I 'spose he was. He always wore that belt to play cards. Don't know why he loved it so much. Kermit never went to a Texas ranch or saw a real cowgirl in his life."

Nicki set the glass on an end table. "When they found my dad's body in St. Martin Parish, they didn't see the belt, even though he still had most of his clothes."

"Nobody came back into the cabin wearing it if that's what you're getting at." Andre narrowed his eyes. "The sheriff searched the place. There was no belt, no wad of cash, and no gun that had been recently fired."

"Just the same, I'd like to drive out to the cabin. You can come with me or I'll go alone. Just point me in the right direction."

Andre tossed a lock of graying hair off his forehead. "I'd be happy to oblige, niece, but that cabin is long gone. That last hurricane sent a surge up the Atchafalaya, and those old piers just gave way. I drove there when the floodwater went down, and nothing was left but splintered posts and busted furniture caught in a logjam downriver. I got a letter from the government saying I had to clean up the debris or pay a fine. My insurance covered the cleanup, but there wasn't enough money to rebuild. You won't find Kermit's belt or anything else where that cabin used to be."

Nicki peered out the window and saw neighborhood children kicking a ball down the street. "I appreciate the information." She offered her aunt a warm smile. "Thanks for the iced tea, Aunt Rita. I hope to see you at the holidays if not sooner. Let's stay in touch."

Eager to be on her way back to New Orleans, Nicki fled from her aunt and uncle. The walls of their modest home had started to close in on her. She was still determined to find the answers she sought, but she knew now they wouldn't be coming from Uncle Andre or his cabin on the Atchafalaya.

# THIRTY

*T*he air was stale, dead ficus leaves littered the carpet, and a faint odor of something spoiled drifted from the refrigerator. Nicki had never been in a dead man's apartment before. When Hunter had called that morning, she'd been daydreaming about the best weekend of her life—friendly people, delicious food, dancing under the stars with the world's most attractive man, all in the wild Louisiana bayou. Who would have figured?

Funny how love changed your outlook on everything.

Falling in love with Hunter would doubtlessly be a mistake, but she couldn't seem to stop herself. He'd been so attentive, so gentle. She would gladly listen to his slow drawl for the rest of her life. And then there was that high-octane kiss that sent every nerve-ending on red alert. She felt so safe and protected with him, even without her new nine millimeter Beretta.

*Something bad is just around the next corner.*

*The ax is about to fall.*

*Don't get too comfortable because disappointment is just a stone's throw away.*

Those were the maxims her mother had taught her. This was how Nicki lived her life until coming to New Orleans.

Hunter had changed everything. Hunter Galen—the man

Detective Saville thought was a murderer. The man James Nowak thought was a cash cow in his self-enriching scheme. The man Ashley Menard now thought was a sewer rat.

In St. Martinville, Nicki had glimpsed a life she yearned to be part of. His aunt's house wasn't flashy like the French Quarter apartment or elegant like his brother's mansion. It was warm, friendly, and relaxed. His relatives had welcomed her despite the fact the last they heard he was engaged to someone else. Memories of his passionate kisses on the boat dock would carry her through her golden years, but was she striving for the impossible? She certainly didn't want to be a mere amusement to help him recover from his breakup with Ashley. Nicki tried not to think about how many society girls were waiting for their chance at bat.

*"What you got goin' for you, Nicki? A dead shot with a squirrel rifle?"*

*"Rich people—they marry their own kind."*

*"Old lady Galen ain't inviting you to no tea party in the Garden District."*

Detective Saville's words had stung, cutting her right to the bone. They still brought a flush of shame to her cheeks days later, but she tried to take comfort in the thought that because Saville was wrong about Hunter, maybe his romantic prognostications couldn't be trusted either.

Unfortunately, now that she was with him in Nowak's condo, Hunter was all business. "We're missing something, Nicki, something not on the office computer or his laptop," he said. "James's parents gave me permission to look at everything, so let's get started."

Nicki peered around the forlorn room. "What more do we need than the computer files of his scams and the phony statements? We already have a complete picture of Nowak's creative accounting system."

"I don't know, but there has to be more. I'll take the bedroom." Hunter flexed his fingers. "Why don't you start with his desk?"

"You got it, boss."

It didn't take long before she uncovered something unexpected and something she knew Hunter wouldn't like. Nowak recorded in his checkbook register the source of every deposit to his account. He listed notations such as "April commission check" or "parents' birthday gift" or "expense reimbursement." Nicki supposed it had made yearly income tax preparation that much easier.

It also made it easy to spot a series of deposits from Ashley. Why would she have given James a thousand dollars a month for the past year? Perhaps James had loaned Ashley money to buy a car or pay off an expensive credit card debt and she was simply paying him back. Then again, why wouldn't she go to Hunter or her father for the loan or the old-fashioned route—a bank? Nicki rubbed the bridge of her nose and then massaged her temples. She decided to keep looking and not run to Hunter with the information quite yet

James's parents had given Hunter the key to his home safe, so a few moments later Nicki had the contents spread out in front of her on the dining room table. After perusing several contracts, an alarming picture began to emerge. If these documents were to be believed, James hadn't worked alone in his quest to separate clients from their money.

Hunter's masculine scrawl, complete with a flourish on the final *n*, was on every major financial transaction for the past two years. She recognized the signature from their contract and her recent paycheck. Either the man monopolizing her dreams was a liar and a thief, or James was also a world-class forger.

Nicki was praying for the latter when the doorbell rang. Hunter emerged from the den and opened the door to a middle-aged couple with weary faces and the body language of the defeated. She knew who they were without introductions. Mr. and Mrs. Nowak walked into their son's townhouse looking as though they hadn't enjoyed a decent night's sleep in weeks. She rose from the table to greet them.

"Nicki, these are James's parents, Elizabeth and Stephen Nowak." Hunter shook hands with James's dad. "Mr. and Mrs. Nowak, this is my investigator, Nicolette Price."

"Good morning," she murmured, stepping forward. "I'm truly sorry for your loss."

Mrs. Nowak accepted her hand but didn't meet her eye. "Thank you, Miss Price." An uncomfortable silence ensued.

"Thank you again for allowing me access into your son's private life. Would you care to sit down?" Hunter gestured toward the sofa.

Mr. Nowak shook his head and crossed his arms over his chest. "We want his killer caught, Hunter. The longer the police focus on you, the longer his killer gets away with it."

The man looked tired but sounded angry. Nicki remembered Hunter mentioning James was their only child.

"There's something else. Our son had recently retained legal council. He knew he was being investigated for securities violations. He said these check-ups were routine and assured us he had done nothing wrong, but he didn't want to worry *you* unnecessarily." Looking uncomfortable, Mr. Nowak withdrew a packet from an inside pocket. "According to these papers, he was about to be indicted for fraud and other...crimes. We don't understand how this happened. How did things get so out of control?" Mr. Nowak looked to Hunter for an explanation, as though all they were going through was due to some grievous misunderstanding.

Hunter scanned the three-page document and turned back to the couple, his posture sagging. "Miss Price and I are still piecing together what James was involved in. Whatever it was, he didn't deserve to die. We will bring his killer to justice." He passed her the packet of papers.

Mrs. Nowak began to sob, her face twisting in anguish. "I want this nightmare to end so James can rest in peace. I hate what the newspapers are saying about him, that he was some kind of flimflam man. I hope my son's name will be cleared once this is over." She looked at each of them in succession and then hurried toward the door, tears streaming down her face.

"Let us know if we can do anything else." Mr. Nowak followed his wife. They obviously couldn't wait to leave the dismal place.

Nicki sorrowfully watched them go. Their son *was* a thief, but how did you tell parents that? Mrs. Nowak didn't see the damaged man. She remembered a little boy who picked bouquets of dandelions for her on Mother's Day.

"This doesn't look good," she said softly.

"He had to know his house of cards would come tumbling down eventually." Hunter spoke with little emotion.

"I don't mean for James. I mean for you."

He stared at her. "What are you talking about?"

She sighed heavily. "Your signature is on all currency transfers, Hunter. Your name appears as often as Nowak's on every financial transaction."

"That's impossible!" He pulled the papers from her fingers and perused them for less than a minute. "He forged my name, Nicki," he said with less vehemence. "I assure you I wasn't part of this. I had no idea what he was up to. No doubt I should have, but I didn't." He tossed them down on the coffee table.

"The signature looks *exactly* like the one on my last paycheck. Maybe homicide doesn't have enough to indict you for murder, but there's plenty of evidence linking you to Nowak's fraud. Federal investigators have access to these buy and sell orders."

Hunter stared at her without blinking. "I don't care what it looks like. I *didn't* sign those contracts."

"I don't think you're grasping the seriousness of this, Hunter. It's not *me* you need to convince," Nicki said, trying to soften her tone.

"What are my chances of avoiding prison when I can't even convince the woman trying to clear my name?" Hunter shook his head. "Let's pack this stuff up and get out of here. We can work at my apartment." He began inserting the papers into an already bulging briefcase.

Nicki had a bad feeling in her gut. All the wonderful moments they shared in St. Martinville evaporated like fog in sunlight. Hunter was everything she wanted in a man, everything she needed. He made her feel feminine and desirable, besides having faith in her ability as a PI. Yet every time they were together, she stuck her size-eight foot in her mouth.

"I'm on your side, boss, but we need to act fast before your reputation gets tarnished." Nicki followed him out the door, as usual voicing whatever came to mind. "People invest money in your company because of who you are. Innocent until proven guilty sounds nice in the movies, but the real world operates differently. Even if the feds don't indict you, any hint of scandal could ruin you forever. What's more, any connection to the scam could give Detective Saville what he wants—a motive to arrest you."

Hunter stopped midway down the steps. "You have my attention. What do you think we should do?"

She hesitated only a moment before answering. "If you examine the facts, all roads lead to Ashley." Nicki saw his expression of incredulity but forged ahead. It was now or never. "First, Nowak ripped off her father's investment account for a ton of money. And second, Ashley paid Nowak thousands of dollars during the past year. Maybe there's a logical explanation for this, but I found proof she paid it."

He shook his head, sighing deeply. "If there is a logical reason, I'm not aware of it."

"I'm sorry, Hunter, but this smells like blackmail from where I come from in Mississippi."

"That sounds like motive down here in Louisiana too," he said, but his expression revealed little joy in the supposition.

"Maybe Nowak demanded more money or maybe she got tired of paying it. Or maybe something was going on between them, and Ashley decided to end it. A bullet between the eyes is a handy way of removing a thorn from your foot."

"No way, Nicki." Hunter went down the rest of the steps with her at his heels. "Ashley hates squishing a bug with her shoe. Besides, she was on the *Queen Antoinette* at the time of his murder."

"Maybe if Nowak broke off with her—"

Hunter turned to face her. "Hold up there. Instead of spinning this into a daytime soap opera, let's go find out the truth."

"Sure, but where exactly would that be?" Nicki glanced at her watch and then at his weary face.

"Where else? Ashley's apartment. If she's not home, I still have my key." He clicked open the doors on his car and, like the gentleman he was, held hers open for her.

Nicki climbed in and buckled her seat belt. His little debutante could be a murderer, and they were on their way to the Bates Motel.

# THIRTY-ONE

Nicki checked the passenger's side mirror for the tenth time to make sure no one was following them. Then she said a prayer that Ashley wouldn't be home. The last thing she wanted was an ugly scene. Nicki wanted to stay focused on solving the case while keeping a safe distance from Miss Fashion Plate. Assault and battery from a tacky hair-pulling incident wouldn't look good on her background check. And if she failed to get Hunter off? *Say, Mr. Galen, would you write to me while serving ten-to-fifteen for fraud, and another twenty-to-life for homicide? Maybe we can schedule non-conjugal visits the third Tuesday of every month.* No, she needed to keep her mind on the case.

"Any thoughts about your signature appearing on every fraudulent financial transaction Nowak was conducting?" Nicki stole a glance at Hunter from the corner of her eye.

"Only that it does look like my signature." He kept his focus on the traffic ahead. "I know only know one person who can write my name as well as I do, and that's Ashley."

"How do you know that?"

"I've seen her practicing it more than once. When I questioned her, she scribbled a 'Mrs.' in front and said she was preparing for when she became Mrs. Hunter Galen. The second time I caught her, she said she wanted to be able to cash my paycheck at the bank—except I don't draw a paycheck like the other brokers."

"You think she's desperate for spending money?"

He shrugged. "I wouldn't think so. Her chain of hair salons is supposedly doing very well. According to my sister, new customers wait weeks to get an appointment."

"So what did you make of her writing your name like that?"

"At the time it was just another unexplainable female mystery, but now who knows?"

"Hunter...could she have been James's real partner?"

He worked his neck from side to side at a red light. "I doubt it. Ashley knows every fashion designer in America and Europe. She can recite who is dating whom in the television and movie star world with perfect accuracy. And she can describe the latest trends in hair, makeup, and cosmetic procedures in great detail. But could she get involved in a scam to swindle client portfolios? I think she would view that as somehow beneath her." Hunter stepped on the accelerator as the light turned green. "She once told me that 'dwelling on money in any manner other than how to spend it is boring.' That was her assessment of my chosen career."

"Perhaps you were blind to her true nature." Nicki winced slightly once that was out of her mouth. Investigating a lead was one thing. Sounding like a jealous woman was another.

A muscle in Hunter's neck tightened. "Well, we're about to find out just how naive I've been." He came to a stop behind Ashley's warehouse district townhouse.

Nicki jumped out without waiting for him to open her door. At the front door, she steeled herself for an unpleasant encounter as he rang the bell. When no one answered, Nicki rang the bell again and then knocked, all to no avail.

"She must still be visiting friends and shopping in Baton Rouge.

She'd planned to stay a few days to give me a chance to come to my senses." He spat out the words like bad tasting food. "Apparently, I proposed to a complete stranger."

"What do you want to do? You make the call, boss. Breaking and entering is a class C felony if she gets mean over your breakup."

Hunter pulled out his keys from his pocket. "You're the one with a decision to make, Miss Price. At this point I couldn't care less about adding to my already lengthy list of crimes. But you're at the beginning of what I'm sure will be a long and successful career." He inserted a key into the lock.

"Wild horses couldn't keep me out." Nicki looked over her shoulder and then followed him inside.

He paused in the foyer. "Come to think of it, I've never been here before. Ashley usually came to my French Quarter apartment or I went to her father's house in the Garden District."

Nicki peered with interest at the preferences of a woman unknown to both of them. Ashley's decor was expensive but strikingly austere: an Italian leather sofa, silk side chairs, glass end tables and étagère. A teak entertainment unit concealed a large TV and sound system. Persian rugs covered polished hardwood floors, and modern pieces of art hung on the walls. There was no clutter, no dust, and no knickknacks. There was no warmth or humanity. The room felt like an upscale furniture showroom or a model home in a gated community.

Hunter walked to a wall where a pastoral watercolor hung amid contemporary art. "My sister painted this to emulate the style of Alfred Sisley, an English impressionist. Do you think it looks out of place?" Sadness underscored his question.

"I don't know much about art, but I think it's beautiful," she said softly. "Everything in this place looks way too perfect. I'll bet you no one ever watched a Saints' games or ate a plate of nachos in here."

Hunter nodded as he scanned the room. "She spends most of her time at her father's."

Nicki walked into an equally spartan kitchen. Silk magnolias bloomed on the Tuscan country table, but there was no blender, toaster, or microwave on the counter and no glasses drying in the dish drainer. In fact, there was no dish drainer. Hunter started opening cabinets and drawers as though curious about the woman he had been engaged to. They found a small microwave hidden in a cupboard and the coffeemaker in the pantry. It was unplugged but had a paper filter ready to go. Ashley took meticulous to a new level.

They wandered down the hallway peering into the streak-free bathroom with towels stacked with military precision. The Martha Stewart guest room probably never enjoyed a single overnight guest, but there were signs that someone lived in the home in the master bedroom. Although the bed was perfectly made, one high heel peeked out from beneath the dust ruffle. Her armoire stood polished and dust-free, but a bit of lace hung from the third drawer.

*And to think Hunter had considered marrying this slob.*

They discovered further signs of life in the bathroom. Only in this large, windowless room did Ashley reveal her true identity. Cosmetics, toiletries, and accessories littered every surface. Rattan shelves from floor to ceiling were jammed with framed photographs, mementos, jewelry cases, photo albums, and newspaper clippings of Ashley in various pageants. Stacks of paperbacks waited beside her Jacuzzi tub, along with more bath and body products than at a mall kiosk. Empty wine glasses and Evian bottles were lined up around the tub like sentinels. Towels overflowed her hamper, while another basket was mounded with clothing headed for the laundry. A pair of socks was balled up under the pedestal sink, and shoes of every color, shape, and heel height were scattered across the floor.

Ashley behaved like a human being in this room.

Nicki experienced a pang of guilt for spying into the secret world of Hunter's former love.

"We're not going to find anything in here to connect Ashley to James's scam," said Hunter.

"I wouldn't be so sure. If any mysteries will be revealed, it'll be in this bathroom."

"Then go for it, but I can't invade her privacy like this." He abruptly left the room.

*Time for burying your head in the sand is long past.* Nicki put aside her misgivings and began snooping through the woman's stuff. It didn't take her long to find a few interesting items. On the rattan shelf was a prom picture of Ashley and her date. The young man was powerfully built, with a sunburned face and thin goatee. He didn't look quite relaxed in his white tuxedo with boutonniere and cummerbund, but who felt comfortable in formal clothes at eighteen? Ashley wore a beauty queen smile and a daringly low-cut dress for a high school dance. Another photo sharing the frame piqued Nicki's interest as well. Taken about the same time, Ashley faced the camera surrounded by her friends. Everyone wore jeans and flip-flops and held up cans of beer on a boat dock in the bayou. The same boyfriend as prom night, with plenty of tattoos and a ball cap proclaiming the Muskrats, had his arm around Ashley's waist.

Nicki rummaged through the scrapbooks and the high school yearbook with a bad feeling about the skinny, vapid-faced woman smiling from all the photographs. Ashley had attended Forrest High School in Terrebonne Parish, a rural district that encompassed a great deal of geography. Their football team was called the Muskrats, and the team colors were orange and white.

*I couldn't see much from where I was hiding, but one of them wore an orange ball cap with a picture of a muskrat on it.* If Nicki hadn't voiced her recollection to Hunter aloud, she never would have remembered details from that night in *La Maison de Poisson*. Perhaps more than one team used a muskrat logo in the Cajun parishes, but as she studied the photo of Ashley's high school pals, she could easily imagine them in the back of a pickup with shotguns. But why would Ashley remain friends with her former cronies from Terrebonne? Surely they didn't possess the necessary social class she reached for now. And what possible ill will could they harbor toward a new PI from Mississippi?

Nicki replaced the yearbook and photographs and then searched through stacks of more recent pictures. She found many from the engagement party at Ethan Galen's, and an equal number of candid shots of Hunter and...herself. Nicki's uneasy feeling about privacy invasion morphed into fury as she held up photo after photo: One of her parking the Escort in Hunter's driveway, another of her on the steps of Christine's trailer, another of her studying a tourist map in the French Quarter, one of her and Hunter dancing in the dance hall, and recently their meeting in Lafitte's the day he visited Philip in Terrebonne.

"Hunter! You need to see this." Nicki lined up the photos on Ashley's vanity.

A minute later he was peering at the montage with an ashen face. "Ashley or someone on her payroll has been stalking you."

"That's for certain, but for what purpose? To gather proof that I work for you? You already told her that. And who actually has prints these days with digital cameras and smartphones? None of this makes any sense."

"I don't know, but we need to tread lightly. Let me find out what this is about. Ashley is up to something and I don't want you in danger. Put everything back exactly where it was except for the ones of you and me."

"Do you still have the evidence you gathered at the fishing

camp?" she asked. "I'm calling Nate. His license may have been suspended until the hearing, but I'm sure he still has contacts with local forensic labs. It's time to find out if those good old boys in the bayou are Ashley's friends."

"Fine, but you're not going anywhere without me." Hunter selected Nate's number on his phone and put it on speaker. "Nate," he said when the man answered. "Hunter Galen. I need to drop over with some beer cans and—"

"Bring a bucket of chicken as well or don't bother coming at all. Man, it's been a while since I heard from you. Call your brother and bring him too. Ethan can't be a perfect husband all the time."

Nicki smiled in spite of herself.

"I'll look forward to male bonding some other time," said Hunter. "Right now, we need some DNA work done, and you know which labs are the quickest. We need to identify who drank the beers at the fishing camp if they're in the system."

"Quick is going to cost you, Hunter. And why isn't my delight-ful cousin making this request? Did you fire her for sleeping on the job already? I tried to warn you."

Nicki didn't want Nate spooked about a potential stalker when it might amount to nothing. She had no real proof—yet—that Ashley knew the thugs from the bayou. Taking pictures of her might be nothing more than catty behavior. Debating how much to divulge, Nicki spoke up. "I'm just fine, cousin. Thanks for asking. And I'm handling the investigation just fine too, but we need your discretion with this."

"You've got it, Nicki. Come on over and tell Hunter to bring his checkbook. DNA work costs an arm and a leg. Even so, the quickest you're looking at is a week. Everything you see on TV is pure fiction."

They retraced their steps in the townhouse, Hunter locked the door behind them, and they drove to his apartment as fast as traffic would allow. On the way, Nicki mulled over scenarios of what might have happened in the bayou. No matter how she looked at it, she couldn't think of how it had anything to do with James or his death.

Once they were inside Hunter's home, he immediately went to the kitchen and rummaged under the sink. Behind a bag of recyclable newspapers he took out the sack of beer cans and shell casings.

"So that's where you put those. Thank goodness Jeanette didn't throw them out."

"So unlike her nosy self to overlook something," Hunter murmured.

"Did I hear my name, *mes petites*?" Hunter's housekeeper wandered into the kitchen carrying a basket of folded towels.

"Yes, ma'am. I was hoping to see you again, Mrs. Peteriere." Nicki produced her friendliest smile.

"Good day, *O'lette*. Would you like a Diet Coke? I bought you two six-packs and hid them from you know who."

"Yes, ma'am. That sounds good." Nicki tried not to giggle.

"Why do you keep a bag of old beer cans?" Jeanette asked Hunter. "What are you up to?"

"And what are you doing here today?"

Jeanette poured the soda over ice with great deliberation. "When I was cleaning here the other day, I smelled something bad coming from your hamper."

Nicki took a long swallow of her drink and locked gazes with Hunter, lifting one eyebrow.

"My laundry doesn't smell, but thank you for your concern." He held up the sack of evidence. "This is important, Jeanette. Did you touch what's inside in any way?"

"No. With your sneaking around like a thief in the night, I knew you were up to something."

"Thank you, Mrs. Peteriere." Nicki took the bag from him. "We need to have these analyzed for possible fingerprints."

"You're a little Agatha Christie, and he is Hercule Poirot?" Nodding at Hunter, Jeanette released laughter akin to a cackle. "*N'est-ce pas?*"

"Yes, ma'am. I loved those kinds of stories when I was growing up."

"Why don't I fix you two a nice dinner? By the time you return from your clandestine sleuthing, everything will be ready to eat." The housekeeper grinned at each of them in succession.

"Thank you, Jeanette, but I've made reservations for dinner. Please take the rest of the day off." Hunter nudged Nicki in the direction of the door.

"I'll give my cousin your fond regards, Mrs. Peteriere, and thanks for the soda." Nicki smiled warmly at the elderly woman.

"*Alors*, you should avoid *Monsieur* Price like Bourbon Street on a Saturday night. He was a thorn in your foot, remember?"

"Good night, Jeanette." Hunter swept open the door and then discovered that visiting Nate or dinner in the Quarter wouldn't be in his and Nicki's near future.

Two plain-clothes detectives in expensive suits stood in front of them. One of them held up a badge. "Hunter Galen, you're under arrest for fraud and securities violations. You've been ordered to surrender your passport and come with us for questioning. If your passport is on premises, Agent Anderson will accompany you to retrieve it. You may call your attorney on the way downtown."

Hunter glanced at Nicki as though waking from a dream.

"You go get the passport while I call your lawyer, your brother, and my cousin." Nicki shifted the bag of evidence behind her leg. "May I have your card, sir, so I know where you're taking Mr. Galen?"

The federal agent nodded his head politely as he handed her a business card.

Nicki watched helplessly while Hunter was led from his comfortable French Quarter apartment in handcuffs. He would be locked in a cell that would be neither comfortable nor remotely justified. She knew without a doubt that he hadn't bilked his clients out of their savings, just as he hadn't killed his college chum and business partner, but her faith in her ability to prove either of those things slipped to one notch above sea level.

# THIRTY-TWO

*A* few days later, when Hunter walked into *Grand-mère's* formal parlor, he was blindsided by a sense of loss. *Grandmère* was almost ninety years old and had lived a long, productive life, but Hunter wished she could have stuck around until he straightened out the mess he was in, which probably would have made her the oldest living human in recorded history.

Arranged around the perimeter of the elegant room was an assortment of Galen family members. Ethan and Cora greeted the endless stream of friends and neighbors in the foyer who arrived bearing enough food to feed the entire Garden District. People wanted to be helpful, even if it was just baking a pan of pecan brownies. Aaron and Chloe sat on the sofa, their faces awash with misery. Jeanette perched on a straight-back chair by the fireplace. For once his grandmother's best friend wasn't doing anything except clutching rosary beads. Her employer and friend for the past fifty years was gone. Hunter's mother, usually so indomitable, looked as fragile as a porcelain doll. Ken Douglas, the attorney responsible for his release from federal custody on bail, hovered nearby, eager to comfort but reluctant to intrude.

Hunter slouched in a wingback chair, wishing Nicki were with him. She had captured his heart without trying. Lately, he found himself thinking about her in the most peculiar circumstances and during not so peculiar ones as well. He'd called her repeatedly since his release and left several messages on her voice mail, all to no avail.

"You look like you could use this." His brother held out a glass filled with something amber.

Hunter shook his head. "No, thanks. Alcohol will only make me feel worse."

"Agreed. That's why I brought iced tea brewed by our sister." Ethan set the glass on the end table at Hunter's elbow. "Judging by the color, she must have used a dozen teabags, but her heart was in the right place. So drink up."

Hunter swallowed some of the bitter brew. "Tell me what happened to *Grandmère* and leave nothing out. I can't believe I was in jail when she died. I hope she didn't know."

"Rest easy. She went out on her own terms and knew nothing about your arrest. She got up early to bake cookies and cook a pot of oyster stew for a neighbor who just had a baby. So like her—always thinking of others. Later she told Jeanette she felt light headed and had some indigestion. Jeanette wanted to call the doctor, but *Grandmère* wouldn't hear of it. She insisted on taking antacids and lying down. When Jeanette checked on her an hour later, she was gone. The doctor said she probably had a massive coronary while asleep. Mama said she'd been complaining about dizziness and fatigue for the past month but didn't want anyone to worry." Ethan swallowed a mouthful of Chloe's tea with a grimace.

Hunter stared out the window at another neighbor arriving with yet another casserole. "What on earth will you do with all this food?" He made conversation so he wouldn't think about his grandmother dying alone in her room instead of surrounded by her family.

"Invite the entire island of Hispaniola for the funeral luncheon. What are *you* going to do, Hunter? Ken was able to get you out so you could attend the funeral, but he isn't a criminal lawyer. Your case is out of his league."

"I know that. I contacted Mark Kirby. He's from Washington and familiar with federal prosecution of financial crimes. I can't think of a better use for my trust fund than high-priced attorney fees."

"Don't worry about the cost. Our family isn't bankrupt yet. What I'm asking is do they have a case?" When his elder brother locked gazes, Hunter noticed for the first time how gray Ethan's temples had become.

"If you're asking if I had any part in James's scams, I didn't. But according to my investigator, you're not innocent until proven guilty in the investment business, not when people trust you with their entire net worth."

"Miss Price is absolutely right. What evidence prompted the feds to file charges?" Ethan dropped into an adjacent chair.

"They have a stack of documents, including lines of credit and unauthorized buy and sell orders for accounts James had been churning. My signature is right beside his. James—or somebody—can execute my signature with amazing accuracy." Hunter saw no need to name whom he suspected.

"You will need to take copies of the documents to a handwriting expert. Maybe Aaron can help with that." Ethan ran a hand through his hair, his usual response when frustrated.

"Nicki is one step ahead of you. She already talked to our future brother-in-law. Aaron contacted his Atlanta office and lined up a handwriting analysis. Of course, with the FBI involved, whatever they find becomes federal evidence that can't be swept under the rug."

"Miss Price is that certain of your innocence?"

"She is, and because I never signed those papers, this innocent man can relax and enjoy another glass of his sister's special brew." Hunter toasted Chloe across the room with his empty glass. Her sweet smile nearly broke his heart.

"Good to hear." Ethan rose to his feet. "We'll get through the next couple of days and then concentrate on putting your troubles behind you."

But Hunter knew his troubles wouldn't go anywhere soon, because at that moment Ashley walked into the room. She greeted Cora wearing black from her Jimmy Choo stilettos to the Chanel pillbox hat atop her upswept blond hair. Her skin was pale and her makeup understated—Ashley had even her mourning *operandi* nailed down.

With rage building in his gut, Hunter approached the two women hugging in the doorway.

"There you are, Hunter," said Cora. Dark circles ringed her red-rimmed eyes. "Ashley is here." Apparently unaware of their breakup, Cora squeezed Ashley's fingers once more before walking toward the kitchen.

"My father sent a case of Maker's Mark with his deepest condolences. Could you have someone retrieve it from my trunk?" Ashley's drawl tinkled like wind chimes, but right now Hunter would rather listen to fingernails dragged down a chalkboard.

"Phil thinks a funeral for a ninety-year-old woman needs a case of bourbon?" Hunter muttered under his breath.

"Oh, Hunter, don't be difficult. I came the moment I heard." Ashley stepped forward, extending her arms in sympathy.

With half the room watching, Hunter had no choice but to accept her embrace. "Thank your father for his generosity."

"I can't believe she's gone." Ashley laid her head on his shoulder. "*Grandmère* was always so unselfish. She was a paradigm for women. I wish I hadn't been too busy to learn a few lessons."

*Truer words were never spoken*, Hunter thought, pulling Ashley to arm's length. Surprisingly tears were flowing down her cheeks. He automatically dug his handkerchief from a back pocket, which she accepted with a half smile.

"Thank you, Hunter. I'm so sorry for your loss. She was an exceptional woman. I so wanted her to be my mentor. There's no denying I certainly could use one. Now I'll never have that chance." A fresh batch of tears streamed from her eyes.

Hunter hated it when women cried. He felt so helpless, and in this case, culpable. He no longer had feelings for her, but it was impossible to remain unaffected by her sorrow. He wrapped an arm around her shoulders and tried to offer whatever comfort he could.

Ashley turned herself against his chest, sniffling and whimpering softly. "I can't believe she's gone," she said again.

Hunter patted her back with growing disgust. The repetition made it seem as though she were using stock replies from googling "appropriate sympathy responses" and felt as sincere as handshakes following a grudge match in sports. When several cousins surrounded them, squeezing Ashley's arm and murmuring words of solace, Hunter realized many didn't know about their breakup. He'd told his mother, sister, and brother, but apparently word hadn't gotten around.

"Let's go to the kitchen," he said, eager to quit the limelight. "Chloe made iced tea. Would you like some? And give me your car keys. I'll have someone take the case of bourbon out of your trunk." Hunter stopped one of his teenaged cousins along the way with the request.

"I would love some of your sister's tea," she said, finally extracting herself from his shirt. "I must tell Chloe how very sorry I am and your mama too." Ashley's voice sounded as weak as a child's. In the kitchen she blotted her face with his handkerchief and went to the window. "Oh, my. Would you look at *Grandmère*'s garden? I mean, Ethan and Cora's now."

*Bad choice of rooms*, Hunter thought, struggling to summon a single charitable thought for her. He should have known the backyard would remind Ashley of the recent party. "She did as much work as the gardeners."

"How pretty the flowers look with everything in bloom. Seems like we were just celebrating our engagement here. Everyone was so happy that day. I know I couldn't have been happier." Ashley was starting to sound like a character in a Tennessee Williams play.

"As my grandmother's death reminds us, everything in life changes. Nothing stays the same." Hunter wanted no misinterpretations. He poured her some iced tea and then emptied the pitcher into his glass to protect the unsuspecting.

"Well, I don't like it! This reminds me of when my mother died. The normal routine and things I could count on were taken from me. Once you and I got engaged, I thought I had found stability. You were my rock. I planned to settle down and become a real wife and mother, just like Mother was to Daddy." She set down her glass untasted and turned to face him.

Her luminescent blue eyes failed to have their usual effect.

"Then you broke our engagement," she continued, "and the rug was again ripped from beneath my feet." She paused, waiting, while tears welled up in her eyes.

Hunter would have to be less than human if he didn't regret the pain he caused, but his compassion didn't include even an ounce of love. "I'm sorry today brought back sad memories and that I caused you so much heartache." Even if Ashley's sorrow was genuine, he stood on a slippery slope. He needed to keep their breakup permanent—no cooling-off period, no stepping back to assess the situation. "What other news did you hear? Did word of my arrest reach Baton Rouge?"

Her glassy eyes rounded with surprise. "Arrested for James's murder? What could they possibly have to tie you to that?"

"No, not for murder. For fraud and securities violations, many counts of each."

Her expression of astonishment faded a tad. "What do you mean?" She took a small sip of her beverage and frowned.

"My name appears on all kinds of documents found at James's. I have copies and so do the feds. Apparently, they have been gathering evidence for months to prepare formal indictments."

"Of course your signature would be on Galen-Nowak paperwork." Ashley pulled her hat from her head and tossed it on the counter. "You were business partners. Both signatures were needed for major transactions."

Hunter lifted an eyebrow. He'd never mentioned that particular detail due to her previous disinterest in financial matters. "These are trades James made without investor consent, part of his little scheme to enrich himself using our clients' assets. I never signed any of those buy and sell orders. He or someone else forged my signature." He lowered his voice as Aunt Donna entered the room with an empty ice bucket and a warm, loving smile for him.

Ashley didn't so much as blink at his words, but a muscle twitched along her jawline while her nostrils flared. "That's ridiculous. Why would James forge your signature? He had to know you would spot it during the end-of-month review." She marched to the refrigerator. "Is there anything else to drink? That tea tastes dreadful." She pulled out a bottle of wine and reached for a stemmed glass.

"He forged my name because it was the only way trades would have gone through. James dummied up fictitious statements for each client he defrauded to cover his tracks. I reviewed the bogus statements at the end of each month." Hunter chose not to mention that her dad had been last month's larceny victim.

She swallowed a gulp of wine. "Why, that little thief! You never would have found out if he hadn't been killed and you started snooping in his home."

An interesting choice of words, but Hunter let it pass. "That's true, and I have Miss Price to thank for the full picture of his deception."

Ashley didn't even try to hide her displeasure at the mention of Nicki's name, but she only said, "Well, I'm glad she earns the salary you pay her. Now she has plenty to keep her busy with the fraud indictment and your partner's murder."

"Getting the fraud charges dropped won't be too hard. Nicki sent samples of my handwriting, along with copies of financial transactions I never signed to a handwriting expert. He should be able to conclude those signatures were forged. Maybe they'll even be able to tell who did sign my name." It was pure bluff, but Hunter gave it a try.

She didn't grab the bait. "I hope so. With *Grandmère*'s death, we have other things on our minds besides bogus charges against you." Ashley quickly swallowed her wine and then crossed the large kitchen to set her empty glass in the sink. In the doorway, she looked back over her shoulder. "Please tell me I can sit with your family at the funeral, Hunter. I know things are...different between us, but I did love your grandmother and I wish to pay my respects." The crocodile tears returned, called to duty once more.

"All right, Ashley. I can't stop you from attending her Mass."

She offered a thin smile and walked into the living room, where even more friends and neighbors had swelled the ranks of mourners. Ashley went straight to his mother, who wrapped her in a warm embrace. "Oh, Mrs. Galen," she drawled. "I'm so sorry about your mother-in-law. I know you two were very close. Is there anything I can do to help? My daddy and I are at your disposal." Ashley's musical voice sang the words in near parody of Southern womanhood.

Yet his mother didn't seem to recognize an actress in her midst. "Your sympathy is all I need, my dear. You know what it's like to lose a mother." Clotilde dabbed her eyes with a lace-edged handkerchief. "And you were so young when you lost yours. At least I had my mother-in-law for many years." She wrapped a steadying arm around Ashley's thin waist and led her to the sideboard, where she poured them each a small glass of bourbon.

*Throwing gasoline on the fire.* Hunter clenched down on his back molars as he watched the performance. It took him mere seconds to regret his decision about the funeral. He'd had no idea how to refuse, but he should have found a way. Ashley would use the occasion to worm her way back to the fold, making the breakup that much harder. How much of her emotional outpouring was real, and how much was just another attempt at manipulation? He had been engaged to a duplicitous liar and a cheat, but was she also a murderer? He didn't think so. But then again, he'd played by everyone's rules for years and ended up the fool.

For now he couldn't let Ashley suspect his true feelings for his private investigator. Not until they ruled out any connection between Ashley and the thugs who had frightened Nicki half to death. He needed to find out if someone was still threatening Nicki and take care of them. He'd stood on the sidelines keeping the peace long enough.

The moment Ashley walked into the house, he'd realized he was in love with Nicki. Not intrigued with or smitten by...but in love with. He wanted her by his side at the funeral and no one else. Allowing Ashley to sit with the family portended a long, stressful afternoon. Not just for him, but also for Nicki if he could get her there. Ashley's machinations always spelled trouble. Hunter punched in Nicki's number and started to leave yet another message on her voice mail.

But before he had a chance to plead his case for her to return his calls, Nate walked through the front door with his cousin on his heels. She wore no Chanel suit and veiled hat, no designer shoes or perfect coiffure. Nicki looked sad, a little scared, and...wonderful. Her gaze swept the room filled with mourners, paused on Clotilde and Ashley with glasses lifted in tribute to *Grandmère*, and finally landed on him. Hunter practically trampled his Aunt Donna trying to reach her side.

"I came as soon as I got your message," she said softly. "I'm so sorry to hear about your Mamaw."

As Hunter accepted her shy hug and Nate's handshake and heartfelt condolences, he felt the walls closing in around him. It was only people approaching: Ethan to accept sympathy from his best friend; Aunt Donna to say hello to Nicki; his mother to make the acquaintance of Nicolette—something he should have taken care of already; and Ashley to wreak mischief. All the times he should have taken a stand, all his missed opportunities to do the right thing, crowded in around him like specters.

Hunter felt doomed and that there was never a man more deserving of the gallows.

# THIRTY-THREE

On the day of Helene Galen's funeral a light drizzle was falling from gray, overcast skies. Thankfully, Nicki had remembered her umbrella as she squeezed into a tight parking spot on Bienville, a street several blocks from the church. True to form, she stepped out of her car into a puddle.

Hunter had asked her to meet him that morning to ride in the limousine, but she'd declined. Just as she'd refused to stay for lunch at Ethan and Cora's home two days ago. Hunter had looked disappointed and upset. Perhaps he wasn't accustomed to being told no by an employee, but at that moment Nicki didn't care.

She had been in Baton Rouge transferring evidence to the federal prosecutor assigned to his case when Nate called with the news. Despite road construction, traffic snarls, and faulty air-conditioning in her car, she returned to New Orleans as soon as possible. Her heart broke for Hunter, knowing how much her Mamaw meant to her. Nate explained that the Galens would receive family and friends in the Chestnut Street mansion. So Nicki expected to see expensively dressed people talking in low voices and sipping bottled water or coffee. The shell-shocked family would try their best to welcome a throng of mourners.

But Nicki hadn't expected to see Ashley in the comforting

embrace of Hunter's mother. *So much for them breaking up.* When she and Nate walked into the living room, all eyes fixed on her as though she'd sprouted a second head. Only one girlfriend per person per funeral, and Ashley had beaten her to the punch. Again.

Looking genuinely happy to see her, Hunter had wrapped his arms tightly around her. Then she ruined the moment by referring to the Grand Dame of New Orleans society as his *Mamaw*, loud enough for everyone to hear. Nicki didn't need her gun to shoot herself in the foot. All she had to do was open her mouth and talk.

Ashley whispered something to Mrs. Galen that Nicki was unable to lip read.

A little girl asked her mother what a "Mamaw" was.

Nicki wanted to slink out the door.

Now as she hurried up the steps of St. Louis Cathedral, which had anchored Jackson Square for centuries, she was regretting her decision to attend the funeral. She would never fit into Hunter's world no matter how much she wanted to. When they were alone together, her dreams carried her away. She loved him and felt real affection from him in return. But today in this magnificent church, Nicki knew she could never take Ashley's place in his life. Some chasms were impossible to cross.

Nicki breathed a sigh of relief when she spotted her cousin. "Good morning," she whispered as she slipped next to him in the pew.

"Hey, Nicki. How ya doing?" He wrapped an arm around her shoulders. "You look downright conservative."

"Thank you, I think," she said softly, smoothing wrinkles from her black linen skirt. The boxy jacket with silk tank top felt appropriate without going over the top. Or at least that's what she hoped. And her black wedge heels made her almost as tall as her arch nemesis, who sat up in the third row next to Chloe's fiancé.

Ashley was wearing a chic sheath dress with that blasted pillbox hat. Nicki's unkind thoughts—in church, no less—made her bite her lip and heave a big inward sigh.

Suddenly the massive pipe organ began *Pachebel's Canon* and the assembled parishioners respectfully quieted their chatter. An ornately carved white casket was wheeled up the aisle behind a troupe of clergymen bearing sacred items to be used during the Mass. Members of the Galen family followed the procession with solemn faces.

Hunter walked beside his sister, who looked weak from grief. As the processional passed her pew, Hunter stopped and reached for her hand. "Sit with me, please, *O'lette*. I would like that very much."

How could she decline? How could she do anything but concentrate on putting one foot in front of the other before her knees buckled?

When they reached the front of the church holding hands, Ethan and Cora entered the pew first. Hunter guided Chloe to sit on his left and pulled Nicki in on his right. Nicki held her breath in case the skies opened to rain down fire and brimstone. She wasn't Roman Catholic and was sitting in the first pew. Yet nothing disastrous—or miraculous—happened as a soloist began to sing and the priest said the Mass of Christian burial.

During the next hour, Mrs. Etienne Galen, Sr. was eulogized by several friends, New Orleans civic leaders, her eldest son, and finally by Jeanette Peteriere. The elderly woman walked to the podium on the arm of a young woman. Her gait was painfully slow, but she held her chin high.

At the pulpit, Jeanette glanced over the assemblage before speaking clearly into the microphone: "Helene Galen was a fine lady. She treated everyone fairly and lived by the golden rule. Do what's right even if you think nobody's watchin', because God is watching. He gonna take care of us, one way or the other. We'll be okay if we all remember that. Helene told me once that whichever of us gets to heaven first, they gotta dust, wash the windows, and make the roux for gumbo." Jeanette turned her focus toward the ornate ceiling high overhead. "Well, Helene, I suggest you get busy. I'll be there before you know it."

If there had been a dry eye in the house, there wasn't now. She dabbed her damp face with a handkerchief and returned to her pew even less steady than before. Tears cascaded down the pretty face of her caregiver too. Nicki, who barely knew the older woman, tightened her grip on Hunter's hand and cried with everyone else. Seeing the man she cared about in pain left a hollowness in her chest. After the rites of Communion and prayers for the dead to comfort those who mourn, the priest issued his parting benediction.

Hunter and his family trailed the casket from the sanctuary to the waiting hearse, and Nicki ducked down a hallway to find the ladies' room. She needed a moment to fix her face and straighten out her thinking. Everything was happening too fast and she understood none of it. What was she doing sitting with the family in the box seats? She was merely an employee on the payroll. But hearing Hunter utter the words, "Sit with me, please, *O'lette*," had made her feel special, valued...maybe even loved.

"Oh, there you are. I was wondering where you had run off to."

Nicki pivoted to meet the cool blue gaze of the oh-so-sophisticated Ashley. "Hello, Miss Menard."

"Ashley, please. Considering that we have so much in common, we should be on a first name basis." Her smile revealed sparkling white teeth, but the gesture contained no warmth. "I'm curious as to what you're doing here." Ashley spoke without animosity, as though casually inquiring about the weather.

"I beg your pardon?" Nicki asked, but she didn't wait for a

response. "I'm here because Hunter asked me to come." Defensiveness lifted her voice a full octave.

Ashley perused Nicki from her shoes to the top of her head, slowly and deliberately, intending to intimidate. "I'm sure he did. He's fascinated with you. Maybe because you're so unusual. Rather like the three-legged stray that followed him home from college one day. Goodness, that dog had a bad case of fleas! I couldn't believe Hunter took him in." Ashley bent toward the mirror to touch up her flawless makeup.

Nicki had had enough of the evil debutant. She'd had a bellyful of Ashley-clones her whole life. "I'm no homeless pet. Hunter hired me to do a job and that's what I'm doing. If he has grown to respect me and we've become friends, that's none of your business." She sucked in a gulp of air, not sure where her backbone had come from. "The last I heard, you two were broken up."

"You're here doing a job?" Ashley's voice grew shrill. "What kind of detective carries no gun? In case you haven't noticed, New Orleans is a dangerous place these days."

Nicki wasn't about to explain she was licensed to work, just not to carry a firearm yet. What was happening here had nothing to do with licenses or gun permits. This was about staking territories and making a claim on another human being. Nicki shouldered her purse and tried to step past the woman.

"You just smelled his money, didn't you, Miss Backwoods Mississippi? You took one look at his nice apartment and unlimited trips to Walmart flashed through your head. You might get four new tires for your Escort *and* fill your shopping cart at the dollar store." Her thick drawl dripped with scorn.

Nicki's fingers froze on the doorknob as she turned to face her tormentor. "Oh, I'm the gold digger? I've taken nothing from Hunter other than the paycheck I earn. Maybe you're the one trying to marry the gravy train."

"Do I look hard up to you, Miss Price?" Color rose up Ashley's neck into her pale cheeks. "I don't need to marry money. My daddy's loaded, and I'm his only child. In the meantime, I own four hair salons that keep me in all the designer clothes I can wear." Her eyes narrowed like a feral cat's. "I love Hunter, so I'll bide my time. Sooner or later he'll go back to saving whales and the environment instead of poor people he feels sorry for."

Despite her upbringing to turn the other cheek, Nicki wanted to slap Ashley or at least push her down like children on a playground, but her stomach turned queasy as an image of her mother scrimping between disability checks came to mind. Any possible clever retorts evaporated.

Ashley swooped in for the kill. "Keep your distance from Hunter, Nicki. You'll only end up making a fool of yourself. Did you really think you could play in his league? You'll embarrass him in front of his family, friends, and business associates." She resumed her primping before the mirror, but added in a kinder, gentler tone, "Hunter is too much of a gentleman to tell you."

Nicki left the room without responding and pushed past ladies milling in the narrow hallway. She could still hear subdued voices in the foyer as mourners filed out of the cathedral. Not wishing to run into Hunter with her face streaky with tears, she hurried in the opposite direction. Down two more corridors and up one short flight of stairs, she emerged outdoors on a side street, away from the heavy scent of magnolias clogging her senses. Nicki glanced over her shoulder to make sure no one was following her and then circled the block to where she'd left her car. At the moment, she didn't care that Hunter had asked her to ride with him or about any of the other responsibilities she was shirking.

Ashley was right about a few things. She didn't belong in Hunter's rarefied world. She had deluded herself that class could be learned like strategy in a game of chess. Ashley had it...and she never would. Nicki started the car, rolled down the windows, and breathed in the thick, humid air. A group of college-aged girls walked past, talking animatedly about their evening plans. Nicki would go back to Christine's trailer, open a Diet Coke, and eat an entire bag of salt-and-vinegar chips. *Isn't that what women do when they are whipped?*

Except when they had a job to do as a professional private investigator. She'd turned over proof to the investigators that Hunter had been duped in the fraud with James's second set of books and the handwriting expert's evaluation, but she was no closer to finding the real killer than on day one. And didn't murderers love to go to funerals? Pulling into traffic, she headed toward Lafayette Cemetery in the Garden District, where the priest had indicated final interment would be made. The salt-and-vinegar chips with a cola chaser would have to wait.

Funeral processions with police escorts arrived ahead of those fighting traffic and red lights. The family was already encircled about the Galen family crypt when Nicki joined them. With his head down, Hunter stood close to Ethan with tiny Chloe sandwiched between them. Clotilde looked pinched and pale on the arm of the family lawyer. Aaron, the kindly FBI agent and Chloe's fiancée, stood in the second row, while Ashley was practically imprinted on Hunter's jacket. The rest of the crowd had squeezed behind them into a very limited space.

"You just gonna stand there and glare at that woman?"

The unexpected voice behind her caused Nicki to jump. She turned to find that Jeanette had also arrived tardily, cemeteries not easy ground for the elderly to maneuver.

"You startled me, Mrs. Peteriere." Nicki murmured. "For a moment I thought I had irritated a restless spirit."

"No, *O'lette*. These folks are all asleep in Jesus. Nobody restless. This is my granddaughter, Renee." Jeanette nudged the lovely young woman with high cheekbones and caramel skin next to her. After Nicki shook hands with her, Jeanette bobbed her head toward the street. "You go on back to the car and sit in air-conditioning. You don't need to stand around in this heat."

When Renee protested, Jeanette held up a thin, blue-veined hand. "Do as I say, Renny. Don't sass me. I'll hang on to Miss Price's arm on the way back. She gotta be here anyway 'cause she's working." Jeanette drew away from her granddaughter and grabbed hold of Nicki's jacket.

"Of course you can," Nicki whispered. "Would you like to lean against this crypt? The stone feels cool."

"Go on," Jeanette demanded. With a shake of her head, Renee started down the path toward the gate. Jeanette grabbed Nicki's arm and hissed in a low voice, "Don't be leaning on nobody's tomb unless you knew them and know they would want you to."

Despite everything, Nicki couldn't help smiling a little as she straightened and wrapped her arm around the elderly woman's waist. They found an obscure spot to stand behind the last row next to a crypt in serious disrepair. While the priest read from Scripture, led the assembled group in prayer, and offered his final blessings, Nicki felt Jeanette sag against her side. The woman's face was damp, but she neither sobbed nor sniffled. Despite the beautiful day in the cemetery, despite the comforting words from the priest, and despite the fact Hunter paid no attention to Ashley, Nicki couldn't stop staring at the silky blond head of her rival.

"Why do you let that skinny gal get under your skin?"

The housekeeper's words were nothing more than breath beneath Nicki's ear. "Excuse me?"

"You heard me."

"I...I don't." The lie sounded lame even to her.

"What do you care what she says or if she don't like you? You still worried 'bout the number of Valentines inside your shoebox?

You still hopin' to be invited to the popular gal's sleepover?" Jeanette huffed. "You don't like her. She don't like you. So what? That's life."

Nicki glanced around to make sure no one was listening as she suppressed another smile. She remembered the grammar school shoebox all too well—lifting the lid to see if her stack of Valentines was on par with everyone else's.

"Ashley doesn't even know me." Nicki lowered her mouth to Jeanette's ear. "She doesn't like me because my family's from Red Haw instead of Prytania Street. And I didn't go to a fancy private school in a starched white blouse every day."

Jeanette whispered while they were supposed to be offering personal prayers for the deceased. "Your daddy never got asked to join the country club?"

Nicki waited until the priest concluded and the funeral director instructed mourners where to go for the luncheon. "My daddy never owned a suit and tie, let alone a set of golf clubs. He spent most of his free time drinking with his cronies. That's pretty much what killed him, by the way." Nicki was shocked at how callously she described him.

"You bothered that you got nobody to send a Hallmark card to on Father's Day?"

Nicki tried to gauge if Jeanette was being sarcastic, but her aged face was the picture of sincerity. "Nah. I'm over that."

"You still mad because your ma was stupid enough to marry him?"

That hit a tender nerve. "Maybe she wasn't stupid at all. Maybe she just wanted to be a mother and didn't have tons of options knocking on her door."

Jeanette's black eyes sparkled. "So you love your mama despite her messing up."

Nicki glanced around at the mourners. People were placing

roses one at a time on the crypt's steps. "Of course I love her. Before she got sick, my mother worked sixty hours a week to help me get through college. Now she's on government assistance and can't even afford clothes from the Goodwill store."

"Do you think she's proud of you?"

"I guess so."

"Don't sound like you had it so bad, *O'lette*."

Nicki stared at the stream of expensively dressed mourners taking their sweet time to lay down one flower. "I grew up living with my Mamaw and Papaw in a cabin with an outdoor well, a generator for electricity, no phone, and a wringer washer on the back porch. In a world of wireless Internet and cell phones, they still collect rainwater in a barrel to wash clothes. Their chickens scratch around in the dirt. When hens stop laying eggs, into the stew pot they go." Nicki paused uncomfortably.

Jeanette appeared to be chuckling. "Go on. Get it all out. Those folks will take all morning."

"When I told my grandmother we call those 'free-range chickens,' she said that there was nothing free about them. She paid a fair price for her hens at the grain elevator and just let nature take over."

Jeanette's web of wrinkles deepened with her smile. "Your granny sure right about that."

"This is the twenty-first century, but Mamaw still uses a woodstove to bake biscuits and oatmeal raisin cookies just for me."

"Don't fix something that ain't broken." Cocking her head, Jeanette peered up. "Don't you go to see her no more?"

"Of course, as often as I can."

"Her cookies any good?"

"They're the best. I eat a dozen each time I'm home." Nicki swallowed, trying to loosen the lump in her throat.

"Why then do you care if your kin are poor? Whether your

people came on the *Mayflower* or a slave ship like mine, it don't make you who you are. *You* make you who you are. Don't worry 'bout nothing but what to say to your Maker when you die." Jeanette tightened her grip on Nicki's arm. "You're better than that yellow-haired scarecrow, but telling you won't do you no good, *O'lette.* Not till you believe it in your heart."

The crowd thinned as mourners whispered final words to Clotilde and headed to their cars or the streetcar. They would regroup at a French Quarter restaurant, where a lavish meal would be served. Only the immediate family remained at the crypt—and one yellow-haired scarecrow.

"Why don't you take our flowers up while I wait here on level ground?" Jeanette nudged Nicki in her ribs. "And go say something to Hunter. That boy is hurting and could use a friend."

After she had been elbowed a second time, Nicki approached the Galen family behind Ashley's father.

"This might be tough going right now, Hunter," said Philip, "but everything will work out better for you and Ashley in the long run." With that, Ashley collapsed into Hunter's arms.

Nicki's opportunity was lost. She'd waited too long.

If she stayed a minute longer, she would scream like a banshee. She placed their flowers on the crypt's steps and returned to the elderly woman, wrapping an arm around her waist. "Are you ready, ma'am? Let's get you back to your granddaughter. These walkways are a nightmare and it's probably a hundred degrees out here."

As they moved in tandem away from the ornate Galen tomb, Nicki distinctly heard a clucking sound. Without a shadow of a doubt, Jeanette was clucking like one of Mamaw's free-range chickens.

# THIRTY-FOUR

*F*unerals had a way of putting things into perspective, of allowing a man to see his life as it was and implement necessary changes while there was still time. *Grandmere's* funeral forced Hunter to see what a mess he'd made of his professional and personal relationships. When the SEC finished their investigation, he most likely wouldn't have a client still willing to invest their lunch money. He had brought disgrace to the Galen family, a proud and respected name in New Orleans for more than two hundred years. His family had used their wealth to help rebuild after Katrina. Now with the stigma of James's murder and his recent indictment as a white-collar thief, his mother wouldn't want to show her face in society.

But it was his personal quagmire troubling him today. He should have told Nicki he loved her and taken his chances. And he should have told Ashley not to attend the funeral. Now Nicki neither trusted nor believed in him and he couldn't blame her. She was probably on her way back to Natchez. Working as a greeter at a discount store had to be better than getting a two-timing swindler off the hook for murder.

Alone in his apartment, Hunter stripped off his jacket and tie and then draped them over a kitchen chair. He considered getting drunk but nixed that idea. Nicki's influence had changed him in more ways than one. How could he wallow in self-pity while James's murderer remained free to walk the streets, eating fried catfish and hushpuppies all day long? Although Nicki claimed she had the evidence from a handwriting expert to get his fraud charges dropped, they were no closer to finding the killer.

Reheating a cup of coffee in the microwave, Hunter watched heavy clouds darken until the sky opened with a deluge. Two hours later, elbow deep in the same financial papers that weren't getting him anywhere, a knock on the door distracted his attention. The knock didn't sound friendly.

Detective Saville was waiting with an unpleasant smile. "Afternoon, Mr. Galen. Mind if I come in?" Without waiting for an answer, he stepped into the foyer.

Hunter sighed in frustration. "By all means, Detective. Make my bad day complete."

"Oh, yeah, that's right. I read in the paper your grandma died. Sorry 'bout that. I heard she was a fine old lady. Must have been pretty upset with you lately." Saville swaggered into the living room, his eyes assessing every detail.

Hunter chose not to take the bait. "If she was, she never said. What do you want, Saville? I'm sure you didn't come down to the Quarter to express your sympathy. You could have just sent a card like everybody else."

Saville feigned a shocked expression. "Man, I couldn't send what I've got through the US mail. There are federal laws against that."

"What exactly shouldn't be sent through the mail?"

The detective's grin stretched from ear-to-ear as he pulled a manila envelope from his pocket. "Take a look, lover boy. See what that sweetheart of yours has been up to while you were robbing and pillaging your clients." He tossed a glossy five-by-seven on the coffee table with dramatic flair and dumped the remaining photographs into a heap.

Hunter picked up one to peruse. It was of his late partner and his former fiancée sitting in a booth with glasses of wine in front of them. James had his arm around Ashley's shoulders and both were smiling. Hunter felt his gut tighten. "Ashley met James for a drink to discuss something. So what? They were friends." Even though Hunter spoke the words, he didn't believe them.

"Come on, Galen. You're supposed to be a smart man." Saville selected a couple of others from the stack and held them up: Ashley undressing in James's living room; Ashley and James locked in a sensuous embrace. Both photos were grainy in quality, as though taken with a telephoto lens, but they left no doubt that the two had been involved in inappropriate activities for friends.

Hunter couldn't hide his revulsion that Ashley and James were lovers. He was nothing but a gullible fool who had been duped financially and romantically by the people he trusted most. The sandwich he ate after the funeral churned in his stomach. Uttering an oath, Hunter smashed his coffee cup against the fireplace bricks.

"My, my, you have a temper." Saville clucked his tongue. "There's no telling what a guy like you would do with something stronger than coffee under his belt."

"Where did you get these?"

"I sure didn't take them or I would have waited to get close-ups of Miss Louisiana *au naturele*. Get my drift?" The detective snickered like an immature adolescent.

Hunter lunged at him and grabbed the lapels of his suit jacket.

"Easy there, Galen." Saville shoved Hunter away. "I'd hate to arrest you for assaulting an officer when I got bigger plans for you, rich boy."

"The last time I checked, it's not illegal to be cheated on by your girlfriend," Hunter said through clenched teeth.

"True enough. I've got other charges in mind. Say, that Miss Menard is one fine lookin' woman. I might hang on to one of these after logging them into evidence. You know…to keep under my pillow for sweet dreams." Saville stuffed the photos back into the envelope.

"I don't think so." Hunter reached for the envelope, but Saville jammed it into his pocket. "Who took those?"

"That's a real good question. Some upstanding citizen sent them anonymously to my attention at the precinct. They must not know 'bout the obscene mail laws." Saville patted his jacket pocket. "And what these are, besides highly entertaining material, is proof of motive." His happy-go-lucky tone turned malicious. "Now we've got motive coming out the ears. You and the deceased were caught in a flimflam operation that went sour. Then you found out your little beauty queen was getting her toast buttered by both partners."

"Get out of my house, Saville. You turn everything dirty and perverse to suit your incredibly low standards."

"I'm going, Galen, because I have an appointment with the DA. I just stopped to pay you a courtesy call and give you a chance to confess and save the taxpayers of Orleans Parish the price of a trial." Saville laughed heartlessly on his way out the door. "And it's not me adding a dirty spin. These pictures speak for themselves."

As Saville went down the steps to the courtyard, Hunter punched in Nicki's cell number. The photographs the detective so enjoyed were evidence all right. Ashley was the one with motive because she didn't like not getting her way. He had been blind to what was going on between his partner and the so-called love of his life. Ashley may have slept with James, but she never would have married him. Nowak didn't bring enough to the table to satisfy her expensive tastes. Something had gone wrong between them; something had upset the apple cart. Maybe James had threatened to expose her secrets, so she did what any frantic social climber would do—eliminated the obstacle.

The call went straight to voice mail. "Nicki, we need to talk as soon as you get this. Don't play games with me, *O'lette*."

Hunter ended the call and began pacing the room. If Ashley killed James, she had nothing to lose by hurting Nicki. In desperation he called Nate, who picked up on the first ring.

"Hunter, what can I do for you?"

"Thanks again for coming to the funeral, Nate," he said. "Do you know where Nicki is? It's urgent I talk to her now, not when she gets around to checking her voice mail."

"I haven't seen her since the graveside in Lafayette Cemetery. She was in some serious discussion with Jeanette and then marched back to her car without saying goodbye to anybody. So very like my cousin—temperamental and impetuous. What's going on, Hunter? Has she been any help whatsoever with this investigation? I only believe half of what she reports back."

"Yeah, she's a big help, but I need to make some changes, ones Nicki isn't going to like. Things are getting out of hand, and I don't want her getting hurt. I can't go into details now, but I need her off the case. Can't you send her on assignment to Timbuktu for a while?"

Nate exhaled through his teeth. "Her license won't be good in Mali, and Nicki sure won't like getting fired from her first job."

"Then don't tell her. Let me do that. If you hear from her, just have her call me."

"I'm sorry, man. I knew we shouldn't have handed your case over to a greenhorn—"

Hunter shook his head impatiently. "That has nothing to do with it. Just have her call and tell her not to go anywhere near Ashley!" He hung up before Nate could pepper him with more questions. The last thing in the world he wanted to do was fire Nicki.

He would prefer having her close twenty-four seven, but knowing her knack for blundering into things, how could he protect her?

The ring of his phone spiked his heart rate, but one glance at the display indicated it was not the woman he was hoping to hear from.

"Hunter? It's me."

"I'm in a hurry here, Ashley. What do you want?"

"We need to talk." A note of panic affected her cultured drawl. "There are a few things I would like to explain."

"No doubt there are, but I don't have time or see the point. It's over between us. I don't know how to make it any plainer than that."

He heard a deep intake of breath. "I know that Detective Saville came to see you." She waited several moments for him to respond.

But Hunter had nothing to say. Ashley Menard already felt like an unpleasant memory from the distant past.

"I haven't seen the photos he said he had, but I can just imagine." She sounded indignant, as though shame rested with the photographer instead of with her. "You have to hear me out! I tried to tell you about James, but you wouldn't listen. You didn't want to know what evil your best friend was capable of."

"Let it go, Ashley." Hunter tried to stem the tide of useless excuses. He didn't care enough to listen to her reasons for her actions.

But she refused to be deterred. "James knew about my past, about the mistakes I made after college. He was blackmailing me to get what he wanted."

*Is there no end to the "poor me" spin she puts on everything?* "I saw the pictures. You didn't look like an innocent victim to me." Hunter gritted out his words in frustration.

"I did it for us! James would have told everyone just to spite you. He wanted everything you had, even me. He was so jealous, but it was just a game to him." Her voice cracked with emotion.

"You slept with my best friend so your tidy life would remain the same?" Hunter couldn't tell if she really believed she'd behaved nobly or if this was simply more manipulation. He'd already stomached enough of the conversation, along with her lying and cheating.

"I know I made bad decisions and then my world careened out of control. But that's over with. James can't hurt us anymore."

A cold shiver ran up Hunter's spine. *Did she just admit to murder?*

"What are you talking about? Did you kill James to stop his blackmail?" Hunter couldn't believe any woman was capable of such cruelty.

"Of course not, but I told him I wouldn't pay another dime. Now the problem has been eliminated."

Hunter was trying to talk rationally to a madwoman—a woman who already killed one person who stood in her way. "I gotta go, Ashley. Let me think it over, and we'll talk in a few days." He planned never to talk to her again, but inciting a psychopath wouldn't be smart.

The last sound he heard before ending the call was "I love you, Hunter."

His disjointed feeling of doom fanned into a full-fledged nightmare. He had to get Nicki far away from New Orleans. If Ashley killed once to save her grand plan, she would do it again. Hunter would stop at nothing to keep Nicki safe. She was the reason Saville's photos generated no emotion other than disgust. Nicki had filled his life with joy.

He could deal with his grandmother's death. He could even deal with the SEC trying him for fraud and embezzlement. But he wouldn't lose Nicki. For the first time in his life, he was in love. He just hoped he hadn't waited too long to tell her.

～

Ashley dried her tears on an Hermes scarf. She wouldn't waste time feeling sorry for herself. If she was going to win Hunter back, she had to act. He had changed. He had never been vindictive and unforgiving before. And when she pondered what might have caused his change in personality, only one possibility came to mind: Nicolette Price—that cheap little tramp from Natchez or whatever lay outside of nowhere along the Mississippi.

Ashley reached for her phone as a plan galvanized her to action. Ms. Price had ignored the first warning and continued to interfere. Although her old pals had tried, they had failed to deter Nicki's interest in Hunter. The two of them had been spotted dancing in the Quarter at one of Ashley's favorite haunts. When Hunter took her sailing on the *Queen Antoinette*, it was more than she could bear. This time her friends needed to utilize more forceful persuasion. Too much was at stake to allow Hunter the time to tire of tacky Nicki and come home where he belonged. Her girlfriends were already whispering behind her back. Even worse, they were starting to cluck their tongues in pity. *Poor Ashley. Hunter dumped her for a woman who worked for him. Tsk, tsk.*

And pity was something Ashley couldn't tolerate.

On the third ring the biggest and meanest of her former boyfriends from Forrest High picked up the phone. "Bobby?" she asked in her sexiest voice. "It's Ashley Menard. Are you busy? I have another job for you and the boys."

# THIRTY-FIVE

*T*ypical of her luck lately, the moment Nicki stepped into the shower, her phone rang. She fumbled with it, trying to answer without dripping water on the tiles. "Hello?" she said after a long pause.

"Good morning, Miss Price. Did I catch you at a bad time? Forgive me for calling on a Sunday, but this had just slipped my mind until today," said a singsong voice.

"It's fine, ma'am, but who is this?"

A hearty chuckle preceded introductions. "And here I thought you sat by your phone night and day, waiting for my call. It's Sophie Godrey from St. Landry Parish. You gave me your business card."

Nicki stopped worrying about puddles on the floor. "Yes, ma'am. I remember. Did you contact Sheriff Latanier on my behalf?"

"I did. He said you should come see him if you wanted to ask questions. He doesn't like discussing open cases over the phone. Old school, you know. He said he would be home this weekend."

"I would be happy to drive out this afternoon. May I call him to confirm the time?"

"No, he told me to just give you his address and directions. You can arrive anytime. He no longer attends Mass since his wife passed on. Poor dear," she added. Her accent deepened with her final assessment.

Unsure which Latanier was the "poor dear," Nicki pressed on. "If you could supply an address, I can use my GPS."

"Just jot down my directions. GPS won't do much good where he lives."

Without further argument, Nicki wrote down every landmark and twist in the road, thanked Mrs. Godrey, and ran to her closet. She had never got dressed and out the door so fast in her life.

It proved fortuitous that Nicki had noted every detail from the helpful dispatcher. The route to the home of the retired sheriff of St. Landry Parish was trickier than Dorothy's yellow brick road. She didn't know what kind of house she expected for a retired public servant, but it wasn't a double-wide trailer set half a mile from the road. The plastic flower boxes beneath the windows were filled with dead geraniums, and rolled supermarket flyers sat in a pile next to the steps. It looked as if the sheriff simply retrieved them from the driveway and tossed them into the weeds.

Nicki approached the entrance cautiously. The front door was open, the screen door closed but not latched. Drone from the TV indicated somebody was home, yet no one answered when she knocked or called out a friendly greeting. No way did she want to enter the home of someone who had worn a gun on his hip throughout his career. However, peeking in the window wasn't beneath her dignity.

Clutter covered every surface of the room. Apparently, when the sheriff ran out of surfaces, he began stacking things in corners—DVDs, books, magazines, and crates of old board games. Someone in the household must have loved garage sales, perhaps bargaining for "one price buys the lot" merchandise. Nicki suspected nothing had been thrown out since the man's wife had passed.

With no sheriff in sight, Nicki crept around to the back of the house and discovered a very different world indeed. An oyster shell path led through the manicured lawn down to a broad bayou, where not a single bullrush or cattail grew along the bank. Unlike the interior of his home, Sheriff Latanier maintained a *Better Homes and Gardens* backyard. Matching Adirondack chairs provided comfortable spots for two anglers. A fishing pole rested in an aluminum bracket, while the world's largest tackle box sat at the feet of the dock's sole occupant.

"Sheriff Latanier?" Nicki approached cautiously.

"Miss Price, I presume."

"Yes, sir. I hope I'm not interrupting you."

"Not at all. I've been expecting you since Sophie Godrey called." He finally pivoted enough to meet her gaze.

Nicki choked back a gasp. If forced to venture a guess, she would surmise the sheriff was a radiation or chemo patient of the strongest potency. His skin was tightly drawn over his facial bones, his eyes deeply set within the sockets. "I'm grateful you were willing to see me, sir."

"Have a seat, Miss Price." Latanier pointed at the other chair. "I don't know what help I can be. You've read my report, which I reviewed again recently in anticipation of this visit, and I have no further information to add. No new leads, if that's why you're here."

Nicki sat primly and crossed her legs. "I realize you didn't have the same forensic capabilities back when you first investigated my father's death that you would now, sir. Perhaps new evidence would lead to his killer."

He studied her for a moment. Then he said, not unkindly, "We did our job, Miss Price. None of the guns on the premises had been recently discharged. No one in the cabin tested positive for gunshot residue. Nobody heard a shot. There was no blood on the dock or by the water's edge. I agree that your daddy's death was no accident, but I can't arrest somebody without hard evidence— not back then and not now."

Nicki dug her fingernails into the wood. "If you could have arrested somebody that night, who would it have been?"

Latanier grinned but shook his head. "You're a professional now, Miss Price, so act like it."

"You're retired now, sir, and I'm Kermit Price's daughter. This conversation is off the record."

The sheriff gazed at the water, where fish jumped at low-flying insects twenty feet away. "Those Cheval brothers had rap sheets longer than your arm. Junior Cheval wouldn't like somebody cheating him at cards, but I had nothing to arrest him on. Nobody saw Junior or Terrence or Louis with blood or anything else on them. I interviewed those witnesses on Saturday and then came back the next morning to talk to everybody again, including that little boy."

Nicki's breath caught in her throat. "What little boy? Your report doesn't mention a child."

Latanier shrugged. "Probably because he wasn't a witness. The kid was asleep during the poker game and whatever took place afterward. I saw no reason to put his name in my official report."

Nicki pulled her water bottle from her purse, her throat suddenly dry. "Who was he?"

Latanier's brows knit together. "Don't recall his name, but he was the son of the guy who owned the cabin. The kid went to bed before the craziness started."

"How old?" she gasped. "How old would you say he was?" Nicki suddenly remembered Nate's warning about turning over rocks.

The sheriff rubbed the bridge of his nose. "Can't say for sure, but probably around seven or eight."

Nicki released her death grip on the chair and struggled to stand. "I appreciate your seeing me today, Sheriff. At least I know which direction to head in. Lovely place you have here, by the way. I'll see myself out."

Seven or eight? Nicki placed one foot in front of the other and forced herself to walk away from the dock. Not Nate. It had been Sean, his younger brother.

# THIRTY-SIX

St. Landry Parish, home of the retired sheriff, was only a couple of hours from Natchez. But Nicki wouldn't have cared if it were a thousand miles. She wasn't going back to New Orleans until she talked to Sean. Seventeen years was long enough to wait—she wouldn't let one more night go by. She punched in Nate's number as soon as her phone found a signal.

He answered on the first ring. "Hey, Nicki, where are you?"

"I'm on my way to Natchez. I should say none of your business."

"Don't get huffy. I ask only because Hunter is looking for you."

"I'll call him later. Right now I need Sean's address. Could you give that to me?"

"Why would you need his address?"

"I heard he's moving in with that sweet girlfriend of his without first marrying her. I intend to do my womanly duty and set that boy straight."

Nate was silent for a few moments. Then he said, "Okay, why do you really want to know? I doubt you would poke your nose into my brother's business. You haven't seen him in over a year. Me, on the other hand—"

"Just give me his address, Nate. Why do I have to tell you everything? Can't I have a little privacy?"

He had no answer to that. He recited an address on a street just east of the city limits. "What should I tell Hunter?"

"Tell him nothing. I'll call him the first chance I get." She hung up before her cousin decided to resume his questions.

When she pulled into the driveway of a duplex on a quiet street, Sean opened the front door before Nicki could ring the bell.

"I take it your brother warned you I was on my way," she said in greeting as she stepped past him into a tidy living room.

"Nate called, but apparently he has no idea as to why you would want to see me." Sean met and held her gaze.

"But you do, don't you, cousin?" Nicki's hands balled into fists.

"Yeah. I've been waiting for this visit for ten years, ever since my dad died." Sean pushed the door shut against the evening air.

Nicki shrugged off a prickle on the back of her neck. "Is your girlfriend home?"

"I sent Angela to the mall for extra memory sticks even though I have several in my desk drawer." Sean lowered himself to the couch much slower than a man of twenty-five, the same age as her, should.

"Sounds like you have something you need to get off your chest. Something that's long overdue." Nicki didn't hide her wounded disappointment.

He lowered his face into his hands, muffling his words. "I prayed this day would never come. Even after my dad died I was too ashamed to face you...or the rest of my family."

With the realization she was about to get the answers she'd been waiting for, Nicki grabbed the back of a chair for support. "You saw what happened to my dad at the cabin?"

He nodded mutely.

"You saw my dad's murder but said *nothing*?" Nicki's trepidation gave way to rage. "You'd better start talking now, Sean Price, or I will beat it out of you!"

A ridiculous threat, to be sure, but effective just the same. He peered up at her with a pale, stricken face. "I wasn't sleeping that night like everybody thought. The argument during the card game woke me up. It sounded mean, hateful, with foul language I'd never heard in that cabin before. I lay in bed listening to them for a while. One of those Chevals brought out a bottle of whiskey to pass around. And your dad kept raising the stakes, fattening the pot. They'd never played for stakes that high. I had a bad feeling the louder those brothers got. Then Junior called your dad a cheat and a liar and a whole lot of other things I'd never repeat. Uncle Kermit denied dealing from the bottom and tried to calm Junior down; everybody did. But there was no talking to Junior Cheval. Your dad said he was going to smoke a cigarette and stormed outside, furious. Those three brothers went after him."

Tears began to leak from his eyes, but he kept talking. "My dad tried to follow them down the path, but the biggest guy, I think his name was Louis, punched him in the gut. He told Dad to get back inside if he knew what was good for him. Junior told Louis to make sure nobody interrupted the friendly little chat he was going to have with Kermit." Sean pulled out a handkerchief to wipe his face. "I crawled out of my bedroom window and hid in the bushes. I knew how to reach the water without being seen."

Nicki forced herself to take a deep breath. "Did my dad paddle away in the pirogue?"

Sean nodded. "He tried to, but Junior caught up with him on the dock. They argued. Uncle Kermit said that he won fair and square and they were just sore losers. Junior said nobody had that kind of luck. Then your dad said he had a good luck charm and showed them his alligator belt with the fancy buckle. 'These Texas cowgirls never let me down.'"

Sean actually sounded like her father, a fact that sent a chill up Nicki's spine.

"That made Junior even madder and he pulled out a gun. It was down by his ankle under his pant leg. I didn't know what to do, Nicki. I thought about going back for help, but I was scared they would catch me spying on them. So like a coward I just sat there, motionless."

"You were only eight years old. Don't beat yourself up." Nicki wasn't sure where her sudden empathy was coming from.

An incongruous cuckoo clock nearly jarred them both from their seats. "I hate that clock, but Angela insisted on hanging it on the wall."

Nicki looked at it and then turned her gaze back to her cousin, waiting for the rest of the painful story with damp palms.

"When Uncle Kermit saw the gun, he took out his money clip and held it out to Junior. 'Fine,' he said. 'Take everything I won tonight. Me having a little fun is no cause for people to get hurt.' He tried to make a joke out of it."

"'You cheated us, Price. You invited us into this bug-ridden swamp and tried to rip us off.' Terrence tried to calm his brother down, but Junior wouldn't have it. 'I'll take your money along with that gator belt. From now on those cowgirls are my good luck charm.'"

"'No way,' said Uncle Kermit. 'Keep the money, even what I started the night with, but you ain't getting my belt.' He tossed the cash down on the dock and spit on it. Then Uncle Kermit climbed into the pirogue."

"Junior said, 'You stinkin' thief! I'd say your luck just ran out.'"

Sean covered his face again with his hands. "Are you sure you want to hear this? Maybe it's better if you don't know every detail."

Nicki moved to sit next to him on the couch. "I've waited so long. There's nothing you can say that would be worse than my imagination."

Nodding, Sean focused on the floor. "Junior pulled a piece

of PVC pipe from his pocket, some kind of homemade silencer. What kind of man carries one of those to go fishing?"

The rhetorical question required no answer.

"Before Uncle Kermit could push away from the dock, Junior shot him in the head. Your dad fell back, half in the water and half out. Junior picked up the money and tossed the gun into the pirogue. He told Terrence to tie our old pirogue—the one with a slow leak—onto the back of Kermit's. Terrence was to paddle far up the channel and come back with nothing but that fancy belt."

Nicki closed her eyes as her father's final minutes on earth played out in her mind. Had the bullet killed him instantly? Or had he drowned when Terrence swamped the boat once he reached a strong current. "What happened next?" she prodded.

"Terrence asked how he was supposed to get back. Junior said to paddle back in the small boat, swamp it a hundred yards out, and swim the rest of the way. Terrence said, 'Swim? There're gators in that bayou.' Junior said, 'Then I suggest you swim fast.' Junior went back to the cabin mad as a hornet. He told the men that Kermit took off with their money and Terrence went after him in the other pirogue."

Sean wiped away his tears. "Andre, Eugene, and Louis went to bed, but my dad stayed up with Junior. I think Dad was afraid to go to sleep. Once I figured out what Terrence planned to do, I prayed that gators would eat him. But a few hours later he walked in dripping wet. Terrence said dad's boat sunk and he had to swim back."

"Terrence said he never caught up with my dad?"

Sean nodded. "I stayed in that tree a long time, too afraid to come down. But when I finally crawled through my window, Dad was sitting on the bed, waiting for me."

"You didn't tell Uncle Charles what happened?" Nicki croaked, her voice raspy.

"I told him everything, but Dad made me promise to keep

quiet. He said the Chevals were bad blood. No telling what they might do. Junior might hurt me or my mom or Nate. He said nothing would bring Uncle Kermit back, so no good would come from ever telling the truth."

Nicki jumped to her feet and began to pace "And nobody found the gun or either pirogue?"

"Do you have any idea how many busted up boats sit on the bottom of the Atchafalaya? And guns, for that matter."

"What about the belt? Didn't Junior order Terrence to bring it back with him?"

"Terrence didn't walk in wearing it, if that's what you mean. And nobody called the police until late the next day. When the sheriff arrived, he had no grounds to strip-search people. The Chevals had a full day to hide it."

Nicki stood and hiked her purse to her shoulder, but she paused on her way to the door. She couldn't leave with one question hanging over her head like a cloud. "Why didn't you tell after Uncle Charles died? Are you still afraid of the Chevals?"

Sean shook his head. "No, I don't care what those river rats do. I was ashamed to face you...and my brother. I'd passed a point of no return years ago without knowing it."

"Nate doesn't know any of this?"

"He knows nothing. My dad wouldn't let me tell him either. When you called today, I felt only relief that the nightmare was finally over." He wiped his face with the handkerchief again and said, "I'm sorry, Nicki. Can you ever forgive me?"

"I already have, Sean." She offered her cousin a small but genuine smile. "But the nightmare may not be over. With what you told me, I plan to go back to the St. Landry Sheriff's Department. Sheriff Latanier had a bad feeling about Junior Cheval. We have probable cause to reopen the investigation if you're willing to make a statement."

"You don't think seventeen years is too late?"

"There's no statute of limitations on murder, but if there's enough evidence for the prosecutor to indict, you'll have to testify in court. So don't say you're willing if you're not one hundred percent sure."

"I'm in, Nicki. I'll do whatever it takes."

"Good. Keep your phone turned on." She strode out the door toward her car.

"Wait, it's too late to drive to New Orleans tonight. Sleep in our guest room and go home tomorrow. Then you'll be able to meet my fiancée."

"Thanks, but I plan to sleep on my mom's couch. Considering everything you told me, she and I have a little catching up to do." Nicki slipped behind the steering wheel and lowered the window. "I'll mention that Angela inhabits the guest room until the big day. That tidbit will get back to Aunt Rose and she can relax."

"I owe you, cousin. If there's anything I can do between now and the day you die, just say the word."

"I'll keep that in mind." Giving him a final wave, Nicki backed down his driveway and headed across town. Sean wasn't the only one who would sleep better tonight. Somehow knowing the truth made all the difference in the world.

By the time she'd walked in the door of her mom's apartment and seen her sweet face, the last bit of her anger was gone. Her mother wrapped her arms around her and welcomed her home. Home. Maybe it wasn't as chic at Hunter's Rue Royale address, but it was tidy and comfortable and had everything a person needed.

# THIRTY-SEVEN

An employer could always count on getting their money's worth from Nicki Price. Hadn't she filled all the saltshakers and catsup bottles after her restaurant shift even though officially off the clock? Hadn't she straightened the stacks of T-shirts in Chic Chicks at the mall before heading home? Hunter Galen deserved at least as much in exchange for four hundred a week plus expenses.

*Hunter.* An ache filled her heart remembering his tender words and his sweet kisses. But that's where she went wrong. She'd filled her head with what-ifs and maybe-some-days instead of what she had come to town for. Did all women fall into the same rut? Let an attractive man treat them decently, and suddenly they were hearing church bells and picking out wallpaper for the nursery. Hunter was a nice guy, no doubt about it. And he was a good man to work for, but he wasn't the right man for her. Even if he liked her, even if he found her reasonably attractive, one day he would wake up and realize she didn't belong in his world.

Unfortunately, unlike Dorothy from Kansas, Nicki couldn't go home anymore, not permanently. She came to New Orleans to earn a living and send money to her mother. Nate had given her a chance, and in return she'd spent her time with stars in her eyes dreaming about Hunter Galen. Knowing what she needed to do, Nicki took a long, hard look at the silly woman in the mirror. She was smart, well trained, and well motivated. Bridesmaids, picket fences, and playgroups would have to wait.

This Monday morning, Nicki had the evidence from the handwriting expert proving Ashley had forged Hunter's signature. And the fingerprints on the shell casings and beer cans came back to her old pals from high school. The same old pals had left their prints on the photos taken of her and Hunter. But was Ashley a murderer? What she needed was a recorded admission, and the woman might just hate her enough to provide one. Women like Ashley loved to rub defeat into the face of their adversaries. Nicki decided to stop at home to pick up her micro recorder. She would get the truth from the conniving Ms. Menard and prove how formidable a foe she could be. After all, what did she have to lose?

Smoke started filling her nostrils while still blocks from Christine's trailer in Chalmette. In an area of bizarre and often noxious odors following Katrina, the smell of smoke was unusual. And this wasn't the familiar scent of wood smoke, evoking campfires, marshmallows, and s'mores. This was the acrid smell of burnt plastic, rubber, and electrical components. As sirens wailed in the distance, traffic slowed to a crawl. Ducking down a side street, Nicki wound her way into the trailer park. Each street looked like every other except for flags, pennants, and decorations used to point the way home for the confused.

As she approached Christine's street, her throat tightened. For no apparent reason, goose bumps rose on her arms in the sweltering heat. Cars from local residents, spectators, and various police, fire, and rescue vehicles blocked her access. Nicki pounded the wheel in frustration and laid on her horn until a few cars moved from her path, but the street remained blocked. No one would get through this traffic jam anytime soon.

In exasperation Nicki parked in a driveway where no one appeared home—or were uninterested in the commotion—and left her name and cell number under the windshield wiper. Oddly, as she drew near to her temporary home, the crowd of rubbernecks parted. Toddlers and their weary mothers watched her from doorways. While her eyes burned and watered, Nicki fought the impulse to gag from the foul metallic taste in her mouth.

The police had erected a perimeter of wooden barricades where she usually parked her car three trailers away. White smoke hung heavy in the air, obliterating the scene beyond their cordon. Nicki saw no fire, no flames, and no fireman scurrying with their hoses and ladders. Only red and blue lights on the police cars spun eerily in the thick air.

Nicki squeezed between two barricades until stopped by a strong hand and a gruff voice. "Ma'am, stay back! You can't go any farther." The fireman tightened his viselike grip on her arm.

"I live here!" Nicki pointed in the direction of Christine's trailer, struggling to free herself from the man's grasp. "Please, I must see if my roommate is okay. Her name is Christine. Christine Hall." Her voice sounded unrecognizable in her own ears as fear crawled up her spine.

"What unit number, miss?" The question floated from the smoke before a thin, middle-aged man appeared. "I'm Mike Merrell, the Chalmette fire investigator."

Nicki tried to stop gagging, but the more she coughed, the more the smoke irritated her lungs. "Number...number twenty-eight. Please let *go* of me!" She wrenched free from the fireman.

Merrell looked down at the clipboard in his hand. "Looks like number twenty-eight is where the fire originated. The blaze had already spread to adjacent trailers before fire personnel arrived."

Just then the breeze partially cleared the air, allowing the outline of three windowless and roofless trailers to appear, their smoke-blackened walls puckered and warped from the intense heat. The middle trailer, the one Nicki had called home, was nothing but a mass of twisted metal and smoldering debris. Although her lungs ached from coughing, she couldn't leave the surreal dead zone.

"Did you say you're Christine Hall? Do you live in number twenty-eight?" Merrill's voice brought Nicki's attention away from the horror.

"No," she rasped. "I'm Nicolette Price. I've been staying with Christine for a few weeks."

"You weren't with Miss Hall this afternoon?" Merrill jotted something down on his soot-spotted tablet.

"No, but I talked to her a couple hours ago. She wasn't planning on going anywhere."

The fireman and arson investigator exchanged an odd glance—or maybe it was her imagination. Nicki felt on the verge of hysteria.

Just then two firemen in breathing apparatus stepped from the smoke and herded the crowd back, trying to get everyone behind the barricades.

"Let's step away to talk, Miss Price. The fumes from these trailers as well as much of their contents are toxic and can cause short-term respiratory distress in addition to long-term problems." Merrill pulled her into a yard five trailers away from Christine's. "Fire personnel have the blaze contained. All we can do is wait for the debris to cool. I assure you, any victims of smoke inhalation have already been transported to the hospital."

"Where's Christine?" Nicki demanded. "Send your men to find her. She may be wandering around the village hurt or confused."

"We've searched the general vicinity, ma'am." The investigator waited until she met his eye. Then, more gently, he said, "I'm afraid we brought a body out of unit twenty-eight. It appears to be female, but I'm afraid positive identification will take a while.

We're waiting on the county medical examiner. I will also have the fire marshal called in due to the fatality."

When she swayed on her feet, Merrill reached out to steady her. Fighting back the impulse to wretch, Nicki's eyes felt like dry cinders that peered through slits in her face. She cleared her throat and wiped her nose on her sleeve. "Only one body? You didn't find two little kids?"

"Only one body, Miss Price. Rest assured, the firefighters found no one else in the trailer. No children."

Nicki heard the words as though deep underwater. Her roommate, confidante, and friend was dead. She clenched her eyes shut, trying not to envision the final minutes of Christine's life. She had been frightened of fire. She wouldn't even burn candles. She didn't buy her first box of votives until after she moved to the trailer park. "After all, tin cans don't burn," she had told Nicki.

"How did this happen?" Nicki dug in her tote bag for her water bottle. The first sip hit her stomach hard. "How can a tin can burn?" she asked through tears of frustration.

Merrill shook his head as he pulled a white handkerchief from his pocket. "Please take this, Miss Price. And because you also lived in the unit I'll tell you what I know, but all facts are unsubstantiated until the investigation is complete and an autopsy performed. I'm fairly certain we're looking at foul play...arson with murder or manslaughter specifications. I believe an incendiary device was tossed into the home that ignited whatever combustibles lay nearby. Apparently, the device landed near the water heater, which may have had a small propane leak, one Miss Hall wasn't aware of. We're lucky that tank didn't blow up or the number of casualties would have been much higher. A propane explosion could have leveled the block. That leak probably caused the rapid acceleration."

Staring at the wiry man, Nicki wiped her eyes and nose with different ends of his pristine hanky. "This wasn't an accident?" She sounded like a bullfrog.

"I'm sorry, ma'am. Somebody torched that trailer. Whether or not they planned to kill Mrs. Hall, the end result remains the same."

With her face streaming with tears, Nicki heard someone calling her name.

"Nicki!" A terrified voice wafted through the smoke and mist.

"I'm here!" She answered, unsure if it was she they sought.

A few moments later Hunter's handsome face was visible through the haze. "Hunter!" she choked out, going to him. "The firemen think Christine is d-dead."

He enveloped her in his arms and pulled her against his chest. "Oh, Nicki. I'm so sorry." His words were soft as a prayer.

"I mean, some poor soul is dead, and most likely it's Christine because that was her trailer," Nicki rambled, incoherent with grief.

He just held her, and Nicki was grateful he didn't offer pointless phrases like *It'll be all right,* or *Let's hope it's not her* because they both knew it was Christine, and things wouldn't be all right for a long time.

Nicki drew back a little. She blew her nose and then peered into Hunter's blue eyes. "What are you doing here?"

"I called Nate, but he only knew you were on your way home from Natchez. I left several messages for you, but when you didn't call me back I became worried and couldn't wait any longer. I had to come looking for you." He pulled her close again, resting his cheek on her hair. "What else did the fireman say?"

"They think it was arson. Somebody tossed something into the trailer that set off a gas leak on the hot water tank. Whatever happened, someone did this on purpose to poor Christine—"

Hunter had a bad feeling, but he tried to keep his voice calm even though his heart raced as he asked, "Who would want to kill Christine?"

"I don't know. Maybe her ex-husband? It could have been Preston Hall. He lost his temper with his kids more than once."

"Did Preston ever threaten her? What do you remember?"

She pulled away from him. She saw that his demeanor had changed from comforting to something fiercer. "I don't know exactly. Hunter, why are you—"

"*Think*, Nicki. Were Christine and her ex fighting? What did she say?"

She tried to recall everything Christine had mentioned about the father of her children. "No, Preston had been more reasonable lately. He'd even talked about unsupervised visitation and possible joint custody down the line. Apparently, full-time parenting wasn't as much fun as he thought it would be." Her words trailed off as reality hit home. As of today, Preston's custody would be one hundred percent.

Hunter turned from her and approached Mr. Merrill, who was interviewing other witnesses. "Excuse me," he interrupted. "I'm Hunter Galen, Miss Price's employer. This wasn't an accidental fire? Are you talking murder?" Hunter handed the investigator his business card.

"We won't know until the fire marshal completes his report. In the meantime, Mr. Galen, you need to step behind the barricades. This is a police matter that doesn't concern Miss Price's employer."

Hunter leaned forward so that they were nose-to-nose. "If this was attempted murder, Mrs. Hall may not have been the intended target. And that concerns me plenty."

Merrill jotted that down on his clipboard and summoned a policeman with a wave of his hand. "There will be a full arson investigation, I assure you. Although I can't discuss the case with you, you may report your suspicions to a police detective. Miss

Price will need to give a full statement as well. This policeman will point you in the right direction." With that, Merrill strode toward a cluster of gawkers at the barricades.

"What is the matter with you?" Nicki hissed. "Why would you bully him?"

"Let's get away from these trailers." He took her firmly by the hand. "I want to keep you safe until we give our statements, and that won't be here."

Nicki had had enough people poking, pushing, and pulling her for one day. She yanked her hand free and glared at him. "Stop dragging me around! I'm not leaving. I will stay here because this is where I live."

His determination softened. "There's nothing left, Nicki. Christine's home, your possessions, they have been destroyed. You can stay with me until you make other arrangements—"

"You're not the Red Cross, Hunter Galen. I can take care of myself. I will stay here until I find out if the person who died was Christine, for one thing. It could be an unfortunate Avon lady for all we know. And if it is her, I'm going after who killed her. So stand back and let me do what you pay me for!" She took a final swipe at her nose and stuffed the handkerchief in her pocket, certain Mr. Merrill wouldn't want it back. "I'm tired of everybody treating me as though I'm a nincompoop in need of coddling."

"I never said you were a nincompoop, and I only coddle you because I thought we are...we were..." Hunter curtailed what he planned to say as Merrill returned with his clipboard and a police detective. "Have it your own way," said Hunter, his expression suddenly thunderous. "Give your statement to the detective and help with the arson investigation. Once they learn you may have been the target, they will probably put you under police protection. But as of this moment, you're off the Nowak murder case.

Only people who can follow orders work for me." He stomped away as though suddenly in a big hurry.

Nicki turned to the investigator. "Could you give me a minute? A personal emergency just came up."

She ran after Hunter without waiting for an answer. "You're firing me? My best friend gets killed, everything I own is incinerated, and you pick *now* to can me? Of all the insensitive, poorly thought out..."

But Hunter wasn't listening as he maneuvered his way through people with nothing better to do than watch trailers smolder.

"Hunter! Stop! Why would you think this has anything to do with me? It could have been that creep Christine dated. She and Travis broke up on bad terms."

Nicki had to dodge residents and ambulance chasers all the way back to Hunter's car. The shiny black Corvette was coated with a heavy layer of soot. Coughing, out of breath, and afraid he would leave, she threw herself in his path and put her hand on his chest. "What is the matter with you? Talk to me."

He stopped fumbling with his keys and looked her in the eye. "From the day we met, you never trusted me or gave me a chance. Always ready to believe the worst, that's your motto." Hunter shrugged off her hand. "I'm sorry about Christine, but now you know how it feels to lose a friend. James was my friend, despite everything that happened. Remember? You, on the other hand, never wanted my friendship or cared about me. This was nothing but a job to you." He jumped into his car and lowered the window with a press of a button.

"Where is all this coming from?" Nicki slapped her hand down on the convertible top in sheer frustration. "Let's give our statements to the police and find someplace to talk."

"No. I've already said my piece. Go prove yourself, *O'lette*.

Show the world what a great private investigator you are. But you'll be doing it on someone else's dime. You're fired."

Hunter didn't hear her gasp as he started the engine with a roar of horsepower, offered her one last scowl, and drove away.

Flummoxed, Nicki stood in the street until his taillights disappeared around the corner, thinking that maybe three little words—words she had never bothered to say—may have changed her run of bad luck forever.

# THIRTY-EIGHT

*T*he hardest thing in the world was not looking back. Hunter drove away from the chaos and confusion without looking in his rearview mirror at the woman he loved more than he thought possible. Had he looked at her tear-stained face a moment longer, witnessed her grief from losing her friend in an awful twist of fate, he couldn't have done what he had to do. Foreboding tied his stomach into knots, heightening his awareness of the grim neighborhood as he drove away from the cruel and senseless murder. He didn't want to fire Nicki, but no rational explanation would keep her from danger. She could sniff out trouble like a beagle after a fox.

Nicki Price...no artificial sweeteners, no hidden agendas. What you saw was what you got. And what Hunter saw he wanted for the rest of his life.

Besides, it was time for him to take a stand. No more trying to keep everyone placated. No more pleasing people to keep the peace. That was what got him into this mess in the first place. If he had confronted James after his initial not-quite-kosher stock trades, maybe he would still be alive. If he had confronted Ashley at his grandmother's wake with the truth—that no amount of feminine machinations would get them back together—maybe

Christine would still be alive. He couldn't stand around trying to convince Nicki that a psychopath had her squarely in her sights. Better to hurt her feelings, even if she ended up hating him, than allow anything to happen to her.

Hunter knew with certainty that Ashley hadn't acted alone. Maybe she could kill a lover who knew her secrets—a man who held all the aces in a rigged game. Maybe she could manipulate Hunter's assistant into sending Nicki on a wild chase into the swamp that was meant to scare her off the investigation. But construct an incendiary device and then use it to kill an innocent woman? For that Ashley would need a little help. And who better as an assistant than the man who had lost a fortune at the hands of James Nowak? Daddy Menard—the man who lived and breathed to make his daughter happy after his wife died.

Hunter wasted no time getting out of Chalmette and back to town. He drove down North Claiborne back to the Garden District, every mile fueling his own personal fire. He thought about calling Nate, knowing he owned several firearms; he even contemplated calling his brother. Ethan had the uncanny ability of getting whatever he needed in the blink of an eye. But when Hunter pulled into the cobblestone driveway of the Menard Garden District home, he was alone and armed with nothing but his rage.

It was high time for him to make a stand.

He parked on the crushed oyster shell drive and headed toward the front door. Since their breakup he could no longer go around back, walk into the enormous kitchen, and greet the household staff with a casual "How ya doin?" Instead, he knocked and waited for someone to open the carved wooden door.

"Good afternoon, Mr. Galen," said the housekeeper curtly. The familiar "Mr. Hunter" was gone.

"Good afternoon, Mrs. Taylor."

"Miss Ashley isn't home. I suspect she's at one of her salons or her townhouse." The housekeeper tried to shut the door, but Hunter wedged his foot against the frame. "I've come to see Mr. Menard. Would you please tell him I'm here?"

Looking confused, the woman sniffed indignantly. "Mr. Menard isn't here either."

Hunter stepped into the foyer and glanced around. The Christmas open houses and holiday parties in the three-story center hall seemed so long ago. "If you don't mind, I'll wait for him in his study. I have an urgent matter to discuss."

His brashness took her by surprise. "He's not in New Orleans, Mr. Galen. Mr. Menard packed a bag a few days ago and left. He told me not to call him unless the levees gave way or it was a matter of life or death."

"Where did he go, Mrs. Taylor? This *is* life or death."

She clasped her hands together and then shrugged. "Where he always goes when he wants to be alone. He's at his house in Terrebonne."

"Thank you, ma'am." Hunter left before the housekeeper regretted revealing so much to the man who jilted the girl she had practically raised.

According to Ashley, Phil holed up in the swamp when he wanted to get blistering drunk so as not to frighten her or the hired help. Hunter headed to the bayou as fast as possible so Menard didn't get drunker than he already was.

Instead of dwelling on the folly of visiting the father of a sociopathic killer alone and unarmed, Hunter focused his thoughts on Nicki. Even after she learned the true reason for her dismissal, she probably wouldn't want anything to do with him. She was a country girl from Mississippi. Once he'd caught her studying him while reconstructing the Galen-Nowak accounts as if to ask, *How could you let things get so out of hand?*

Indeed, how had he? How could he become engaged to a woman he didn't love, get swindled by a partner who systematically destroyed his company, and, worse, place Nicki in the cross-hairs of a dangerous woman? Female jealousy could be deadly even without Ashley's lack of a moral compass. At least for now, Nicki was safe. Without a job or place to stay, she would have to return home to Natchez. Once James's killer was behind bars, he would look for her there. Maybe she would give him a chance to make things right or maybe she wouldn't, but at least she would be out of harm's way.

Ashley didn't like being told no. And she didn't like figuring out he was in love with someone else.

A light rain turned into a downpour during the drive out to Lake Boudreaux, causing the Corvette to hydroplane across the slick pavement. Hunter breathed a sigh of relief when he turned into the drive and noticed for the first time how dilapidated the house had become. Spiky weeds had sprouted throughout the lawn, the kind that pinched your feet if you walked barefoot. Several trees sagged from heavy vines and broken branches, while tattered Spanish moss and dead leaves swirled around the foundation. The house resembled a setting in a Faulkner novel right before an arsonist reduced it to a smoldering ruin. Hunter spotted Menard's vintage Mercedes under the portico as he crossed the leaf-strewn porch and knocked. Tired of waiting for servants, he would break down the door if he had to.

When the door opened, the butler peered at him. "Can I help you, sir?"

"I need to see Mr. Menard," he announced. "I know he's here and I know where to find him." Hunter strode through the expensive but shabby main rooms toward the back of the house.

"He's in the library," the man called as an afterthought.

Menard had remodeled an old porch into something one

would expect in an English manor house. The servant didn't follow Hunter down the hallway.

"Mr. Menard?" He rapped on the closed door. "It's Hunter Galen. I would like a word with you, sir." His choice of words struck him as absurd. He wanted far more than a word. When no one replied, Hunter pushed open the door.

Philip sat alone in the dim room behind an antique walnut desk. As expected, an open bottle of one-hundred-proof bourbon reposed on his left, along with a crystal tumbler on his right. The bottle was three-fourths gone, the glass dull with smudges. The room reeked of cigar smoke. But the real ruination lay with Menard himself. Why hadn't Hunter noticed how paunchy and bloated Ashley's father had become? Deep lines ringed his bleary eyes—the whites tinged with yellow jaundice—an ominous indicator of a distressed liver. Despite the stifling temperature in the room, a moth-eaten cardigan covered a shirt that looked as though it had been worn for days. Philip's thick, silver hair was striated by greasy comb tracks, while his aristocratic nose flamed with broken capillaries, another mark of a life ruled by alcohol.

"Come in, Hunter. I was wondering when you would pay me a social call." His voice sounded hoarse and thick but not unfriendly. He motioned to the leather wing chair in front of his desk. "Have a seat. Care for a drink?"

"Don't you think you've had enough?" Hunter tried to sound concerned, as though he cared about this madman.

"What difference does it make?" Menard tipped the smudgy glass to his lips. "They turned me down for a liver transplant, so I'm dying. You here 'bout that money you owe me, boy, the money your slimeball partner stole?" He filled another tumbler with an inch of bourbon and pushed it toward his visitor.

Hunter decided to see what information Menard offered on his own. "Partly." He took a small sip and set the glass down.

"That thief robbed me of almost a million dollars when you tally it all up." A slight slur betrayed his inebriation.

"As I told you earlier, an independent accountant has both sets of books—Nowak's fictitious set and the one reconstructed from his laptop. When he arrives at the dollar amount you were scammed and not normal investment losses, I will make full restitution even if I have to mortgage everything I own. But that's not why I'm here."

"Then you're here 'bout my Ashley. You ready to make amends and patch things up? I don't like how you shamed her in front of her friends, breaking up with her like that. But I'm willing to let it slide since her slate ain't exactly clean as a whistle." Menard refilled his glass to the rim. "That gal is impetuous like her mother, and she don't always think clearly. She's made some foolish decisions."

Prostitution and blackmail weren't impetuous mistakes. Did Menard equate his daughter's behavior to skinny-dipping during spring break? "I'm not here for advice on winning Ashley back. Nothing can be farther from my mind. I'm here to find out what you know about arson and murder in Chalmette today."

Menard straightened in his chair. "Chalmette? I don't know anybody living in Chalmette. What's left out there since Katrina? What are you talking about, boy?"

"I'm no boy, Mr. Menard. I'm the man who will make sure Ashley goes to jail once I get proof. And so will you if you helped her in any way."

Fierce color rose up Menard's neck into his face. His hand gripping the glass trembled with fury. "I don't know anybody out there, so I got no reason to start fires. You'd better talk sense, Hunter, or I'll throw you out so—"

"My private investigator was living in Chalmette with a roommate. Somebody torched their trailer this morning and killed her friend. I believe Nicki was the target, not her roommate. Nobody had motive to go after Nicki but Ashley, but it's doubtful she would do something like this alone."

Menard gazed into the amber liquid as though fitting jigsaw pieces together in his mind. "Your investigator that blond-haired gal who came to your grandma's funeral, the one you made a scene with?"

"There was no scene in the church. I merely wanted Nicki where she belonged, which is by my side."

Menard threw his tumbler at the wall, shattering the glass into dozens of shards. Amber liquid dripped down the paneling. "You are a fool, Galen! Throwing away a quality woman like Ashley for some...some Mississippi trash like Nate Price's backwater cousin."

Hunter chose not to point out that if any location constituted backwater, it was the house they were arguing in, but it was Menard's other misconception he couldn't resist. "So you believe *quality* women have affairs with their fiancé's business partners? The same partner that she helped to scam clients out of their life savings? I would say Ashley made her decision long before I made mine."

Menard leaned precariously back in his chair as a string of curses spewed from his mouth. "I don't care about the money. You can tell that accountant to forget tallying what I'm owed. I know Ashley made some big mistakes, but I had a little talk with her and she won't make any more."

He sounded sure of himself, but how could he possibly control the actions of a grown woman? "What are you talking about?"

"Look here, Hunter. You patch things up with my daughter. Tell her you're willing to forget the past and start over. I know that's what she wants, but she's too stubborn to ask. You two can get hitched in someplace small but nice. Then take her away from New Orleans for a while. Maybe go to Europe. She always wanted to spend time in Tuscany. Rent an Italian villa for a few months—my treat. We'll forget the million dollars Nowak stole and consider it her dowry." Menard chuckled as he reached for the bottle and a fresh glass, his large belly quaking beneath his wrinkled shirt.

Hunter shook his head to make sure this wasn't a nightmare he'd wake from in a cold sweat. He swallowed a mouthful of bourbon and then set the glass out of reach. "No, Mr. Menard, there won't be any wedding, small, intimate, or otherwise. You're not following this, are you? Your little girl, the one you doted on since birth, is a murderer. That's a tad worse than sleeping with my best friend and helping him steal from a company that would have been half hers one day. She burned a trailer to the ground in Chalmette and killed a mother of two children who had nothing to do with this sordid soap opera. And she killed James Nowak. He may have been a slimeball like you said, but he didn't deserve to be shot and killed at close range."

Menard pushed back from the desk as his face morphed into something grotesque. "I don't know nothing about a Chalmette trailer, but I know for a fact Ashley didn't kill Nowak." An evil glint sparked in his dull eyes. "Because I did."

Hunter stopped trying to gauge how far Phil would go for his daughter. "*You* killed him?"

"That's right. He wasn't just blackmailing Ashley. He started blackmailing *me*. All she could pay was a grand a month to keep her indiscretions quiet. Nowak figured he could squeeze me for a lot more. So not only did he steal from my investment account, he demanded five thousand a month in cash or he would tell you Ashley was a tramp."

Hunter could feel the blood drain from his face when Menard voiced Nowak's tawdry description of his daughter. "I couldn't let him do that. She was about to marry into the best family in Louisiana. She would be set for the rest of her life. And that son of a gun was about to ruin everything." Menard's cold, steely eyes were fixed on Hunter's. "*Nobody* messes with my little girl's happiness. Not Nowak and not you, Galen. So what's it going to be?"

Menard modulated his tone as he pulled a large handgun from under the desk. "You think about it. I'm offering you a chance to put all of this behind you. I'm still a powerful man. My influence will go a long way in reassuring your clients—maybe some will even stay with your firm. I'll help you shake off the scandal and put the blame squarely where it belongs—on Nowak's dead shoulders. I'll issue a press statement releasing your company from personal culpability." He paused and sighed wearily. "I'm an old man, Hunter. I'm ready to take my chances with the hereafter as long as I see my wife again. I'm leaving everything to Ashley. Think about what you're throwing away for some trailer trash from Mississippi."

# THIRTY-NINE

*Trailer trash from Mississippi?* Nicki heard the hoarse, scratchy words and stiffened her spine. That red-faced old man had better not be referring to her. Ashley must have learned her sweet-talking style from dear old dad. Nicki pressed her ear to the library door and felt her temper shoot into the stratosphere. In the last twenty-four hours, she had been insulted, ridiculed, burned out of her home, lost a friend, and fired—and then she'd watched the only man she ever cared about drive away from her.

She loved Hunter. She must, or it wouldn't have hurt so much when he walked out of her life. Nicki had never fallen so hard for anyone, let alone someone as rich, powerful, and sophisticated as he. What could she possibly offer a man like him?

It didn't really matter that she'd been fired. She was going to stay on the case until the job was finished. *After all, don't fired employees get two weeks' notice?* And she had no intention of answering her phone or checking voice mail for the next few days. Hunter hadn't killed James Nowak. Whoever killed Christine probably had, and Nicki had finally figured it was the bad man on the other side of the door. She would bring Mr. Menard to justice and *then* Hunter could write her out of his life.

Drawing her Beretta from the waistband of her jeans, Nicki gently nudged the door with her knee. Her concealed carry permit had been waiting in the mailbox at the entrance to the trailer park. Also in the box was a cell phone bill and a letter from her grandmother. Nicki had moved her weapon to a lockbox in her trunk, far from curious fingers if Christine's kids came for a visit. Now the shiny handgun bolstered her confidence as she nudged the door another inch. Pure adrenaline had fueled her high-speed race from Chalmette to Terrebonne Parish, and one additional surge should carry her through.

"I'm giving you one last chance to do the right thing, Hunter. Think about your family. Wouldn't they prefer you to put this behind you?"

"Let me think a minute," said Hunter. His mellow drawl practically curled Nicki's toes. "Would my family want me to marry a beautiful, hardworking, nice girl from Natchez whom I happen to love? Or a lying, manipulative hooker who's most likely an arsonist and a murderer?"

"Why, you ungrateful—"

Nicki heard the sound of scraping wood and scuffling feet, followed by the roar of a high-caliber gun fired in confined quarters. She pushed into the room, dropped into a crouch, and raised her weapon. The tang of gunpowder overpowered the smell of dusty books and spilled alcohol. "Freeze!" she shouted. She tried to take aim as two men flailed on the other side of the desk, but everything was happening too fast. "Freeze!" she repeated, seeing the large revolver in Menard's hand. "Drop the weapon!"

As Nicki took aim, the two men jostled like caged bears, punctuated by a string of French curses. Hunter held Menard's forearm while the gun's barrel swung dangerously between a spot on the ceiling and the center of his chest. Unable to get a clear shot, she shouted again. "I'm not telling you again, Menard. Drop the

weapon!" A second ear-shattering blast obscured any further discussion on the topic. With her ears ringing from the discharge,
Nicki holstered her weapon and launched herself across the desk
at Ashley's father. The two of them hit the polished library floor
with a resounding thud, along with an ominous crack of bones.

Menard released a howl of pain, giving Nicki an opportunity
to kick the weapon out of reach and slap a handcuff on his right
hand. When she grabbed his left wrist, Menard bellowed in agony.
"My arm's broken! Have some mercy."

*Like the mercy you showed James Nowak?* The uncharitable
thought crossed her mind until her Christian upbringing took
control. Nicki attached the other handcuff to the leg of the five-
hundred-pound mahogany desk and turned her attention to
Hunter. He was slouched against the wall several yards away, his
expression an odd grimace.

"Are you all right?" She dropped into a crouch by his feet.

"I'm fine, *O'lette*. Never better. You saved me." He licked his
thumb and tried to clean a smudge from her cheek.

The feel of his fingers on her face was heavenly, but she had a
job to do. Nicki called nine-one-one, gave specific instructions
as to her location, and requested an ambulance. After furnishing
identification and assuring the dispatcher she was in no immediate danger, Nicki ended the call and slid down next to Hunter.
"They'll be here in three shakes of a lamb's tail."

"How did you know to come here? When did you guess it was
Philip and not Ashley?"

"It was just a hunch. I planned to have it out with the Ice
Queen. You know, wring a confession from her using my bare
hands around her throat. I stopped home to get my micro
recorder. That's when I found the fire and Christine...and you."
Fighting back tears, Nicki swallowed the lump in her throat. "I
knew something was off the mark. Ashley might spike someone's

drink or scratch out a woman's eyes in a jealous rage, but toss a firebomb into a house? I don't think so. She would be too afraid of breaking a nail or singeing her eyebrows." Nicki released a sigh. "No, setting a fire wouldn't be her style...at least, not without help. Then I remembered something I overheard at James's funeral. Mr. Menard said, 'This might be tough going right now, Hunter, but everything will work out better for you and Ashley in the long run.'"

"I remember," Hunter said as he settled his right arm around her shoulders.

"I thought it was an insensitive thing to say at the time, but later it got me thinking and I started putting two and two together. Nowak had been blackmailing Menard for a lot of money in addition to swindling his portfolio. When Menard realized he was being scammed, he went to see your partner and in a rage killed him. Then he tried to make it look like a suicide as an afterthought. He must have figured he wasn't the only one being swindled and many clients would have motive. And the cops probably wouldn't look too hard at your future father-in-law."

"You think you're so clever." Menard's voice could be heard from the other side of the desk where Nicki had handcuffed him. "You don't know anything. You think I did this for money...to get out from under blackmail? I was willing to pay that creep five grand for the rest of my life if he would have kept his mouth shut. But Nowak was drowning in gambling debts and got scared. He said he was going to tell Hunter everything—how he ripped off the company and about the blackmail. Ashley hadn't been helping him—she was being blackmailed too—all because she sold herself to rich men after college." His voice dropped to a whisper. "I couldn't let Nowak ruin my little girl's life. She is all I have left in this world."

For an instant, Nicki pitied the man who loved his daughter

so much that he would commit murder. Then she remembered Kerry and Evan Hall, who would grow up without their mother and her compassion waned. "What about torching the trailer? Did you do that for love too?" She felt Hunter's arm tighten around her shoulder.

"I'm saying this for the last time—I don't know anything about a trailer fire. Ask my butler. He will verify I've been here for three days drinking myself senseless. The farthest I've gone from this room is the bathroom."

Nicki locked gazes with Hunter. His cool blue eyes reflected her own opinion. For once in his sorry life, Menard was telling the truth. Someone else must have helped Ashley with her dirty work.

Hunter enfolded Nicki in an embrace, and for a few precious moments, she allowed herself to be comforted by the man she loved. "How ya doing, *O'lette*?" he asked softly, stroking her hair. "You've had quite a day to write down in your diary."

"I've been better, to tell the truth, but at the moment I'm feeling pretty good."

"You handled yourself magnificently."

"In that case, is there any chance of getting my job back? Going to interviews will be hard because all my fancy clothes burned in the fire."

"I have something more permanent in mind for you if you'll have me. Something that includes an apartment above an art gallery in the Quarter, whatever new clothes you want, and a lifetime supply of devotion." Hunter kissed the back of her fingers.

She swiveled to face him. "This almost sounds like a proposal. What exactly are you saying, boss? Spit it out before the cavalry arrives." Her stomach felt as though it would sprout wings and fly away.

"I'm saying I love you. And I want to marry you."

Nicki smiled gloriously at him. "I love you too. And that's the honest truth. But since I'm finally getting the hang of investigation, I'd really like my job back too."

"I think that can be arranged." Hunter pulled her close for a kiss.

When Nicki nuzzled against his chest, she felt a quiver of pain shoot through his body. She reared back and demanded, "Hunter, are you hurt? Were you *shot*? Why didn't you say something?" Opening his jacket, she saw the crimson stain on his left shoulder. "You're losing a lot of blood." Instinctively, she pressed her palm to the wound to staunch the flow.

Hunter winced. "Easy, sweetheart. It looks worse than it is. What did Clint Eastwood say in the spaghetti Westerns? Just a flesh wound, ma'am. I will live...I hope happily ever after."

"You had better live. Gals from Red Haw take marriage proposals very seriously."

Flashing blue and red lights beyond the window signaled the arrival of law enforcement. Nicki breathed a sigh of relief at the sound of heavy boots on the porch. Soon Philip Menard would be taken into custody and headed to jail and Hunter would be on his way to the hospital. With their poignant moment curtailed, Nicki jumped to her feet and took charge. When the police and EMTs entered the room, she pointed at Hunter and said, "This man needs medical attention for a gunshot wound in his shoulder."

Then she looked over at Menard, who was leaning against the desk, his breathing raspy. "That is Philip Menard, the owner of the house. He shot Mr. Galen and also admitted to the murder of James Nowak in New Orleans last month. I have his confession on tape. Detective Russell Saville of NOPD is handling the murder investigation. I'm Nicolette Price of Price Investigations." She flashed her PI license at the officer in charge. For several minutes, Nicki answered a string of rapid-fire questions.

"Don't go anywhere, Miss Price," instructed a Terrebonne Parish deputy. "One of our detectives will want your full statement." He barked orders into his radio and then hurried to secure the prisoner.

Paramedics surrounded Hunter to assess his wound, monitor his vitals, and start an IV. None were pleased when he vehemently refused their gurney and walked to the ambulance with his left arm in a sling and his right arm around Nicki's waist. Hunter also refused to be transported to the hospital until Menard was led from the house and placed in a squad car. While paramedics worked on Hunter's shoulder, Nicki gave her statement to a detective, who then took statements from the butler and Menard's maid. A deputy returned to Nicki brand-new handcuffs, ready to subdue criminals on the next case.

Nicki returned to Hunter's side with one question still troubling her. If not Menard, who was responsible for the fire at Christine's?

Her answer soon arrived in a flurry of dust and gravel. Ashley brought her car to a stop and jumped out. She approached the officer loading her father into a cruiser like a madwoman. "What's going on here? Where are you taking my daddy?"

"To the sheriff's department in Houma, miss. You can call his attorney and ask him to meet you there." The deputy turned his back on her without a second glance—something Ashley wasn't accustomed to.

Hunter reached for Nicki's hand with his good arm. "Unmentionable words are about to hit the fan," he said with a wry smile.

"I insist you sit down, Mr. Galen," said a paramedic. Her tone had a take-no-prisoners quality. She pulled his arm back, attached a blood pressure cuff, and secured him on the gurney.

While Hunter finally complied, Nicki kept her focus on her

rival but left her hand off her weapon. It took Ashley only a few seconds to spot them in the melee.

"What have you done, Hunter?" cried Ashley, approaching like a dervish. She stopped short a foot away, her face contorting with rage as she looked at Nicki. "You're alive? I guess even fire can't kill a cockroach like you."

Her shock at seeing Nicki unharmed erased any doubt as to who'd burned the trailer and killed Christine.

Nicki forgot her pledge to keep quiet. "Had you succeeded, at least I'd know where I'm headed when I die. You, on the other hand, are going to jail and I'm looking forward to testifying. You might like jail, Ashley. Those orange jumpsuits are totally cool."

"Oh, shut up!" She pivoted toward Hunter. "Why is my father being arrested?"

Hunter's expression turned cold. "Let's see...he admitted to killing James because he was about to expose your fondness for rich, old men. And I almost forgot he tried to kill me when I didn't like the idea of us getting back together." Hunter lifted his sling, where blood had already stained the gauze bandage.

"Daddy shot you?" Ashley sounded genuinely surprised before turning on Nicki like a feral cat. "This is your fault, you little hick." She took a step closer.

Smoothly, as though she had rehearsed the move a thousand times, Nicki pulled her gun from her holster and leveled it at the approaching threat. "Stay where you are, Ms. Menard. I'm fully licensed, have my gun permit, and will defend myself if you threaten me one more time."

Ashley stopped in her tracks. The women eyed one another with deadly intent until an officer stepped over to take Ashley away. Apparently, the police had a few questions for her too. Nicki kept the gun trained on her.

"Easy there, Annie Oakley." Hunter cautioned. "Law enforcement frowns on shooting bad guys in the back."

"Are you kidding? Any female on the jury would recognize extenuating circumstances once they met her." Nicki lowered the gun and returned her weapon to her holster.

"That might be, Miss Price, but why don't we spare the taxpayers the expense?" Detective Russell Saville stepped from the glare of headlights.

"Good evening, Detective," said Hunter. "Still think I'm the one who killed my partner?"

"Nah, I gave up that supposition as soon as I heard from the feds you weren't in on the scam. That's when I went to see Robert Bissette. He copped to sending me those pictures of Ashley, but he swore on his mama's grave he had nothing to do with killing Nowak. Apparently, he suspected your partner was up to something and paid someone to keep an eye on him. The photos were meant to get you in hot water since he thought you'd scammed him." Saville rubbed his temples with his fingertips. "That's when I decided to chat with the other person who lost a lot of money, Menard. Good thing I picked tonight or I would have missed all the excitement."

"Timing is everything, Detective." Turning away from him, Nicki asked the paramedic if she could ride with Hunter to the hospital.

"She's my fiancée," he said, anticipating their initial objection.

The grinning EMT gave his consent and assisted Nicki as she climbed inside and tried to take up as little space as possible in the confined interior. Once they were situated and underway, she whispered in Hunter's ear. "Hey, what did Mr. Menard mean about Ashley selling herself for money? Dish the dirt. I have an inquiring mind."

With his good arm Hunter reached up to touch her face. "That, my favorite employee, is a story for another day. And I'm hoping you and I will share lots of them. I have a few questions of my own."

Nicki felt a curl of warmth that began in her belly spread up her spine. The thought of spending a lifetime with Hunter was like no lines at the amusement park, a barrel of Moose Tracks ice cream, and free gasoline for life rolled into one. Because the paramedic was surreptitiously watching her while she monitored his vitals, Nicki decided not to spoil the perfect moment by saying something idiotic. She allowed his fingers to caress her cheek for another delicious moment and then tucked his hand under the white blanket. "Conserve your energy, Galen. You'll need your strength to get down the aisle once they stitch you up." Nicki couldn't stop herself from grinning as happiness filled her to the bursting point. "I have something wonderful in mind for you."

# FORTY

When Nicki woke, she didn't immediately recognize her surroundings. She was wearing an oversized Saints T-shirt in an antique, four-poster bed with expensive silk sheets twisted in a heap by her feet. *Oh, yeah. Hunter's guest room.* Her fiancé's soft snores drifted from the next room through vents in the wall. Memories of the horrific events from the previous two days drifted back. Nicki covered her head with the top sheet to blot out the fire, Christine's body being removed from a mass of twisted metal, and a sodden Menard trying to draw a bead on Hunter in a last-ditch attempt to protect his daughter. And then there had been Ashley…kicking and screaming with indignation as her father was hauled away to jail, followed shortly thereafter by her own detainment for questioning. When the ambulance left the Menard Terrebonne retreat, Ashley was being led to a separate police cruiser.

Hunter had been taken to surgery immediately upon his arrival at the Terrebonne General Medical Center. The doctor assured Nicki that Hunter would survive and that his wound would heal nicely. The bullet had torn through the fleshy part of his shoulder, missing major blood vessels, tendons, and bone. After the operation and recovery room, Hunter was admitted so he could sleep off the anesthetic and be monitored overnight. Nicki slept fitfully on a vinyl chair next to his bed. She called no one—not Nate and none of his family to tell them the news. What could she say? *Hunter was shot by his almost father-in-law, but he's okay now?* After the longest day of her life, she had been too tired.

Hunter checked himself out of the hospital by one the next day. He submitted to several injections for infection and put prescriptions for antibiotics and pain relief in his pocket, but he overruled the doctor's insistence he remain twenty-four hours for observation. Hunter had looked the man in the eye and said, "Thanks, but we're going home. We won't get a good night's sleep until we're back in the quiet, restful French Quarter." The tired physician probably thought Hunter was still loopy from the anesthetic, because anyone who had ever been there would not describe the Quarter in those terms. But Nicki knew what he meant. A person slept best in their own bed.

One of the sheriff's deputies had brought Hunter's car to the hospital, so they had a means of transportation. Nicki's Escort had been left at the isolated retreat. She would send Nate to retrieve it as she planned to avoid that part of Louisiana for a long time. At Hunter's insistence, they stopped at the sheriff's department in Houma to give their statements. Hunter also had no desire to return to Terrebonne Parish anytime soon. They gave their videotaped statements separately to overworked deputies. With Hunter's shoulder stitched up and the sheriff satisfied he had the right people behind bars, Nicki drove them back to New Orleans, Hunter dozing in the passenger seat. Dark purple shadows ringed his eyes, evidence that his wound and the string of events had exacted a toll on his body. Nicki crossed the Crescent City Bridge never so glad to be back in a city. Even abandoned houses and vacant lots overgrown with weeds no longer looked alien to her country-girl eyes.

There had been no discussion as to where they would go. With her temporary home in Chalmette destroyed along with virtually everything she had brought with her from Natchez, she accepted Hunter's invitation to stay the night in his guest room. Especially as he'd accompanied the invitation with "I love you" and "I want to marry you." Those words had lifted her spirits and filled her heart with joy.

Love changed everything. No longer was gaining independence and autonomy so important in her life. No longer did she want to prove herself at any cost. She still wanted to work and loved being a PI, but when Hunter chose to confront Menard alone, he had put his life on the line. She could certainly adjust to New Orleans' tight parking, odd sights, peculiar smells, and revelers all night long to make a life with Hunter. The city was struggling to rise like a phoenix after Katrina. Nicolette Price was overdue for her own revival.

After she had tucked the car into the alley on Rue Royale, Nicki had to help Hunter up the steps into his apartment while he leaned heavily on her. It was all she could do to get him to his room and help him carefully onto the bed.

"Thanks, Nicki," he said, sounding exhausted. "I owe you one. That pain pill has kicked in and turned me to putty."

"All you owe me is a paycheck, Galen, and maybe a nice, fat Christmas bonus."

Sprawled across his quilt, Hunter crooked his good arm behind his head. "How 'bout a frozen turkey and a big box of chocolates?" he asked, his focus on the ceiling.

"That will do for a start."

Suddenly, he sat up and pulled her into an embrace. He planted a string of kisses across her forehead.

"Whoa. Hang on there, boss. Aren't you afraid of ripping open your stitches?"

"That's way down on my list of worries, right after black mold on the foundation and calcium plaque in my arteries." His mouth found hers in a deep, searing kiss that seemed to go on forever.

Finally Nicki straightened and patted down her already messy hair. "Well, I'm in charge of your postsurgical care, and I fear acute blood loss. Get some rest. I'm going to take a shower. Maybe you can take one later." As he slumped back on the bed and closed his eyes, she covered him with a soft throw she found folded over a chair and tucked in the edges. Then she grinned over her shoulder as she walked from the room. "I'll check on you later. Holler if you need another pain pill. I don't want you walking around by yourself."

After calling her cousin and giving him the short version of the day's events, along with a request for her car, she'd taken a long shower to rid herself of an accumulation of dirt, sweat, smoke, and blood. Nicki stood under the shower spray until she wrinkled like a prune trying to wash away everything that had happened. She couldn't remember when she drifted off to sleep, but it was definitely after midnight. The mournful wail of a saxophone from a blues club wafted its way into the darkened room. She'd slept off and on through the night, getting up every few hours to make sure Hunter drank fluids and took his meds. Now the Quarter was coming back to life. Nicki felt a raw, overwhelming hunger that made the bowl of mints on the nightstand look gourmet.

She brushed her teeth and hair, rummaged in the kitchen for a roll of plastic wrap, and then padded quietly into Hunter's room. She was relieved to see that he was beginning to stir. She gently placed her hand on his uninjured shoulder and whispered close to his ear, "Hunter, wake up. I'm starving!"

"I'm here for you, sweet *O'lette*." He opened his eyes and smiled at her. Groggily, he lifted his hand to touch her face.

"None of that, sir. I want food and lots of it. When was the last time we ate?" She tossed the roll of plastic wrap on the bed. "How do you feel about showering and getting dressed?"

He swung his legs over the side and with her help sat up. He was still wearing the same bloody, ripped clothes from the day before. The hospital had refused him a fresh pair of scrubs to wear home because he'd refused to follow doctor's orders. "Should we call for pizza delivery? I doubt you'll find anything edible in my fridge. We could order a double cheese deluxe with extra crawfish and eat right here." He patted the spot beside him on the quilt.

"No way." Nicki shook a finger like a grade school teacher. "Goodness, that bullet sure didn't slow you down much. While you shower, I'll call for takeout delivery but no pizza. Then I'll get the bag from my car. Since coming to the big city, I've kept a change of clothes and toiletries behind the driver's seat. After all, a private investigator never knows when she'll go undercover on an all-night stakeout." She dropped her voice low and sultry and drew two fingers across her eyes.

"Sorry, my love. You'll have to remain as is. Your car is still in the bayou. But I think you look beautiful in my T-shirt."

"Hold on a minute." She went to the window overlooking the alley and peeked out. "I called Nate after you fell asleep last night and asked him to bring my car back to the city. It was the least he could do since I solved the case and saved his agency's reputation." Nicki smiled, knowing she'd stretched the truth to the breaking point. "And there she sits, dusty but ready for my next adventure. So I will have clean clothes for our *al fresco* dining on your balcony, Mr. Deep Pockets. I'm ordering shrimp and crawfish, along with rice, red beans, Caesar salad, hush puppies, fried okra, and broccoli."

"*Broccoli?* You're adding broccoli to a veritable Cajun Creole feast?" Hunter shook his head with a laugh.

"Of course. We need something healthy. Now get moving."

Even as she gave orders and pointed at his bathroom door, she looked carefully at him to make sure he was up to the task. She didn't want him to overdo and end up back in the hospital.

"Will that be it, Miss Price? No dessert?"

When he started to unbutton his shirt, revealing a tanned and toned chest, Nicki blushed to the roots of her hair. "Peach pie, à la mode," she said. She shook off her shyness and came closer to cover his bandage with the plastic wrap. Once it was as secure as she could make it, she kissed his cheek and then left the room. She didn't stop until she reached her little Escort, which was squeezed next to Hunter's flashy Corvette. Giddy excitement welled in her belly just like the time they called her name at a church fund-raising raffle.

So this must be what all those romance novelists wrote about.

This must be what love felt like.

And it felt even better than winning a toaster oven.

# FORTY-ONE

*T*he ringing of a phone broke an otherwise perfect moment during a perfect engagement dinner in the Blue Lotus. Why wouldn't Nicki and Hunter select the restaurant where they first met? Even if she'd been hiding behind a tall menu at the time. Two men pinned her with their expressions—one her fiancé and one her boss.

"Who could be interrupting such an auspicious moment?" asked Hunter.

"Let it go to voice mail," said Nate.

Nicki dug her phone from her bag. "I think I should look." Her pulse quickened when she read the name on her screen. "Hello, Sheriff Latanier. I trust you're calling with an update?"

While Hunter and Nate watched curiously, Nicki listened to news that surpassed her wildest dreams. The sheriff summarized a string of events with professional succinctness. She couldn't keep from grinning over recent developments in the case.

"I can't thank you enough, sir. Yes, whenever you need my deposition, just let me know." Ending the call, Nicki turned to her companions.

"Well?" they both asked simultaneously.

"With Sean's deposition, the DA was able to obtain a search

warrant for the current residence of Theodore Cheval, aka Junior. Junior was living with his mother seventeen years ago when my dad met him in a bar. Fortunately for us, he moved back in with Mama when his third wife kicked him out six months ago. Detectives for St. Landry Parish converged on the house early this morning."

Nicki paused to take a breath. Her audience waited with rapt attention.

"They found my father's belt hanging from deer antlers in Mrs. Cheval's garage. We have people who will testify that the belt was my dad's. Both Junior and Terrence have been arrested and charged with murder. A warrant is out for Louis Cheval for accessory to murder, after the fact. He helped his brothers conceal evidence. Bond has been set for Junior at a million dollars." Nicki bit the inside of her mouth to keep from crying from joy. This was no time for tears.

"At long last, cousin." Nate slapped her on the back.

"Well done, my favorite Nancy Drew." Hunter leaned over and kissed her cheek. "I'd say this calls for a celebration."

"I solve my first big case and all I get is slapped and a kiss on the *cheek*?" Nicki snorted with disgust. "I need to hang out with a better crowd."

# FORTY-TWO

*F*unny how things worked out. Nicki carefully folded her new tops, jeans, and skirts and then laid them in her suitcase with her new socks, underwear, and pajamas. Two pairs of sandals were in the outside compartment along with a hairdryer and assorted toiletries. Everything paid for from Nate's bonus because she'd cracked the case.

Because the DNA collected weeks ago during her previous visit to *La Maison de Poisson* turned out to belong to Ashley's high school sweetheart, NOPD detectives took arson investigators out to Terrebonne to question Bobby "Bubba" LaSalle. Once they dangled a little white lie that his truck had been seen in the vicinity of Christine's trailer, he cracked like an egg. Apparently, he wasn't going to jail alone for something that hadn't been his idea. The firebomb meant to scare Nicki back to Natchez had turned into felony manslaughter when it ignited a propane leak.

Ashley was cooling her four-inch heels in jail, waiting for someone to post bond. And it wouldn't be daddy dearest because he was sitting in a cell on another floor. Rumor had it Philip was going to plead guilty to second-degree murder of James Nowak to avoid a trial and chance a first-degree conviction. Louisiana still believed in the death penalty.

That got Hunter off the hook, which was the reason for Nicki's paycheck and motivation for the much-needed bonus. The fed's preliminary report, based on the evidence Nicki supplied, confirmed Hunter had no culpability in Nowak's shell game. A statement to that effect would be released to the press and would perhaps quell client uneasiness and stem a mass exodus from his investment firm.

Hunter. He turned out to be the biggest surprise of all. Not exactly the rich, arrogant, self-serving con man she had pegged him for the first time they had a meal at the Blue Lotus. He'd paid for Christine's funeral following the confirmation of her identity and set up college funds for her children at a local bank. This at least somewhat assuaged her guilt. She had planned to help her friend stop making bad choices, but instead she only brought more evil into her life.

Next, Hunter sent letters to his clients, thanking them for their loyalty and assuring them of full restitution if James's sticky fingers touched their accounts. Fortunately, it appeared that Philip Menard and Robert Bissette were the only ones seriously defrauded, and Ashley's dad certainly wasn't going to be reimbursed. And Hunter sent letters to the junior brokers informing them of new company rules regarding risky investments for the renamed Galen Investments.

Hunter had insisted she use his credit card to replace her wardrobe, but a woman needed to maintain some autonomy. It was enough he had moved to Ethan and Cora's and given her his apartment until their wedding. She was glad he shared the same conviction that there would be no comingling until after they were married. Fortunately, she had passed the new daughter-in-law test with his mother.

Hunter's final test lay ahead. Would he be shocked when he saw exactly who she was and where she came from? Her world was very different from the smooth-sailing lifestyle of the rich and infamous. Or maybe the test would be hers.

Nicki pressed everything down in her suitcase and retrieved her makeup bag from the bathroom. Despite all that she'd accomplished, the time had come for an overdue visit back home. Not to her mother's apartment in Natchez, but to their real home in Red Haw, Mississippi, to the two people who had influenced her life the most.

Mamaw and Papaw would be waiting on their porch when they drove up. He would have on a ball cap, a plaid shirt—cotton in summer, flannel in winter—and work boots; she would be in a floral print duster with fuzzy slippers on her feet. Her gray hair would be a helmet of tight curls thanks to the home permanent a neighbor gave her from time to time. When Mamaw had turned sixty, she lopped off the long plait she wore down her back and opted for an easier coiffure. She hung the braided hair on a hook in the barn and insisted it kept horseflies away from her ancient mare. She had once told Nicki with a chuckle, "When Papaw gets lonesome for the long-haired gal he married, I send him out to the barn."

A stew full of carrots, potatoes, turnips, dried beans, and whatever meat her grandfather took with his squirrel rifle would be simmering on the woodstove, although her mom would probably bring beef shanks bought on sale at the market and kept in the freezer for just such an auspicious occasion—such as Nicki bringing home the man she loved and planned to marry one day in the not too distant future.

Mamaw would have baked cakes, pies, biscuits, and the oatmeal raisin cookies cherished by her granddaughter. She would set out jars of blackberry jam and strawberry preserves. There would be no wine in the house, or vintage champagne, or expensive microbrewery beers, but there would be plenty of sweet tea, lemonade, and strong coffee with a pinch of chicory to start the day. There would be mason jars of pickled beets, pickled cucumbers, and chow-chow to garnish each meal. No frilly calico caps covered these lids like those in gift shops—just a label indicating content and canning date. However, her grandparents weren't totally without modern vices. Papaw bought peanuts in bulk and stored them in a twenty-five-gallon canister. He took a bowl most evenings to eat on the porch and gave any that went stale to the squirrel who peeked in the window. And Mamaw had discount cards for every grocery chain in Natchez for snatching up bargains on her occasional trips to town.

Nicki's throat tightened and her stomach felt hollow, even though she wasn't hungry. This was what heartache felt like. She hoped she wouldn't spend the entire visit teary-eyed from childhood memories.

*Nicki Price goes to town and comes home a crybaby.* That's what her grandparents would say, and the thought made her smile. She checked the bag of spices, seasonings, and herbal concoctions she'd picked up locally. Papaw was a fabulous herbalist and could cure asthma attacks, hot flashes, snakebites, migraine headaches, and the common cold. *Hmm. I wonder what he has on his shelf for Hunter's gunshot wound? He'll probably recommend a poultice and echinacea tea.*

"Are you about ready, darlin'?" Hunter's soft words pulled her from her reverie.

"Just about. I'm checking what I bought to take with us. It doesn't look like much of a homecoming offering."

A slow smile spread across his tanned features. "I picked up a few things too while you were sleeping in. They're packed in the trunk, the food on dry ice."

Nicki narrowed her gaze. "What did you buy, Hunter? Nothing fancy, I hope. You know my kinfolk don't cotton to fancy."

"Simmer down. Everybody likes to try new food. I picked up andouillie sausage, smoked alligator, Creole hog's head cheese, and a five-gallon tub of fourteen-bean soup mix. None of that needs refrigeration. And for the first night of our visit, the fish vendor packed a crab-and-shrimp boil to cook over the open fire, along with two-pounds of fresh red snapper. Oh, and a quart of olive salad." Hunter looked mighty pleased with his purchases.

"That's it? No frogs legs or turtle soup?"

His grin faded a tad. "Would they like that? We can swing by the French Market on our way."

"I was joking, Hunter. They have frogs and turtles where they live too, should anyone develop an unbearable craving." She slipped her arm around his waist. "You packed all that in your trunk?"

He nuzzled a kiss into her hair. "Yeah, and rechargeable battery packs for the new table lamp and radio I picked up, just in case your papaw wants to listen to an LSU or Ole Miss game when his generator isn't running."

"Will there be room for my suitcase?" she asked. "I sure don't want to leave my new clothes behind."

"Hmm...either behind the seat or you might have to hold it on your lap. Sorry 'bout that."

She tightened their embrace, feeling the heat build between them. "Are you sure you're ready for this much rusticity? You realize there won't be a crystal flute, silver ice bucket, or espresso machine within miles."

Lifting her chin with one knuckle, he bestowed a kiss that pretty much answered every question. "Are you joking, *O'lette*? Woods for playing hide-and-seek? A rowboat for fishing at dawn? A porch swing for watching the stars come out? I've been itching for a quiet getaway for a while." His hug threatened to crack her ribs. "And you know the best part of all?"

"What's that, rich boy?" Nicki thought her heart might burst in her chest.

"When we finally tire of stargazing, there won't be any TV, wi-fi, or fax machines to distract us from the truly important things in life. We'll be forced to *retire* to the porch swing for some old-fashioned entertainment." He kissed her lips softly and drew her head down to his chest. "I, for one, am ready. *Laissez les bon temps roulez*," he whispered.

"Me too. Let the good times roll." That tidbit of French Nicki already knew by heart.

# DISCUSSION QUESTIONS

1. The characters of Nicki Price and Christine Hall illustrate how certain decisions can profoundly affect the future. What were some of the mistakes these women make that are difficult to overcome?

2. Nicki is often embarrassed by her poverty-stricken upbringing. How do those roots actually help her to become the woman she's destined to be?

3. On the other hand, Hunter grew up with every advantage. How did his silver spoon upbringing adversely affect his growth of character?

4. Why do you think Hunter was reluctant to confront his business partner as soon as he suspected financial improprieties?

5. What are some other ways people keep their heads in the sand, much to their detriment?

6. Ashley Menard was a manipulator of people and situations. Discuss people you've encountered in life with similar abilities. How are they able to get their way so often and for so long?

7. Why is it so important that Nicki solve the cold case of her father's death, besides the obvious fact that she loved him?

8. The characters of Kermit Price and Philip Menard serve to illustrate how parents are seldom all-good or all-bad. What are some challenges you had to resolve with your own father in order to find peace within yourself?

9. Why does Hunter have just as difficult a task of proving himself to Nicki as she does to him?

10. Nicki's fear of swamps began during her childhood, yet God forces her to deal firsthand with that fear over and over. Discuss some of your own pet phobias and how you learned to overcome them.

# ABOUT THE AUTHOR

**Mary Ellis** is the bestselling author of 12 novels set in the Amish community and several historical romances set during the Civil War. *Midnight on the Mississippi* is the first of a new romantic suspense series, Secrets of the South.

Before "retiring" to write full-time, Mary taught school and worked as a sales rep for Hershey Chocolate. Her debut book, *A Widow's Hope*, was a finalist for a 2010 Carol Award. *Living in Harmony* won the 2012 Lime Award for Excellence in Amish Fiction, while *Love Comes to Paradise* won the 2013 Lime Award. She and her husband live in Ohio.

Mary can be found on the web at
www.maryellis.net
or
https://www.facebook.com/#!/pages/
Mary-Ellis/126995058236

# The Quaker and the Rebel

**What Happens When an Underground
Railroad Conductor Falls in Love with
a Man Loyal to the Confederacy?**

Emily Harrison's life has turned upside down.
At the beginning of the Civil War, she bravely
attempts to continue her parents' work in the
Underground Railroad until their Ohio farm is sold in foreclosure. Now
alone and without a home, she accepts a position as a governess with
a doctor's family in slave-holding Virginia. Though it's dangerous, she
decides to continue her rescue efforts from there.

Alexander Hunt, the doctor's handsome nephew, does not deny a
growing attraction to his uncle's newest employee. But he cannot take
time to pursue Emily, for Alexander isn't what he seems—rich, spoiled,
and indolent. He has a secret identity. He is the elusive Gray Wraith, a
fearless man who fights the war from the shadows, stealing Union sup-
plies and diverting them to the Southern cause.

The path before Alexander and Emily is complicated. The war
brings betrayal, entrapment, and danger. Amid their growing feelings
for each other, can they trust God with the challenges they face to provide them with a bright future?

# The Lady and the Officer

### Love, Loyalty, and Espionage...
### How Does a Lady Live with All Three?

As a nurse after the devastating battle of Gettysburg, Madeline Howard saves the life of Elliot Haywood, a colonel in the Confederacy. But even though she must soon make her home in the South, her heart and political sympathies belong to General James Downing, a Union army corps commander.

Colonel Haywood has not forgotten the beautiful nurse who did so much for him, and when he unexpectedly meets her again in Richmond, he is determined to win her. While spending time with army officers and war department officials in her aunt and uncle's palatial home, Madeline overhears plans for Confederate attacks against the Union soldiers. She knows passing along this information may save the life of her beloved James, but at what cost? Can she really betray the trust of her family and friends? Is it right to allow Elliott to dream of a future with her?

Two men are in love with Madeline. Will her faith in God show her the way to a bright future, or will her choices bring devastation on those she loves?

# The Last Heiress

### She Crossed the Sea to Save a Legacy...
### Finding Love Was Not Part of Her Plan

Amanda Dunn set sail from England for Wilmington, North Carolina, hoping to restore shipments of cotton for her family's textile mills, which have been severely disrupted by the American Civil War. But when she meets Nathaniel Cooper, her desire to conduct business and quickly return to England changes.

Amanda's family across the sea deems the hardworking merchant unsuitable for the lovely and accomplished heiress. And when Nate himself begins to draw away, Amanda has her own battle for a happy future on her hands.

As the Union navy tightens its noose around Southern ports, Nate's brother, a Confederate officer, comes for a visit. Nate contemplates joining the Glorious Cause—not in support of slavery but to watch his brother's back. Yet will this potentially life-threatening decision put the union between him and Amanda in jeopardy?

To learn more about Harvest House books and
to read sample chapters, visit our website:

**www.harvesthousepublishers.com**

HARVEST HOUSE PUBLISHERS
EUGENE, OREGON